Ties That Bind

Also by Brenda Jackson

Family Reunion

Welcome to Leo's
(Anthology)

Brenda Jackson

Ties That Bind

St. Martin's Griffin
New York

www.stmartins.com

Library of Congress Cataloging-in-Publication Data

Jackson, Brenda (Brenda Streater)
    Ties that bind : a novel / Brenda Jackson.—1st St. Martin's
    Griffin ed.
        p. cm.
    ISBN 0-312-30611-3
    1. Married people—Fiction. 2. Friendship—Fiction. I. Title.
PS3560.A21165 T54   2002
813'.6—dc21

                                                    2002005047

First Edition: November 2002

10 9 8 7 6 5 4 3 2 1

Acknowledgments

To the man who has been the love of my life for over thirty years, Gerald Jackson, Sr.

To my family and friends for always being so supportive.

To Deirdre Sherard Thompson and Leslie A. Arthur for their much appreciated assistance in providing information on Howard University.

To Dr. Clifford Muse, University Archivist, Howard University, for all the historical information that he provided on Howard University.

To my Heavenly Father. I'm everything I am because you love me.

Book One
1965 - 1968

Woe unto them that call evil good, and good evil; that put darkness for light, and light for darkness; that put bitter for sweet and sweet for bitter.

Isaiah 5:20

One

October 1965
Howard University, Washington, DC

"For crying out loud, Jenna, the least you can do is act like you want to go," Ellie Stanhope said, glancing at her watch. "What else do you have to do tonight?"

"Study," was Jenna Haywood's reply as she turned away from the closet and walked over to the bed to put on her shoes.

"All you ever do is study."

Jenna glanced over her shoulder at Ellie. "Have you forgotten this is college and getting an education is the reason we're here?"

"Whoa, speak for yourself. That's not why I'm here. I came to Howard for a different reason altogether."

Jenna shook her head. It hadn't taken long for Ellie to explain when they first met two years ago that the reason she had come to Howard University was to find an educated man to marry who could give her the good life she wanted.

Jenna couldn't understand any black woman still thinking that way. That had been the norm for women years ago, to go off to college to find a husband. But now all across the country more and more women were demanding equal rights, although for most black women and men, civil rights were the main thing they were fighting for. But still, women were finally coming into their own, getting recognized for their accomplishments. There was even a women's liberation movement that had recently gotten started. And as far as black women were concerned, thanks to the Civil Rights Act that was passed last year, you could now enter jobs that used to be considered for "white women only".

Ellie was right. Her reasons for coming to Howard were altogether different from Jenna's. Jenna wanted to one day become an architect, a field a lot of women had not yet ventured into. Besides, she owed it to her parents, who had scraped and saved their last dime to send her to college to do her very best in school.

"Will you please hurry up, Jenna!"

Jenna turned and saw Ellie impatiently tapping her foot on the floor. "What's the rush?"

Ellie rolled her eyes heavenward. "Jenna, this is the biggest, most important fraternity party of the year. Everyone who is anyone on campus was invited."

Jenna smiled. "Then how did *we* get invited? We aren't anybody. At least we aren't anybody important."

"Speak for yourself, Jenna Haywood. I *am* somebody. I'm a woman with my eyes on Sonny Cahill."

Jenna didn't have to ask who Sonny Cahill was. He was the senior who was the son of New Jersey's first Negro mayor. And everybody on campus knew that like his father, Sonny had political aspirations. Everybody also knew that he was seeing Terri Whitelaw on a steady basis, who happened to be this year's homecoming queen. Jenna couldn't help wondering how Ellie thought she would fit into the picture. "Okay, I'm ready to go."

Ellie headed for the door. "It's about time."

The sound of Fontella Bass' hit single, "Rescue Me," was blasting when Jenna and Ellie neared the building where the party was being held. Black and gold streamers and balloons were all around the courtyard. Jenna heard that when the Alphas held their annual party, it was indeed a party. She also knew the most popular guys on campus belonged to this fraternity, which no doubt was another reason Ellie was eager to attend. Last year they hadn't received an invitation. But this year was different.

"And for pete's sake, Jenna, try not to look bored tonight. A lot of the AKAs and Deltas will be here. I know you aren't interested in joining a sorority but I am, and I don't want them to get the wrong idea about me just because we're roommates."

Jenna lifted a brow. "And just what idea is that?"

"That I'm a fuddy-duddy bookworm. I have plenty of time to buckle down and hit the books during senior year. Right now I want to enjoy college life and make sure my future is set. Hopefully I'll have good news for my parents when I go home for Christmas."

Jenna knew from what Ellie had told her that her parents were the driving forces behind her finding a husband at college. According to Ellie, her parents had met that way at Howard years ago. Her father was a pharmacist and her mother was a schoolteacher. Ellie had also explained that although she didn't think her parents were in love or anything like that, the most important thing was that they were well suited for each other, which made things even better. Jenna couldn't understand why anyone would think that way, or why anyone would want their daughter to follow in their footsteps and enter a relationship so clinical and loveless.

Jenna thought about her own parents. Neither had gone to college but her father was proud of his job as a meat cutter and her mother enjoyed working as a cook in the school's cafeteria. And as far as love was concerned, John and Jackie Haywood had plenty of it for each other as well as for their four children.

By the time Jenna and Ellie reached the building where the party was being held, a number of people were coming in and out, and others were hanging around outside talking and having what seemed to be a good time. There was no doubt in Jenna's mind that Ellie would enjoy herself tonight. But Jenna doubted that she would. Her mind would be preoccupied with thoughts of the test she would have in her history class on Monday. Because of this party, she would have to spend most of Sunday studying.

As they entered the building Jenna hoped that Ellie wasn't planning to stay too late. If so then she wouldn't have any choice but to leave her here, although she didn't really want to do that. But Ellie was determined to be a part of the in-crowd, no matter what it took. She and Ellie were two different people with two different sets of goals and ambitions. Jenna had accepted that and was fine with it. But she knew Ellie had a long way to go to accept her way of thinking and to understand that there were more important things in life besides husband-hunting.

●　●　●

"Hey, how about if we ditch this party and go to my dorm and make out?"

Jenna smiled at Johnny Lane as he came to stand beside her just as her favorite song, "Rainbow 65" by Gene Chandler, began playing. Johnny, six foot four, muscular, with good dark looks, was one of the first persons she had met upon arriving at Howard and was a known flirt around campus. "Sorry, Johnny, I have a headache," she said grinning. "I'm surprised to see you here though. I thought you didn't do the fraternity thing."

He shrugged. "Normally I don't but a man has to eat sometimes and the food here is always good." He glanced around the room then smirked at her. "I see Princess Ellie was able to talk you into coming."

Jenna shook her head. Johnny and Ellie didn't get along. In fact they disliked each other intensely. Ellie claimed he lacked any kind of breeding and polish. On the other hand, Johnny thought Ellie was a snob. "I didn't mind."

"Yeah, right," he said grinning, knowing better. "How you put up with her beats me. She's operating under the misconception that she's popular on campus when in fact very few people actually like her."

Jenna shrugged. Feeling loyalty to her roommate she said, "Ellie's okay. She just tries too hard at times."

Johnny snorted. "In trying to get people to like her she somehow manages to get them not to like her."

Jenna took a sip of her punch. She knew that in the beginning Johnny had had a thing for Ellie. When she all but made him feel he wasn't worthy of her affections, whatever feelings he'd felt for her had turned into animosity. Jenna hated that because she considered both Johnny and Ellie her friends and often found herself right smack in the middle of their fray. More than once, Ellie had tried making her choose sides but she had refused to do so. As far as she was concerned, whatever Johnny and Ellie felt for each other didn't involve her.

"So, is Leigh still spending most of her time over at Noah's place?"

Jenna nodded. Leigh was her other roommate who didn't get along with Ellie either. Instead of tolerating the situation like Jenna, Leigh spent most of her time with her boyfriend, Noah Wainwright, who lived off campus. He was three years older than Leigh and a law student.

"Can't say I blame Leigh too much," Johnny was now saying. "You have to be the most tolerant person on earth, Jenna."

Jenna smiled. "I don't let Ellie get under my skin." Changing the subject to one that was Johnny's favorite topic lately, namely civil rights, she asked, "I heard there may be another march on Washington next year."

Johnny shook his head. "Don't count on it. President Johnson is definitely not John F. Kennedy. Right now he's too worried about what's happening in Vietnam to give a damn about a bunch of black folks. But what this country has to realize is that young men like me have no reason to go to some god-forsaken country I know nothing about and shoot up a bunch of people I personally don't have anything against, when I'm being treated like a second-class citizen in my own country."

Jenna raised a brow upon hearing the anger in Johnny's voice. "Are you saying you won't go into the armed services if you're drafted?"

"Hey, don't look so surprised. I heard Muhammad Ali is thinking the same way. He went all the way to Italy and won that gold medal, and came back here and couldn't go into a five-and-dime store and sit at the counter because he's black."

Jenna took another sip of her punch. Muhammad Ali, the famous boxer, who had been known as Cassius Clay until last year when he changed his name, had started speaking out against the injustices against blacks. "I hear the Muslims have held several meetings on campus."

"Yeah, and I've attended a few and found them pretty interesting. Maybe you could go to one of the meetings with me," he said, knowing full well that she wouldn't do such a thing. Jenna was a good Southern Baptist girl who wouldn't be caught associating with any group believed to be of a radical nature, and with such a different viewpoint than her own religion. Not to put her on the spot, he decided to change the subject and discuss a recent rumor he had heard. "Did you hear there may have been a conspiracy with Malcolm X's death?"

Jenna lifted a brow. She wasn't surprised. There were some people like her parents who also believed there had been a conspiracy behind President Kennedy's death, too. Malcolm X, the onetime spokesman for the Nation of Islam and leader of the Organization for Afro-American Unity, had gotten slain earlier that year. "No, I hadn't heard that."

After a few minutes of filling her in on the latest rumor, Johnny said, "Well, since you won't leave this party to go somewhere and make out with me, I guess I'll move on. I'm sure there's some woman here tonight who'll be interested."

Jenna chuckled. "Yeah, I'm sure there is." She watched as Johnny left her side and crossed the room to a group of ladies standing nearby. She checked her watch. It was close to twelve o'clock already, the midnight hour. She searched the crowd for Ellie. She had only seen her twice since they had arrived. She spotted her standing across the room talking to Tyrone Wells, one of the star players on the football team. Jenna knew that now would not be a good time to approach Ellie to let her know she was ready to leave.

Deciding to take a step outside to get a bit of fresh air, Jenna made her way through the crowd and for the door. Once outside she took a deep cleansing breath, thinking she much preferred being outside than inside.

She happened to glance across the yard where a group of guys stood talking, and blinked when she noticed that one of them was staring at her. And for the life of her she couldn't help but stare back. From the floodlights shining off Drew Hall she could see his features clearly—he was such a dreamboat! He had medium-brown skin and black curly hair. She would guess his height to be at least six foot four and his shoulders were broad. From the Howard Bisons jersey he was wearing, she wondered if he was a member of the football team. He had, she thought, the most handsome face she had ever seen and that thought suddenly played havoc on her nerves. This was the first time she had seen any guy on campus who had even slightly interested her.

Suddenly, she realized he had left the group of guys he'd been standing with and was coming straight toward her. Jenna felt some sort of an electric current passing between them that was irresistible, undeniable. She experienced a sense of panic and for a quick moment was about to turn and go back inside. But something about the way he was looking at her stopped her, and she somehow knew that even though there was this raw energy flowing between them, she had nothing to fear from him. So she remained where she was, watching him approach. Her gaze locked firmly with his while the sound of Wilson Pickett's "In the Midnight Hour," drifted through the air. When he finally reached her, he smiled, took her hand in his and said in what she thought was the deepest male voice she'd ever heard, "Will you go back inside and dance with me?"

Jenna thought his hand felt warm as he led her back inside where they joined other couples dancing. As they moved their bodies in formation to do the swing, it occurred to her that not once had she thought of turning him down when he'd approached her.

For the longest time he didn't speak. Neither did she. They merely stared into each other's eyes as if they thought dancing together, in this place, at this time made perfect sense. Although they would probably be the first to admit that this intense attraction didn't. She had never felt anything like this in her entire life, not even for Jeremy Fields and they had dated all through their last two years of high school. They had broken up after graduation when he had decided that he wanted to escape the prejudices in the South by moving to California.

"Who are you?" she finally asked, thinking she should at least know the name of the person who had miraculously warped her senses.

"Randolph Devin Fuller. And who are you?"

"Jenna. Jenna Marie Haywood."

A smile lifted the corners of his mouth. "Hi, Jenna Marie Haywood."

Jenna could help returning his smile. "Hi, Randolph Devin Fuller."

"You're a junior?" he asked with interest.

"Yes. What about you?"

"I'm a senior. Funny we never ran into each other before on campus."

Moments later when Wilson Pickett's song ended and a slow number by Solomon Burke immediately began playing, Randolph gently pulled Jenna to him, holding her close, but not too close as to be considered indecent or disrespectful. But it was close enough to breathe in the tantalizing scent of her perfume.

With mixed emotions bombarding him resulting from holding her in his arms, Randolph tried to calm himself down. "So, tell me about yourself," he said, swallowing hard.

"What do you want to know?"

"Everything."

She smiled. "That would take more than this dance, Randolph."

He barely suppressed the chuckle rising in his throat as he kept his gaze leveled at her face. He thought she had a beautiful smile. The last thing he had expected when he showed up here tonight was to run into a woman he would find himself irresistibly attracted to. "Then tell me the important stuff like what brought you to Howard."

Jenna nodded before she began speaking. "I'm in the school of architecture. What brought me here is my parents' lifelong dream that I get educated at a prestigious college. They worked real hard to send me. It's my dream to return to Knoxville and open a business there."

"Knoxville? Is that where you're from?"

"Yes. I'm the oldest of four kids and the only girl. Now what information would you like to share?"

He smiled. "I'm majoring in business with plans to go on to law school here. The Fullers have deep roots in Richmond, Virginia, where my father was born. My paternal grandparents still live there. My mother's parents are in Glendale Shores, South Carolina."

She nodded. She had heard all about Glendale Shores, which some people claimed was the most beautiful of the sea islands off the South Carolina coast. "Do you ever go to Glendale Shores to visit?"

"Not as much as I'd like. When I was a kid growing up, I spent most of my summers there."

"Do you have any sisters or brothers?"

"Yes," he replied, smiling fondly, thinking of the brother he was very close to. "I have a brother named Ross. He's a law student. I heard my parents wanted a third child but once they saw what a holy terror I was, they decided two was enough." He then studied her features, thinking how young she looked. "How old are you?"

She smiled. "I'm eighteen. I graduated from high school at sixteen. Since my mother worked in the school system, I was able to start school a year ahead of schedule."

"Is your mother a teacher?"

"No, she's a cook in the school cafeteria. And how old are you, Randolph?"

"I'm twenty. I'll be twenty-one in April."

"April? What day in April?"

"The fourth."

Jenna blinked. "My birthday is April fourth, too," she said, grinning from cheek to cheek. "Isn't that a coincidence?"

"Yes, it is," Randolph said warmly, thinking she was simply beautiful, although she hadn't done anything to accentuate that beauty. But in his opinion, she didn't have to. She wore her hair up in a knot that showed just what a graceful neckline she had. She had applied minimum makeup and was dressed conservatively in a skirt and blouse. But there was something about her that had grabbed his attention the moment she had walked outside.

"Why were you standing outside?" he asked curiously. "Were you getting bored already?"

Jenna didn't say anything at first. If he was an Alpha she didn't want to offend him by saying she wasn't enjoying the party, so she said, "I'm not used to being up this late unless I'm studying. I was hoping my roommate would notice I wasn't inside and take the hint that I was ready to leave. I want to go to church in the morning, then spend the rest of the day studying for a test I have on Monday."

"Who's your roommate?"

Jenna's gaze searched the room. "Ellie Stanhope. She's the girl dancing with Tyrone Wells."

Randolph's gaze followed hers. "If you're ready to leave I can walk you back to your dorm."

Jenna shook her head. "We came together and I can't leave without making sure Ellie gets back to the dorm okay."

He smiled. "Then I'll make sure she does. Come on." Sliding his hand around Jenna's waist and drawing her to his side, he began walking in the direction where Ellie and Tyrone Wells were dancing. He tapped Tyrone Wells on the shoulder. "Ty, make sure this lady here gets back to the dorm okay. I'm walking her roommate home."

Tyrone nodded, smiling. "Okay, Rand."

"You're leaving already, Jenna?" Ellie asked. Her voice definitely indicated she wasn't pleased at the thought.

"Yes. I'll see you later."

Ellie looked at Tyrone and smiled. "Yes. Later."

Jenna shook her head, wondering what had happened to Ellie's plan to snare Sonny Cahill, since it now seemed she was enamored with Tyrone Wells.

"Ready?"

Randolph's question intruded into her thoughts. "Yes, I'm ready."

With his hand curling around her arm, Randolph led Jenna across the room, through the doors and out into the yard.

The grounds were well lit as Randolph and Jenna strode along a paved lane that led to several dormitory buildings. They talked about everything, from the Temptations' newest single, "My Girl," and how fast it was climbing the charts, to the fact that some white folks had started growing their hair long, hanging big beads around their necks, wearing bell-bottom pants and calling themselves hippies.

Randolph also told Jenna that he had participated in the march on Washington two years earlier and the Selma march earlier that year. "I was there for Bloody Sunday, too," he said quietly, remembering what had started out as a peaceful demonstration. No sooner had they reached the city line, there had been a posse of Alabama State Troopers waiting for them on Governor Wallace's orders. The troopers had immediately attacked the crowd who had bowed their heads in prayer, using tear gas and batons and whipping the peaceful demonstrators with no signs of mercy.

"Your parents let you participate?" Jenna asked with keen interest. She had wanted to participate in the march but her parents had not allowed her to, although she knew her father had participated. He had written to her about what had happened and it had been just as Randolph described it. A number of peaceful demonstrators had gotten beaten and jailed.

"Both my parents were killed in a car accident when I was ten. Our paternal grandparents raised Ross and me. My grandfather is a good friend of A. Philip Randolph and he thought it would be a good experience for me and Ross."

"Your grandfather is friends with A. Philip Randolph?" she asked, making sure she had heard him correctly. Besides Martin Luther King, Jr., Mr. Randolph was one of the most prominent leaders in the fight against segregation, especially in the military and labor forces. He had also been the one to organize the march on Washington two years ago. Jenna had heard her parents speak highly of him on numerous occasions, especially her father, who was now a part of the Teamsters Union because of Mr. Randolph's fight for fair and equal employment practices.

"Yes. They served in World War Two together. In fact I was named after him."

They stopped walking when they came to the building where Jenna lived. "You won't get into trouble for coming in after midnight, will you?"

She smiled. "No. I told our dorm mother that we would be getting back late. She's usually more lenient on the weekends."

Randolph nodded. He wasn't ready to part company with her yet. There was something going on here, something between them that had started from the moment he had laid eyes on her tonight. It was definitely worth exploring since nothing like this had ever happened to him before. "What are your plans for tomorrow?"

Randolph's question took Jenna by surprise. She hadn't considered the possibility that he might want to see her again and her heart began beating rapidly at the thought. But another part of her heard her mother's voice, warning her to be aware of smooth talking guys around school. They were guys who were only out for one thing. She hated to think that Randolph might be that way. She tilted her head and looked up at him. "Why do you ask?"

"I was hoping you would go to the movies with me tomorrow afternoon. James Bond's new movie, *Thunderball*, is out and I heard it's good."

"I'm going to be busy tomorrow studying," she responded, playing it safe and feeling awful that she felt she had to.

"What about next weekend? Can we go out then?"

Jenna gazed at him thoughtfully. "I don't know if that's a good idea."

He lifted a bemused brow. "Why wouldn't it be?"

For the life of her, Jenna couldn't rightly say at the moment.

A smile came to his lips when she couldn't provide him with an answer. "I'll tell you what. How about going to a concert with me two weekends from now?"

"A concert?"

"Yes. The Ramsey Lewis Trio is doing a benefit concert on campus. Would you go with me?"

Jenna hadn't been to a concert since the free one on campus last year. "Yes," she said, making a decision.

A huge smile spread across his face. "Good. Can I call you during this week, too?"

She smiled back. "Sure."

"What's your phone number?"

As she rattled off the number, he mentally stored it in his head. "Are you going to the game next Saturday?"

"I hadn't planned on it. I'll probably be too busy studying."

He nodded then reached into his pockets and pulled something out. "This is a free pass if you change your mind and decide to come. You can get in as my guest," he said, handing it to her. When their hands touched he heard her quick intake of breath. He was glad. If being around her was playing hell on his senses he was happy to know that she was suffering that same effect.

"Thank you and thanks for making sure I got home safely."

"It was my pleasure." He smiled.

"Good night, Randolph."

"Good night."

Quickly turning, Jenna raced up the steps to the building, opened the door and slipped inside.

For a long while after she had gone, Randolph stood watching the closed door.

Bronson College, Boston, Massachusetts

"Aren't you worried about not passing Professor Dunbar's class?"

Angela Douglass smiled up at a fellow student as they walked together from the library. Already the air was filled with a chill and the weather reports indicated there would be light snow on the ground in the morning. "No, I'm not worried. Professor Dunbar will assign me a tutor before letting me fail."

"Must be nice to have connections."

She heard the deep sarcasm in Sandra Sawyer's voice but chose to ignore it. "It is." She then glanced at her watch, a present from her parents on her eighteenth birthday two years ago. "I've got to run. This is the night Mrs. Hightower is entertaining and I promised her that I would help. See you later."

Sandra watched Angela until she had disappeared from view, thinking some people had it too easy. Just because Angela was a descendant of Frederick Douglass, everyone treated her like she was a queen. She went to class when she was ready and did half the work and still managed to get good grades, all because her family was close friends with Dean Hightower.

As Sandra crossed the street, heading for her dorm, she thought of how unfair that was.

"You did an outstanding job tonight, Angela. The next time I talk to your parents I'm going to let them know just what a big help you were."

"Thank you, Mrs. Hightower." Whenever she had to deal with Leanne Hightower Angela knew to be on her best behavior. She was well aware that her parents often checked up on her.

"The last time I talked to your mother she said that things were pretty serious between you and that Fuller boy."

Angela pasted on a smile as she washed the last plate. Tonight the Hightowers had hosted a dinner party for some rich white man named Robert Morgan, who had recently donated a huge sum of money to the all-girl college that she attended. "Yes, ma'am. Everyone is hoping that Ross and I will marry when he graduates. He's attending Howard Law School."

The older woman smiled as though impressed. "A Howard law graduate will be a good catch, young lady. Especially one with a good family name. I understand the Fullers are a very respected family in Virginia." After a while she asked, "I understand he has a brother?"

"Yes, his name is Randolph," Angela responded to the older woman. *And he's the one I really want and not Ross. And although Ross is the one my parents have selected for me, I will get who I want in the end.* She couldn't help but wonder what it was about Randolph that made her want him so. Her obsession with him had started the first time she had seen him at a birthday party for Massachusetts' black attorney general Edward Brookes. At the time she hadn't known that he was Ross's brother and although he did nothing more than toss a glance in her direction, she had felt a deep yearning inside of her like she had never felt before. She liked the way he walked, the way he talked, the way he looked and the way he carried himself, all self-assured and confident, like he knew exactly what he wanted in life. Ross, although the older of the two, didn't seemed quite as assured and confident as his younger brother. From that night on she knew without a doubt that Randolph Fuller would be the only man for her and that somehow, some way she would have him. And from that time almost a year ago, she had become more and more obsessed with having him, to the point that she would fantasize about him constantly.

"It's getting late, Angela; too late for you to walk across campus alone. I'll have Herbert take you home."

"I don't want to be a bother."

"And you won't be. Now get your coat while I let him know that you're ready."

• • •

Dean Hightower took a few puffs from his pipe as he put the car in reverse and backed out of the driveway. "Did you get everything?"

"Yes."

He nodded. "I'm sure Leanne appreciated your help tonight."

Angela smiled. "I didn't mind. In fact I enjoyed it."

"What did you think of Mr. Morgan?"

Angela shrugged, thinking of how she had noticed him looking at her a number of times during the evening. "He seemed nice."

Amusement danced in Dean Hightower's eyes. "He's been more than nice by donating a lot of money to the school. It's money we'll need to keep things running. Parents aren't sending their girls to private schools anymore, and I think it's a sin and a shame. We and Spellman are the only two institutions left for colored girls."

Angela cringed. She hated it when someone still referred to African-Americans as colored.

A bump in the road snapped her back to the moment and it was then that she noticed Dean Hightower had made a turn down Minger Road. She glanced over at him.

"Leanne expects me to come right back," he said, bringing the car to a stop and cutting off the engine. "So this can't take long."

It will be the first time if it doesn't, Angela thought.

He was already out of the car and at the passenger side before she could draw her next breath. He opened the door for her. "Come on and sit on the hood. I want it that way."

She felt heat thicken between her legs when he picked her up and sat her on the hood of his car. Automatically she spread her legs, wondering what Mrs. Hightower would have thought had she known she hadn't worn any panties tonight.

As she watched Dean Hightower remove his belt and lower his zipper she remembered the first time they had done this, right in the kitchen while Mrs. Hightower took a nap upstairs.

"I wish there was more light out here," he said, pulling his erection out of his pants. "I love looking at your sex."

She smiled. That wasn't all he liked doing to it. He had even tasted it a few times and she wondered if he would do so tonight. She had really liked it.

She watched him hold himself in his hands, thinking that for an old man of forty-five, he was still in good shape. He was big and healthy looking.

"Lie down," he instructed. He had barely shoved her down on the warm hood when he climbed on top of her. Without wasting any time, he thrust deep inside of her, not bothering with the use of a rubber, knowing she had started taking the pill six months ago.

"I'm flunking English, Dr. Dunbar's class," she told him, thinking that now was a good time.

"Don't worry about it. You'll pass with an A."

She smiled. He'd said just what she had wanted to hear.

With talk out of the way, he began pumping fast and furious inside of her while holding her in place so she wouldn't slip and slide all over the freshly waxed surface. To help him along she wrapped her legs around him. Doing that unleashed the oversexed beast within him. He clamped down on her shoulders while he continued to thrust inside of her. Each time he bore his hips down on her he moaned, groaned. He also began murmuring vulgar words about what he was doing to her.

Angela felt herself getting aroused by what he was saying. The ache between her legs throbbed and intensified and his hard, deep thrusts were making it feel better. She squeezed her eyes shut, thinking just how much she enjoyed this. Ross thought she was a virgin. He also thought she was a prim and proper lady because she always carried herself as such around him. If he were to see her now, he would be shocked out of his skin.

"Tell me!"

Dean Hightower's demand interrupted her thoughts. She opened her eyes. She knew the one word he loved hearing and wanted her to say but she wasn't ready to say it just yet. Her sex still throbbed and she wanted more.

Her silence made him push deeper, harder, ramming into her, which only aroused her more. She closed her eyes, fantasizing. In her mind, the man having sex with her on the hood of the car was no longer the dean of Bronson College, but the man she wanted, Randolph Fuller. She pretended it was Randolph's strong fingers that were digging almost painfully into her hips while his sex thrust in and out of her like a lunatic.

She bit her lips to stop from calling out Randolph's name when she felt herself pulled toward a climax.

"Tell me!" he demanded again.

Yes, Randolph, I'll tell you anything. When she began shivering toward an orgasm, she uttered the word Dean Hightower wanted to hear that would push him over the edge. "Shoot!"

And he did. As usual that single word fragmented his mind and he shot his semen into the depths of her sex, totally drenching her womb. His snarl of pleasure made her come and she cried out, thankful they were on a road no longer used.

He pushed her thighs wide, taking the word she had shouted literally as he continued to flood her insides. He was loaded with the stuff, and had once told her that once it got backed up inside of him, he couldn't function properly. She couldn't help but wonder how many other girls on campus were helping him to relieve himself.

For the longest time they both just lay there, on top of the car, trying to regain their strength. Moments later he slowly lifted his body and his eyes flickered to her face. "Mr. Morgan likes you. I saw how he kept watching you tonight." He smiled. "I bet he'll give anything to taste you."

Angela waited until Dean Hightower had pulled out of her and lowered himself to the ground. She slowly sat up and drew her knees up to her chest and hugged them. "You mean that he'll want to . . . you know?"

Dean Hightower smiled. He knew just how much she enjoyed being tasted. "Yeah. White men prefer doing that sort of thing more than they do sticking it in and shooting off." He reached out and placed a gentle hand over hers, transforming himself from her lover into the man who was a father figure as well as good friend of her family. "I wouldn't suggest it to you unless I thought you'd like it. And I think he might give the school additional money if you cooperated. Will you?"

She thought about what he was asking. She had heard stories about white men and their tongues. It was time she found out if what she'd heard was true. "Yeah, I'll do it if you're sure it will be for a good cause."

Dean Hightower's lips tilted into a smile that reflected both gratitude and appreciation. "It definitely will be for a good cause, Angela."

She returned his smile. "Then, yes, I'll do it."

Two

Howard University

"Aren't you going to tell me about last night?"

Jenna lifted her head from her book and looked across the room at Ellie. "What is it you want to know?" she asked dryly. She really did need to study. Tomorrow's test would cover an entire segment on the Revolutionary War.

"Everything."

"I don't have time to tell you everything, Ellie, I'm trying to study. Can you be more specific?"

With a definite frown on her face Ellie crossed the room and dropped down on the floor in front of Jenna. "I want to know about Randolph Fuller. You do know who he is, don't you?"

"Yes, he's a nice guy I met last night and who walked me home," Jenna replied, hoping that would be the end of the conversation but somehow knowing it wouldn't be. Ellie was interested in her love life or lack thereof.

"Randolph comes from a family of prominent attorneys. I understand his grandfather once dated Josephine Baker and is good friends with A. Philip Randolph."

"Umm," Jenna said disinterestedly, returning her attention to her book.

Ellie became annoyed. "Doesn't that mean anything to you?"

Jenna looked back up at Ellie. "No. I don't measure a person's worth by his family or his family connections. I thought Randolph was a nice person and appreciated him seeing me home safely. He was a gentleman to do it. That's all there was to it."

"Are you saying you aren't seeing him again?"

Jenna thought about the football pass in her dresser drawer as well as their plans to attend the concert together. "Possibly. I don't want anything or anyone to take my mind off school work." And she knew Randolph could certainly do that. He was doing so already. She had awakened that morning thinking about him, and that thought made her a bit uneasy. Her main focus was finishing up at Howard and going back home to open her own business. Then she would be able to help her parents send her three younger brothers to college. All three had dreams of attending Morehouse.

"Well, I wouldn't put too much stock in anything developing between you and Randolph anyway if I were you."

Jenna met Ellie's gaze, wondering why she would say that with such confidence and certainty. "I hadn't planned on doing so but I'm curious as to why you would say something like that."

Ellie shrugged. "You and Randolph don't fit. His grandmother is on the board here and I've seen her a few times at various functions on campus. She's one of those women who're the epitome of style, grace and elegance. I heard she's handpicked Randolph's brother's girl-friend, who is a direct descendant of Frederick Douglass. She intends for them to marry when he finishes law school. The girl goes to some private all-girl college in Boston."

Ellie stretched out on the floor as she continued talking. "The reason Randolph was never on my list of eligible men is because his grandmother will probably pick out his future wife as well. And not to sound mean or anything, but I doubt you have a chance. Rumor has it she's looking at Lena Weaver."

Jenna didn't have to ask who Lena Weaver was. She was a stunning-looking girl; a senior on campus. Her grand-uncle, Robert C. Weaver, was rumored as being President Johnson's top pick for secretary of Housing and Urban Development, a new cabinet position that been added that year. If Johnson chose him for the position, it would make him the first black cabinet official in U.S. history.

"So if you're interested in Randolph, you're only wasting your time."

Jenna snapped her book closed, bothered by what Ellie had said and not wanting to hear anything about Randolph any longer. "I think I'll go down to the Blackburn Center and finish reading," she said quietly.

Ellie stared up at her. "I hope you don't think I'm being cruel by telling you this, Jenna, but I wouldn't want you to be hurt by Randolph."

As Jenna grabbed her sweater and headed for the door, a part of her thought that she was already hurt, just a little. She had thought Randolph was different. Last night he'd acted like he was interested in her and all along he already had his future wife picked out for him. Her mother had been right. You had to be aware of smooth talking guys.

The next afternoon Jenna sat on the bench in the park near campus studying the designs of the buildings she saw, jotting down information about each for her Architectural History and Theory class. As she glanced at the Washington Monument that loomed in the distance, she thought the nation's capital was such a beautiful city. You could scarcely look anywhere and not see some historical building or landmark. Where most cities had skyscraper buildings that jutted discordantly into the sky, what you got in DC was a scene that resembled a rural theme park, complete with grassy fields and large reflecting pools of water.

After finishing what she was doing, Jenna packed everything into her tote bag and began walking back toward campus. She thanked her lucky stars Ellie hadn't been there when she'd gone to her dorm room after class earlier. Ellie had been spending a lot of time with Tyrone since Saturday night. He had come around yesterday afternoon to take her to a movie, and from what Leigh had said, he had shown up again today to take Ellie to the library so they could study together. The thought of Ellie studying was almost comical.

"Is he the one she's selected for her husband?" Leigh had asked, grinning when they had seen each other earlier that day. "Maybe she'll get so wrapped up in him that she'll stay out of our business."

Jenna doubted that, but she had kept her thoughts to herself since she knew how Leigh felt about Ellie.

She had just reached the Aldridge Theater when she saw Randolph and Lena Weaver walking together on their way to class. Jenna's grip tightened on her tote bag. At first she hadn't wanted to believe Ellie's allegations, but now she was seeing Randolph with Lena with her own eyes. She inhaled deeply, thankful they hadn't seen her. Feeling the need to walk off her hurt and disappointment, Jenna headed in the opposite direction, not ready to go to her dorm yet.

It was late afternoon when Jenna opened the door to her room just in time to hear the phone ringing. The private telephone in their room was a luxury that she, Leigh and Ellie had agreed to chip in and pay for for the convenience of not having to use the public one down the hall. She quickly crossed the room and picked it up, thinking it was probably Noah calling for Leigh. "Hello."

"May I speak to Jenna, please?"

Jenna frowned, recognizing the deep, masculine voice immediately. "This is Jenna."

"Jenna, this is Randolph."

"Yes, I know," she said, wanting to add, *And I know you have a girlfriend, so why are you calling me? I saw the two of you together.*

"How did you do on your test today?"

"I think I did all right. Thanks for asking." *Resist him!* her mind screamed. *Tell him good-bye and hang up!* it screamed again. *Tell him that you know what game he's playing and you don't want to be a part of it.*

"I forgot to ask what time you wanted me to pick you up for the concert next weekend."

Jenna swallowed. She had forgotten about their plans for the concert. "I've changed my mind about going. Maybe it will be a good idea for you to ask your girlfriend."

"My girlfriend?"

"Yes, your girlfriend, Lena Weaver."

There was a slight pause then he said. "Lena is not my girlfriend. We're just friends."

"Yeah, right. Look, I'm sort of busy right now. It was nice talking to you." And with that closing statement she hung up, thinking he probably wouldn't ever call her again.

"So, you got short with Randolph Fuller because of what Ellie said?" When Jenna didn't respond quickly enough to suit her, Leigh Murdock continued. "When are you going to learn not to take Ellie's word as gospel? Most of the time she doesn't know what she's talking about, Jenna."

Jenna took a sip of her Coke. "But this time she did. I saw Randolph and Lena, Leigh. They were walking on campus together," she said with a sad smile.

"Is that all? Noah walks to class with a lot of girls and they mean nothing to him."

"Well, it really doesn't matter."

Leigh reached out and captured Jenna's hand in hers. "Try telling that to someone else, Jen. We've been roommates for over two years and I can tell when something really matters to you."

Jenna knew Leigh was right. "Okay, it does matter," she confessed moments later with a shy smile. "I kind of liked him."

"And you should. He's a nice guy."

Jenna lifted her brow. "You know him?"

"Not personally but I've heard nice things about him. Noah and Randolph's brother, Ross, are best friends and share a house off campus. And from what I understand, Randolph isn't going with Lena Weaver, so he wasn't trying to pull a fast one over on you."

Jenna's conversation with Leigh stayed in her mind as she got ready for bed later that night. She couldn't sleep, since she couldn't stop thinking about Randolph Fuller.

Moments later when she finally drifted off, her mind was still filled with thoughts of the guy with dark eyes and warm smile who had walked her home from the party on Saturday night.

*   *   *

Two days later Jenna glanced across the length of the Founders Library and saw Randolph at the exact same moment that he saw her. She suddenly remembered their last conversation and how short she'd been with him and wondered if he would simply ignore her.

Then it occurred to her that he couldn't ignore her any more than she could him. That same attraction that had brought them together Saturday night was pulling at them again with an intensity that almost scared her. A shudder rippled through her with his intense stare and a purely feminine unease settled deep within her when he began walking toward where she sat. Her heart skipped a beat when he stood before her table.

"Hi, Jenna," he said, smiling warmly at her. He was also looking deep into her eyes and the sheer power of his gaze made her tremble inside.

"Hi." She didn't know what else to say.

He glanced around and saw the librarian looking at them, to make sure they kept it quiet. He met her gaze again. "Is there someplace where we can go talk?"

His voice was deep and throaty. It was also gentle, she thought, looking back at him. "Uh, sure."

After she gathered her things, they walked outside. Jenna was grateful she had brought her sweater. The weather had turned chilly since she had entered the library a few hours ago. For a few minutes they didn't say anything to each other, they just continued walking. She was letting him take the lead and wondered just where they were headed.

"You been doing okay?" he asked her moments later.

"Yes. What about you?"

"I've been doing fine. I'm just ready for this semester to be over."

She couldn't help but smile. "It just started last month."

He laughed. "Yes, I know."

When they got to the Blackburn Center he held the door open for her. "I thought we could sit and eat something while we talk. You don't mind, do you?"

She shook her head. "No, I don't mind."

"Good. It will be my treat."

"You don't have to do that. I can pay for my own."

"I want to. Please let me."

She met his gaze and nodded. "All right."

They got a table near the jukebox and then he asked what she wanted.

"A hamburger and a milkshake."

"What flavor?"

"Strawberry."

He nodded. "Will you share an order of fries with me?"

She smiled, knowing he was teasing her a little. He was doing the very thing he had set out to do from the first. Take her out. Anyone who saw them together sitting at the same table, sharing a meal, would assume they were dating or something.

Before walking off he moved to the jukebox and selected a couple of songs. Her breath caught when "In the Midnight Hour" began playing. It was the song that had been playing the moment they had noticed each other in the yard Saturday night. She knew he had played it deliberately to make her think about that night. And she *was* thinking about it as she glanced around. There were a number of couples sharing food and talking. There were also people alone, sitting at tables studying. Usually she was one of them. But not today. Randolph had seen to that.

Moments later he returned with their food. After he had spread everything out in front of them, and after taking a sip of her milkshake, she asked. "What did you want to talk to me about?"

He took a sip of his soda before responding. "Your misconception that I'm trying to run some game on you. I meant what I said the other night, Jenna. I'm not going with Lena Weaver. Because of our families, Lena and I are friends, nothing more."

She nodded, holding his gaze. For some reason she believed him. "All right, and I apologize for sounding so cold the other night, but . . ."

"You weren't sure you could trust me?"

"Yes," she said quietly.

"And that's understandable. All I want is for us to get to know each other better. Is anything wrong with that?" he asked, whispering hoarsely.

"I always thought there was. At least for me. My main focus is to concentrate on my studies and nothing else."

"Do you see me as a threat to that, Jenna? If you do then let me assure you that I'm not. Staying on top of my schoolwork is important to me as well. Uncle Sam is pulling men who aren't making the grade out of college and shipping them off to Vietnam. I have no desire to go into the armed services any sooner than I have to."

Jenna nodded, knowing that was true. The draft deferral was good as long as a person was in school making good grades. Leigh had mentioned how hard Noah was working to keep his grades up, too. No one in their right mind wanted to go to Vietnam. Each day the news reports indicated that more and more American servicemen were losing their lives, and there were a number of demonstrations being held across the country protesting the war.

"All I'm asking is that we get to know each other better by spending some time together. And just how much time we spend together will be your call."

Panic rushed through her with what he was saying. The only time he would share with her was what she allowed him. "Why?" she whispered, wanting to know why he was letting her set the conditions, the rules, the guidelines.

"Because I care."

"And why do you care, Randolph?"

For the longest moment he didn't answer. He just continued to look at her. Then suddenly he slowly reached out and took her hand in his and then she knew. She felt the same thing he did. The current. The electricity. The charge. The passion.

It flowed from his body to hers then back to his again. The feelings he experienced from touching her were gut-wrenchingly deep. Then there was the heat that flowed between them.

"That night when I first saw you at the party, Jenna, the moment I looked at you, a part of me knew there was something going on between us that I couldn't explain. I'm not crazy about it any more than you are, but I'm not going to deny that it's there."

Jenna let out a shaky sigh. A part of her couldn't deny it either. But then, she didn't want to become involved with anything or anyone who could make her lose sight of her whole purpose for coming to college. Her parents depended on her to do the right thing. Her brothers depended on her to help make sure their dreams came true. There were others she had to think about more so than herself.

She met Randolph's gaze again. His stare was unnerving. It made whatever it was between them, that neither of them understood, bigger than life. She had gone to bed each night since meeting him with thoughts of him on her mind. And tonight, at the library, a part of her had responded to him, against her will, against her desire and best intentions. The plain fact was that what they were experiencing couldn't be normal. No attraction could be that deep. That intense. That volatile.

She closed her eyes briefly against all the emotions she was feeling. They were the same emotions he was feeling too. And he was right. They owed it to themselves and to each other to find out where all this would lead.

She opened her eyes and met a gaze that was holding hers with such intensity that for a split second she thought everything around them was at a standstill, except for the beating of their hearts. She finally dragged her gaze from his and took another sip of her milkshake. The cold substance felt thick, refreshing as it flowed down her hot throat.

"All right," she finally said, softly. "I prefer that we don't see each other during the week but I'm okay with us going out occasionally on the weekends."

He nodded. "That's fine with me but I can call during the week, right?"

"Yes, if you'd like."

The slow smile on his lips indicated he would like. They finished eating the rest of their food. They had discussed what was happening on campus: the Vietnam War and how it was becoming more and more on everyone's mind, and the civil rights movement and how some of the leaders working with Dr. King were getting impatient, annoyed and intolerant of the growing amount of racism they faced each day. They had begun questioning whether or not his approach of nonviolence was the way. And if it was, why was it taking so long for results?

Randolph walked Jenna home while holding her hand. When they reached her dorm building, he said softly, "If there's ever anything you want to know about me, just ask me. Please don't believe everything that you hear." Pulling her out of the light from the building to a dark, secluded spot on the building's steps, he leaned down and his lips touched hers, gently, but with a passion that was blatantly male and made everything about her that was ultrafeminine react. He was bringing her to a sizzle without a whole lot of effort and she heard the low sound that erupted from her throat the moment his tongue touched hers.

She might not fully understand what was happening between them but she definitely understood the burning sensation that was flowing through every part of her body. It felt strange to experience such feelings since she had never slept with a man and didn't know a thing about passion.

He ended the kiss and stared at her unblinking as he drew in a deep, labored breath. He then smiled in a way that was so sensuous it made her heart began pumping wildly. "Good night, Jenna. I'll be by around six next week to take you to the concert. Will that time be okay?"

She swallowed deeply, thickly, then nodded. "Yes."

He pulled open the door for her and she looked at him once again before going inside. When she heard the door click shut behind her she drew in a deep breath, inhaling air into her lungs. Confusion shook her with the intensity of their attraction to each other. Startled by the giddy pleasure she felt, she slowly walked down the hall toward her dorm room. Randolph Devin Fuller had definitely turned her world upside down.

Three

Randolph walked along the paved lane, too wired to go back to the dorm room he shared with two other guys. He thought about going to one of the popular hangouts on campus, but didn't want to be around a lot of people just yet. He needed to walk and think.

He had never been this tied in knots over a woman in his life. Girls had always been there, hanging around, being available. And because he'd been raised to treat all females with respect, he never played games with them. He was either interested or he wasn't. But under no circumstances had he ever let any female call the shots in their relationship. He never had the time or the inclination to do so.

His life had always revolved around some purpose. Before college he had concentrated on making the grades he needed—that was expected of a Fuller—to get into college, namely Howard, a tradition his great-great grandfather had started back in the late eighteen hundreds. Then once he got to Howard and had gone out for the football team, academics and sports had joined forces in his life, taking up most of his time. He dated occasionally, but he'd never given a thought to getting serious about anyone. Even when his grandmother, who was as tenacious as they come, tried pushing Lena Weaver at him, he had staunchly refused to succumb to any member of the opposite sex.

Until Saturday night.

He still wondered what had happened to him. He seriously didn't have a clue. All he knew was that when he had seen Jenna, a part of him had known—at that exact moment—that she was meant to be the woman for him whether he was looking for her or not. He remembered his maternal grandfather who lived in South Carolina once telling him that was how it had been when he had met his grandmother—love at first sight. Once they had met, it was as if no other woman existed or mattered.

He then thought of his paternal grandparents—the ones who had raised him and Ross after their parents' death. At times he wondered if Robert and Julia Fuller ever truly loved each other. He knew they respected each other. But love? He always believed Robert and Julia's parents had arranged their marriage, although he'd never asked them or had been given any confirmation of such a thing. But for some reason, in his grandmother's mind, the suitability of two individuals was more important than if those persons loved each other. Love, she claimed, could come later. Evidently she believed what she was preaching enough to push it onto him and Ross. It was a harder sale for him than it was for Ross. Ross always strove to please their grandparents, where Randolph was considered the rebellious one.

He smiled when he thought of Ross. It wasn't that his brother was a weakling by any means. Ross was just very careful in choosing his battles and a fight with Julia Fuller was a battle no mortal person would want to take on. So in some things, Ross meekly gave in. Like his dating of Angela Douglass. Even after dating her for almost eight months, Ross hadn't managed make it to first base yet. She was too dignified, too refined, too prim and proper and too damn restrained. Ross had even admitted she hadn't allowed him to kiss her until they had dated for three months. Yet he continued to date her to keep their grandmother happy and off his back.

Randolph noticed that he had walked from one end of the campus to the other while he'd been thinking, and yet he still wasn't ready to go to his dorm room. After checking his watch and seeing it wasn't yet seven o'clock, he made a quick decision to walk the two miles to where Ross shared a house with Noah Wainwright. Ross had lived on campus for four years and had decided that while in law school he wanted the freedom and privacy living off campus afforded. Their grandparents had agreed and his grandfather had helped to locate a two-bedroom house not far from Howard Law School. Ross had chosen Noah for a housemate, the two having met when Noah first came to Howard. They had remained best friends ever since.

Pulling his jacket closer together to ward off the cool chill of the night air, Randolph began walking the two miles to where he knew his brother was probably at home studying.

• • •

Ross Fuller looked up from the huge textbook he was reading when he heard the solid knock on his bedroom door. "Yeah?"

"It's me, Ross. You got a minute?"

Ross closed the book and called back, "Yeah, Noah, come on in." He watched as the door opened and his best friend, Noah Wainwright, stepped into the room.

"You still at it?" Noah asked Ross, indicating the book he held in his hand.

"Yeah, I still have a good twenty more pages to read tonight. What about you? Did you complete that paper you were working on?"

"As much as I plan on doing tonight. If I have to write anything else about property ownership I'm going to go nuts. It's not like black folks own a whole lot of property anyway."

Ross smiled. "But we can dream can't we?"

"The only thing I do these days is pray this damn war will be over before we graduate next year."

"It will be. It doesn't take a rocket scientist to figure out we have no business in 'Nam. I feel confident President Johnson is going to wise up to that fact so we can get the hell out of there. Those 'Congs are crazy and don't fight fair. Besides, I don't fully support the reason why we're there."

"Which is the main reason I don't want to go."

Ross nodded. They felt the same way, yet he knew if either of them got called to go, they wouldn't hesitate to do so. They were Americans and they would defend their country or die trying. He glanced around his bedroom. "I would invite you to sit down, but as you can see I have no idea where the chair is. It's probably over there under that huge stack of clothes." He had yet to fold up the laundry he had washed two days ago.

"I'm fine standing. I just need to talk to you about something."

Ross noted the serious expression on Noah's face. "Okay. What is it?"

"It's about Leigh."

Ross lifted a brow. Leigh Murdock was Noah's girlfriend. "What about Leigh?"

"I appreciate you letting her hang out here with me sometimes. It really means a lot."

Ross had an idea just how much it meant. Anyone who saw Noah and Leigh together knew how much in love they were. From what Noah had told him, Leigh's brother had been his best friend in high school, so he had hung out over at Leigh's house quite a bit. He had known for a long time that he loved Leigh, but since he had been three years older than she, he had never let those feelings be known. Leigh's brother Zachary, with no plans to go to college after graduating from high school, had entered the police academy and become an officer on the streets of Miami. Zachary hadn't been on the force two years when he was killed in the line of duty. On the night of Zachary's funeral, Leigh, who had been very close to her brother, had sought comfort in Noah's arms and things had officially started from there. Leigh had made a decision after she graduated from high school to join Noah at Howard.

"Hey, I don't mind, Noah. You know I like Leigh. She's a nice person. Besides, this place always looks a thousand times better after she's spent a few days over here," Ross said, teasing. But it was the truth. Not only did Leigh straighten up after them most of the time, but she knew how to cook and usually made a number of good-tasting dishes whenever she stayed over.

Noah laughed. "Yeah, it does, doesn't it? But still, Leigh and I appreciate your letting her stay occasionally."

"Think nothing of it. But I guess the reason you're mentioning it is to let me know she'll be here when I wake up in the morning, right?"

Noah gave him an ingratiating grin. "Yeah, right."

Ross shook his head, laughing. "Thanks for the warning. I would hate to show up for breakfast wearing my underwear not knowing a lady was in the house."

Noah joined him laughing. "I would hate for you to show up that way, too."

Although Ross knew Noah was a responsible person and it probably wasn't any of his business and was nothing one guy could ask another unless he felt sure of the close relationship between them,

Ross stopped laughing, leaned back and looked up at Noah. "You're using protection, aren't you?"

The two men's gazes met and Noah knew the significance of the question Ross was asking him. If Leigh wound up pregnant that meant he would have to drop out of school. Dropping out of school and getting married would eventually lead to getting drafted. Being married with a baby on the way might work as an excuse before the draft board for a white man, but it would be a waste of time if you were black.

Noah didn't answer right away. Then he said, "Yeah, I'm using protection, although sometimes I wish I didn't have to. If things were different and Leigh and I were married, with me having finished school and no threat of going off to war, I wouldn't hesitate to get her pregnant, Ross. I want her to have my baby bad. Real bad." His eyes met Ross's and he saw his best friend's surprise. "Don't you ever feel that way about Angela?"

"No," Ross said without thinking about it. He couldn't see the prim and proper Angela pregnant with anyone's baby, least of all his. "Angela and I don't have that kind of relationship, Noah." In truth, at times he didn't think they had a relationship at all. They were merely two people whose families had decided they were a perfect couple.

"In that case you don't know what you're missing. There's nothing more meaningful in a man's life than to love a woman. I mean truly love a woman, Ross. You'll know what I mean when it happens to you."

Noah's words were still on Ross's mind an hour or so later when the doorbell rang. He knew it wasn't Leigh since she had arrived already with her overnight bag. He hoped it wasn't his grandmother, arriving in town to check up on them. All he needed was for her to find out Leigh was spending the night with Noah.

He breathed a sigh of relief when he opened the door to discover it was his brother, Randolph. "Damnit, Rand, you had me scared there for a minute. I thought you were Grandmother Julia."

Randolph chuckled. "Is she still coming to town unannounced?" he asked, entering the house.

"Not as much as she did last year. Granddad must have said something to her about it."

Like that would mean anything, Randolph thought. "Or she got tired of dropping by and finding this place a mess. Sometimes you and Noah can be real slobs."

"Yeah, well, if the reason you came by was to hurl insults then I'm not in the mood. But if you happen to have a beer in that bag you're clutching so tightly to your chest then you can stay for a while. Just as long as you brought enough to share."

Randolph huffed loudly. "It was either that or run the risk of you guzzling down all of mine," he said, following his brother into the kitchen. "Where's Noah tonight?"

"In his bedroom. He has company."

Randolph nodded and smiled. Although he'd never met Noah's girlfriend, he had heard from Ross that she was good looking, and that she and Noah were deeply in love. He also knew from talking to Ross that she spent a lot of time, especially nights, at their place with Noah. No wonder Ross had been nervous about their grandmother showing up unexpectedly. Julia Fuller would have a hissy fit if she knew a woman was sleeping over. "Do you ever get jealous?" he asked as he sat down and handed his brother a beer.

Ross lifted a brow as he joined Randolph at the table. "Jealous about what?"

Randolph smiled. "About the fact that there's always action going on in Noah's bedroom but never any in yours."

Ross thought about the woman he'd been seeing now on a steady basis for the last eight months. He shrugged. "Angela is in Boston. Besides, she isn't into sex before marriage."

Randolph chuckled. "Are you sure she's even into sex *after* marriage? I would find that out if I were you. Doing something like having sex might be too undignified for her."

The corners of Ross's mouth quivered into a smile. "You don't like Angela, do you?"

"No," Randolph replied without hesitation. "I can't rightly say that I do. I think you can do better. I admit she looks okay, but you need a woman with passion, Ross, and I doubt Angela Douglass has a passionate bone in her body."

Ross wasn't stunned by his brother's statement. In a way he had to agree with Randolph, but still . . . "Passion isn't everything," he said unconvincingly.

Randolph grinned. "I bet you couldn't convince Noah of that about now."

Ross chuckled. "Yeah, well, probably not." He took a swallow of beer, not wanting to discuss Angela any longer. "So what brought you by?"

Randolph looked down at the beer bottle he held in his hand. A few moments later he looked up and met his brother's curious stare. "I met someone."

Ross lifted a brow. "Someone like who?"

"A woman I'm attracted to."

Ross took another sip of his beer before saying, "Okay, so what's the problem? I'm sure in your lifetime you've met a lot of women you're attracted to. Can you be a little more specific than that?"

Randolph shook his head, wondering why he had wasted his time coming to see Ross. His brother clearly didn't understand the ramifications of being attracted to someone, probably because he'd never been attracted to *anybody*. Academics had always been the number one thing in Ross's life. That and his love for music. Ross had a gift for being able to pick up and play basically any instrument. "What is there to be more specific about, Ross? I met this woman at a party Saturday night and I can't get her out of my mind. From the moment I laid eyes on her, I knew I wanted her."

"And what do you know about her?"

Randolph was not surprised by Ross's question. After all, he was studying to be an attorney and everyone knew attorneys had inquisitive minds. "Her family isn't well known if that's what you're asking."

"Then you might as well forget her. Grandmother Julia would never go along with you getting involved with someone she would consider a nobody."

Randolph leveled a dark frown at him. "Then it's a good thing I don't lose sleep at night caring what Grandmother Julia will or won't go along with. I'm more like Dad than either one of us." Both of them knew that their father, Ross Senior, had defied his mother when he married Adrianna Denison, a girl from what Grandmother Julia referred to as the backwoods of South Carolina, a girl without any strong family connections or ties. Julia Fuller was determined to make sure her two grandsons didn't make the same mistake.

"Why cause yourself unnecessary grief?" Ross shuddered at the possibility of having to deal with his grandmother's wrath. She could be very unreasonable when she wanted to be, which unfortunately was most of the time. But then he knew Randolph was the defiant one and had stood up to their grandmother on a number of occasions.

A smile touched Randolph's lips after taking a hefty sip of beer. "Why cause myself unnecessary grief you ask? One good reason is for something you seem to know nothing about, Ross. Something that's called passion."

Noah and Leigh lay together on rumpled sheets after having made love once already. Yet as far as they were concerned, it wasn't enough. He quickly put on another rubber to protect her, lifted her into his arms and placed her on top of him as sweat sheened his skin and dampened hers.

His sex was thick and hard again and jutted proudly and boldly from the apex of his thighs, waiting for her to take it inside of her. A shudder went through him as he watched her straddle him, parting her legs wide to flank his hips, but not settling her weight on him yet. Instead she leaned down and kissed him, the way he liked, sweetly, tenderly and with a hunger that made every part of him burn.

Using his fingers he reached out and found what he wanted, that part of her he loved, craved and needed. Touching her, he saw she was still wet. His fingers gently slipped into her, stroking her to make her body ache with the same need as his. He heard her inhale a gasp then slowly exhale a rush of pure pleasure as his fingers withdrew then slid inside her again, moving to the sound of the rhythmic music he heard in his head. Heat poured through him as she continued to attack his mouth, her tongue mating with his with an intensity that was depriving him of all thoughts except for one—making love to her again. "Now, Leigh," he whispered softly, not able to take any more. He wanted her now.

He felt her shift as she lowered her weight onto him, fitting the opening of her hot center to the tip of his arousal. He shuddered when they made contact. The scent in the room was male, female—sex. He placed his hands on her hips to lead, to guide. And when she eased down on him, taking him into her body, hot pleasure tore through him, making a whispery rumble pour forth from his throat, setting fire to his flesh. Like always, his need and desire for her was so intense, everything about her inflamed his senses, driving him near the brink.

And when he was embedded deep within her, he felt her move, slow at first, up and down, in and out, while she continued to kiss him long and hard, using the same rhythm on his mouth that her body had set in motion below. His hand moved from her hips and began rubbing her back as she rode him over the edge, her every movement branding him as hers more and more, and making every cell in his body fully charged and ready to explode at any minute.

And then it happened, the explosion—that intense pleasure he knew he would find with her. Only her. The sensation hit straight in his loins. He knew she felt it as well and he hardened even more inside of her as she continued to ride him wildly with mindless passion. His mouth captured the scream she threatened to make, as ecstasy ripped through them both and they soared high among the clouds.

Moments later when they finally came back to earth, Leigh's body sank down on Noah. Still connected to him, her breathing was hard and fast. "I love you," she whispered, knowing he meant everything to her and knowing how life could end in an instant, like it had for her brother.

"And I love you," he answered softly, nestling her in his arms as she lay atop him, still a part of him. He kissed her before pulling the sheet over them.

"I'm tired," she said sleepily.

He smiled. "And you should be, baby. Go to sleep."

And she did as he held her in his arms, close to his heart where he knew she would always and forever belong.

Four

Saturday evening, after finishing all the school assignments she needed to complete, Jenna decided to go to the football game using the free pass Randolph had given her. They were playing the Hampton University Pirates.

Green Stadium was already crowded by the time she got there. She quickly found her seat before the pregame show began. Turning when she heard someone call her name, she looked up and saw Leigh and Noah sitting not far away. She smiled and waved back at them. There was another guy sitting with them who was looking at her strangely, and she immediately knew he was Randolph's brother. She didn't want to stare but she could clearly see the resemblance, and like Randolph he was a very good-looking man.

During halftime she and Leigh met up at the hot dog stand. "So what do you think?" she asked Leigh as she put mustard and ketchup on her hot dog.

"We're going to win," Leigh said, pretty sure of herself.

Jenna wasn't too sure. "You think so?"

"Yes. A lot of our key players haven't been on the field yet, including Randolph."

Jenna nodded. She couldn't help the smile that touched her lips. While standing on the sidelines, Randolph had looked up in the stands and had seen her and smiled. "That guy sitting with you. That's

Randolph's brother, isn't it?" she asked after taking a sip of her Coke.

"Yes, and I hope you don't mind but I mentioned to him that Randolph was the one who gave you your pass to attend today's game."

No wonder he had looked at her funny, Jenna thought. He was probably trying to figure out what his brother saw in her. "No, I don't mind," Jenna assured Leigh.

After returning to her seat for the beginning of the third quarter, Jenna looked over her shoulder. Randolph's brother was staring at her, and surprisingly, he smiled. Recognizing it as a friendly gesture, she smiled back at him.

Leigh had been right. In the end the Bisons won, beating the other team by five points. She had watched with admiration when Randolph had gone onto the field, earning his team points with a touchdown, and at another time stealing the ball from their rivals with an interception.

After the game it had been her intent to leave and return home. She was surprised when Leigh approached her with Noah and Randolph's brother in tow. "See, I told you we would win," she said happily, grabbing her arm.

"So you did," Jenna said, smiling, as she gave Noah a hug.

Leigh then introduced her to Randolph's brother, Ross.

"Nice meeting you, Jenna," he said, smiling down at her.

"It's nice meeting you too, Ross."

When Leigh and Noah invited her to join them for something to eat, she declined, saying she was going back home.

"You're not going to wait around for Rand?" Ross asked her. He actually seemed surprised at the notion that she wouldn't be.

"No, I hadn't planned on it. Besides, I'm sure he has plans."

Ross chuckled. "I doubt it." He could see why Randolph was taken with Jenna. He thought she was a very pretty girl and she didn't act like the other girls Randolph had dated before who treated him like he was the next best thing since bread pudding. "I plan on waiting around for him. Would you wait with me?"

Jenna wondered why he would want her to do that and decided to come right out and ask him. "Why?"

Ross smiled and Jenna immediately thought it was a smile very similar to one she had seen on Randolph. "I think he'll be glad to see you."

Jenna wondered why he thought that but instead of asking him she told him she wasn't sure that would be a good idea.

"And I happen to think it's a wonderful idea. Trust me."

And for some reason she did, which was why moments later the two of them were standing outside the players' locker rooms talking while waiting for Randolph to appear. She was enjoying Ross's company. She noticed there were other girls around, too, waiting for players as well. She noted Ellie among them.

Tyrone was one of the first players to come out amidst the loud cheering from the crowd. He went straight over to Ellie and kissed her soundly on the lips. Other players soon followed and it seemed that each had a special girl waiting for him whom he greeted with a kiss. Jenna began to feel uncomfortable. She wondered what Randolph's reaction would be when he saw her standing there waiting for him. Although he had pressed her about them seeing each other again, he hadn't made it clear exactly what their relationship was.

Her heart nearly stopped when he walked out. He wasn't looking around the crowd for anyone in particular and Jenna's breath caught when she noticed Lena Weaver walk over to him.

Randolph greeted Lena with a smile but didn't kiss her. Then, as if he had some kind of internal radar where Jenna was concerned, he glanced over in her direction and saw her.

Surprise flitted into his eyes and the smile on his face widened. Excusing himself from Lena, he quickly headed over in their direction, his gaze dead center on Jenna.

Jenna couldn't take her gaze off Randolph any more than it seemed he could take his gaze off her. Her stomach twisted nervously in knots and the rest of her insides began to stir with the heat from his gaze. In the distance she thought she heard thunder rumbling—or was it the sound of her body trembling?

Moments later he was standing in front of her and without saying a word, he leaned down and captured her lips with his. Sharp thrills of sensation flooded Jenna's body, taking her breath away.

"Hi," he said, smiling after ending the kiss. "I'm glad you came."

A part of Jenna was glad she had come, too. She didn't know why but she was glad he had kissed her. That kiss had basically made a statement to everyone that she meant something to him.

Taking her hand in his, he turned his attention to his brother. "You two know each other?" he asked curiously.

Ross smiled. "No. We met officially after the game. Leigh introduced us."

"You know Leigh?" Randolph asked Jenna.

Jenna chuckled. "Yes, Leigh and I are roommates. Small world, huh?"

"Yeah, but not small enough," he said, frowning at his brother, wondering how he could get rid of him so he could be alone with Jenna. Thankfully, Ross caught his drift.

"Well, I guess I'll be going."

Jenna turned to him, surprised. "You're leaving?"

Ross chuckled. "Yes. I was only waiting around to make sure Rand didn't have any broken bones or anything. You know how it is, big brother looking out for little brother and all that nonsense."

Jenna felt the brothers' closeness and thought it was wonderful that they were friends as well as brothers. "It was nice meeting you, Ross."

"It was nice meeting you, Jenna, as well."

After Ross walked off, Randolph's hand on Jenna's tightened. He looked down at her. "You want to go and get something to eat?"

Since she had eaten a hot dog and drank a Coke earlier, she wasn't very hungry but she figured that he would be after playing such a grueling game. "I'm not hungry but I'll go with you if you'd like."

He smiled. "You don't know just how much I would like."

"So what do you think of Ross?" he asked as they walked down the paved lane toward her building, after leaving the restaurant where they had gotten something to eat.

"He's nice," she said, looking at him under lowered lashes. "You may want to keep him around as a brother."

Randolph laughed. "Believe me, I intend to."

"Do you remember a lot about your parents?" she asked him,

remembering that he had been ten when his parents had gotten killed in a car accident.

"Oh, yeah. They were the best. My father was a prominent attorney in Virginia, but he still found the time to spend with Ross and me. He and my mother were very close, too. They loved each other very much. I think that's why God took them away together because he knew it would have been hard on one without the other, even with me and Ross."

When they reached her building, they stood and talked a while under the light. She finally got the nerve to ask him something she had been wondering about all evening. "Today when you saw me, why did you kiss me?"

He thought about her question for a minute before answering. "Because it seemed like the right thing to do," he responded quietly. "It was something that I wanted to do." He looked at her, studying her. "Did it bother you?"

Jenna shook her head. "No, it didn't bother me."

"I'm looking forward to our date next Saturday night," he said, drawing her to him.

"Me too," she said honestly, allowing herself to be drawn into his arms when he reached out and lifted her mouth for his kiss. Just like earlier that day, the kiss was special, sweet and tender. It tempted her to put her arms around his neck and get closer to him.

Moments later when the kiss ended, he continued to hold her. "What will you be doing tomorrow? Studying?"

She shook her head. "No, I've completed all my homework."

He nodded. "Would you like to go to the movies?"

She smiled. "Sure. What time do you want me ready?"

"How about around five?"

"Okay."

He then leaned down and kissed her again. This kiss was a little deeper and lasted a little longer than before, and she gloried in the feel of his lips on hers.

"I think I better let you go inside while I have the mind to do so, Jenna."

She nodded. "Good night, Randolph."

"Good night. I'll see you tomorrow."

Jenna nodded before turning to go inside her building.

Jenna awoke the next day to hear the news that a big demonstration had erupted on some college campus up north that was protesting the United States' involvement in Vietnam.

At breakfast in one of the cafés on campus, Johnny was glad to fill her in about it. He also told her that a group calling itself the Black Panther Party was growing in membership across the country and demanding the end of racism and class oppression on constitutional grounds. Johnny even admitted that he had gone to one of the secret meetings and said he was thinking seriously about joining the group. He claimed the leaders of the party weren't street thugs, but highly educated individuals who had gotten sick and tired of the government dragging their feet to do what was right by black people.

When Randolph picked her up for the movies, Jenna asked him what he thought of the group. "I think that like a lot of organizations, they started out with a really good cause but now their ideology is questionable, especially with the group on the West Coast. Rumor has it that one of its leaders was arrested for the assassination of a police officer. I don't know if it's true or if the group was framed. If I were your friend Johnny, I would be very careful before thinking of joining. I hear J. Edgar Hoover's men are watching them like a hawk, just waiting for them to make a wrong move."

Jenna nodded, hoping Johnny was doing as Randolph suggested and thinking things through before joining the group.

The following weekend Randolph and Jenna went to the concert and afterward met with some of his friends for dinner. The more they were around each other, the more they enjoyed each other's company.

"So, Jenna, you and Randolph have been dating for a couple of weeks now. What do you think of him?" Leigh asked her one night while they were still awake, lying in the darkness listening to the soft music playing on the radio. Ellie claimed she was staying out all night with a friend. Both Jenna and Leigh had a feeling that friend was Tyrone.

Jenna smiled. "I really like Randolph, Leigh. I like him a lot."

"Oh, is that all?" Leigh said grinning. "I was hoping it was a little deeper than that."

"We've only known each other for three weeks, Leigh. We're trying to take things slow."

"Why bother taking things slow?"

Jenna raised her eyes to the ceiling. She knew Leigh was only teasing but she felt the need to answer her anyway. "Because we don't want to rush into anything. We want to make sure what we have and what we feel is right."

"Trust me, Jen, it is. I think of how right it is every time I see the two of you together. You and Randolph make such a cute couple. Nearly as cute as me and Noah."

And with Leigh's statement they both laughed.

"Leigh, can I ask you something?" Jenna whispered hesitantly, a few minutes later.

"Sure. What?"

"When did you know that you loved Noah?"

Leigh smiled as she lay in bed thinking. "I think it was the first time my brother Zachary brought him home with him from school. I was twelve and they were about fifteen. I thought he was so—so cute and I developed a crush on him then. As I got older, things got worse but I kept my feelings to myself. When I was fourteen he left home to come here for college and Zachary entered the police academy. After that I only saw Noah when he came home for the holidays since he always made it a point to drop by the house to visit with Zachary. Then when I turned sixteen and was in the eleventh grade, Zachary was killed in the line of duty. Noah's family got word to him and he came home immediately."

Leigh rubbed the goose bumps she felt on her arms as she remembered that time. "Noah took Zachary's death real hard, but so did everyone else, especially me. He was the big brother I adored. After the funeral Noah asked me to go for a car ride with him. He said he wanted to talk to me about something. What he did was share with me the last letter he had gotten from Zachary. In that letter, which Zachary had written a week before he'd died, he asked Noah to look out for me if anything ever happened to him."

Leigh inhaled a deep gulp of air as she fought the tightening she felt in her throat. "It was as if my brother had known he would be dying or something. After Noah told me about the letter, I fell apart and he tried to comfort me. Somehow we started kissing and couldn't stop. He finally pushed me away but not before I told him that I loved him and had always loved him."

"What did he say? Was he surprised?" Jenna asked curiously.

Leigh chuckled. "What he was, was mad as hell. He was mad at himself for being weak. He felt he had taken advantage of me although I tried to convince him he hadn't. He immediately took me back to my parents' house, saying I was too young to know my own heart. When he left I thought I had ruined things and that I would never see him again. And he deliberately didn't come home that Christmas. Everyone assumed the pain of Zachary's death was the reason, but I knew he was avoiding me."

"Then what happened?"

"He didn't come back home until the summer before I was to start my senior year of high school. I came home from spending a day at the community pool and there he was, sitting in the living room talking to my dad. The moment he looked at me, I knew. I knew in my heart that as much as he had tried fighting it, deep down he loved me, too."

"How did you figure that?"

"By the way he looked at me. Noah has very expressive eyes and I was able to read how he felt in them, and later when I got him alone I made him admit it."

"How?"

"By coming on to him and kissing him again. This time he didn't push me away but kept right on kissing me. Before he left to return to Howard at the end of the summer, I was no longer a virgin and we've been together ever since."

Jenna drew in a deep breath, thinking that had been such a beautiful love story. That night after both of them had drifted off to sleep, she couldn't help but dream of Randolph.

Bronson College

Many miles away, someone else was also having dreams about Randolph.

Angela opened her eyes and shook her head in disappointment, realizing she'd only been having a dream.

Being careful not to wake up her roommate, she swung her legs over the side of the bed and came to her feet. The lower part of her body still throbbed.

With a small sigh she grabbed her robe and put it on before opening the door and quietly easing out of it, deciding to go for a walk. She needed relief and finding it wouldn't be easy when the entire student body was nothing but girls.

As she walked she thought about the first time she had seen Randolph last year at a birthday party given for A. Philip Randolph. Her mother had explained that Julia Fuller was looking for debutantes from good families as potential future wives for her two grandsons.

Angela had known that matches between well-known African-American families were often made. She had also known that if such a match was made between her parents and the Fullers, she much preferred Randolph over Ross. But her mother and Julia Fuller got the notion in their heads that she and Ross were a perfect fit. So she played the part of the prim and proper woman around him, often extending her role to act like a total prude who didn't like sex. She had hoped that would turn him off but so far it hadn't. The man had the patience of Job.

"What are you doing out here this time of night with your bedclothes on?"

Angela turned to the sound of the deep, husky voice. It was Mr. Adams, the security guard. He was short, stocky and a good fifty years old. But he was a man and that's what she needed right now. And from what she'd heard, some of the girls had slept with him and in return he kept his lips zipped when they sneaked off campus.

Her lips quivered into a smile when she looked at him. "I couldn't sleep. I got restless."

He frowned. "Well, it's not safe being out here this time of night by yourself. You need to go back inside."

She knew he was being cautious with her since it was well known that her family was close friends with the Hightowers. She forced tears into her eyes, something she had learned to perfect as a child. "But I don't want to go back inside. I need to think. I'm not doing so well in one of my classes, and I'm afraid I'm going to get kicked out of school."

As she'd known they would, her tears got to him. He walked over to her. "There, there," he murmured, trying to stop her from crying. "Nobody is going to kick you out of school. All you have to do is study a little harder and things will be fine."

"You think so?" she asked, sniffing.

"Yeah. Your family is friends with Dean Hightower. So I doubt you're going anywhere."

I doubt so, too, but not for that reason. The dean likes poking me too much, Angela thought, deciding not to waste any time talking to Mr. Adams. They were standing under a huge oak tree and couldn't be seen. Without warning she dropped to her knees in front of him.

"Hey! What's the matter with you? What are you doing!" he asked as she snapped the button off his pants and tore at his zipper. He tried pushing her away but she was intent on getting just what she wanted. Before he could push her back she had taken the man-tool out of his pants and had it in her mouth. The hair covering his stomach tickled her nose but she ignored it as she nearly swallowed him whole—the way Mr. Morgan had taught her to do during the week he had stayed with the Hightowers. In that one week he had shown her a lot, and she was glad to use her newfound knowledge on someone and see the results. She wished it was Randolph, but again she could fantasize.

Locking her mouth firmly on Mr. Adams, she began purring and saw that he was no longer fighting her. In fact he had grabbed the back of her head to push himself deeper inside her mouth. She knew the way she was working her mouth, as well as the kissing and sucking sounds she was making, were driving him insane.

Knowing he was about to come, she pulled back and quickly stood up. "Stick it in me now!"

Wasting no time, he shoved her back against the tree and rammed deep inside of her, tearing the top of her robe in the process. She closed her eyes and began fantasizing while he was pumping into her like a madman.

That's it, Randolph, take it all. Take it all, baby. Take it all!

She didn't open her eyes when he ripped the rest of her robe and the top part of her gown. She felt his hands all over her breasts. In her mind they were *Randolph's* hands, big and strong. The thought that this was *Randolph* touching her and thrusting back and forth inside of her made her desperate.

Holding onto his shoulders for support, she wrapped her legs around his waist as he held her against the tree trunk, pumping into her at every angle he could.

When she heard him let out a loud, harsh grunt, just seconds before he ejaculated, she almost wept with intense pleasure, loving the feel of *Randolph* exploding inside of her. As Mr. Adams continued to rock against her, enjoying her to the end, she slowly opened her eyes. She had fantasized about Randolph all the while he had taken her and she had enjoyed it. She smiled. Her dreams and fantasies would serve their purpose until she got the real thing.

And one day she intended to have Randolph Fuller.

Five

October turned into November and with it came cooler weather in the nation's capital. The Vietnam War was still being fought and more and more American troops were being sent to Saigon each day. The bloodiest battle to date had been fought a few weeks ago, and in one engagement the North Vietnamese ambushed a battalion, nearly wiping out an entire company and killing close to two thousand American soldiers. Around the country, more and more people had begun protesting the war.

On the home front, now that the Voting Rights Act had been passed, Martin Luther King, Jr. had begun focusing on poverty and racial inequality in the North. Out West and in other parts of the country, the Black Panther Party began challenging King's leadership of the civil rights movement as well as his policy of nonviolence.

Everyone at Howard University left campus the day before Thanksgiving, heading home. Because they had the farthest to travel, Leigh and Noah left a day earlier than the others, catching the train to Miami. Ellie's parents arrived to pick her up at noon on that Wednesday.

Ross, who owned a late-model Chevrolet that his grandfather had given him, offered to take Jenna as far as Richmond, Virginia where she could purchase a ticket with a lower bus fare to Knoxville. Both Randolph and Ross had entertained her along the way with stories of their childhood and all the trouble they had gotten into.

When they reached the Greyhound bus station, Randolph walked her inside. He then sat with her and waited for her bus to come, refusing to leave her alone.

"I miss you already," he said before she boarded the bus. They had seen a lot of each other during the past six weeks and the thought of not seeing her for four straight days had him in a state of misery.

She had given him her parents' phone number and he had promised to call. "I'll understand if you don't get around to calling," she told him, smiling up at him, knowing how much she would be missing him as well.

"Don't even entertain that thought, baby," he said, holding her tight in his arms. He kissed her and then released her to get on the bus before the driver closed the door.

"You really like her a lot, don't you?" Ross asked him when he made it back to the car. Randolph had appreciated his brother waiting patiently while he had stayed with Jenna.

"Yes, I like her a lot, Ross. She means a lot to me."

Ross nodded, smiling. "I can tell and I'm really happy for you, Rand."

Hearing Ross give his blessings on his and Jenna's relationship meant a lot to Randolph. "Thanks, Ross, I'm glad to hear that you feel that way."

Randolph was not surprised that his grandmother knew he was seeing a girl around school. He wasn't even surprised that she knew Jenna's name. But he had been surprised to discover within minutes of arriving that she had taken the time to find out everything she could about Jenna, including her family history.

When he and Ross arrived she was sitting on a burgundy leather couch in the living room. Like the rest of the house, everything in this room spoke of elegance, from the huge crystal chandelier that hung overhead to the huge gold sconces that graced the marble fireplace. Then there were several framed pictures that hung on the walls by renowned African-American artists Romare Bearden, Jacob Lawrence and Clementine Hunter.

His grandmother stood when he and Ross entered the room, along with their grandfather who had opened the door. She didn't bother with a greeting but lit right into him.

"I ordered a report on that girl you've been seeing at school, Jenna Haywood, and I can't believe you would even think to associate yourself with someone who is clearly out of your class, Randolph," she said in a huff. A dignified huff but a huff nonetheless.

He gave his grandmother the same stare she was giving him. If she wanted a showdown she would get one. As she continued talking, expounding on all the reasons he should be paying more attention to developing a relationship with Lena Weaver, he took the time to study the older woman who for some reason felt she had the right to interfere in his life.

He couldn't help but think his grandmother was a beautiful woman. And as she always did, on today she looked refined, sophisticated and pampered. And of course she was impeccably dressed, a model of elegance from her head to her toes. Dressed in a beige linen suit, she was the epitome of a Southern-bred black woman whose educated family, as well as the family she had married into, had somehow managed to have a little more than others, a fact she relished and took pride in. And she was determined to make sure the young women her grandsons selected as future wives had her same breeding.

"Are you listening to me, Randolph?"

Her question drew his attention back to what she'd been saying. He crossed his arms over his chest. "Not really. This is my life we're talking about and the woman I decide will share it will be of my choosing and not yours, Grandmother Julia. We've discussed this numerous times. Why are you so determined to saddle me with Lena Weaver?"

"Saddle? You should be honored that her parents think you're worthy enough for their daughter. Do you know the connections she will bring to this family?"

Randolph rolled his eyes toward the ceiling. "When will you realize that connections and family ties are only important to you? They mean nothing to me."

"And I guess that little chit from Tennessee who has no family ties or connections does?"

"Yes."

Julia Fuller waved an elegant hand in the air, letting him know his response meant nothing. "Of course you would think that way. Don't you think it's time to return to reality and remember your place in life, Randolph? Your playtime with that girl has gone on long enough, and Lena has graciously tolerated your foolishness. At the risk of sounding crass, I would think after two months you would have gotten just what you wanted from her by now and moved on."

Randolph's jaw twitched in anger. "And just what do you think I want from her?"

Julia glanced at her husband and Ross. Both were used to her and Randolph's arguments but for some reason the expression on their faces, as well as the looks they were giving her, indicated they felt she may have gone too far this time. But she had no intentions of backing down.

"Since you have pushed me to be totally frank with you, Randolph, then I will, although I'm uncomfortable with what I'm about to say." She hesitated briefly. "I do understand that you're a young man with certain needs; needs you wouldn't ask a well-bred lady like Lena to take care of. So quite naturally you would want to seek out another woman to take care of those needs for you."

Randolph had listened to his grandmother's words quietly, all the while fuming inside. He decided to state his feelings for Jenna once and for all. "You evidently misunderstood my relationship with Jenna, Grandmother. So I think I better set you straight on the matter."

A smile suddenly came to his lips when he thought of Jenna, who in his opinion was the best thing to happen to him. "I love Jenna and if I marry anyone, it will be her."

He saw the anger flare in his grandmother's eyes. "You're bewitched. She's bewitched you the same way that Denison girl bewitched your father."

Randolph's smile widened. "Yeah, and it's a good thing *that* Denison girl bewitched my father, or Ross and I wouldn't be here today, now would we? Now if you will excuse me, I've suddenly lost my appetite to eat anything, so don't expect me at the table to partake in Thanksgiving dinner." Without giving her a chance to say anything, he turned and walked out of the room.

Randolph ate his dinner in his room, refusing to sit at the same table with his grandmother. Later that night his grandfather came to visit with him. After asking him how school was going, the older man sat on the bed and began talking to him. "Your grandmother loves you," he said wearily.

"She has a strange way of showing it," Randolph muttered, still upset. "She has no right to try and dictate who I should be involved with. No right at all."

"She only wants what's best for you."

"Then she has nothing to worry about because Jenna is the best thing to ever happen to me. I refuse to become involved with a girl who will make me miserable for the rest of my life, just for the sake of making Grandma Julia happy. Ross may be willing to do it but I won't."

His grandfather looked at him, slightly surprised. "Are you saying Ross isn't happy dating Angela?"

Randolph raised his eyes to the ceiling. Was his grandfather really *that* unobservant? "What do you think, Grandfather? When do they ever see each other with her going to school in Boston? And she is so prim and proper it's downright sickening. Next time you see them together take a real good look at them. Then take a real good look at Ross and you'll see just how miserable he is. I have no intentions of being miserable. Jenna makes me happy and nothing is going to make me change my mind about her. Nothing and no one."

Julia Fuller angrily paced the confines of her bedroom. Every so often she would take a puff off her cigarette. Randolph had defied her for the very last time. She had just spoken to Maureen Weaver and had assured the woman Randolph would start paying more attention to her daughter. Now it seemed that would not be the case.

She took a huge puff off her cigarette thinking of a plan. There was no way Randolph would make Jenna Haywood a member of their family. How could he even consider such a thing? Why couldn't he be like Ross and happily accept the woman she had picked out for him?

She smiled. Angela Douglass was such a well-bred young lady and the fact that she was a descendant of Frederick Douglass and came from an impeccable family made her perfect. The same held true for Lena being a relative of Robert C. Weaver.

In addition to their family and social connections there was another reason she wanted Angela and Lena for granddaughters-in-law. They were both light skinned, just like her. Any smart African-American man knew to choose a light-skinned woman for a wife, especially if he wanted to move up in the world. In this day and time, the color of a person's skin mattered.

Sighing, she picked up the phone. A few minutes later when the party on the other end answered she said, "There's something I want you to do."

Howard University

Randolph was thrilled when he returned back to school and saw Jenna. Over the following weeks they grew closer and their relationship became stronger. During the weekdays they spent a lot of time together studying and then on the weekend they did a number of activities together. She even went with a group that followed the football team out of town to a game.

One night after they had gone to a movie, Randolph asked her if she planned on going home for Christmas. "Yes, I can't imagine not being with my family on Christmas. Why?"

He looked at her tenderly. "Because I plan to spend Christmas in South Carolina with my maternal grandparents and was wondering if you could come and spend some time with me there for a few days."

Uncertainty tugged at her heart. "I don't know if my parents will allow it," she said to him. She knew they would frown at the thought that she was going somewhere to spend some time with a boy, especially one they hadn't met yet.

"Would it help if I come up and meet them first and have my grandmother call with an invitation?"

Jenna nodded. She figured that might work. It wasn't that her parents were overly strict or anything, they just had a certain set of moral values they had established for her and she had always abided by them. "Would your grandmother do that?"

"Yes, she's dying to meet you anyway. I've told her a lot about you."

Jenna smiled. "You have?"

"Sure I have. I'm very close to Gramma Mattie and I want her to meet the woman I plan to marry one day."

Jenna's breath caught. That had been the first time either of them had ever mentioned marriage. "You want us to get married one day?" she asked him shyly.

He smiled. "Yes, that's what usually happens to people who fall in love. They eventually marry, have babies and live happily ever after. And that's what I want for us, Jenna. I know it won't be any time soon since I plan to go on to law school after I graduate, but I want you to know my intentions are honorable. One day I intend to make you my wife."

Tears clouded her eyes. "Oh, Randolph. More than anything I want to marry you one day, too."

Later that night Jenna shared her good news with Leigh. "Oh, Jen, I just knew Randolph had marriage on his mind. It's plain to see that he simply adores you. Even his brother knows how much he cares for you and has mentioned it to Noah on several occasions. Ross really likes you."

Jenna then told Leigh about Randolph's invitation to spend a few days with him and his grandparents in South Carolina over the Christmas holidays.

"Are you going to do it?" Leigh asked her excitedly.

"It's up to my parents. Randolph said his grandmother would be calling to invite me personally. I'm hoping my parents will agree."

Leigh nodded. "Does Randolph ever talk about his paternal grandmother? The one who lives in Virginia. The one Noah refers to as the Society Queen."

Jenna smiled. "No, not often. I don't think the two of them get along."

Leigh nodded, deciding not to mention to Jenna what Noah had shared with her regarding Randolph and his grandmother's huge fight over Thanksgiving regarding her. Ross had told Noah about it. At that moment Leigh decided to change the subject. "So what's going on with Ellie? She's been acting pretty weird lately."

Jenna hated to agree with Leigh but she had also noticed the change in Ellie. It seemed that she intentionally went out of her way to avoid the both of them and when she did encounter them she was totally rude. "I have no idea but I'm glad I'm not the only person who's picked up on it."

Leigh smiled. "I think she's jealous."

Jenna raised a brow. "Jealous of what?"

"Not of what, but of who. I think Ellie is jealous of you, Jenna. She's never seen you as a threat before but now she does."

Jenna shook her head, not understanding what Leigh meant, so Leigh decided to explain things to her. "In my psychology class last week, we talked about people like Ellie. They are people who have insecurity complexes and feel threatened by anyone that they perceive as possibly better than they are. Before, in Ellie's mind, neither of us was better than she was because your father is a meat cutter and your mother is a cook. My father is a bus driver and my mother does hair. And because of our parents' occupations, in Ellie's mind neither of us should have anything going for us here at Howard. We certainly shouldn't be well liked nor should we have popular boyfriends. But what I have is a boyfriend in law school who loves me and who treats me like a queen and who is working his butt off in school so that one day he can give me all the things he thinks I will ever want. And you have a guy who is the best catch on campus and who loves you to distraction. As far as Ellie is concerned, good things like that weren't supposed to happen to girls whose parents are lower class."

Jenna shook her head. "But Ellie has Tyrone and one day he will give her the life she's always wanted, so she has nothing to be jealous about. So what's her problem? Can't she see that in the end all of us will be happy?"

"It doesn't matter, Jen. Only Ellie was supposed to be happy, not us. She scratched me off her 'be nice to' list a long time ago. But with you, since you didn't have a boyfriend and weren't involved with anyone on campus, you were tolerated. But now since the two of us have received personal invitations to join a sorority, the same one that she's been dying to get into and hasn't yet been able to, that really has her dander up. Be careful around her. I don't like her and I don't trust her."

Jenna thought about what Leigh had said when she got into bed that night. She couldn't understand how some black people could think they were better than other black people. When it all came down to it, all black people were fighting for equality. So in her opinion, although our ancestors may have traveled from Africa on different ships, right now all of us were in the same boat. She was glad Randolph had not looked down on her parents' occupations when she'd told him what they did for a living. He had said that he admired a man who worked with his hands and that his maternal grandfather had made a living being a furniture maker. "My paternal grandmother is the one who has a hang-up about what people do for a living, Jenna, I don't," he said. "Neither does my Gramma Mattie. You're going to love her, trust me."

Randolph had been right. Jenna received a call from Mattie Denison two weeks before Christmas inviting her to spend three days around the holidays. She had then asked Jenna for her parents' phone number and said that under the circumstances, she felt she should speak with them as well.

Jenna received a call from her mother the following day letting her know that Randolph's grandmother had called and that the two of them had had a very pleasant conversation. Mattie Denison had asked Jenna's parents for their permission to allow Jenna to visit during the holidays, assuring them that she and Randolph would be properly chaperoned during the entirety of her visit. After talking with Mrs. Denison, Jenna's parents felt comfortable about her going as long as they got to meet Randolph beforehand. It was decided that he would come up a day early and spend the night at her parents' home before taking her to South Carolina to meet his grandmother.

Randolph was ecstatic when she shared the news with him later that day while they were eating at the café on campus. He would use his grandparents' car to come and get her in Knoxville the day after Christmas, and the following day, bright and early, he would drive her to Glendale Shores, South Carolina, where they would arrive before nightfall.

"Will Ross be there?" she asked him after taking a sip of her Coke.

Randolph shook his head. "He plans to spend Christmas with Angela and her parents in New York and will arrive the day before you leave."

Jenna nodded, smiling. She was glad she and Randolph would be spending some time together over the holidays.

A week later Jenna got summoned to the financial aid office. She met with Mrs. Naomi Portsmouth, the woman in charge of student loans and financial aid. A short, stocky light-skinned woman who wore a no-nonsense, down-to-business, nonfriendly expression, Mrs. Portsmouth's office wall was covered with various framed degrees and a number of plaques commemorating her work with various charitable organizations.

"Miss Haywood, I note that you have signed up for classes next semester, and we need to know how you plan to pay for them."

Jenna frowned. As usual she had applied for a student loan to cover those expenses that went beyond what her parents had taken care of, and immediately told Mrs. Portsmouth so.

"Unfortunately your student loan was denied."

Jenna lifted her brow in surprise. "Denied? But why? It's never been denied before. I've always gotten a student loan to cover my balance."

"Well, it wasn't approved this time so the balance is now your responsibility. Perhaps your parents can come up with some more money," the woman declared curtly.

Jenna shook her head, knowing that wasn't possible. Her parents were providing too much toward her education as it was. They still had her brothers to take care of. "Is there some way I can get on a work-study program to pay as I go?"

"I'm sorry, that's not possible. The balance will have to be paid before you leave for the holidays."

Jenna sat up in her chair. "But there's no way I can come up with five hundred dollars in a week!"

"Then I guess that means you won't be returning to Howard after the holidays," the woman responded, not showing any mercy.

"But—but, surely there is something—"

"No there isn't," Naomi Portsmouth all but snapped, getting to her feet.

"Good day, Miss Haywood. I have another appointment."

In tears Jenna left the woman's office, not believing the conversation that had just taken place. The thought of not returning to Howard was devastating.

She was on her way back to her dorm when she heard Randolph call her name. She turned and watched as he crossed the courtyard toward her. He looked into her face and immediately knew something was wrong. "What is it, baby?"

She shook her head, too ashamed to tell him. The thought of not returning to Howard and to him next year brought fresh tears to her eyes.

"Jenna, tell me what's wrong."

She hesitated briefly before responding. "I just came from the financial aid office. My student loan didn't go through. I have to pay the balance on my account before I leave for the holidays or I can't come back."

Randolph frowned, wondering who had told her such nonsense. The financial aid office was good at working with students and usually helped in finding alternate ways to pay. Both of his roommates had gotten student loans and one of them had gotten bad grades this semester. He couldn't imagine them not working with Jenna who was a model student. "There must be some mistake. There has to be some way they can work with you and help you find other ways to pay the balance."

"There isn't any way, according to Mrs. Portsmouth."

Randolph raised a brow. "Naomi Portsmouth?"

"Yes. You know her?"

"Yes, I know her." Randolph frowned. Naomi Portsmouth was not only a sorority sister of his grandmother, but they were good friends as well. He couldn't help wondering if his grandmother had anything to do with Jenna not getting a student loan. He wouldn't put it past her to go that far, especially if she thought it would keep him and Jenna apart.

"I'll give you the money."

Jenna blinked. "What?!"

He smiled with a tender look on his face.

"I said that I'll give you the money."

Jenna sighed. "Randolph, you don't even know how much it is. Besides, I can't let you do that."

"Why not?"

"Because I can't. It wouldn't be right taking money from you. What will people think?"

"It wouldn't be anyone's business. And it doesn't matter how much it is. I have the money, Jenna. My maternal grandparents had set up funds for Ross and me to contribute toward our college expenses, but of course Grandmother Julia's pride wouldn't let her accept their contribution. So the money is just sitting there, not being used."

Jenna shook her head. "No, I can't let you use your money for me, Randolph. I can't."

He saw her defiance. "Then what will you do?"

She sighed sadly. "I don't know. I can't ask my parents for anything else. It wouldn't be fair on them and my brothers."

"Then let me help."

"Randolph, I've told you that I can't take your money."

He inhaled deeply, before saying, "Let's treat it as a loan then. You can pay me back."

She looked at him thoughtfully as she tossed his offer around in her mind. "But I won't be able to pay you back until after graduation."

"That's soon enough. Like I said, the money is just sitting there and you're welcome to use it."

Jenna thought about his offer some more then said, "I'll pay you back with interest."

Knowing she wouldn't accept things any other way, he said, "That's fine. And if it makes you feel better I'll have Ross draw up the papers."

She nodded. "Yes, that would make me feel better. We should handle this strictly as a business transaction between us."

Randolph smiled. "Okay." Although he would have Ross draw up the papers, he had no intentions of ever calling in the loan. A wife wouldn't be legally liable to pay her husband anything, and he had every intention of making Jenna his wife one day.

"Now that we've got that settled, how about the two of us going to get something to eat?" he said, taking her hand in his.

Jenna smiled, her love for him washing over her. "I'd like that."

Yes.

Bronson College

"I'm pregnant."

Because her gaze was intense, Angela saw the sweat immediately pop out on Dean Hightower's forehead. She would have laughed out loud if the situation weren't so serious. She moved her gaze from his to glance around his office. He had numerous plaques on the wall and a number of framed photographs of him and other important individuals, including John F. Kennedy. Angela knew she didn't have to tell him that if her parents had any idea he had been sleeping with her for almost two years, he would lose every single thing he owned, including his respectability.

He finally collected himself enough to ask, "Are you sure?" After she nodded, he looked at her thoughtfully, then shook his head. "I thought you were on the pill, Angela."

"I am. But last month I got a cold, and I guess the medicine I was taking diluted the effectiveness of the pill."

He frowned and in an agitated tone said, "And I guess you're here to tell me the baby is mine?"

Angela smiled. It could be his, Mr. Morgan's or Mr. Adams's. But she was putting her money on him. "Yes, sir. There hasn't been anyone else," she lied.

"What about Mr. Morgan?"

"He only spent his time tasting me like you said he would." She decided that he didn't have to know that the man had taken advantage of a good thing and had ended up doing a lot more than that.

"What about your boyfriend? The one who's a law student at Howard?"

She sighed, beginning to get upset. She didn't appreciate him trying to weasel his way out of this. "I haven't seen Ross since the beginning of school. In fact the last time we were together was at a Labor Day cookout his grandparents gave. And not only that, but Ross thinks I'm still a virgin."

"A virgin? How in the hell can he think that?"

Angela frowned. "Ross has no reason to think otherwise. In the year we've dated, we have only kissed once or twice. His grandmother wants a prim and proper young lady for her grandson, and I'm doing my best to play the part."

Dean Hightower thought of all the not so prim and proper things she had done with him. "You must be some damn good actress."

She smiled. "I am." And her best part was yet to come. Some way she would get Ross out of the picture and become available for Randolph. She knew Julia Fuller had hopes and dreams of Randolph and Lena Weaver becoming an item, but Angela had no intention of letting Lena or any other woman have Randolph. And how she would get Ross out of the picture was something she needed to work on. She would need a valid reason to break things off with him. And it would have to be a reason his grandmother would accept, and feel so badly about that she would then consider the best solution would be to match her up with Randolph.

Her best friend Kathy Taylor, who was attending Howard, was keeping tabs on Ross's activities. So far Kathy hadn't reported anything that Angela could use as an excuse to end things between them. According to Kathy, Ross was studying too hard to become involved with anyone. But Kathy had told her some disturbing news that Randolph was spending a lot of time with a girl on campus—and it wasn't Lena Weaver.

"You know what you're going to have to do, don't you, Angela?"

Dean Hightower's question reeled her thoughts back to the issue at hand.

She knew, but decided to play dumb. "No, sir. What will I have to do?"

"Get an abortion. I have a friend who can handle it. She has a good reputation. She can do it as early as next week and by the time you go home for the holidays you'll be good as new."

"Will I miss any of my classes?"

"Yes, but don't worry about them. I'll handle things with your professors."

Angela nodded, knowing that he would. His future, like hers, was at stake. "And what about other babies? Will having this abortion stop me from having other babies in the future?"

"No, you'll be able to have other children."

She nodded, satisfied. "All right, Dean Hightower, please make all the arrangements."

"You haven't mentioned your condition to anyone, have you?"

There was no reason to let him know that she had called and told Kathy. The two of them had been best friends for life and didn't have any secrets from each other. "No, I've told no one."

Howard University

Everyone on campus was excited about going home for Christmas although more and more troops were being sent to Vietnam each day. Three days before she was to leave for home, Jenna got a call from her mother telling her that Jeremy, the guy who had been her boyfriend in high school, had gotten killed in Vietnam. Jenna took the news hard. She had known Jeremy most of her life and even before they had gotten serious, they had been good friends. His family was in the process of making funeral arrangements and had called her parents, wanting her to know. After talking to her mother, tears Jenna couldn't contain rolled down her face. After they had graduated Jeremy had gone to California to escape the injustices of the South but he hadn't been able to escape the horrors of Vietnam.

She had been so upset over the news she had skipped her history class and stayed in her dorm room and cried. She wished she could see Randolph but knew that he was in his important Business Law class. Deciding to go to the café for lunch she dressed and walked across campus, thinking how brokenhearted Jeremy's parents must be. He had been their only child and to make things worse, they had lost him right before Christmas.

She'd been sitting alone eating when Johnny Lane joined her. "I was hoping I would see you before I left," he said. Then, after seeing her red puffy eyes, he asked with concern, "Hey, are you all right?"

She looked at him and smiled. She hadn't seen him in a while and had recently asked Leigh about him. Leigh was in several of Johnny's classes and had mentioned he was not attending class like he should. It had come as surprising news. Johnny was smart as a whip and had always taken his studies seriously.

"I'm fine," she said softly, fighting back more tears. "My mom called earlier to tell me a good friend of mine was killed in Vietnam. My heart aches for his family. He was their only child."

Johnny nodded and handed her his handkerchief as more tears fell from her eyes.

She accepted his handkerchief. "Thanks. I'm sorry for falling apart like this but Jeremy was a very special friend. We dated our junior and senior years of high school." After a few more sniffs she looked up at Johnny and asked, "How have you been? I haven't seen you around lately."

He nodded. He always considered Jenna a good friend. "I've been around but not for long. I've decided not to return after the holidays."

His news came as a shock to Jenna and she looked at him, stunned. Like her, he was a junior with only one year of school left. "You aren't coming back? Why?"

He smiled warmly at her. "Because I can't live a lie anymore, Jenna. I can't continue to go to class every day when there is so much injustice in the world. I'm tired of being judged by the color of my skin. I'm tired of being told I'm not good enough when my ancestors are the ones who built this country. Yet they think I *am* good enough to send to the jungles in some godforsaken country to fight a war. I'm sick and tired of it." He took a deep breath before continuing. "I called and told my parents this morning and they're upset. My father even told me not to come home."

Jenna reached out and took his hand in hers. "What will you do, Johnny? Where will you go?"

He looked across the table at her and gave her one of his ever-loving flirtatious smiles. "I've decided to join to Black Panther Party. They need more black men who understand and support their cause."

Jenna's hold on Johnny's hand tightened as she remembered some of the things Randolph had told her about that organization. "Oh, Johnny, are you sure that's what you want to do?" Just that morning there had been an article in the papers about the Black Panther Party and their involvement in the killing of policemen in Los Angles. A number of the leaders had been brought in for questioning.

"Don't believe everything you read, Jenna. Slandering the party is the white man's way of discrediting an institution they feel threatened by. But it won't work. We will rise and be supreme and people will see there is such a thing as black power."

Jenna shook her head, knowing Johnny believed everything he was saying and that there was no way she would be able to get through to him. More tears began filling her eyes. "Oh, Johnny, please take care of yourself and no matter what you do or where you go, remember that I'll always be your friend. If you ever need me for anything, please let me know. I'll be just a phone call away."

"Thanks, Jenna, and I'm going to remember that. Just keep me in your prayers."

She smiled through her tears. "I will, every night. I promise."

He leaned over and kissed her cheek. Then he stood and walked out the door. A part of Jenna felt she was losing another good friend, just like she had Jeremy. She couldn't help but wonder when she would see Johnny again, if ever. She cried as she left the café and began walking back to her dorm.

She cried for a country that was letting some of its people down—the black people—people who had always loved it but wanted the same thing the next man had, equal rights and equal opportunities.

And then she cried for a country that was losing a lot of its men—future leaders of tomorrow—every minute and every hour to a sense-less war. She wondered when it would end; the injustices, the hating, the killing and the fighting.

A light blanket of snow covered practically everything and Jenna noticed a number of people she passed pulling their coats tighter around them to ward off the cold. But a part of her didn't feel the cold because that moment, her entire body felt totally numb and empty inside.

Six

"Everyone, I'd like you to meet Randolph Fuller."

The first thing Randolph noticed about Jenna's parents was that they seemed genuinely friendly. What he noticed about her three younger brothers was that they seemed very protective of their sister. As Jenna made the introductions, Randolph discovered that the tallest of the brothers, the one who stood toe-to-toe with him, was sixteen-year-old Jarvis. The fourteen-year-old twins were Jason and Jared.

"So you're Randolph Fuller? I've heard quite a lot about you, young man," Jenna's father said, giving him a firm handshake. He was tall with a muscular build.

"Yes, sir." Although Randolph felt he was under the man's micro-scopic gaze, he had a feeling that John Haywood was a fair person. He also got that same impression from Jenna's mom who immediately made him feel welcome.

"I hope you don't mind sharing a room with my sons," Mrs. Hay-wood said softly, smiling at him.

"No, ma'am, I don't mind at all."

That evening at dinner he and Mr. Haywood got into several con-versations and Randolph discovered that a lot of John Haywood's views on the Vietnam War and the civil rights sit-ins and marches were identical to his. They were both hoping President Johnson would soon pull the troops out of Vietnam and both believed the Black Panther Party would do more harm than good to the civil rights movement.

"You're doing the right thing by staying in school to avoid the draft," Mr. Haywood said to him as Randolph loaded another helping of mashed potatoes onto his plate. He thought Jenna's mom was a great cook and thought the students at the school where she worked were fortunate to have her preparing their meals.

"I'm hoping by the time I finish law school the war will be over. In fact I'm hoping it's over before my brother finishes law school next year. I wouldn't want him involved in it, either."

"We've gotten ourselves into a big mess," John Haywood said, after taking a generous sip of iced tea. "I hope Johnson knows what he's doing."

Dinner had been delicious and Randolph had eaten every mouthful. He didn't hesitate to tell Mrs. Haywood just how much he had enjoyed the meal, especially her apple pie.

The older woman smiled. "Since you liked it so much, the next time I bake one I'm going to put an extra one in the oven for you and ship it to Jenna."

Randolph smiled. "Thank you, Mrs. Haywood." A part of him knew she would keep her promise.

After spending time with Jenna's parents, he knew they believed in the three H's—honor, honesty and hard work. Now he understood Jenna's dedication to doing well in school and always wanting to do the right thing. She was raised in a family that expected no less.

He wondered how things would have been for him and Ross had their parents lived. One thing was for certain, his father would have stood up to Grandmother Julia like Randolph was doing. His grandmother Julia had told him more than once that he was definitely his father's son. Randolph knew Ross was their father's son, too. He just hadn't found anything he wanted badly enough to fight for yet. But if that time ever came, Randolph had no doubt Ross could and would hold his own with Julia Fuller.

He shuddered as he remembered his last conversation with her.

She would not admit to having anything to do with Jenna's student loan being turned down. But he knew he had rendered her speechless when he had told her that Jenna had come up with the money and would be returning to Howard.

Bright and early the next morning, after eating a delicious breakfast Mrs. Haywood had prepared, Randolph walked Jenna out to his grandparents' car. Opening the trunk he placed her suitcase and his overnight bag inside. He then walked around the car and opened her door for her. Jenna's father had left for work already but her mother had given him strict orders to drive carefully and had told Jenna to call and let them know when they had arrived safely.

Once inside the vehicle, before he placed the key in the ignition, he reached over and caressed Jenna's thigh, needing to touch her. Yesterday had been the first time he had seen her in the two weeks since they had left school for the holidays. He couldn't do what he had wanted to do upon first seeing her, which was to take her into his arms and kiss her. In fact, he hadn't been able to do anything with her, not even hold her hand. A shudder ran through him when he felt her tremble slightly beneath his touch. It was still there, that automatic reaction they always got whenever they touched or kissed.

They had driven several miles heading out of Knoxville when Randolph couldn't take it any longer and pulled the car off the highway onto the shoulder of the road. He reached across the seat and pulled Jenna into his arms.

The moment their mouths touched, sizzling sensations passed through both of their bodies as they engaged in a hot, tongue-thrusting, curl-your-toes, red-blooded kiss.

Moments later, the unexpected blast from a tractor trailer's horn broke them apart. Both leaned back against their seats, panting for breath.

"I needed that. I don't think I could have driven another mile without it."

Jenna smiled. "And I don't think I could have let you driven another mile without doing it."

Randolph grinned as he glanced over at her. She was wearing a green dress, one a woman would probably wear to church on Sunday, and he knew she had done so to make a good impression on his grandparents. Her hair was neatly curled and she wore very little makeup if any at all, and her lips were still moist from their kiss. He wanted to lean over and get another taste of them. "You look good," he said finally. "Every time I see you I think you get prettier and prettier."

Her smile widened, pleased with his compliment. "Mr. Fuller, if you're fishing for brownie points you're definitely on the right road to getting them."

Randolph laughed. "Speaking of roads, I guess I better get back onto this one if we're to make it to Glendale Shores in a reasonable time. Your parents and my grandparents expect us to arrive before dark." He started the car again and rejoined traffic.

"Randolph?"

He took his eyes off the road for a quick second and glanced over at her. Her face appeared flush with heat and her eyes were filled with desire. "Yes, sweetheart, what is it?"

"You're going to behave yourself around your grandparents the same way you behaved around my parents, aren't you?"

His lips twitched into a smile. "Do you want me to?"

"No, not really but I think you should. I want your grandparents to like me. I don't want them to think I'm not a nice girl or anything like that."

Randolph heard the nervousness in her voice and knew meeting his grandparents and making a good impression was important to her. "You *are* a nice girl and they will know it whether I behave or not. But I won't do anything to make you feel embarrassed or uncomfortable. Like your parents, my grandparents love each other very much. Gramma Mattie knows and understands how it is to be in love, Jenna. She knows just how important you are to me and because of that, you will be important to her as well. She knows I plan to marry you once I finish law school."

He chuckled then. "She also knows me and knows it's going to be hard for me to keep my hands to myself around you, but she has assured your parents that you will be properly chaperoned and you better believe she meant it. But . . . my grandparents have to go to sleep sometime."

Jenna kept her gaze focused on Randolph as a thought came to her. She frowned. "You're not thinking of sneaking into my room when they are asleep, are you?"

He grinned at her. "Yeah, I was seriously thinking about it."

"Oh, Randolph, please don't. What if they find out? What if you're caught? What will they think of me?"

When the car came to a stop at a traffic light, he reached over and cupped her chin with his hand. "They will think that you are the most beautiful woman in the world who has totally captured my heart. And I love you." He leaned over and brushed her lips with his. "Relax. I promise to be on my best behavior for the next three days."

"You promise?"

"Yes, I promise." He smiled. What he wouldn't tell her was that her definition of "his best behavior" was totally different than his.

Jenna felt the beginnings of a nervous lump in her stomach when they caught the ferry over to Glendale Shores. Randolph hadn't said a lot about how his grandparents came to live on the sea island or how many other families lived there. Jenna knew from one of her history lessons that like Hilton Head, Glendale Shores was a sea island occupied since the late eighteen hundreds by free black men who formed a number of communities on the island. These communities consisted of farmers, fishermen, basketweavers and fishnet makers. Jenna also remembered that just like on Hilton Head, the Gullah culture was still preserved. The Gullah were a strong group of African-Americans, many of whom were born on the islands and spoke the Gullah dialect. However, unlike Hilton Head, which had been home to several thousand blacks since the end of the Civil War, Glendale Shores was an island once owned by a wealthy white plantation owner. He had willed the sea island to descendents of the slaves who had worked for him a number of years before his death.

When the ferry arrived at Glendale Shores, Jenna couldn't do anything but hold her breath when she found herself surrounded by the

peaceful beauty of nature. Everything on the remote island, every towering tree, every flowering plant, and every blade of green grass was
painstakingly beautiful. And with a sweeping view of the Atlantic
Ocean as the backdrop, it made a breathtaking picture.

Rolling down the car's window, Jenna breathed in the warm fra-
grances of flowers that were unknown to her, thinking that this had to
be the most beautiful land on the East Coast. Sighing with pleasure
she turned to Randolph. "How long have your grandparents lived on
this island?"

Randolph smiled. He understood what she was going through.
Glendale Shores always had the same affect on him whenever he
returned after a lengthy absence. "My grandfather was born on this
island. He brought my grandmother here when they married and the
two of them have been here ever since. I remember my mother sharing
stories with Ross and me about her days growing up here. In order to
go to school she and her cousins would catch the ferry to Beaufort."

He slowed the car down as he turned the corner onto the only road
she saw, a long gravel road that ran the length of the ocean before wind-
ing into an area surrounded by underbrush, needle grass, palmettos and
pine trees. "The island," he continued saying, "was willed to the Denison
family in the mid eighteen hundreds. For a while, during the Civil War,
General Lee commanded all the islands along the coast of South Carolina. When a hurricane hit he and his troops moved inland to Savannah."

"I think it's beautiful," she said, her gaze returning to look out the
car window. A part of her felt encompassed by nature as they drove
through a dense and wooded area. "Do you have a lot of relatives living
on the island?" she asked.

"No, right now the only ones living here are my grandparents and
two of my grandfather's brothers and their wives. For a long time there
was no electricity. Everything was done by primitive means. So when
the young Denisons could escape to modern civilization, they did.
Most of them moved to Savannah and Beaufort. This island is private
and the Denison family wants to keep it that way."

Glancing around at her surroundings once again, Jenna could

understand why. Suddenly she realized Randolph had turned off onto another road, this one with a surface that felt like hard clay. An uncontrollable fluttering began in the pit of her stomach, and a shiver of apprehension rippled up her spine as she began feeling nervous again about meeting his grandparents. Then the car stopped and she turned in her seat to look at Randolph. Without saying anything he leaned over and lowered his head, bringing his mouth to hers, and she immediately responded to his kiss. Unlike the other one, it was soft, tender and languid. The nervousness in her body was replaced by a sensuous sensation that started at her toes and began moving upward to the crown of her head.

Moments later, releasing a heavy sigh Randolph ended the kiss but placed tender nips around the corners of Jenna's mouth and bottom lip. "You don't have a thing to worry about," he said huskily. "You're with me and like I told you before, they will love you," he said, giving her a reassuring hug. He then pulled back and hooked a knuckle under her chin, prompting her to look at him. "I love you," he said softly.

"And I love you," she whispered back, remembering a time she hadn't wanted to get involved with him or anyone else. But he was such a wonderful person. She would never forget how he had graciously offered to loan her the money she needed to stay in school. That had meant a lot to her.

Randolph let go of her face then caught both of her hands in his. He tightened his hold on them. "Promise me something."

"What?" she whispered, looking up at him.

"Promise me that at night, if I come to your room, you won't turn me away. All I'll want to do is hold you in my arms and sleep with you that way, nothing more. Promise me."

Jenna started to tremble and as a defeated sigh broke forth from her lips she leaned forward and rested her forehead against Randolph's. As of yet they had not gone all the way. A lot of nights while at school, they would study together in his room and occasionally would fall asleep in each other's arms. She had felt such contentment and such peace whenever she was in his arms while he held her. As far as she was concerned, it was a profound experience of the rarest form, one she had missed the past couple of weeks they had been apart.

With her forehead resting against his, the warmth of his breath on her face seemed to derail her entire thought process. At the moment she didn't want to think about the risk of his grandparents finding out. All she wanted to think about was finding a special time they could spend together. She pulled back and saw him gaze at her through the darkness of his eyes. She felt dizzy, light-headed and completely in love.

She brushed her lips against his and said softly, "I promise."

Albany, New York

Angela took a sip of her tea, very much aware that her parents were closely watching her and Ross, noting how they were interacting with one another. There was very little conversation between them at the dinner table. She preferred it that way, but from the look her mother was giving her, she knew she wanted things to be otherwise. Evidently it was time to prove to Ross that she was a great conversationalist.

Sighing softly Angela took her mother's cue and turned her full attention to Ross. "Are you looking forward to graduating in the spring?" she asked him.

He looked up from his meal at her, as if surprised she had spoken, and smiled. Whether it was genuine or forced, she couldn't tell.

"Yes. This last year has been loaded with reports and essays to complete. None of my professors have shown any mercy."

She nodded. "I know what you mean. Things were pretty hectic at Bronson as well."

"Did Angela tell you she made straight As this semester, Ross?" Her father beamed proudly. "We're so proud if her."

Ross's smile widened. "Congratulations, Angela! That's wonderful. I'm proud of you, too."

She nodded, smiling. "Thanks, Ross. It took a lot of hard work but the results were well worth it." As she took another sip of her tea she wondered what Ross and her parents would think if they knew just what type of hard work it had taken. She was glad they would never, ever know.

"So, Ross," Henry Douglass said, leaning back in his chair after pushing aside his dinner plate. "What are your plans after graduation?"

Angela frowned. She knew her parents were hoping his plans were to marry her.

Ross met her father's gaze. "I haven't decided yet, sir. I guess what plans I make will depend on the state of the nation. If there's still a war going on then—"

Henry Douglass waved away whatever words Ross was about to say. "There won't be. Johnson isn't stupid. He knows he has played this Vietnam thing long enough and it's time to pull out and bring our boys home. It wouldn't surprise me in the least if they returned in time for Easter."

Ross didn't think that would be the case but decided he didn't feel much like debating with Angela's father. The man could be fairly pigheaded about things when it suited him. Deciding he needed to escape her parents' scrutiny for a while he turned to Angela. "How would you like to take a walk?"

Angela smiled. "I'd love to."

"Get your jacket, honey, it's chilly outside," her mother said when she stood.

"I will, Mama."

Ross and Angela walked quietly through a park that was located a few blocks from where her parents lived. He had come to New York to spend Christmas with her and her parents before going to spend the rest of the time with his grandparents in South Carolina.

For Christmas he had given her a brooch. He knew it hadn't been the engagement ring her parents had been counting on, but he was not ready to make such a commitment. Besides, something Randolph and Noah said kept nagging at him. They were convinced that he and Angela didn't share any sort of passion.

They continued walking, side by side, not holding hands like most couples would normally do.

"So, is Randolph spending Christmas with your grandparents in Virginia, Ross?"

Ross lifted a brow and smiled. "No, Randolph is spending Christmas with my grandparents in South Carolina. I'll be joining them there in a few days." He knew Angela and his Grandmother Julia talked occasionally, and decided not to mention that Randolph had invited Jenna to Glendale Shores. If his Grandmother Julia found out it wouldn't be with his help.

He stopped walking and, automatically, so did Angela. He turned to her and captured her wrist in his hand, ignoring the fact that he felt nothing. No love, no passion, no attraction.

Her head rose and she looked at him curiously. "What is it?"

He shook his head. It showed a sorrowful state of their affairs if she had to ask. Didn't she even have a clue what he was about to do? "I want to kiss you," he said, spelling it out for her and searching her face to garner her reaction to his statement.

She shifted nervously. "Here?"

"Yes."

"Out in public?"

His lips curved into a smile that made heat suddenly curl between her legs. Angela blinked, she had never reacted to Ross like this before and could only assume it was because he reminded her of Randolph more so than ever today. Or it could be that she hadn't had a man since her abortion last month and her body was getting hungry, restless. But still . . . she had to be careful. He might be testing her.

"A lady never kisses a man in a public place, Ross," she said, deciding to play it safe.

He pulled her off to the side, under a shadow of trees. "Now it isn't as public, Angela," he said smoothly.

She searched his face as he leaned closer to her and followed his lead when he settled his mouth gently on her lips. He just barely tasted her lips, their chests not even touching. But still, she could tell from that brief exchange that with the right woman, Ross Fuller could be a highly charged, highly passionate man. It was there in his taste and the gentleness of his lips as they traced over hers.

Too bad he wasn't Randolph.

When he released her and stepped back, she studied his eyes but couldn't read his expression. It *had* been a test but one totally different than she'd expected.

And as they began walking back toward her parents' home, a part of her wondered if she had passed.

Seven

Jenna could see the top of the house as the car rounded a bend in the road. Then it was there, looming before them, this huge Southern-style home that looked like a throwback to the Civil War era. The architect in her appreciated the design that was two stories, spacious and welcoming. There was a porch in front that seemed to wrap around the entire circumference of the house.

She leaned forward in her seat to look out the windshield to get a better view. When Randolph brought the car to a stop, Jenna stared at him then back at the huge wooden structure that seemed to be built of strong, solid oak, painted a light gray and surrounded by a number of moss-draped oak trees and many flowering plants.

"Your grandparents' home is simply beautiful," she told him softly, thoughtfully and truthfully.

"I'm glad you like it. It was originally built right after the Civil War but not this big. Every generation that lived here added their own finishing touch. Grandpa Murphy extended the porch as well as enlarged the kitchen. He also added a guest bedroom and another bathroom when I was a kid."

Jenna drew in a deep, steadying breath when an older couple opened the front door and stepped outside onto the porch. "Your grandparents?" she asked Randolph, swallowing the thickness in her throat.

"Yes, that's Gramma Mattie and Grandpa Murphy but everyone around here calls him Bush." He walked around to her side of the vehicle to open the door. Walking her up to the porch, he held her hands in his, squeezing them reassuringly.

"Gramma Mattie and Grampa Murphy, I'd like you to meet Jenna Haywood, a very special friend of mine."

Taking Jenna's hands in hers, Mattie Denison smiled at the woman her grandson had wanted her to meet. "Welcome to Glendale Shores, Jenna. Grampa and I are glad you could come."

Jenna smiled at the small-framed woman with soft brown eyes that immediately made her feel welcome. "Thanks for inviting me." She then turned her attention to the huge bulk of a man who stood next to the small woman. He was staring at her with such intensity that she began to feel uncomfortable all over again. Then suddenly, she saw the corners of his mouth lift into a smile. It was a smile that reminded her of Randolph and Ross whenever they smiled.

"She's pretty, Randolph," his grandfather said as his smile widened. "You may have to keep an eye on your uncle Duncan while she's here," he added with good humor, taking Jenna's hand in his. "Duncan is my seventy-year-old brother who thinks he's twenty and still appreciates a pretty girl when he sees one," he said as an explanation. "I'm glad you could visit, Jenna."

"I'm glad I could visit, too," she said, returning his smile. Her small hand was almost swallowed by his and she wondered how a woman as small as Mattie Denison could be married to a man as huge as Murphy Denison. He wasn't big in an overweight sense, but big as in tall and muscular. She wondered if this was where Randolph and Ross had gotten their height and muscular build.

Mattie Denison had Randolph bring Jenna's luggage inside while she showed her the room she would be using during her visit. Jenna thought it was a beautiful room with handcrafted furniture. She found out later that Randolph's grandfather had built much of the furniture in the house.

"Don't forget to call your parents to let them know you made it here all right, child. There's a phone in the kitchen and another one in the living room." At Jenna's nod, Gramma Mattie smiled again and said, "It will be another hour or so before dinner is ready. You can take a nap and rest up if you like."

After she was left alone, Jenna glanced around. It was the type of room one could spend hours reading in or being downright lazy. There was a huge window that overlooked the backyard which had a barn-type structure painted the same color as the house. There was also a pier with creek-fed pockets of marshland on both sides, jutting into a huge waterway that eventually led to the ocean. As she unpacked her things she wondered where Randolph's room was. Deciding to call her parents, she left the bedroom and walked to the kitchen, which was easy to find due to the aroma of fresh bread baking. Mrs. Denison was in the kitchen, taking the bread out of the oven when Jenna entered.

"I thought I'd call my parents now," Jenna said, wondering where Randolph was as she picked up the phone and began dialing. The question on her face must have been obvious when she saw his grandmother smile at her. "Don't worry none. Randolph ain't deserted you. He and his grandpa are out front talking. He'll be inside shortly."

Jenna nodded. She hadn't meant to be that obvious. "Thanks." Her father answered the phone and moments later after talking to both her parents she hung up. "My mom wants to thank you again for inviting me."

The older lady turned to her. "You'll always be welcome here, Jenna. And I have a feeling that this won't be the last time Randolph brings you here. I suspect there'll be other visits."

Jenna smiled. She hoped so. "Is there anything I can help you with, Mrs. Denison?" she asked as she watch her mix ingredients into a pot over the stove. The smell of chili filled the air.

"Nah, and you may as well get used to calling me Gramma Mattie, especially since Randolph says you're the one he's gonna marry. And if you are, I'm downright tickled pink. That grandson of mine has good taste. You're such a pretty thing."

"Thank you."

"I mean it. I can tell you're a person who will make him happy, although I know the two of you have a long road ahead of you."

Jenna nodded. She and Randolph really hadn't talked about what they would do once they were finished with school. She had another year left in college and he had two years of law school to complete. "This is such a beautiful island," she said as she sat down at the table.

"That's what I thought the first time Bush brought me here. I knew how much he loved this place and knew if I loved him I might as well be prepared to love it as well since this would be my home."

"Do you ever get lonely? Especially since the only way off the island is by ferry."

Gramma Mattie smiled. "There's too much around here to do to get lonely. Bush had me pregnant within the first year that we married, so there was our boy, Murphy Junior, to take care of. Then two years later our Adrianna was born. That's Randolph's mother. Murphy Junior died in a boating accident a week short of his fourteenth birthday, and that was probably the only time I ever regretted living here. There was so much around here to remind us of him. He loved the outdoors, especially the water and that was what took him away."

The older lady stopped stirring the ingredients in the pot. "That's why Ross Fuller, Senior became so much like a son to us when he married our Adrianna. He was such a wonderful person and he loved our daughter very much."

"How did they meet?"

Mrs. Denison began stirring the pot again. "Over yonder on Hilton Head. That's where my family is from. I had a sister living there at the time and Adrianna had gone to spend a week with her. Ross Senior, who was twenty-two at the time, just happened to be there that particular week visiting a friend from college." She chuckled. "Must have been love at first sight for those two. Before he left to return to school, he and his friend took a boat over here and talked to Bush and me. He wanted us to know that he intended to marry Adrianna once he finished law school. In one week he had made up his mind that he was in love with her and wanted her for his wife. Since she was seventeen and had just finished high school, Bush and I told him he would have to wait a little while beyond him finishing law school, since we intended for her to go to college. Her daddy and me had made plans for her to attend Savannah State. We figured if he loved her as much as he said he did, he would be willing to wait for her."

"Did he?"

Mattie Denison smiled as she placed a lid on the pot she'd been stirring. "Almost. Adrianna got pregnant during her second year of college. That's when we found out that she and Ross Senior had been sneaking around seeing each other. We didn't know that on several occasions he had come down from DC and visited her at school. I guess one of those times their hormones got the best of them." She wiped her hands on her apron as she walked over to the refrigerator to take something out. "But one thing I can give the boy credit for," she continued, "is that when he found out Adrianna was pregnant, he married her without wasting any time, even when his own mother told him she would disown him if he did. He proved just how much my girl meant to him and married her without his mother's blessings. And I can truly say that he loved her completely until the day they died in that car accident."

At that moment Randolph and his grandfather wandered into the kitchen and Randolph smiled when he saw her. "You're all settled in?" he asked as he joined her at the table.

"Yes, and I have such a beautiful room and the bed looks so comfortable."

For the next hour or so Jenna listened as the older couple brought Randolph up to date on what had been happening on the island since the time he had left for Knoxville. It seemed a group of white men had visited the island and made everyone on Glendale Shores an offer to buy their land. And the price they offered wasn't all that bad.

"Will you sell?" Jenna asked, then blushed after wondering if she had stepped out of line by doing so. She quickly apologized.

Murphy Denison waved off her apology. "There's no need to apologize. If what Randolph tells me is true, then you'll be in this family one day," he said, leaning against the counter of the spacious kitchen. "And the answer to your question is no. I won't sell. The way Old Man Denison had his will set up when he deeded this place over to his former slaves was that only a person with Denison blood can inherit this land. Now there is one exception and that's the case of a godchild or an adopted child. If a Denison legally declares someone as their godchild or adopted child, then even without Denison blood that person can inherit land on this island as well, although a situation like that hasn't happened yet. So far all Denisons on this island are Denisons by blood. And the ones who are in a position to inherit this land have pledged they won't sell. That's the only way we can keep what is ours. There aren't too many places in this country where black folks own beautiful land such as this, and can boast of all-black communities and townships. Hilton Head, Glendale Shores, St. Simons and Sepalo are all that's left of a black heritage we need to hold onto. We owe it to our ancestors to keep our land and not let others come in and take it away."

During dinner Randolph mentioned to his grandparents that this summer after graduation he and Ross had thought about working for Martin Luther King, Jr. as he went about increasing black voter registration.

Everyone remembered two summers ago, when three civil rights workers who had volunteered for the Mississippi Summer Project to register black voters, had been murdered by law enforcement officers and members of the Ku Klux Klan. Their killers had still not been brought to justice.

"Do you think things will be better this summer?" Mattie asked Randolph as she passed around the bread. She didn't want to think that her two grandsons would put themselves in any danger.

"I hope so," Randolph said, taking a huge piece of bread off the platter. "It's bad enough that Americans are over in Asia fighting the Vietcongs and then here they are fighting each other."

"The boys will be fine, Mattie," Murphy Denison said, seeing the look of worry on his wife's features. "I think it's admirable that Ross and Randolph are willing to stand up for what they believe in." He then shook his head. "But what really has me concerned is this group that calls themselves the Black Panthers. Where King is preaching nonviolence they are preaching violence and that worries me."

Jenna nodded. She was worried as well, especially since Johnny had decided to leave college and join the group. She mentioned as much to Randolph when they went for a walk after dinner.

"The only thing you can do, Jenna, is pray that he keeps his head on straight and doesn't get caught up in the hatred that group is preaching. Although I do understand their issues and concerns, I don't believe violence is the way to go about changing things. I hate to see so many brilliant minds creating their own ideology as to what the correct measures should be in order to ensure equality for black people. The last thing we need is to become a divided people. Blacks need to stay united for the cause. That's the only way we can get what we want in this country."

As they continued to walk Jenna found it hard to believe that it was less than a week before the new year and that it was the dead of winter. Here on the island there was a tropical warmth to the point that she didn't need a sweater. The early evening was quiet and shadowy and the only sounds that disturbed the peaceful setting were those of various insects swarming about in the thickets. Large lanterns that hung from several posts illuminated the path leading to the area where they were headed. Randolph wanted to show her a pond that was fed by an underground spring. They walked together holding hands, sharing that special closeness they always shared whenever the two of them were alone.

When Jenna heard the ripple of water she knew they were close to their destination. And then she saw it when he led them through a small clearing. Her heart stopped beating for a split second when she gazed at the beauty of her surroundings. "Oh, Randolph," was all she could manage to say.

"Do you like it?"

"Yes! It's beautiful." And although she didn't say it, the first thing that came to her mind was that this would a beautiful spot for a wedding. It was so picturesque. She could just see herself pledging her life to him in this very place.

"When we used to stay here during the summers, Ross and I would go swimming in this pond all the time. We used to have loads of fun, just the two of us."

Jenna tilted her head and stared up at him. She knew the answer to the question she was about to ask but decided to ask anyway. "You and Ross are very close, aren't you?"

He released her hand and placed an arm around her shoulder, bringing her closer to his side, pulling her body into the hard muscles of his body as he gazed across the pond. He smiled as some fond memory came to mind. "Yes, Ross and I are very close. We've always been close, even before our parents' deaths. Then after that, we became even closer. We felt we were all that was left of what had once been a very happy family. My parents loved each other very much and they loved us as well."

Jenna felt his body become tense and she glanced up and saw his jaw go taut. She was just about to ask him what was wrong when he began speaking again.

"After my parents' death my grandmother, Julia Fuller, orchestrated a custody battle. She thought Ross and I were too good, too filled with rich Fuller blood, to be raised by Gramma Mattie and Grampa Murphy. She thought they were uneducated backwoods Carolinians. They didn't have a chance against her and her influential friends, and eventually they had to be satisfied with us just spending our summers here with them."

"What about your paternal grandfather? Couldn't he do anything?"

Randolph shrugged. "He knew what she was doing was wrong but I guess over the years he learned to just let her have her way to keep peace." He frowned. "Ross has formed that same attitude."

She moved closer and came to stand in front of him. She remembered what Ellie had said about his paternal grandmother having already picked out the woman she wanted him to marry. "What about you, Randolph?" she asked him quietly, as she gazed up into his eyes. "Have you learned to give into her wants as well just to keep peace?"

He met her gaze, looking down at her, fully seeing her features from the soft lighting cast off the water. He leaned down until she could see the flecks of light in his dark eyes. "No. That's one lesson I haven't learned and don't plan on learning, either. I make my own decisions about anything I do."

Jenna felt the warmth of his breath on her face when he leaned forward. She could smell the coffee he had drunk at dinner along with the peppermint candy he had placed in his mouth afterward. She could also smell his natural scent that was all male. When his lips touched hers and he slipped his tongue into her mouth, she realized that he was the one who had taught her more about passion than she had ever known. She was still a virgin, but had given him liberties with her body that she had never given anyone else. He had touched her everywhere. She lifted her arms from around his waist and draped them around his shoulders, interlocking her fingers behind his neck, returning his kiss with all the emotions of a woman in love.

A warm breeze off the pond surrounded them but did nothing to cool the heat of the kiss they were sharing. She felt the hardness of him press against her middle which started blood pounding through all the most intimate parts of her body, making the nipples on her breasts tighten as hot sensations flowed through her veins. She leaned forward and stood on her toes, loving the taste and texture of his mouth. Loving the way his tongue was mating with hers.

Moments later Randolph broke the kiss but continued to hold her in his arms, trying to get this breathing under control. "It's time for us to go back," he said huskily, against her ear. "Or they'll wonder what we're doing out here."

Jenna nodded. She then rubbed her palms across her dress as she tried to get any wrinkles out. She glanced back up at Randolph. "How do I look?"

"Like you belong to me," he said softly.

Jenna's breath caught. The strong conviction in his voice made her want to kiss him all over again but she knew that although she had the inclination, she didn't have the time. "That's because I do belong to you, Randolph," she said softly.

Randolph expelled a long breath, thinking that the next two days would be pure torture. His grandfather had taken him aside earlier that day and had given him a not too-subtle hint that lately he had the tendency to wake up during all hours of the night and roam about. In other words, he was warning Randolph to stay in his bedroom and leave Jenna alone in hers. "Come on, let's head back," he said, taking Jenna's hand in his and wondering if she was beginning to feel just as frustrated as he was.

"Randolph really loves that girl, Mattie," Murphy Denison said to his wife as he slid in bed beside her. All the lights were out and every living body under his roof was in bed. "He couldn't take his eyes off her at dinner."

Mattie lay flat on her back and stared pensively up at the ceiling. "Yes, I know and she loves him, too. I could feel their emotions and they are strong ones."

A frown marred Murphy's forehead. "Stronger than the ones Adrianna and Ross Senior had?"

She glanced over at her husband in the darkness. "Yes." A short while later when she knew Murphy had gone to sleep, Mattie took in a deep breath. Her ancestry was Gullah, a rich culture that had been developed over the years of slavery. It was still in existence today, with most of them living on Hilton Head. She had been born the seventh daughter of the seventh daughter. Her mother was said to be clairvoyant and psychic. Although Mattie refused to claim she had inherited either of those talents, she did on occasion have the ability to read strong emotions in people. She wasn't even sure how she did it, she just knew that she did.

The first time had been when she was a child of nine living on Hilton Head and had read the emotions of Mr. Armstrong. Everyone had adored and respected him as a teacher but there had been something about him that had always made her leery. There had been strong emotions radiating from him whenever he looked at her that always made her keep her distance. Less than a year later she understood why when everyone discovered that he had been sexually molesting some of the little girls at school.

She didn't experience another episode of reading emotions until she had met Murphy. Each year the residents of all the sea islands along the Georgia and South Carolina coast got together for a huge celebration of their African-American heritage. That particular year when she turned eighteen and was fresh out of high school, the celebration had been on Sapelo Island. There had been fun and games for everyone and plenty of food to eat. She had seen Murphy across the distance and when he had looked at her, she had felt the strong emotions radiating from him and had known at that moment that their lives would forever be entwined. He had covered the distance between them and without saying a word, he had taken her hand in his. After introducing themselves they had gone walking to make plans for their future. Less than a month later they had married, and he had brought her to Glendale Shores to live in this house with him and his parents.

She had also known when Ross Senior asked for Adrianna's hand in marriage that he had loved her with an intensity that was all-consuming. The emotions radiating from him whenever he looked at her daughter had been just that strong, potent and powerful. The emotions that had radiated from her daughter to Ross Senior had been those things as well.

But nothing, she thought as she gazed up at the ceiling, had prepared her for the emotions that were radiating between Randolph and Jenna. The love Randolph had for Jenna was stronger, more potent and even more powerful. And that's what had her worried because where she had seen total happiness in Ross Senior and Adrianna's future, she saw a glimpse of pain, heartbreak and betrayal in Randolph's and Jenna's. And knowing just how much the two young people loved each other, she couldn't understand why she was picking up on so many negative forces. For reasons she couldn't understand there would many years of unhappiness before they would finally find true happiness. And as much as she wanted to, there was nothing she could do or say to warn them of what lay ahead.

There was no way she could change or reset the future that was predestined for Randolph and Jenna.

Eight

January emerged with a new year and with it the United States' involvement in Vietnam increased. There were one hundred and eighty thousand American troops in Vietnam, but General Westmoreland was asking the government for two hundred and fifty thousand more.

Back at home, Robert C. Weaver was named the first Secretary of Housing and Urban Development, making him the first black cabinet secretary under any president. The Black Panther Party was growing in numbers and whenever any of their faces flashed across the television screen, Jenna would strain her eyes to see if Johnny was among them. When she had returned to school after the Christmas holidays, she discovered Johnny was not the only student who had left college to join some political movement or another.

January soon disappeared into February and most of the students on Howard University's campus were busy studying to make sure they had all their credits before the school year ended in May. Football season was officially over and without practice to take up a lot of his time, Randolph began spending more and more time with Jenna. They ate breakfast together in the school's café each morning, walked to class together whenever they could and made it a habit to eat dinner together as well. For Christmas he had given her a beautiful blue cardigan sweater and for Valentine's Day had given her a huge box of candy and a beautiful card. For Christmas she had given him a copy of John F. Kennedy's book, *Profiles in Courage*, and for Valentine's Day she had given him an album by the Temptations.

February eased into March and it was getting harder and harder for Randolph and Jenna not to go all the way. Their kisses were becoming more and more heated, and whenever he touched her, her body would tremble in desire. Every time he looked at her, passion so thick you could cut it with a knife consumed her. She was having a hard time sleeping at night and she could tell he was too. And there were times when the two of them were together where they were so aware of each other it was almost unbearable. But she kept telling herself that holding out and not going all the way was the best thing. And although she knew he was frustrated, he never forced the issue with her. He merely took whatever she gave him and never complained.

Leigh was spending more and more time with Noah. She was concerned that with Noah about to graduate from law school in a few months, he might get drafted to go fight a war she thought was senseless.

Jenna knew from talking to Randolph that he was also concerned with the possibility that Ross would be drafted. Jenna also had concerns. The longer the war lasted the greater the chance of her brother Jarvis reaching the age where he could get drafted. She tried not to think of the possibility of him leaving home for Vietnam.

The Black Panthers Party was claiming that there were more black men being sent to Vietnam than white men, whose families either shipped them off to Canada or made sure that once they entered the armed services, they were given desk jobs in Washington for safekeeping.

Randolph had just gotten in from a meeting with one of his study groups when he noticed his grandmother's car parked in front of his dorm. "What does she want?" he muttered to himself as he entered his building, wondering what could have possibly brought Julia Fuller all the way from Virginia. The two of them had not been on good terms since that episode over the Thanksgiving holiday. On top of that he had contacted her over the phone after the incident involving Jenna's student loan and they had exchanged harsh words. He had ended the conversation, telling her that until she accepted Jenna, he would not be coming home during the holidays. He had spent his entire Christmas on Glendale Shores.

Mrs. Tucker, the dorm mother, stopped him before he went up the stairs to his room. "Randolph, your grandmother is here to see you. She's been waiting for over an hour in my office."

Releasing a heavy sigh, Randolph crossed the hall to the woman's office and without bothering to knock, he entered. His grandmother was across the room pacing with a cigarette in her hand. She hadn't heard him enter so he silently closed the door behind him.

"Grandmother Julia, you wanted to see me?" He saw her turn to the sound of his voice and watched as she checked the elegant-looking watch on her wrist.

"You're late, Randolph."

He leaned against the closed door and met her annoyed gaze without flinching. "No, I'm not. This is the time I usually get in on Mondays. Besides, I didn't know we had an appointment," he said, deliberately making it seem like her visit was anything but personal.

She patted her hair while taking another puff off her cigarette. "I thought it would be best if we met face-to-face on an important matter that has come up."

"And what important matter is that?"

With barely concealed curiosity, he watched her flip open the strapless purse she carried and pull out a white envelope. Crossing the room she handed it to him. "This is your invitation to Friday night's affair at the White House. The First Lady is hosting a dinner party in honor of Robert C. Weaver's appointment to the president's cabinet."

Although his grandmother was behaving as cool as a cucumber, he knew she had to be pretty proud of herself. An invitation to the White House to wine and dine with First Lady "Lady Bird" Johnson, was probably a dream come true. For her but not for him. "Why am I invited?" he asked, not bothering to glance at the envelope he held in his hand.

"Because you'll be Lena Weaver's date that night."

Randolph frowned. He could see the purpose of her visit very clearly now. "I will not be Lena Weaver's date that night or any other night."

Julia Fuller raised her gaze toward the ceiling. "Of course you will. It's not every day a person gets invited to dine at the White House."

"Then I hope you enjoy yourself and have fun for the both of us since I won't be going, especially not as Lena's date. The only way that

I go is with Jenna." Without hesitation he placed the invitation back in her hand.

A stunned look appeared on Julia Fuller's face. "You can't be serious."

Randolph smiled. "Oh, but I am. If I show up it will be with Jenna and no one else."

Julia Fuller's face went from stunned to furious. "How can you even consider bringing that girl to such a function, Randolph?"

"How can I not consider it when she's my girlfriend? I've told you that but you choose not to accept it. In fact I plan to marry Jenna after I finish law school."

Julia Fuller's features went into shock. "Marry? Surely you aren't serious. How can she help further your career? How can she bring prestige to your life? And just how is she supposed to be the type of wife who can benefit you?"

Randolph crossed his arms over his chest. "In ways you will never know because you are beyond understanding what it is like to love someone, and I mean truly love someone. If you understood then you would know that none of those things you mentioned hold any great significance. Love is the most important factor."

She shook her head. "In the real world things don't work that way." She glanced at her watch again. "Besides, it doesn't matter what you feel or what you think. We'll discuss that outlandish idea of you getting married at another time. Right now I need you to agree to take Lena to that—"

"Haven't you heard anything I've said? I am not taking Lena Weaver anywhere."

"You don't have a choice. I've told her parents that you will be her date for that night. I'm sure they've told her by now."

Randolph shook his head. "That's too bad. I guess you'll have to call and tell them that something has come up and I won't be taking her after all."

"I can't do that."

"Then don't. Just don't look for me to show up that night with her."

Julia Fuller became livid. She was sick and tired of Randolph defying her every wish. She took a step forward. "You will show up, Randolph, or your grandfather and I will cut off any further funding for you to go to law school," she threatened furiously.

Anger flared in Randolph's eyes with his grandmother's threat. She had no right to toy with people's lives to get them to bend to her will. Now more than ever he was determined not to give in to her. "Do whatever you feel you have to do. I'll take out a student loan and get a job to supplement my income if I must. And you evidently have forgotten that Grampa and Gramma Denison have money set aside for me and Ross's college education; money we haven't touched yet."

His grandmother stared at him. And from her expression he could tell she had forgotten. Her lips twisted wryly. "That girl means that much to you?"

"She means everything to me."

Without making a comment to his statement, Julia Fuller turned and walked out of the room.

Jenna was just about to close her book when Ellie flounced in. She had on a short black miniskirt and a pullover green sweater. Although miniskirts were the new rage, Jenna couldn't see herself wearing anything that short yet. She still felt more comfortable in her skirts that reached below her knees. Ellie, it seemed, had no such qualms. She and a number of girls were parading around campus like it was nothing to wear anything that short.

"You're still studying?" Ellie asked as she closed the door behind her.

"No, I just finished. I wanted to make sure I was ready for my English test tomorrow."

"Oh, I had one of those today."

"How did you do?"

Ellie shrugged. "I failed."

Jenna shook her head at how easily Ellie had admitted something like that. "Aren't you worried about getting all your credits this semester to make senior status in the fall?"

"No. Tyrone is looking out for my future. Just as soon as he signs on with that pro football team out in California, he's going to send for me." She then came and sat on the bed next to Jenna. "I just heard something that I find rather interesting."

Jenna lifted a brow. She knew there had to have been a reason Ellie was so chatty. There were some evenings where she literally ignored Jenna's and Leigh's presence. "What?"

"There will be a private party at the White House this Friday night in honor of Robert C. Weaver's appointment to the president's cabinet. Are you going?"

Jenna raised a brow. "Why would I be attending something like that?"

Ellie smiled. "Because I just overheard someone say Randolph is. I also heard that person say he's going as Lena Weaver's date. I would check that out if I were you. He's supposed to be your boyfriend but he's taking another girl to dinner at the White House. I did try to warn you that his grandmother had already picked Lena Weaver out for him."

Usually Jenna had the good mind to ignore Ellie's insensitive attitude and rude behavior, but she'd hit a raw nerve and Jenna's veins felt like they were ready to explode. "You don't know what you're talking about, Ellie. Randolph would not take Lena Weaver anywhere."

Ellie glared. "Well, don't get mad at me, Jenna Haywood. I was just telling you what I heard."

Without saying anything more to Ellie, Jenna grabbed the sweater Randolph had given her for Christmas off the bed and stormed out of the dorm room.

Randolph looked up from reading his Business Law book when his roommate Evan came in.

"Jenna is outside and wants to see you, Randolph," Evan said as he tossed his car keys on the desk.

A surprised expression covered Randolph's features as he closed the book. He glanced at his watch. It was past nine o'clock. "Jenna's outside?"

"Yeah."

Randolph grabbed his jacket and slipped it on as he quickly headed out the door, then took the stairs two at a time. He wondered what had brought Jenna to his dorm this time of night. Reaching the bottom step he pushed the door open that led to the outside.

He saw Jenna standing ten feet away underneath an oak tree with her profile to him. She hadn't seen him yet so he took time to study her, the woman he loved with all his heart. The moonlight was bright enough so he could see that she was wearing the sweater he'd given her for Christmas. He had seen her in it before, but hadn't noticed the way it hugged her body, following the curvaceous lines from her shoulders to her waist, fitting snug at her breasts; breasts he knew were firm, perfectly shaped with a gorgeous set of nipples. They were the kind he enjoyed licking, sucking and tasting. Then there was the skirt she was wearing, knee-length and pleated. But what was suddenly making his breathing hard and making sweat form on his brow was this throbbing need for what was under that skirt.

He closed his eyes in pure agony, feeling disgusted with himself for having such lustful thoughts. But then he remembered a class he had taken a few years back where they had discussed Charles Darwin and some of his theories; one of which was that men were animals—of the highest class, but animals nonetheless, with the ability to survive and most importantly to mate. The desire to mate was an essential part of life and just as vital as any other basic and elemental need. Slowly opening his eyes, Randolph recognized and accepted everything he was going through, and had been going through since the first time he had set eyes on Jenna Haywood.

He wanted her.

He wanted her with every breath in his body; with every beat that his heart took. Even now, although she was standing a good distance away, he could smell the heated scent of her. He could breathe it, and as crazy as it sounded, he moved his tongue around in his mouth actually tasting it. Giving in to his body's need he felt himself grow hard and felt his entire body begin to hum with pulsating heat.

When he saw her wipe at her eye with the palm of her hand, indicating she was crying, there wasn't even a split second of conscious thought when he shifted his focus. Concern replaced rampant desire. He quickly moved toward her. "Jenna? What's wrong?"

She turned to him and he could see from one of the lights shining off the building the damp tears on her cheeks. Not waiting for her to explain, he pulled her into his arms, gathering her close, enveloping her body into his.

Then she pulled back and looked up at him, as if searching his face for something. "You once told me if I ever wanted to know anything about you to ask and not believe everything I hear," she said softly, giving him a sober smile through her tears.

Randolph kept his gaze on hers. "Yes, that's what I said. Is there something you want to ask me?"

There was a brief pregnant pause before she answered. "Yes."

"Then ask."

"All right." Her chin lifted a little higher as she continued to look at him.

"Go ahead, Jen, and ask. You know I'll tell you anything you want to know."

Jenna nodded, savoring the feel of his strong arms around her. "Are you taking Lena Weaver to a dinner at the White House on Friday night?"

A frown came into his eyes and he wondered where she had gotten that information. He would find that out later because right now the most important thing was to set the record straight with the one person who mattered the most to him. "No. My grandmother was here earlier tonight and made the suggestion but I flatly refused." He knew he was putting that mildly. His grandmother did more than make a suggestion. She had all but threatened him to comply with her wishes.

"She wants you to take her?"

"Yes, and it's my understanding she's already told Lena's parents that I would be her date for that night. She did so without consulting me about it first. So if Lena mentioned to anyone that I'm the one taking her, it's because that's what she assumes."

Jenna nodded. "She's going to be embarrassed when you don't take her."

"Then it will be my grandmother's fault, not mine. I had planned to talk to Lena tomorrow myself and explain things to her." He studied Jenna's features. "Did you honestly think, knowing how I feel about you and what you mean to me, that I would consider going out with anyone else?"

Jenna shrugged. "I didn't want to think it but then I know I haven't been doing with you what other girls are doing with their boyfriends."

"You mean making love?"

She lowered her gaze. "Yes."

Randolph reached out and lifted her chin with his finger so their gazes could meet again. "One of the reasons I love you so much is because your actions aren't dictated by what others are doing and to me that's admirable. Making love is a big step in a relationship. There should be a firm commitment between the two individuals and should not happen until the both of them are ready to pledge their hearts to each other."

He reached out and took her hand in his. "I would be lying if I said I didn't want you, Jenna. Sometimes I want you so bad that it hurts. Sometimes I get so hot inside thinking about you, that even an ice-cold beer can't cool me down. I've awakened in the mornings aroused, gasping for breath, after a night spent dreaming of you."

He expelled a long breath. "But regardless of any of that, I won't ever force you to do anything you aren't ready to do. I will wait as long as it takes." Forcing a smile on his face he added, "Even if it's not until our wedding night . . . although I'd probably be dead from wanting you so much by then."

Jenna chuckled and dropped her head onto his chest. "Oh, Randolph." She wrapped her arms around his waist. "I love you."

"And I love you, too."

She lifted her head up and met his. "I know you do." And she honestly did know, and logically there was no reason not to consummate the love the two of them shared. He had shown her time and time again just how much she meant to him, just how much he cared. And he had told her of his intentions to marry her once he finished law school.

An idea suddenly came into her mind. This was Easter weekend that led into spring break, and because of her finances she had decided to spend the week on campus getting ahead in her studies instead of going home. Randolph had made plans to spend the week at Glendale Shores in a cottage that was located a couple miles from his grandparents' home. It was a small house his parents had owned that now belonged to him and Ross. His grandparents would be gone for two weeks visiting a relative in Chicago.

When he had first mentioned it to her, he had invited her to come spend the week with him. That had meant they would be alone, unchaperoned, without their families knowing about it. Of course, the risk of the two of them together, sharing a house without adult supervision was bad enough, not to mention the feeling of guilt of doing something her parents and his grandparents wouldn't approve of, so she had turned down his invitation. But now she was beginning to rethink that decision since they had already done things the older adults wouldn't approve of, either, like them necking and petting to the point where he had touched her body in every single place.

"Randolph?"

"Umm?"

"Is your invitation still open?"

He glanced down at her. "What invitation is that?"

"The one where I get to spend a week with you on Glendale Shores during spring break." She saw the exact moment his eyes darkened in desire. It was the same moment she felt his body, which was so close to hers, react to her words. She could tell her question had caught him totally off guard.

After considering her for a minute he said, "Yes, it's still open." He then watched her as if his next breath was waiting on her next words.

"Then I accept your invitation."

Randolph took a deep, calming breath. "Are you sure?"

Instead of answering him, she put her words into action when she balanced on her toes and pressed her lips to his. The moment their mouths touched passionate sensations burst inside of her, consuming her mind and her body and shattering any lingering doubt she had about the week they would share. For several glorious moments she

feasted off his mouth and let him feast off hers, as their bodies gener-
ated sparks that began transforming into hot rushes of desire.

Jenna pulled back when she remembered just where they were and
what they were doing. Bracing herself against him it took her a while
to recover from their kiss.

"Jenna? Are you sure?"

She lifted her gaze and said in an unsteady breath, "Yes, I'm sure,
Randolph." A feeling of rightness oozed through her when she added,
"I haven't been more sure of anything in my entire life."

Julia Fuller paced the confines of her hotel room. She was angry to the
point of madness. Randolph was willing to cause her embarrassment
for *that* girl. Color burned her cheeks when she remembered how he
had faced her down, refusing to give in even when she had threatened
to withhold his funds for school. And he was right, if they were to cut
him off the Denisons would gladly come to his rescue.

She balled her hands into fists at her sides. She would have to come
up with a new strategy. Since Randolph was determined to defy her,
she needed a new game plan. The next time she would deal directly
with the girl. If the chit really was in love with Randolph then she
would be more than willing to do the right thing after she was convinced she wasn't suitable and would not be accepted by his family.

Julia smiled. She had a strong feeling that she would be victorious
in the end.

Nine

Jenna looked through the kitchen cabinets of the house she would be
sharing for a week with Randolph, surprised to find them fully
stocked. *At least we won't starve*, she thought, glancing out the window. Randolph was outside placing a huge canvas covering over Ross's
car. Ross had let them borrow the vehicle to make the trip and had

given Randolph strict instructions to keep it protected from the ocean's salty air.

"So what do you think of the place?"

Jenna turned to the sound of Randolph's voice. She hadn't heard him come in. He stood leaning in the doorway, looking at her. "Your parents had the right idea when they built this place," she said smiling. "I think it's beautiful."

Randolph crossed his arms over his chest and continued to look at her. "Yeah, I think it's beautiful too, even more so now that you're here."

Jenna returned his gaze, giving him a saucy little smile. "You think so?"

He rubbed his chin as his eyes moved over her from head to toe. "Yeah, I know so."

Anticipation churned in Jenna's stomach. The house was small and cozy and consisted of one large bedroom, a bathroom, an eat-in kitchen and a living room. There was a huge window in the bedroom that overlooked the ocean. When Randolph had carried their luggage into the bedroom it had reminded her that they would be sharing a bed tonight. Thinking about it suddenly made her feel nervous. "It's past lunchtime. If you're hungry I can fix you something to eat."

Randolph smiled as he shook his head. The only thing he was hungry for was her. "No, I'm fine but there is something I'd like to do before we get a bite to eat."

Jenna swallowed slowly and her heart began thundering at the thought of what that could possibly be. "What?"

"Go swimming. Did you bring your bathing suit like I asked you to?"

Jenna stared at him as she released a deep sigh. "Yes, but like I told you, I can't swim."

"Don't worry about it, I'll teach you how."

She nodded. "We aren't going swimming in the ocean, are we?"

Randolph shook his head when he heard the sound of distress in her voice. "No, I thought I'd take you to the pond."

"The one on your grandparents' property?"

"Yes, that's the one. It's less than a mile from here if we take a shortcut." He walked over to her and spanned her waist with his hands. "If you want you can go ahead and change. I'll wait for you outside."

She nodded, appreciating that he recognized the fact that she wasn't ready to change clothes in front of him quite yet. The feel of his hands on her waist made her shiver and she knew he'd felt it. The darkening of his eyes told her he had. "What about you? Aren't you going to change into swimming trunks?" she asked, barely getting the words out. His hands on her were making her senses so overcharged she could barely think straight.

"They're under my blue jeans," he responded.

"Oh. Then I guess I better go change."

He slowly released her then watched as she quickly disappeared into the bedroom, closing the door behind her.

"What's all the stuff in here?" Jenna asked Randolph as he handed her a canvas sack while he placed a huge, thick blanket under his arms.

"Umm, just a few items I thought we might need," he said as he led her through the wooded path. Like him she had put her bathing suit on under her blue jeans.

During their walk they talked about a number of things including the threat his grandmother had made when he refused to take Lena to that dinner at the White House.

"Do you actually think she would have gone that far?" Jenna asked, finding it hard to believe anyone would want to be that dominating.

"Who knows? At least I won't have to find out since Lena came down with the measles."

Jenna nodded. Randolph had told her that when he had gone to see Lena to explain the situation to her, her dorm mother had told him that Lena could not see anyone because she had caught the measles.

Jenna and Randolph's conversation shifted to what the two of them would be doing over the summer months. Jenna knew Randolph had plans to work with Martin Luther King, Jr.'s voter drive. She told him about her plans to get a job as a counselor at a summer camp. "That way I can earn money for my books and other miscellaneous items I'll need in the fall," she said, shifting the sack from her hand to her shoulder.

Finally, they reached their destination. Although there was plenty of daylight left, a cluster of oak trees surrounded the pond and blocked out most of the sunshine, making the area appear secluded. *There's something peaceful about this place,* Jenna thought, as she watched Randolph spread out the blanket. It was like a secluded paradise. Flowers were in bloom and a wispy midday breeze saturated the air with their fragrance, tantalizing her senses.

"Well, that about does it," Randolph said after completing the task of arranging the blanket on the ground near the pond. He then sat down on the blanket and stared over at her. "Come join me and bring the sack with you."

For a split second Jenna's pulse increased when she gazed at Randolph and saw the look in his eyes. Then she knew. He intended to make love to her here. The very thought of it took her breath away. She could just imagine them lying naked on the blanket together with the gurgling sound of the underground spring in the background while he sank his hard body into the depths of hers, making her his in a way no one had ever done before.

"Jenna?"

She blinked upon realizing that she had not moved from her spot. "Yes?"

"Come here, baby." He reached out and offered her his hand.

Jenna moved to join him on the blanket, taking his hand and holding it steady as she sat down across from him.

"Now let's see what we have in here," he said as he slowly began emptying the sack.

Jenna watched as he pulled out two sandwiches wrapped in waxed paper, a cold bottle of Ripple—the inexpensive wine that was the latest craze on the college campuses, a thick towel, a transistor radio, a handful of rubbers and last but not least, of all things a Bible. She studied the assortment of items then met his gaze as her breathing quickened. She knew what they would do with the sandwiches and wine. She also knew what the rubbers would be used for—although that didn't stop the blush that spread across her face. But the Bible . . . ?

Randolph read the question in Jenna's eyes and picked up the Bible to explain. "This originally belonged to Big Ma, my great-grandmother, who was Gramma Mattie's mother. She passed it on to my grandparents on their wedding day. It was then given to my parents on the day they married. Some people claim Big Ma had psychic powers but I don't know if that's true or not. To me she was the sweetest old woman to ever live on the face of the earth. Although she died when I was seven, I can remember a lot about her," Randolph said as he ran his fingers across the cover of the Bible.

"I recall her sitting me and Ross down one day in this very place and telling us about this Bible. She said it was special and was to be passed on from generation to generation and that if we ever found the person we wanted to bind our lives with, to make sure we pledged our love and said our vows over this Bible. She said doing so would be the tie that would bind us to that person forever."

Randolph placed the Bible on the blanket between them. He then looked up and met Jenna's gaze before reaching out and taking her hands in his. "I love you, Jenna. I love you very much and in my heart I know the love we share was meant to be. Our love will always be the tie that binds us. No matter what happens, our love will survive the test of time. I want this to always be our very special place and one day we'll bring our children here, our grandchildren, and if the Lord is willing, even our great-grands. And together we'll share with them the importance of this Bible and what it means."

He reached out and with his thumb touched the dampness of tears that appeared on her cheek. "You are mine and I am yours. Will you bind your life to mine, Jenna, here, now, forever? Will you accept my love?"

Randolph's words touched Jenna deeply. For the moment, unable to speak, she reached up and lay her hand along his jaw. "I will," she breathed as more tears gathered in her eyes. "I love you," she said softly. "And yes, here, now, forever, I will bind my life to yours."

With the words spoken to bind them, Randolph took an ink pen out of his pocket and recorded their commitment to each other in the Bible before placing it aside. Reaching out he pulled Jenna into his arms. Together they tumbled back onto the blanket. He rained kisses over her face and throat before seeking out her mouth. She parted her lips beneath his as desire rushed through her.

Jenna accepted his kiss and felt the need, desperation, and the passion it conveyed, and began melting under his heat. She caught the distinctive scent of him, male, primal, earthy, as his mouth mated with hers. His tongue claimed hers with a ferocity that made her surrender to whatever demand it was making. The taste of him filled her. It was a taste she had come to know over the past five months.

His hands eased their way to her shoulders to push aside the straps of her bathing suit, seeking the part of her he had come to enjoy. She shivered when his mouth left hers and made its way downward to her breasts. Tipping her head back, a soft moan escaped her lips the moment he captured a nipple in his mouth, lavishing it with his tongue. She lifted her arms and wrapped them around his neck, tilting her breasts upward as his mouth continued a greedy feast on the other breast.

Randolph pulled away from Jenna's body to sit back on his haunches and look down at her. Her mouth was still moist from his kiss. So were her breasts. Long seconds passed as they stared into each other's eyes as the love they shared flowed between them. With a low groan, he reached for the zipper of her jeans and slowly began easing it down. His body and mind had been primed for what lay behind that zipper for a long time. He drank in the scent of her as her entire body began sending off the aroma of her heat. Suddenly he couldn't breathe and his entire body began to hum with a desire it had never felt before. He was so aroused his sex pushed hard against his zipper, making his need for her that much more intense.

He lifted her hips just enough to ease the jeans down the smoothness of her thighs and the shapely outlines of her legs. Tossing them aside, his hand began removing her bathing suit, slowly peeling it down the copper darkness of her skin. He suddenly came to a halt when he moved past her flat stomach and down to the juncture of her legs.

The shock of seeing her completely naked stole breath from his lungs. He had never seen her there. He had touched it before, many times, when his fingers would slide into her, stroke her, loving the feel of her wetness. But now he saw with his own eyes the very essence of what his body so desperately craved. His hands began to tremble as he continued to remove her bathing suit, tugging it down her legs then tossing it aside to join her jeans. When she lay completely naked before him he stood on wobbly legs to remove his own clothes.

Jenna watched as Randolph first removed his shirt to reveal a dark, powerfully muscled chest. She had seen him without a shirt before and each time she did so, she had wanted to touch him, run her fingers over him because he was truly one fine specimen of a man. The shape of his upper torso was magnificent and his dark skin gleamed with perspiration.

Delirious with passion, she bit into her lower lip when he began easing the zipper of his jeans down. Her eyes became huge, mesmerized as his swollen shaft boldly sprang forth from its confinement. A ripple of shock went through her at the unexpected sight. She thought he had been wearing swimming trunks under his jeans. "Randolph . . . ?"

He read the question in her eyes as she continued watching him. "This is how I go swimming here," he said hoarsely, as he continued to push his pants down his thighs. He stepped out of them and kicked them aside.

A shudder ran through Jenna as her gaze took in all of him, from head to toe. But her gaze returned to study that part of him she had never seen before. It was thick, hard, perfectly formed and very much enlarged. She found she wanted to touch it, stroke it and take it inside of her. She stared at him as he reached down and picked one of the rubbers he'd brought, removed it from its foil casing and slid it in place over his erection. "Randolph." She breathed his name in a whispering voice filled with desire, and lifted her arms to receive him.

The guttural sound of a male animal that was about to mate poured forth from deep in his throat as he moved forward, easing into her arms and placing his body directly over hers. Her breasts ached beneath his chest and the feminine folds of her body became even more heated with the feel of his sex pulsating against it. A jolt of antic-ipation raced through her and she closed her eyes when a hot rush of desire lubricated her just that much more. The shudder that went through him indicated he'd felt it, too.

"Hold on, baby," he whispered as the scent of her increased his sex-ual hunger and nipped at his control. Bracing his weight on his elbows he stared down at her, watching her closely. He wanted to see her expression the exact moment their bodies joined as one. His visual focus was entirely on her. His physical focus was on that part of her he so desperately needed to connect with.

The effort of control was etched on his face as his body began eas-ing his engorged shaft into her. She was tight. Almost too tight. He partially withdrew then began a slow penetration again as he watched her. Her expression indicated it hurt. Her fingers sank into his shoul-ders as he continued to ease forward, deeper inside of her. He felt her tense beneath him and a sheen of tears glistened her eyes. He was about to pull out when he felt her legs wrap around him, locking him to her, a silent message for him to stay put—no matter what. She needed to experience this hot, burning pleasure just as much as he did. The feel of her legs around him and the wetness of her feminine folds clutching him pushed him over the edge.

He spread her legs farther apart with his knees at the same time he slipped a hand beneath her hips, lifting her as he pushed into her with one forceful lunge. He saw the flicker of pain that flashed in her eyes just seconds before she cried out.

"It won't hurt again, I promise," he whispered in a strained voice as he felt himself embedded deep within her.

She nodded then he leaned down and kissed her, devouring her mouth as he remained still for a while as his shaft throbbed within her. She could actually feel him growing, getting larger and stretched her body to accommodate him. Her inner muscles gloved him tight.

Randolph then began to slowly move in and out of her body. He knew the exact moment pleasure replaced pain when her hand caressed a path up and down his back, and she began meeting him stroke for stroke. Whimpering sounds poured forth from her throat and was captured in his kiss. Her legs tightened around him as the movements of their bodies intensified.

He groaned.

She purred.

The two sounds infiltrated the quiet peacefulness of their surroundings. Passion—deep and sharp—rammed through them, spurring them to increase the pace of their mating and flooding their minds with unbearable sensations.

He broke off their kiss and looked into her face just seconds before earth-shattering sensations ripped through her, shaking her to the core, making her eyes glaze over in unadulterated pleasure. She screamed his name over and over again. He felt the stirrings of his own desire being shaken to the core by her body's tremors. Throwing his head back and releasing a deep, piercing groan, he joined her in carnal paradise as the throes of ecstasy pushed him over the edge and straight into sweet, sensuous oblivion.

Ten

Jenna didn't want to open her eyes just yet. She didn't think she had the ability to do so even if she wanted to. Nor did she think she could move her body, which was just as well since Randolph was still on top of her. He was still inside of her, joined, connected.

She had experienced the ultimate in passion in his arms. And as she felt the heat of him throb, harden, and enlarge inside of her, her own body awakened to a sensuous stir as powerful sexual urges again consumed her. Her feminine walls once again stretched to accommodate him.

Randolph began nuzzling her neck as his hands cupped her hips, holding her in place when she instinctively began to move. "No, baby, don't move," he whispered hoarsely. "I want to savor the feel of being inside of you this way. I've wanted you for so long. Now that I have you, totally and completely, and now that your life is joined with mine, I won't ever let you go, Jenna. You will always belong to me, no matter what. We will always belong together."

And then he began kissing her with a passion as his body began moving in hers. And this time when she lifted her hips, he didn't stop her. Instead he set the rhythm for her to follow. She began meeting him thrust for thrust.

Tearing his mouth from hers, he concentrated on giving them just what they needed and wanted, pushing her higher as he went deeper, staking a claim on her body, her heart and her soul.

Then it happened again. Jenna felt the tingling that started at her toes and settled dead center between her legs where she and Randolph were joined. There, in that spot, the sensations intensified, overwhelming her, and making it difficult for her to breathe. She called out his name at the same exact moment he called out hers. And then he took her mouth again as he grounded himself against her, inside of her, mating relentlessly with her as the muscles of his body flexed with the flow of his movements as he thrust in and out of her.

Kissing her long and hard, Randolph felt the insides of her gripping him, pulling everything out of him. A part of him wished he wasn't wearing a rubber so he could feel his hot release spurt inside of her, coating her womb with his seed. But he knew now was not the time. They had college to complete.

Vowing his love for Jenna over that Bible made what they were doing now feel right. Their lives were bound together and he felt no marriage vows could make them any more connected and committed. In his heart she was his soul mate, his other half, the woman he intended to share the rest of his life with, the woman who would one day give him children.

That thought made the headiest of sensations spear through him. And when he felt her body muscles squeeze him, extracting from him what it really couldn't have because of the latex separating them, he gave it up anyway when he felt himself falling over the edge. The rapid clenching and unclenching of her muscles as she tried to pull the very essence from him made his entire movement quicken with an agonizing need for release.

A volcano erupted inside of him and it shook with the force of an earthquake as he felt her body climax. Then his body traveled the second time that day to a place called ecstasy.

For the rest of the day Randolph and Jenna shared the essence of what it meant to be totally and completely in love. After making love a second time he had picked her up in his arms and had taken her to the shallow end of the pool and sat down with her in his lap. The heat of the water from the hot spring felt soothing to the muscles her body had used for the first time that day. He had leisurely caressed her body over and over again, reawakening it to his sensual onslaught. Then, taking her hand he had walked her farther into the depths of the pond where he turned her to face him, kissing her with an intensity that melted every bone in her body. He then spread her legs apart in the waist-deep water, wrapping her legs around his hips. Slowly entering her he emitted a groan deep in his throat the moment their bodies connected.

Later, much later, he dried her off and carried her back to the blanket where they ate sandwiches and drank wine. After satisfying their hunger they lay back on the blanket wrapped in each other's arms, looking up at the sky and wishing their time here could last forever.

Jenna knew that being with Randolph without her parents' or his grandparents' knowledge was wrong but at the moment she didn't care. They had seven days to be together before they had to return to school and she wanted to spend all seven with him, savoring every stolen moment that she could. In less than three months they would part ways for the summer and she wanted every single minute to count so she would have memories to draw from.

"Ready for your swimming lessons?"

She looked over at him and smiled. It was a smile of a woman in love, a woman whose body and mind were deeply satisfied and at peace. "You promise not to let me drown?"

He gave her a slow, sexy grin. "Oh, I promise to do a lot of things to you, Jenna, but letting you drown isn't one of them."

Jenna watched as he stood up and then looked down at her. Both of them were naked as the day they came into the world. She watched his eyes darken as he gazed down at her, with love, male appreciation and sexual desire within their depths. The heat of his gaze made her feminine core throb. She couldn't believe she could still want him again and looking at him, at that male part of him that was large and aroused, she could see that he wanted her again, too.

"No, we will never stop wanting each other," he said softly, as if reading her thoughts. "You're my soul mate and my body knows it. It's in tune to the very thing it wants and needs for nourishment and for happiness." She then watched as he reached out and picked up another rubber. After tearing off the wrapping he put it on. "First I gave you swimming lessons . . ."

She smiled up at him as a tingling sensation spread all the way throughout her body. "Then what?" she asked, as if she didn't know after seeing him sheath himself.

"Then I give you something else."

"Something else like what?"

"Some of this," he said, pointing to a certain part of his body. "Want it?" he asked, his voice a rasped whisper.

The nipples of Jenna's breasts tightened. She felt the feminine folds of her body fill with moisture. "Yes, I want it." She suddenly felt wild and hot, wondering just how much pleasure a person could take before dying from it. "How about if we reverse the order of things a bit," she said, gazing up him, all of him.

"In what way?"

"First I get some of that . . . then I have swimming lessons." And to make sure he was just as hot as she was, she lay back on the blanket in a pose that told him she was ready. Her legs spread, her knees slightly raised and her breasts pointed and firm. But just to make sure he got her message, she met his gaze and in a deep, sultry and ultrasexy voice she said, "I want you inside me, Randolph."

He came to her immediately. Covering her with his body, his sex immediately went after that part it wanted. With one forceful lunge he entered her to the hilt. Kissing her, devouring her mouth as his body began mating with hers at a frantic pace, he pumped back and forth into her with a frantic need. She moved against him, with him, taking all he was offering. Within seconds the both of them were overtaken with pleasure so strong it made them lose all manner of control.

Randolph couldn't think straight. The only thing he knew was that he wanted to feel the very essence of Jenna without anything between them. In a moment of madness, without thinking but reacting, he pulled completely out of her, snatched off the rubber, tossed it aside and reentered her in one smooth beat. The feel of her hot wetness on his sex was more profound than he could have ever imagined, and the male part of him that throbbed wanted to flood her with the thickness of his semen.

His animalistic roar vibrated the air at the same time Jenna screamed his name. His release into her was hot, plentiful. He wanted to pull out when he realized what he had done but it was too late. The climax they were sharing surpassed any they had shared before, and they knew in their hearts that their love would surpass any and all things. Happiness was theirs and they intended to savor each and every moment of it, now, today and forever.

As the following days flowed one into another, Randolph and Jenna's love for each other intensified. Their days were spent taking walks, talking, making future plans with their lives as well as discussing the present situation in Vietnam. They had heard on the radio that morning that Vietcong guerrillas had launched an attack against a Tan Son Nhut air base, killing seven American soldiers and injuring a hundred and sixty others. Also, China had downed an American attack plane, killing everyone on board.

Randolph and Jenna didn't talk about where the war might be headed, nor did they speak of the possibility that she might be preg-

nant. They refused to allow anything to invade their peaceful existence. They enjoyed waking up together in the mornings and going
to sleep together at night. They shared a desperate need to fill their
senses with each other and that is what they did. Unlike they
thought it would, the sexual urgency to make love did not wear off
with each passing day. If anything, it intensified, although they
never lost control like they had that first day when Randolph had
taken off the rubber. It was only on their last day at the cottage,
after they had packed and were ready to leave, did he bring the incident up.

He pulled her into his arms after checking the house a final time to
make sure no evidence of her being there with him was left behind. "If
you're pregnant, Jenna, we get married, all right?"

She shook her head vehemently. "No. That would mean your having
to quit school and possibly going to Vietnam."

"I'll take that chance. I'll never have a child of mine born outside of
wedlock. Ross and I made that promise to our father during our talk
about the birds and the bees and it's a promise we intend to keep.
Fuller men live up to their responsibilities no matter what they are and
no matter the sacrifices that have to be made. I knew what I was
doing, Jenna, and a part of me knew I was putting you at risk and for
that I apologize, but I had to have you that way. I had to know how it
felt to be a part of you, skin to skin with nothing betwee us."

Jenna nodded, understanding completely. That was one of the reasons she intended to pay a visit to the doctor when she returned to
school—to go on birth control pills. Leigh had shared with her that
she was on them. Noah had taken her to a doctor across town. Telling
the older man they were husband and wife, the physician hadn't asked
to see the fake marriage license they had obtained. Instead he had
given her an exam while Noah had waited in the outer office and afterward, the prescriptions for the pills. Leigh had been on them for over
three months now and so far she had not experienced any side effects.
And according to Leigh, her and Noah's love life was better than ever
with the risk of pregnancy removed.

"More than likely I'm not pregnant. I'm supposed to start my period in a few weeks so chances are the timing was off," Jenna said softly.

Randolph sighed, knowing he had to be more responsible where she was concerned. "It's going to be hard not sleeping with you every night, sweetheart. I can't wait until I finish school so we can get married."

Jenna smiled as she looked up at him. "We *will* get married one day, won't we?" she asked. For some reason she needed assurance.

"Yes, just as soon as I finish law school. In my heart I feel as though we're already married—not legally but to me we're married in the sight of God and that's what counts. You are my wife, here," he said, placing a hand over his heart.

"And you are my husband, here," Jenna said, taking that same hand of his and putting it to her heart. "It doesn't matter who else knows it as long as the two of us know it."

And then she opened her mouth to him when he leaned toward it, sweeping the insides with his tongue and spreading torrid sensations throughout her body. His kiss was slowly setting her on fire and as she felt his arousal pressing against her, she knew he was on fire as well. A part of her was tempted to tell him to miss the next ferry, and catch the one that would come at midday instead of early morning, but she knew she couldn't. They needed to leave so she could get back to school to call her family. Sunday would be the twins' birthday and she knew they would expect her to call to wish them a happy birthday.

Randolph pulled his mouth from hers, sighing and resting his forehead against hers. "I love you, Jenna. No matter what, always remember that."

"And I love you as well. Always remember that, too," she countered, with the look of complete love glowing in her eyes.

And then he held her close, their hearts beating as one and thinking that the week they had spent together would be one they would always remember.

It was the tie that would always bind them together.

Eleven

The following week Jenna and Randolph were back in school. She knew the moment he joined her at the table in the café one morning that something was wrong. She reached out and placed her hand over his. "What is it? What's wrong, Randolph?"

He tried smiling at her. It had been his intention not to let Jenna know he was bothered by anything but she could read him too well. "I got a call from Grandmother Julia. She plans to host a small dinner party for my grandfather's birthday Saturday and wants me to bring you."

Jenna nodded. She could tell he wasn't thrilled with the idea. "You're not ready for me to meet your grandparents in Virginia?"

He took her other hand in his. "It's not that, Jenna. It's just that I know my grandmother. Not for one minute do I believe she's giving us her blessings, and I don't want to place you in an uncomfortable situation with her."

Jenna smiled. "Don't worry about it. What can she do? I love you and I know you love me. Maybe after she gets to know me she'll come around."

Randolph didn't believe it for one minute but decided not to tell Jenna that. Once Julia Fuller made up her mind about something that was it, and she was totally convinced that Jenna was not good enough to be a Fuller. His parents had been married nearly twelve years and up to the day they had died she'd still considered their marriage a mistake. He would love to think her heart had begun softening but he knew that wasn't the case.

"All right, if you're sure you want to be there. She also wants you to stay overnight. Will that be a problem?"

"No, it won't be."

He nodded. "It's my understanding that Noah has also been invited and more than likely he's bringing Leigh."

Jenna smiled. "Then I'll have a real friend there besides you."

Randolph's hand tightened in hers. "And don't forget about Ross and Noah. They are your friends, too. They know how much you mean to me."

Her smile widened. "I won't forget."

Randolph stared at her, knowing he would always love her and protect her. He was also determined that his grandmother would not come between them.

Jenna realized just what affluent people Randolph's grandparents were when they pulled up in front of a huge brick house in a nice section of Richmond. She could immediately tell that although it was a segregated community, it was where a number of well-to-do Blacks lived, the highly educated ones who'd been fortunate to become attorneys, doctors or politicians.

She felt butterflies take off in her stomach when Randolph opened the car door for her. He took her hand in his and escorted her up the massive walkway to the front door. Moments later an older man that she knew just had to be Randolph's grandfather opened the door.

"You must be Jenna," he said with a welcoming smile that seemed genuine as he took her hand in his.

"Yes, sir," she replied nervously as she studied the man's features, thinking how much both Ross and Randolph favored him.

"Come on in, we'll bring your bags in later," he said, placing her arm in the crook of his. "Ross and Angela arrived an hour ago," he said, speaking to Randolph as he escorted Jenna further into the house with Randolph following in their wake. "And Noah and his date didn't make it. Seems he has come down with the flu." He looked at Jenna and smiled. "But I'm glad you made it, Jenna. You're a beautiful girl and I can see why my grandson is so taken with you."

"Thanks," Jenna said, feeling slightly more more comfortable after such kind words and the warm and friendly welcome Randolph's grandfather had given her. She couldn't help but take note of her surroundings. The inside of the house was just like the outside, impressive. A huge, beautiful crystal chandelier hung in a massive foyer and on the wall a pair of grand-looking sconces flanked a gigantic gold-trimmed mirror.

The architect in Jenna couldn't help but admire how the rooms in the house were situated, each branching off from the foyer, which served as the center of the house. The ceilings were tall, vaulted, symmetrical in design and ornate in detail. So were the furnishings in the rooms she passed. Each piece she knew had been selected to accentuate the lavish feel, even the floral arrangements that were in huge, opulent-looking vases.

Moments later Jenna didn't feel quite so comfortable as she and the elder Mr. Fuller walked into a room where about eight people were standing around drinking wine and chatting quietly. The only person she recognized was Ross, who turned and smiled at her. Taking a deep breath she felt Randolph's hand slip into hers. He leaned down and whispered, "Remember, I love you."

She nodded just seconds before a tall, elegantly dressed older woman turned toward them and gave Jenna the most unwelcome look she had ever seen. The woman crossed the room toward them. Jenna didn't have to be told that the fair-skinned woman was Randolph's grandmother.

Immediately, such words as tall, refined, dignified, graceful, elegant and polished came to mind as she watched Julia Fuller walk toward her. The list could go on and on and the fashionable jeweled-neck silk dress she wore gave her an air of sophistication that Jenna couldn't help but admire. Even the light brown eyes that narrowed at her were striking.

"Randolph, you're late," his grandmother admonished before leaning over and placing a kiss on his cheek. She then turned her attention to Jenna, and hesitated for a moment before saying, "Welcome to my home. You must be Jenna. I'm Julia Fuller, Randolph's grandmother." There was not a touch of a smile on her face or in her voice. And the hand that took Jenna's did not provide a warm handshake.

"We got a late start out of DC," Randolph said, glancing around the room. "I thought you said this would be a private party. What is Lena and her family doing here?"

Julia smiled. She seemed pleased at her grandson's apparent agitation. "Why Randolph, you know that Stuart Weaver and your grandfather are good friends and that Ida is a good friend of mine as well. I couldn't think of celebrating your grandfather's birthday without inviting them. By the way, your godfather is here. Why don't you come say hello to him?" As if it was an afterthought, she turned to Jenna and said, "You can come meet him, too, if you'd like, Jenna. Did Randolph tell you that A. Phillip Randolph is his godfather?"

"Yes, he mentioned it."

"He and Robert are very good friends and have been for years." Without hesitation Julia Fuller then recounted the story of how the two men had been in the armed services together and had been close friends since. And as she led them across the room to the tall, distinguished-looking gentleman who was standing and talking to Ross and a young woman, Julia provided tidbits on the accomplishments of the Fuller family, a family that was known to bred some of the finest attorneys anywhere.

Jenna listened quietly, her confidence dwindling by the minute. It was quite obvious that Randolph's grandmother was telling her about the Fuller family's history and connections to make her realize that she was not a fit. She figured Randolph also caught on to his grandmother's ploy and held her hand in his tightly as they strode with Julia Fuller across the room. Even with Randolph's reassurance, Jenna wished she were someplace else right now. Someplace where she knew she was not on display.

Angela was fuming inside. How dare Randolph pay so much attention to that girl he brought to the party tonight! He was holding onto her like he was afraid if he let go she would disappear!

The only reason she had jumped at Ross's invitation to come tonight was the chance to see Randolph again, in the flesh. He still looked good, and although she admitted Ross was also a handsome man, there was something about Randolph that drove her mad with passion and fueled her fantasies.

She wondered if he and the girl were sleeping together. The

thought of it being even a possibility made her want to scream. She knew from an earlier conversation that Mrs. Fuller did not approve of his relationship with the girl. She also knew that Lena had given up on him and had set her sights on another guy at school who came from a prestigious family, although Lena admitted she hadn't told her parents yet. But she felt when she did they would be fine with her choice.

As far as Angela was concerned that left Randolph wide open. She dismissed the plain-looking girl he was with tonight as competition. Right now her only concern was Ross. Since meeting her at the train station that morning, he was playing the part of the attentive suitor and she was playing the part of the prim and proper lady.

"Would you like some more wine, Angela?"

She glanced up at Ross when his question invaded her thoughts. "No, but I'd like to know who that girl is with Randolph."

Ross smiled as he glanced over to where his brother, Jenna and his grandmother were talking to A. Philip Randolph. "That's Jenna Haywood, Randolph's girlfriend."

"Girlfriend? But what about Lena? I thought it was understood that she and Randolph were an item," she said.

"I guess you weren't the only one who thought that. I believe my grandmother wished it to be so but Randolph has other ideas as to who he wants to spend the rest of his life with. He and Lena are nothing more than friends. She has accepted the fact that Randolph's in love with Jenna and is fine with it."

A frown appeared on Angela's face. "But how can Randolph even consider getting serious with someone like her? Look at her."

Ross raised a brow as he glanced over at Jenna. "I'm looking and I don't see anything wrong. I've met Jenna and think she's a nice person."

Angela raised eyes to the ceiling, fighting to remain calm and to retain her prim and proper demeanor. "I don't care how nice she is, Ross, it's obvious she's not one of us."

Now it was Ross's turn to raise a brow. "One of us?"

Angela sighed in frustration. Was the man that dense? "Yes, Ross. Look at the dress she's wearing. It probably came off the racks and more than likely she did her hair for tonight's affair herself."

Ross frowned. "And that's what draws Rand to her. One thing you're going to discover about my brother is that he detests phoniness of any kind. He also hates people who think they are better than others."

Angela swallowed. She certainly hadn't meant to make Ross upset with her, nor did she want to alienate Randolph. Although he never went out of his way to associate with her, he had accepted her as Ross's girlfriend. "Maybe I was a little hasty in my opinion."

"There's no maybe about it, Angela. You were. Now, if you'll excuse me I want to refill my glass with wine."

As Angela watched him walk off she knew she had to do some backpedaling to get back into Ross's good graces. Evidently any negative comments about Jenna Haywood were a sore spot with him.

"So, Jenna, what sorority are you affiliated with?" Julia Fuller asked, seeming like she was interested.

"I'm not affiliated with any right now. I decided to wait until next year to get involved with one," she said, keeping her gaze on Julia Fuller and not on the others who had assembled at the dinner table.

"Oh." That single word from Julia's lips sounded as if Jenna was lacking in some way.

"I decided to let my studies come first," Jenna decided to add.

"You're a smart young lady," Robert Fuller said, coming to her rescue. "Too many young women get wrapped up in extra-curricular activities when they should be studying."

"There are benefits with joining a sorority, Robert," Julia said, not liking the position her husband had taken. And definitely not liking the fact that he was disagreeing with her in front of others.

"And there are benefits to studying and getting a good education, Julia. She still has time to get involved in that." He winked at Jenna. "I understand you've made the Dean's List quite a few times so the way I see it, you've got your head in the right place."

"Thank you, sir."

Randolph smiled. He could never recall a time his grandfather had disagreed with his grandmother on anything. He wondered what happened to make him stand up to her. Maybe it was obvious to his grandfather, as it was to him, that his grandmother had been trying all night to chip away at Jenna's self confidence.

"Did I mention that I've decided to attend Howard Law School when I complete my studies at Bronson?" Angela broke the silence by saying. "I know you will have graduated by then, Ross, but since you'll be remaining in the area after graduation, I thought it would be nice if I were close by."

If she expected some show of excitement from Ross, she didn't get it. Randolph lifted a brow, when Ross merely said, "That's nice," and continued eating his food.

Randolph sat back in his chair and glanced across the table at the pair. Evidently Ross was upset with Angela about something. He wondered what.

"Well, I think it's simply wonderful that you want to go to law school. Especially since the Fullers have a history of having a line of wonderful and affluent attorneys. Don't you think it's wonderful that she would consider the same profession as Ross, Robert?"

Robert Fuller waved a hand in the air. "Whatever. That news certainly seems to have made your day, Julia."

Randolph couldn't help but smother a grin. Evidently his grandfather had taken his advice and had observed just how dispassionately Ross seemed to be hog-tied to Angela. Maybe now he would keep his eyes open more.

"You're all right?" Randolph leaned over and whispered to Jenna. She had been quiet around him most of the evening.

Instead of answering him, she nodded and kept her attention on her food. He frowned. The two of them would talk later. He needed to reemphasize to her that what his grandmother wanted didn't matter. She was the woman he wanted.

Later that evening when Jenna retired to the elegantly decorated guest room, she wanted to cry her eyes out. Dinner had been a total disaster.

Julia Fuller had used every weapon in her arsenal to make her feel out of place, and every power she possessed to show that Lena Weaver was the one Randolph should be interested in.

First she had seated them at the dinner table with Jenna on one side of Randolph and Lena on the other. It had been the refined and quite beautiful Lena Weaver and Ross's girlfriend, the cool, prim and proper Angela Douglass, who had dominated most of the conversation around the table. They talked about a number of things that were meant to make her feel excluded.

She had observed Ross and Angela throughout the evening, and on several occasions wondered what they had in common. She'd always found Randolph's brother to be totally outgoing, relaxed and friendly. However, the woman he seemed interested in was a total snob.

And although it seemed that Lena had accepted the fact that Randolph was not interested in her, it was evident that her mother and Julia Fuller had not. They kept bringing up past events and situations the couple had shared, including the time Randolph had asked Lena to marry him at the age of fifteen.

Something else Jenna had noticed immediately was the fact that all the women present were fair-skinned compared to her chocolate-brown complexion. It was perfectly clear to her after tonight that she was definitely out of her element around the women and there was no way she could ever fit into Randolph's world.

Jenna lifted her head off the pillow when she heard a knock at the bedroom door. "Yes?"

The door opened slowly and Julia Fuller appeared. "I think we should have a talk, Jenna."

Jenna sat up in the bed and nodded. "Yes, I think we should have a talk, too."

Julia came into the room, closed the door behind her and then leaned against it. "There's no doubt in my mind that you're a nice person, Jenna, but you're not the right person for Randolph. He will need a wife who will be an asset to him."

"And you don't think that I will?" she asked, feeling awful.

"No, I think you would try but society as it is would not accept you since you don't have a good family background. I agree it may not be fair but that's the way things are. Do you want him to suffer because of it?"

Jenna held her head down. "No."

Julia smiled. Convincing her to bail out of the picture was easier than she thought. The chit really did love Randolph. What a pity. "Then I hope you'll find it in your heart to do the right thing. He fancies himself in love with you and can't see how messed up his future will be if he continues to pursue a relationship with you. Randolph marrying you will bring down the Fuller family's name. It will be up to you to call things off, Jenna, then stick to your guns. In time he will get over you, and I do appreciate what you're doing for him."

With tears filling her eyes Jenna stared at the woman who wanted her out of her grandson's life. She was so different from Mattie Denison, who had accepted her with open arms and had acted like she was the best thing to ever happen to Randolph. "You want him to marry Lena Weaver, don't you?"

The older woman didn't hesitate in answering. "Yes, but I doubt Lena's parents will approve of him getting back with Lena after the way he has treated her. But there is another woman out there who is far more suitable for him than you are. And I will get them together."

Jenna wiped at her tears. "Don't you think Randolph has a right to choose his own wife?"

Julia shook her head. "No. He doesn't know what he needs as a helpmate for his career. I do. I'm one of the main reasons my husband is as successful as he is. I came into our marriage with a strong family background and connections. You have neither."

She sighed then, evidently weary of the conversation. "Randolph and Ross went with their grandfather to take A. Philip to the train station. I suggest you leave while they're gone."

"Leave?"

"Yes. Leave. The Weavers are returning to Washington tonight and they have agreed that you can ride back with them."

Jenna nodded. Randolph's grandmother was letting her know she was no longer welcome in her home. "What about Randolph? What will you tell him when he returns?"

"That you made the right decision about your relationship since he couldn't." She stared hard at Jenna. "He'll eventually contact you to try and work things out, but you have to be strong and do the right thing. Understand?"

Jenna sighed deeply. "Yes. I understand. I understand more than you will ever know."

Angela tiptoed back to her room after having stood at the door eavesdropping on the conversation between Julia Fuller and Jenna. She couldn't help but smile. The older woman was letting Jenna know in no uncertain terms that she would never be accepted into the Fuller family. The girl would be a fool to try to hang onto Randolph now.

Angela's smile widened. With both Lena and Jenna out of the picture, things would be smooth sailing from here. Now, if she could only come up with a plan to rid herself of Ross in such a way that would assure her of having Randolph.

She would have to bide her time and come up with an opportunity, but under no circumstances would she let Ross break things off with her. She knew he was annoyed with her after what she had said tonight. If she didn't know better she would think he was kind of sweet on Jenna himself. But she knew to accuse him of it without sufficient proof would be a mistake.

As she went into the bathroom to take her shower she wondered just how Randolph would react when he came back and discovered Jenna was gone.

"Jenna?" Randolph whispered her name a second time and when she didn't answer, he pushed open the bedroom door. The room was empty. Jenna wasn't there.

He went down the hall to his grandparents' room and knocked. His grandfather opened the door.

"Yes, Randolph, what is it?"

"Jenna isn't here. Ask Grandmother if she had to go out or some-thing."

"She's left." His grandmother's voiced carried from within the room, behind his grandfather.

Randolph knew both men's expressions reflected surprise. He quickly moved past his grandfather and entered the room. "What do you mean she's left?"

Julia was sitting up in bed reading like nothing was bothering her, especially the fact that Jenna had left. "Jenna decided to leave," she said.

Anger, immediate and to a degree he had never experienced before, raced through Randolph. There was no way Jenna would have up and left unless his grandmother had said something to her. He took a few steps to stand in front of the bed. "What did you say to her?"

His grandmother lifted her head from her book, hearing the tone of voice he was using on her. "Do not raise your voice to me, Randolph. Robert, tell him not to raise his voice."

Robert Fuller glanced away from his wife to his grandson. "Don't raise your voice to your grandmother, Randolph. Please let me do the honor." He then turned back to his wife. "What did you say to her, Julia?" he asked in a very loud voice.

Julia gasped. Her husband had never raised his voice to her before. "Robert, please, we have guests in this house and I—"

"Answer my question, damnit!"

Julia stopped talking immediately. Her husband had never spoken to her in such a manner. "Robert, please calm down. I won't tolerate you speaking to me that way."

"And I won't tolerate you sticking your nose where it doesn't belong any longer, Julia. For years I sat back and did nothing while you tried to meddle in our son's life. He loved Adrianna, and you knew it but you couldn't be happy for him. Instead you made it nearly impossible for him to come home to even visit. You made him choose between us and the woman he loved and he chose her, and to this day you have never forgiven him for it."

"Ross Senior was my son. I loved him and only wanted what was best for him."

"What was best by your holy standards, Julia, not his. Now you're trying to do the same thing to Ross and Randolph. Ross may go along with your foolishness to keep peace but Randolph won't, and I commend him for it, just like I commended Ross Senior for standing up to you. Now it's time I put my foot down before you do any more damage. I want you to listen to me and listen to me good," he said, leaning over the bed into her face. "If you want us to continue living under the same roof, I would suggest you answer my question and answer it now!"

Julia swallowed. She moved her gaze from her husband's stormy face to that of her grandson's. The look he was giving her was just as angry and filled with bitterness. "Jenna went back to Washington."

"How did she get back to Washington?" Robert Fuller almost growled the question.

Julia swallowed again. "With the Weavers."

"What did you say to her, Grandmother?" Randolph spoke for the first time since his grandfather had interceded.

Julia turned her attention to Randolph. "I made her see reason. I told her that she would never benefit your career as your wife since she didn't bring a strong family background. I also made her see that in marrying you all she would do would be to bring down the Fuller family name. Now she fully understands why the two of you could never have a future together."

Randolph stared at his grandmother, not believing she had said those things to Jenna, and not sure if he would ever forgive her for doing so. "I'm leaving, going back to Washington and will try to convince Jenna that we can have a future together. And you better hope that I can, Grandmother Julia, because I won't set another foot in this house again if I can't. And the Fuller name that you're so proud of, I will disown."

She placed a hand over her heart. "You can't mean that."

"Yes, I do." He then walked out of the bedroom.

Julia met her husband's angry gaze. "You have to stop him, Robert."

"No, Julia, in fact I plan to drive him to Washington tonight myself."

"But—but, it's late and tonight's your birthday."

"Yes, and it's the worst birthday I've ever had because of what you've done. For the first time in my life, Julia, I can look into your face and say that you have truly disappointed me and a part of me regrets the day I married you. Have you ever thought of the fact that maybe you weren't my choice for a wife, either?" He then turned and walked out of the room.

"Hey, what's all the commotion about?" Ross asked, entering his brother's bedroom. He frowned when he saw Randolph packing. "Where are you going?"

"After Jenna."

Ross raised a bemused brow. "After Jenna? But isn't she in the bedroom down the hall?"

Randolph angrily shook his head. "No, Grandmother Julia said something to her about not being the woman for me and then conveniently sent her back to Washington with the Weavers."

At first Ross was too shocked to speak. Then he said, "Grandmother Julia has gone too far this time."

"Yes, and I don't know if I'll ever be able to forgive her for it. Dealing with me was one thing, but deliberately going after Jenna and hurting her was another. She didn't deserve that. I knew I should not have brought her here tonight. Even Angela was rude to her."

Ross nodded. "Yes, I know and I apologize for that."

Randolph stopped packing and stared at his brother. "You shouldn't be the one apologizing. Angela is a grown woman who's responsible for her own actions."

Ross shrugged. "I think she's jealous of Jenna."

"Why on earth would she be jealous of Jenna?"

Ross sighed. "When she made a comment about Jenna, I stood up for Jenna in such a way to make her think that I thought Jenna was very special to me as well. I don't think she liked me sticking up for Jenna the way I did."

When Randolph didn't say anything, Ross continued. "You and Noah were right. There is no passion between Angela and me. But I've accepted things as they are, Rand, since I don't need love and passion anyway. But you do. You need love and passion and you need Jenna. I hope you can work things out with her. She's been dealt a bad hand. Grandmother Julia had no right to do what she did."

Randolph nodded in agreement as he closed his luggage.

When Jenna reached the dorm the only thing she wanted to do was go to bed and cry. Although the Weavers hadn't been deliberately mean, they had practically ignored her during the entire trip.

She was glad she was alone. Leigh was probably spending the night over at Noah's and she figured Ellie was someplace with Tyrone.

She had barely settled into bed when the phone began ringing. She placed her pillow over her head to drown out the noise. She refused to answer it in case it was Randolph. She wasn't ready to deal with him yet. Tears rolled down her face as the telephone kept ringing. Ignoring it, she closed her eyes and forced her mind into sleep.

The next morning Jenna had just finished brushing her teeth and washing her face when the phone rang. Feeling like she was in a better frame of mind to deal with Randolph, she picked it up. "Hello."

"Are you alone?"

She recognized his voice immediately. "Yes."

"Are you dressed yet?"

She lifted a bemused brow and said, "No."

"Then put on some clothes, I'm on my way over."

Jenna's heart began beating rapidly. "On your way over? Aren't you still in Virginia?"

"No, I came home last night. Did you think I wouldn't come after you, Jenna?"

She closed her eyes. Deep down she should have known that he would. "I just assumed you would wait."

"Well, you thought wrong. Put on some clothes. Or if you prefer you can keep them off. Either way I'm on my way over." And with that last statement he hung up.

Jenna nervously licked her bottom lip after placing the phone back in its cradle, thinking that was the angriest she had ever heard Randolph sound.

Jenna was fully dressed when she opened the door for Randolph less than ten minutes later. He walked past her and entered her dorm room, closing the door behind him. When he turned to face her his features indicated he'd had a very sleepless night. His features also indicated he was indeed angry.

"How dare you let my grandmother do this to us, Jenna! We had an agreement that no one would ever come between us," he said in an irritated tone of voice.

"Randolph, don't be mad, please. She only made me realize I would never fit into your world. And she's right."

He said nothing for the longest time, then he took a step toward her. With shaking fingers he reached out and captured her face in his hand. "Don't you know by now that *you* are my world, Jenna? Don't you know that the only way I can be happy is with you? We've pledged our lives together. You are already mine in every sense of the word. In my heart you are already my wife. I chose you a long time ago and in my heart and in the eyes of God, I made it official last week on Glendale Shores. It doesn't matter what my grandmother wants for me. The most important thing is what I want for myself, and I want you."

Tears sprang into Jenna's eyes. "Oh, Randolph."

He leaned down and kissed her wet cheeks. "I love you, Jenna," he said in a voice thick with love. "Don't ever doubt my love for you and don't ever think that something will come up between us that we can't work out. Don't let my grandmother, or anyone, come between us."

Jenna hesitated only a second before she nodded and said, "I won't."

He then leaned over and kissed her deeply and thoroughly. She readily accepted the thrust of his tongue and her body arched against his. When he lifted his head, he smiled and said huskily, "Besides, it's not definite that you aren't pregnant, is it?"

Jenna shook her head. "No, it's only been a little over a week and too soon to tell. But like I told you, I feel certain that I'm not pregnant."

He nodded. "And if you are, I meant what I said, Jenna. We're getting married with or without anyone's blessings. All right?"

She gazed at him with so much love in her heart. "All right."

She didn't hesitate going into his arms when he devoured her lips again. The need to be connected to him in the most elemental and primal way was what she wanted, and she could tell from the way he kissed her that it was what he wanted as well.

Knowing it would be later that day when Leigh and Ellie came home, she began walking backward and pulled Randolph down on the bed with her. In Randolph's arms was where she would always want to belong.

Twelve

As Jenna predicted, she had not gotten pregnant during the week they had spent at Glendale Shores, and since she and Randolph would be apart during the summer months, she decided to wait until returning to school in the fall before going on birth control pills.

With less than two months left before the school year ended, Randolph and Jenna spent most of their time studying and working on various reports they had to turn in. They had put the episode involving his grandmother behind them. He still had not returned home to Virginia, too angry with his grandmother to see her. Although Jenna wanted him to forgive her and put the incident behind him, he hadn't yet found it in his heart to forgive nor forget.

On April the fourth Jenna turned nineteen and Randolph became twenty-one. They celebrated their birthdays together in the privacy of a hotel room in an upscale area of Washington. He gave her a beautiful charm bracelet and she gave him a nice set of cuff links. Their relationship was going smoothly. They enjoyed the time they spent together and since they had become intimate, were closer than ever before. It was obvious to anyone who was around them for any length of time that they were truly in love.

The same held true for Leigh and Noah. Leigh was to return to Miami during the summer to work in her mother's beauty salon, and Noah planned to join Ross after graduation and volunteer his time and services to assist Martin Luther King, Jr. in the voter registration drive. Both Noah and Ross decided that although they opposed the war, they would enlist instead of waiting to be drafted. If they enlisted as law school graduates they could enter the armed services as officers. Noah had his eye on the air force and Ross was looking at the marines.

Noah made a decision not to mention his military plans to Leigh yet. He knew the thought of him going off to war was something she would not be able to deal with right now. After losing her brother she would go bonkers if he went anywhere that would place his life in danger.

News about the war for the past few months hadn't been that encouraging. The air war had increased and the ground war was still reporting a high number of American casualties. Demonstrations against the war were held on a number of college campuses. Howard University had held one such demonstration. Led by a group that called themselves BOTTW—Blacks Opposed To The War—it had been a peaceful demonstration of over two thousand students. Noah and Leigh, as well as Randolph, Jenna, Ellie and Tyrone had all participated.

With so much emphasis being placed on the Vietnam war, the Black Panther Party continued their fight to bring an end to police brutality and the murder of black people on the homefront. The organization was growing in numbers and was still under close watch of the FBI.

Both Jenna and Leigh received their first letters from Johnny. In his four-page letter, he told them he was living in Oakland and was doing okay. He also told them that he was now an official member of the party. His letter went on to read:

I've met the Panthers' founders, Bobby Seale and Huey Newton. The two met as students at Oakland Merritt Junior College and were working at a city antipoverty center. They are good guys and nothing like the media has made them out to be. They are against police brutality of our people in the community, and are working to put an end to that. Please don't believe the negativity you hear in the media about the group.
There are certain parties working hard to discredit us.

Although Johnny's letter indicated he was doing fine, Jenna couldn't help but still be afraid for him.

It was the last week in April with only two more weeks of school left. Noah and Ross were preparing to graduate from law school and Randolph was graduating from Howard's School of Business and would return in the fall to attend law school. Noah planned to accompany Leigh on the train back to Miami. He would stay with his parents for two weeks before joining Ross in Atlanta where they would be given their assignment, finding out where they needed to go on Reverend King's crusade to increase the number of black voters.

April twenty-fifth was Leigh's twentieth birthday. Noah borrowed Ross's car with plans to take her to dinner and to a movie. Noah had a lot of studying to do for his finals but knew Leigh had been uptight a lot lately about the war, and decided to spend time with her to ease her mind.

"Where are we going?" she asked after he had picked her up from the dorm.

He looked over at her and smiled. "It's a surprise." He had reserved them a room at a nice hotel in a well-to-do area of Washington. It was a very old and grand hotel that only recently began opening its doors to black patrons.

"Oh, Noah," she said a while later, stunned when they pulled up in front of the hotel. "It's beautiful."

After opening the car door for her, he gestured toward the huge swinging glass doors and said, "Tonight when we go inside, for their benefit, we are a newly married couple, okay?"

She smiled and nodded. "Okay."

They registered as Mr. and Mrs. Noah Wainwright. Although the hotel clerk looked at the two of them, doubtful that they were married, he didn't bother asking for identification verifying their claim.

Leigh felt like a princess when she and Noah caught the elevator to their room. Everything around them looked elegant, rich and luxurious. And she was in total awe when Noah opened the door to their room. The furnishings were exquisite and on such a grand scale it took her breath away. After taking in her surroundings, a huge smile spread across her face and she turned to Noah. He stood across the room, leaning against the closed door. He had watched her reaction to seeing the room and was pleased that she liked it.

He slowly walked across the room to her. Without saying a word he reached out and pulled her to him and began kissing her passionately, conveying in his kiss just how he felt about her. Leigh melted against him as she returned his kiss. A slow sizzle began working its way up from her toes to settle in the middle of her stomach. When they finally ended the kiss, a little smile curved the corners of Noah's lips. "I think I'd better order room service. I want to make sure we have the strength to handle tonight."

"Hmmm," Leigh moaned as she placed little kisses along Noah's jaw. "Do you have something pretty taxing planned for tonight?"

Noah chuckled. "Yes, you could say that," he said, placing a quick kiss on her lips.

"Then what if I were to ask for a sample of what to expect," she said, dropping her hand to his waist. She begin fumbling with the belt on his pants then eased down his zipper.

He gulped when she stuck her hands inside the opening of his pants to fondle him. "Then I'd warn you to be careful what you ask for because you just might get it," he said huskily, mouthing the words against her lips while at the same time placing his hand beneath the short skirt she wore to cup her bare hips. The skirt, although a shorter length than he was use to seeing her wear, really wasn't short enough to be called a miniskirt. However, Leigh had a gorgeous pair of legs and they were a complete turn-on. When he had picked her up at the dorm he hadn't been able to take his eyes off her.

"It's good to know I'm getting what I want," she said in a sexy voice.

"Baby, you're definitely going to get what you want." Dispensing with preliminaries, he quickly undid his pants and underwear and when they fell to his ankles he stepped out of them. Reaching out he pulled up her skirt, bunching it around her waist. His hands then went to her panties, tugging them down and giving her time to step out of them before lifting her into his arms. "Wrap your legs around my waist, Leigh."

She did as he instructed and placed her arms around his neck as well. She felt him maneuver his sex in a position to enter her body while she did so. The tighter her legs wrapped around him, the deeper he went inside of her. When he was buried deep to the hilt, he walked over to the nearest wall, one that was not connected to another room.

"I don't want to disturb anyone with all our bumping and grinding," he explained in a hoarse voice when her back touched the wall's cool surface.

"Oh," was all she managed to say before he began pumping into her in a frenzy, giving her just what she had asked for and then some. She kept her legs wrapped around him tight as he thrust in and out of her, bumping and grinding her body against the wall in a fast, steady rhythm that made her want to holler out her pleasure.

Each time he retreated she flexed her legs around him to force him back—not that he was going anywhere—but just the feel of him going in and out of her nearly drove her over the edge. When she couldn't handle the pleasure of it anymore, and she felt the scream she knew was about to come, she clamped her mouth down on his and took his tongue into her mouth and nearly sucked it raw when an explosion burst inside of her. Then he took control of their kiss at the same time she felt his release flood her insides with hot, molten liquid. She then did what he had taught her to do—milk him to the ultimate limit. She tightened her legs around him and flexed her inner muscles in a way that pulled everything out of him she desired.

Long moments later, when the both of them were completely drained, he slid her down his body until her feet touched the floor. He then picked her up into his arms to take her into the bathroom so the two of them could get cleaned up for dinner.

Later that night after they had eaten a delicious dinner that room service had delivered, and had made love in the king-size bed a couple of times, Noah presented Leigh with her birthday gift—a beautiful solitaire engagement ring.

"Will you marry me before the summer ends? You won't have to quit school. I'll work and support you while you complete your last year at Howard."

Tears sprang from Leigh's eyes and covered her cheeks. She looked at the ring Noah had slipped on her finger. For the longest time all she could do was cry and nod her head. He left to go to the bathroom to get some tissue to wipe her eyes. When he returned she hugged him and told him she loved him about fifty times.

He held her tightly in his arms, knowing that soon he would have to tell her about his plans to enlist. But there was no way he would leave for the air force without first making her his wife. She would finish her final year of college at Howard as Leigh Wainwright. Unknown to her, he had spoken to her parents about his intentions when they had gone home for spring break. They had given him their blessings.

"You still haven't given me your answer yet, Leigh," he teased as he continued to wipe the tears from her eyes. "Will you marry me, baby, and become Leigh Wainwright?"

"Yes!" she said, hugging him. "Yes, I'll marry you. Oh, Noah, you have made me so happy. This is the best birthday I've ever had."

Weeks later, Jenna, like most of the students, had packed her belongings with plans of going home to get a summer job. Everyone was looking forward to returning to school in the fall, especially Leigh, who was planning a summer wedding, and with plans to return to Howard as a married woman. She and Noah would marry in a beautiful church wedding in Miami during the middle of August.

Jenna felt honored when Leigh asked her to be one of her bridesmaids. Everyone was happy for Leigh except for Ellie. It was obvious she was jealous that Leigh was engaged and she wasn't.

The graduation ceremonies for Noah, Ross and Randolph had ended in a celebration. Leigh and Jenna gave the three a small party at a local restaurant. To everyone's surprise, Angela came and stuck close to Ross' side the entire time. Although she had been invited, Julia Fuller gave some excuse why she couldn't come, however her husband as well as the Denisons were in attendance.

The night before everyone would be leaving campus, in a dark hotel, room on the other side of town, Jenna lay in Randolph's arms, both regretting the time they would be apart over the summer months.

"I'm going to miss you, sweetheart. I love you so much," he said quietly, as he pulled her closer into his arms. They had just finished making love and his voice was warm and tender in her ear. He pulled her closer into his embrace, loving every single thing there was about her. He had never loved anyone like he loved her. He loved being close to her and the way she made him feel. She had brought so much meaning into his life. He was going to miss her so much over the next three months. September seemed like such a long way off.

"And I love you as well." She turned in his arms to meet his gaze. "Oh, Randolph, I wish . . ."

He smoothed her cheek with his finger when she didn't complete her sentence. "You wish what?"

She sighed deeply. "I wish the war was over and you and I could be together."

"I know, sweetheart. Things will be a lot better for us when we come back in the fall."

Jenna nodded, knowing that was true. For starters, he would be moving off campus into the house Noah and Ross would be vacating, which meant that although he would have a housemate, with separate bedrooms she would be able to sleep over at his place every once in a while. "I will get to see you later this summer at Leigh and Noah's wedding, won't I?"

He smiled. "Yes, but hopefully you'll see me before that. My relatives on Glendale Shores always have a big feast on the Fourth of July. If possible I'd like for you to come up for that and stay a few days."

"I'd like that, Randolph, and now after getting to know your Gramma Denison, I doubt if my parents will have a problem with it." After a few moments of silence, Jenna asked, "Will Ross be joining your grandfather at his law firm now that he's finished with law school?"

Something in Randolph's expression told Jenna that would not be the case. She snuggled closer to him when she saw deep concern etched in his features. "Randolph, what is it?"

Randolph sighed deeply before saying, "Ross has decided to enlist in the marines."

"What! Why?"

"Because he knows it will only be a matter of time before he gets drafted and since he has a college education, a law degree at that, he can enter the services as an officer."

Jenna nodded. "How your grandparents feel about him enlisting?"

"Of course no one wants him to go but we can't put our heads in the sand and ignore the fact that there's a war going on."

"And how does Angela feel about it?"

Randolph shook his head. "I have no idea but my thoughts are that she could care less. I don't know if you noticed but they aren't your ordinary couple. They are operating under the premise of an arranged courtship and there's no doubt in my mind that within the next year or so, there will be an arranged marriage as well."

"Ross will marry someone he doesn't love?"

"Yes. He really doesn't think he needs love and passion in his life. I'm hoping that one day he will wake up and smell the coffee before it's too late. Angela Douglass is not the woman for him."

Jenna had to agree. She met Randolph's gaze. "And how do you feel about Ross enlisting?"

Randolph didn't say anything for the longest moment. Then he bent his head close to hers and began speaking in a low, quiet voice. "I don't feel good about him doing it, Jenna, because chances are he'll have to serve time in Vietnam and I don't want him there. You hear all the stories about what's happening over there like I do. Those 'Congs are crazy and will use anything and anyone to be victorious, even their women and children. Ross is a person who'd want to do the right thing. He's not tough and rough enough to handle what he's going to find over there. I'm going to be worried sick about him if he has to go to 'Nam."

"Then let's hope that he doesn't have to go over there. Maybe he'll get to do a tour of duty in some other country."

"Yeah, right. Our government needs to send all the soldiers over there they can. I'm not going to fool myself into thinking he won't have to go."

"Then we'll pray for him each and every night, Randolph." After a few moments she asked, "What about Noah? You don't think he's planning to enlist as well, do you?"

"According to Ross he is. Noah plans to go into the air force in the fall."

Jenna pulled back just far enough to look into Randolph's eyes. "Leigh doesn't know that."

"No, he hasn't told her yet. That's the reason he wants them to marry by mid-August. He wants to make her his wife before he leaves and to make sure she is taken care of. From what Ross said, Noah is going to rent a house for her somewhere near campus. They will live there until he leaves and he'll come back there whenever he's on leave. He's going to make sure she doesn't want for anything while he's gone."

Jenna nodded. Noah and Leigh had caught the train back to Miami that morning. "When will he tell her?"

"Sometime before he leaves to join me and Ross in Atlanta for the voter drive. He didn't want to say anything to her just yet because he knew she would get upset about it. At least when he tells her she'll be surrounded by family and will be able to handle the news better."

Jenna doubted it. She knew that no matter where Leigh was when

Noah told her, she would not be able to handle the news of him enlisting.

Randolph kissed Jenna's forehead lightly. "Can we stop talking now?"

Jenna smiled. "Does that mean you have other ideas of things we can do?"

He rose up and braced his hands on either side of her. The eyes looking down at her were filled with breathless sensuality. "Yes, I have other ideas."

He then proceeded to share them with her.

Thirteen

June 1966

It took Jenna a while to get back into the swing of things at home in Knoxville with her family. She enjoyed her summer job at the day camp working with the children and got frequent letters from Randolph telling her how things were going with the voter registration drive. He ended each letter by letting her know how much he missed her and loved her.

She also received letters from Leigh, telling her how the wedding plans were going. She knew from one of Leigh's letters that Noah had finally broken the news to her about his plans to enlist and as expected, Leigh had not taken the news well. Even surrounded by family she had cried for an entire week. But from the most recent letter Jenna received, Leigh seemed to have accepted his enlistment and was looking forward to her wedding day. She'd explained how she had prayed and asked God to please return Noah back to her safely if he did go to Vietnam. In her heart she felt God would answer her prayer.

At the end of June Jenna received a letter from Randolph, giving her some disturbing news. Tyrone Wells had gotten married, but not to Ellie. He had married some woman he had met in Los Angeles.

Jenna's heart went out to Ellie who had written her just last week to say that she was pregnant and planned a trip to Los Angeles to surprise Tyrone with the news. Ellie had felt certain he would marry her as soon as she told him, and didn't anticipate returning to Howard in the fall. Instead, she had plans to transfer to UCLA to attend school while Tyrone established a promising professional football career with the Los Angeles Rams.

Jenna couldn't help wondering if Ellie had told Tyrone about her pregnancy before he had married the other woman. And regardless, now that he was married to someone else, what were Ellie's plans regarding the baby?

Jenna was counting off the days until she would see Randolph again for the Fourth of July celebration on Glendale Shores. Her parents felt comfortable with her spending the two days with Randolph and his grandparents. According to Jenna's mother, Gramma Mattie called occasionally and it seemed the two women had become good friends.

Randolph and Ross would go to Glendale Shores from Louisville, Kentucky, where they were working in the voter registration drive, and had offered to swing by Knoxville to pick Jenna up. She was packed and ready to go when they arrived.

Randolph's grandparents gave Jenna a warm welcome when she arrived on Glendale Shores. She was surprised that Ross had not invited Angela. When she asked him about Angela he had shrugged and said she and her parents were visiting relatives in Texas.

At the end of the two days Randolph took her back home, but hours before they reached Knoxville, Jenna wasn't surprised when he pulled into a motel off the interstate and got them a room, not caring that it was the daytime.

When Jenna arrived home later that evening she wondered if her parents noticed anything different about her like the satisfied smile that extended to the depths of her eyes. Randolph left, promising to write and call. They wouldn't see each other again until Noah and Leigh's wedding. Her parents had agreed to let her catch a ride to the wedding with Randolph. Ross would be going to Miami a few days early by bus since he was the best man. They figured it would take at least a full day and some of the next for Randolph to drive from Knoxville all the way to Miami, but neither of her parents asked where they would stay for the night. A part of Jenna felt her parents suspected she and Randolph had become intimate although the subject was never discussed. She knew for certain that her mother knew when she approached her the day before the trip and talked to her about birth control. At first Jenna felt sort of embarrassed, but soon she became thankful for the mother-daughter talk.

Randolph arrived on time to pick her up. After saying good-bye to her parents she walked with him down the walkway as he carried her luggage to the car. "Where are we spending the night?" she asked him happily as he placed her things into the trunk.

He smiled at her. "You'll see."

After driving for approximately seven hours Randolph pulled the car into a gorgeous six-story hotel. However, from the hostile looks they received from the all-white patrons when they walked into the lobby, they knew they would not be welcomed there. Instead of enduring any hassles from the prejudiced individuals, they decided to find somewhere else to spend the night. Driving another hour they finally crossed the border into Florida and spent the night at a very nice motel off the interstate.

Jenna loved waking up in Randolph's arms after a night of mind-blowing passion. They dressed and after eating breakfast were back on the road again. It was another seven hours before they finally made it to Miami. Jenna would be staying with Leigh's parents and Randolph with Noah's parents.

The wedding was beautiful and so was the bride. Noah had tears in his eyes as he watched Leigh walk down the aisle to him. Before God and everyone present, they exchanged the vows that joined them as man and wife.

The reception was held at Leigh's parents' church. Later than night Randolph took Jenna for a drive on the beach. She was totally speechless. She had heard about the beauty of Miami Beach and was able to see it for herself. They sat in the car and watched as the moon kissed the waves that rolled back and forth in the ocean. Randolph pulled her into his arms and kissed her until neither of them could think straight. All Jenna cared about was being with him, spending time with him and being loved by him.

"Leigh asked me to move in with her while Noah is away," Jenna said to Randolph as he drove her back to Leigh's parents' home. "Noah found out that he has to report to training camp the middle of next month."

Randolph frowned. He wondered if Ross knew how soon he would have to leave. "Uncle Sam isn't wasting any time, is he?"

"No, it doesn't seem so. The house Noah has found for them has three bedrooms so I can stay there even during the time he's home on leave. The amount I'll be paying them for rent is less than what I'd pay for the dorm and it's within walking distance to school." When she told Randolph where the house was located he smiled and told her it was only a few blocks from where he would live.

Leigh and Noah left the next morning to spend a three-day honeymoon in Daytona Beach. By midday Ross, Randolph and Jenna left to return home. At first Jenna was somewhat embarrassed when they stopped for the night and instead of Ross and Randolph sharing a room, Randolph shared a room with her. She wondered if Ross thought less of her, knowing she and Randolph were sleeping together. She expressed her concerns to Randolph that night while he held her in his arms.

"Ross understands," he told her, holding her gently, although deep down he wasn't sure if his brother actually did. Since Ross had never truly loved and desired a woman it was doubtful he understood the deep desire and passion a man had for the woman he loved. But Randolph knew Ross would not think anything negative about Jenna, nor would he think she was less than the wonderful and beautiful person she was.

When Jenna arrived back home she knew the nights she and Randolph had shared would have to sustain her until they saw each other again in September. She became concerned that she hadn't received a letter from Ellie while she'd been away, and decided to call Ellie's parents. She was stunned when Ellie's mother told her that Ellie had disgraced the family with her pregnancy and they had asked her to leave.

When Jenna asked where Ellie was staying, Mrs. Stanhope indicated she did not know but assumed she was still somewhere in Los Angeles. Jenna could not believe the Stanhopes had actually turned their backs on Ellie because she had gotten pregnant out of wedlock. She knew not having her family's support was probably pretty hard on Ellie right now and on top of that she had to deal with Tyrone's betrayal. Jenna said a prayer for Ellie each night. Although she had not been the easiest person to get along with, Jenna felt Ellie didn't deserve what she was going through.

On the other hand, Leigh, who was still bitter over the way Ellie had treated her the three years they'd been roommates, felt Ellie was getting just what she deserved and was being taught a lesson. Jenna hoped that one day Leigh would find it in her heart to forgive Ellie.

A few weeks after returning from Leigh's wedding Jenna received a letter from Johnny. He apologized for the infrequency of his letters but said he had been extremely busy for the past six months. He told her about the free breakfast program and free health clinic the Panthers had set up in inner Oakland and how Fred Hampton had organized a coalition of black, white and Hispanic youth gangs in the area to assist with the two programs. From his words, she could feel his excitement in being a part of the positive things they were doing. He had ended the letter by asking her not to believe anything negative she heard about the party. The FBI was trying to discredit the organization because of its growing popularity.

Jenna had immediately written Johnny back. Again she pleaded with him to take care of himself, and that if he ever needed anything to write and ask. She knew from his last letter he was still on bad terms with his parents and was bothered by their lack of support in what he was doing. She also included in the letter a picture taken of Leigh and Noah on their wedding day. Johnny had been invited but both she and Leigh had known not to expect him to come.

She received another letter from Johnny, less than a week later. In this letter he told her that he had run into Ellie, and that she had looked so bad he had hardly recognized her. His letter said:

I could not believe it was really her. She was working at a McDonalds, and would you believe that she was actually happy to see me? And it wasn't one of her phony acts. In fact, she has changed. I think what Tyrone did to her broke her spirit and made her see things in a whole different light. I took her back to a friend's place and fed her something to eat and we talked. She said she was living at the Y and that she goes to a health clinic each month to make sure her baby is fine. She's due to deliver in February and you can hardly tell she's expecting since she has lost so much weight. She told me how her parents turned their backs on her when Tyrone refused to acknowledge the baby was his, and then up and married someone else. I told her I knew how she felt about her parents because mine had turned their backs on me as well. I asked how she got to Oakland from Los Angeles and she said Tyrone bought her a one-way ticket and told her that was as far as he would send her. She called her parents and they refused to pay the rest of her way home so she ended up staying. Unfortunately, she doesn't have any relatives she can turn to. But I assured her she has me. In a way we're like two lost souls in a sea of confusion. Although we weren't the best of friends at Howard—and you and Leigh know more than anyone just how much I disliked her at times—I can't turn my back on her because I can actually feel her pain. She needs me and I promise that I'll check on her often and let you know how she's doing.

That night before she went to sleep Jenna said a prayer for both Ellie and Johnny.

Angela smiled as she walked around the house she would be sharing with Kathy while attending Howard Law School. Now that Ross had told her about his plans to enlist she was elated that he wouldn't be in Washington making a pest of himself. However, she knew she still had to be on her best behavior since Julia Fuller might pop up to visit her at any time.

Her smile slowly faded when she thought about how things weren't going as she had planned. First of all, Ross hadn't bothered to invite her to attend Noah's wedding with him, although she had heard through the grapevine that Randolph had taken Jenna with him to Miami. When she had asked Ross about it, he made it seem as if the only reason Jenna had gone was because she had been a part of the bridal party.

The other thing that had Angela upset was the disappointing news that Julia Fuller's plan to break up Randolph and Jenna had backfired. The sight of them together at Ross's graduation had nearly been too much. She had heard from her parents that Julia had decided to leave them alone after Old Man Fuller had threatened his wife with dire consequences if she continued to meddle in Randolph's affairs.

Now Julia was concentrating all of her efforts to bring about a wedding between Angela and Ross now that Ross had finished college. Her parents were thrilled with the idea, and of course she was pretending to be thrilled with the idea as well. However, he hadn't asked her to marry him and deep down she was hoping that he wouldn't.

She was tired of being the nice girl standing on the sidelines. To not give away how she felt about Randolph, she had kept her distance, making a decision to say as little to him as possible whenever they were at the same affairs. Not too much got past Julia Fuller. And heaven forbid if Randolph had shown the least bit of a sign that he was interested in her. She would have been tempted to blow her cover. It was important that everyone assume that she was devoted to Ross, even if it meant alienating Randolph for a while. Gaining Julia Fuller's trust and confidence was a must-do for now. In due time she intended to come up with some kind of plan to snare Randolph.

The two of them would be sharing classes together while attending Howard Law School. She felt confident that she would be able to make him see her in a whole new light and forget all about Jenna Haywood.

Good things came to those who waited and she had waited on Randolph long enough. It was time she made her move.

Fourteen

Washington, DC

The excitement of returning to school was marred with anti-war demonstrations on most college campuses due to several things. One was the United States' War Mission's report which indicated that so far more Americans had been killed in Vietnam than South Vietnamese soldiers. Another was CORE, Congress of Racial Equality's resolution submitted to Congress that urged the withdrawal of U.S. troops in Vietnam, citing the draft was placing a heavy discriminatory burden on minority groups and the poor. A third was French President Charles de Gaulle's condemnation of the American policy and his arguments that a U.S. troop withdrawal from Vietnam would bring the United States greater world influence than it could achieve by continuing its military commitment. Added to those three was the country's protest of the court-martials of three army privates at Fort Dix, New Jersey, for disobeying orders to go to Vietnam.

It was the first week in September. Jenna had spent most of the day unpacking her things. Walking out of the bedroom she looked around the place she would be sharing with Leigh. The older row house had a living room, an eat-in kitchen, two smaller bedrooms and a bathroom on the first floor, and a master bedroom and connecting bath on the second. Leigh had decided to use one of the bedrooms downstairs as a study room.

Jenna liked the way the bedrooms were situated, since they would provide ample privacy to the newlyweds whenever Noah was home. She'd even had a separate phone line installed in the bedroom she would be using. The house was located in a nice neighborhood of other row houses and was within walking distance to campus. With the lump sum Noah had received for enlisting, he had paid for the rental of the house in advance up to the time Leigh would be graduating in the spring.

Jenna's first class was at nine o'clock in the morning. Also on the agenda for tomorrow she had an appointment with the District of Columbia's largest architectural firm to discuss being a part of their internship program. She had a letter of recommendation from a professor who thought she could benefit greatly from the program.

She had only seen Randolph once since arriving in town two days ago. She knew he was busy trying to line up his classes as well as move into his own place. His housemate was a medical student by the name of Ben Lowell who Jenna had liked right away.

Leigh and Noah had left earlier to go to the market. Noah would be in town for another two weeks before leaving for basic training in Warner Robbins, Georgia. Randolph had mentioned that Ross would be leaving the first of October for the marines' training camp in South Carolina. She could tell the news bothered Randolph although he didn't say much about it. He really didn't have to. Since their parents' death Ross had always been the only real constant in Randolph's life, which explained their closeness. The two brothers had remained true and loyal to each other, just like their parents would have wanted.

Jenna decided to take a bath and be ready for bed when the newlyweds returned. She wanted to give them the privacy she felt they still needed and deserved.

"Aren't you going to say something about my decision, Randolph?"

Randolph straightened from leaning against the door and took his hands out of his pockets. "Only if it's your decision and not Grandmother Julia's."

The two brothers said nothing for a long moment. Ross had just told him of his plans to ask Angela to marry him. Randolph wasn't stupid. He knew Ross didn't love Angela and that the only reason he would even think of doing such a thing was because his grandmother was pushing it.

"Although the wedding won't take place until Angela finishes law school in two years, Grandmother Julia thinks we should at least become engaged before I leave so others will know she's spoken for while I'm gone," Ross said as a way of explanation.

Randolph nodded. "I'll support whatever it is you want to do, Ross. I just want you to be happy."

"Thanks, Randolph. I appreciate that."

Jenna picked up her phone on the first ring. "Hello."

"Hey, baby. Did you get moved in okay?"

Smiling, Jenna tugged on the lapels of her bathrobe. "Yes. Everything is unpacked and my room looks lived in. It's so nice, Randolph. I'm going to enjoy living here with Leigh."

"Sorry, I didn't get by to help you."

"Don't worry about it. I know you had to get settled into your own place."

"Yeah, but I had some help. Ross is still here. He won't be moving out until this weekend." Randolph took a deep breath. "He's decided to ask Angela to marry him."

That didn't surprise Jenna. Julia Fuller was expecting the couple to become engaged now that Ross was no longer in law school. "When will the wedding take place?"

"Not until Angela finishes law school."

Jenna nodded. That was another two years. "I'm surprised your grandmother isn't pushing for an earlier wedding date."

Randolph was surprised as well. "Maybe she just wants them engaged for now and plans to convince Ross to move the date up earlier at some point later. Who knows?" Deciding to change the subject, he asked, "What time is your first class in the morning?"

"At nine. Why?"

"So is mine. Do you want to do breakfast?"

"Yes, that sounds like a winner."

"Good. I'll see you in the morning. I love you."

"And I love you, too," she whispered before hanging up the phone.

A few weeks later, the night before Noah was to leave for basic training, Leigh tried putting on a brave face but it was hard. To give the couple privacy, Jenna made plans to spend the night over at Randolph's place.

"Don't look so sad, sweetheart," Noah said to Leigh softly. "It's not the end of the world, you know. I'm just going to be gone for eight weeks and then I'll be back. At least we'll spend Christmas together."

She tried smiling but found that she couldn't. "I know, but I'm going to miss you."

Noah pulled her closer into his arms. "And I'm going to miss you, too, sweetheart. I've only committed four years to Uncle Sam and then I'll be home with you each and every night, and then we'll make all those babies that we want." He could have done two years as a private, but going in as an officer was a four-year commitment. With an officer's salary, he and Leigh would be able to save a lot. It would be more than enough to set him up in private practice, which is what he preferred instead of going to work for a law firm.

"I've asked Randolph to check on you from time to time to make sure you're okay and have everything you need." Noah chuckled. "With Jenna staying here with you that shouldn't be a problem for him."

Leigh nodded, knowing that was true. She then decided to mention something to Noah that she had noticed last night at the small going-away party she'd given him. It was something she hadn't mentioned to anyone. Not even to Jenna. "Noah, did you happen to notice Angela last night?"

Noah lifted a brow. "What was there to notice about her? I admit I was surprised to see her here. She's never gone out of her way to get to know any of Ross's friends. I think the only reason she came was because she's living in Washington now and it would have looked awkward for her not to have come with Ross."

Leigh met her husband's gaze. "I think she came because she knew Randolph would be here."

Noah flashed her a frown. "What do you mean?"

Leigh sat up in bed. Sitting back on her heels she looked down at Noah. "I think Angela has a thing for Randolph."

Noah's frown dissolved into a grin. "Why on earth would you think something like that?"

"Because she couldn't take her eyes off of him. Last night wasn't the first time I've noticed it. I also picked up on it at the graduation ceremony last spring and the dinner party afterward. If looks could kill, Jenna would be dead and Randolph would be her man instead of Ross."

Noah shook his head, finding the very thought absurd. "Honey, you're imagining things. Besides, even if she did prefer Randolph to Ross she would be wasting her time. Randolph loves Jenna."

Leigh nodded, knowing that was true. "But still, I have a bad feeling about Angela, Noah. It's nothing I can put a finger on but there's just something . . ."

Noah shook his head. "I hope you don't tell Jenna what you suspect and get her upset. Randolph is going to have enough to deal with with Ross going away. The two of them are very close."

"But what if I'm right?"

"And what if you're wrong? Look, if you *are* right I have all the confidence in the world that Randolph will find a way to handle Angela."

He leaned over and placed a lingering kiss on Leigh's lips. "I don't want to spend my last night with you talking, sweetheart."

Leigh smiled. "Then I guess you're going to have to give me some sort of incentive not to talk."

"That's not a problem," he said as he pulled her down into his arms.

Three weeks later

"Hi, Randolph, do you have a minute?"

Randolph glanced over his shoulder and saw Angela Douglass standing there. The two of them were in Professor Wayne's class and for the last hour they'd listen to the man give a boring lecture on the Dred Scott decision. "Yes," he said, stopping to let other students pass. He tried to recall in all the time his brother had dated Angela just how many times he'd actually held a conversation with her and quickly concluded there hadn't been many.

He pushed the door open that led to the outside and waited while she passed through. He remembered when he'd seen her the first day of class. She had sat in the back of the classroom trying to look like the perfect student. Although she never had a lot to say in class, whenever she was called on she was very opinionated.

"I was wondering if you've heard anything from Ross? I haven't gotten but one letter from him since he's been gone," she said quietly.

Randolph hesitated, not wanting to tell her that he had gotten a letter from Ross practically every week since he'd left. "Yes, I've heard from Ross and he's doing fine."

"That's good news. I was worried about him."

Randolph stared at Angela. She had said the words so softly, so meaningfully, he wondered for a mere second if perhaps he'd been wrong about her and that she did care for his brother. And maybe the reason she'd been so prim and uptight over the two years he'd known her was due to that rigid all-girl college she'd attended in Boston. He couldn't help but notice since attending Howard she'd become less uptight, less restrained, and wasn't as prim and proper. She was even wearing her hair differently. It wasn't all pinned on top of her head in the conservative style she normally wore but was hanging loose around her shoulders. It made her look younger, he thought as he continued to study her.

"There's no need to worry, Ross is doing fine. He'll be back home before you know it."

"Yes and then what? Will he get orders to stay in the country or will he get sent to Vietnam?"

Randolph sighed. That question had been bothering him as well, but most of the time he just tried not to think about it. "Only Uncle Sam can answer that," he said with a forced smile.

Angela nodded. "Randolph, I know you've had concerns about Ross marrying me, but I want you to know that I really do care for him."

When he didn't say anything she glanced down at her watch, deciding to leave now that he had something to think about. "I'd better go. My next class starts in a little while. I'll be seeing you."

"Okay." Randolph sighed as he watched her walk off and again wondered if perhaps he'd been wrong about her.

Later that day Angela opened the door to the house she shared off campus with Kathy. Going into the bedroom she shook off her fatigue and changed into an outfit less confining. It had been an exhilarating day. She was pleased with the progress she was making with Randolph. Each day he was acting less and less reserved with her.

She couldn't help noticing that he had looked at her differently today. Evidently he'd been pleased with the way she had dressed and the way she had worn her hair. She shivered. Being close to him always did things to her. Things that being around Ross never did.

It meant nothing to her that he thought he loved that nobody, Jenna Haywood. Like his grandmother Julia, she believed that in time Randolph's fascination with Jenna would wear off.

She glanced down at her hand at the engagement ring Ross had placed there before he'd left. She trailed her fingers over the diamond, wondering how much thought he'd put into buying it. It was beautiful but it wasn't anything she would have picked out for herself.

She wanted Randolph, and as always she would eventually get what she wanted.

Jenna received another letter from Johnny. Ellie had contacted him to let him know that her parents were coming for her. Evidently they'd had a change of heart and decided that no matter what, they loved their daughter and would forgive her for any mistakes she had made.

Reading Johnny's letter brought tears to Jenna's eyes. She had been worried about Ellie being without any family in California, and was glad she was going home where she and the baby would be taken care of properly.

She appreciated the way Johnny had befriended Ellie when she needed someone and was sure Ellie was grateful that Johnny had been there for her as well.

Fifteen

As most college students looked forward to a break from school over the Christmas holidays, a number of anti-war incidents occurred on several campuses that involved members of the present administration. Defense Secretary McNamara was mobbed by about one hundred anti-war demonstrators while addressing a small group of students on Harvard University's campus; and when General Earle Wheeler, the chairman of the Joint Chiefs of Staff, addressed a gathering at Brown University, some one hundred and sixty students walked out to protest his defense of the United States' involvement in Vietnam.

Noah and Ross had returned home from basic training with orders to leave for Saigon at the beginning of the year. Although expected, their friends and families were devastated by the news.

Noah and Leigh decided to go home for Christmas to see their families before Noah had to leave the country, and Ross made plans to split the time he had left with his two sets of grandparents, Angela and Randolph.

Leigh tried handling the news as best she could but when she began imagining all the things that could possibly happen to Noah in Vietnam, she became a mass of tears whenever she was alone though she tried putting on a brave face whenever he was around. But she couldn't hold anything back the last night they spent together before he left. Noah had made love to her with a passion that was distinctively his, making memories the two of them would feed off from until he returned. Then he held her in his arms while she cried, and for a brief time tears had formed in his eyes knowing just how much he would miss her.

When she began crying fresh tears he leaned down and kissed them away and held her tighter. "Things are going to be okay, sweetheart. I'll be fine. I promise."

Leigh shook her head as more sobs shook her body. "You can't promise me that because you don't know that for sure. I'm so afraid,

Noah. I love you so much. I don't know what I'll do if you don't come back to me."

"Shhh, don't think such a thing, baby. I'll be back. You are the most important person in my life. You *are* my life. I will come back to you, Leigh."

But what Leigh thought and what she couldn't ask was *how* would he come back. She wanted him to be alive when he returned. She didn't want Uncle Sam returning him to her in a body bag. "I heard the Vietcongs are mean and vicious and that they would use anything or anyone to kill an American, even their women and children. How can you fight a war against people like that?"

He heard the fear in her voice and knew he had to arrest her fears. "I've been trained and I'm ready to do whatever I have to. My year in 'Nam will be up before you know it. When I return you'll have finished school and then we'll start looking for a place wherever I'll be stationed next. And don't forget you'll get a chance to come to Paris when I'm up for R and R. You'll like that, won't you?"

She nodded through her tears. "I love you so much, Noah."

"I know, baby, and I love you just as much." In all the years they had been together, he had never seen her so broken up; not even when Zachary had died. Somehow he had to assure her that things would be okay. He pulled her tighter to him where his heart was pressed against hers. Her face was wet, drenched with tears, but this was the face he wanted instilled in his memory on those nights when he would be just miles outside of enemy lines, not knowing if the breath he took would be his last.

Again, he felt his own eyes beginning to dampen, but he had no shame in crying because tomorrow he would be leaving behind the most important person in his life, the woman he loved. He took his hands and cupped her face and leaned forward to kiss her. He wished this night would last forever. "No matter what happens, Leigh, always remember that I love you and I would go fight a thousand wars if it meant a better future for you and our children. There won't be a day or night that I won't think of you. And as long as the Lord gives me the strength to do so, I'll come back to you. I swear it."

He kissed her again and then he made love to the woman who would always be in his heart. They made love all that night, over and over again and when morning came and the sun shone brightly through the window, they both knew their love would always shine just as brightly and would sustain them through the coming months.

It was two weeks later and Ross and Randolph were spending the last days before Ross was to leave with their grandparents on Glendale Shores. Angela had come down for a few days and again to Randolph's surprise she seemed genuinely concerned about his brother.

The night before he was to leave Ross went into Randolph's bedroom after their grandparents went to bed. Both Gramma Mattie and Grampa Murphy had talked to him about keeping himself safe and not trusting any of the Vietnamese, not even the women and children.

The two brothers stood across the room facing each other, knowing there was a lot they both wanted to say but also knowing there was no need. From the time their parents had brought them into the world they had been taught to love each other and to look out for each other. They both remembered the times before their parents' death and the good times they had shared as a family. Then afterward, at the ages of twelve and ten together they had stood before their parents' caskets and said their final good-byes, promising to always be there for each other. Each had held the other up during that very difficult time and the times following when there was that custody fight. Neither cared which set of grandparents they would end up with as long as the two of them were not separated. There was a strong bond between them. Not only were they brothers, they were the very best of friends.

Ross was the first to cross the room to Randolph with tears unashamedly filling his eyes. It would be the first time the two of them would be separated for a long period of time. "I'm going to miss you, Rand."

Randolph smiled sadly at Ross as tears filled his own eyes. "Same here, brother. But the year will be up before you know it and you'll be home, and I'll be almost finished with law school."

Ross nodded. "Because we are brothers, at least you won't ever have to go to Vietnam and for that I'm grateful. If either of us have to go it seems right that it be me."

"Why?" Randolph asked jokingly, as tears continued to fill his eyes. "Because you're the oldest?"

Ross didn't say anything for a briefest moment, then he said softly, "No, because I'm the weakest." His voice cracked when he added, "If anything were to ever happen to you, Rand, I don't think I'd be able to handle it."

Without hesitation Randolph reached out to his brother and the two men, similar in both height and build, embraced each other as only two brothers could. And at that moment they realized just how blessed they were to share the same blood.

Sixteen

March 1967

The semester passed rather quickly and in less than two months Jenna and Leigh would be graduating. Jenna had received a letter from Ellie a month ago telling her that she had given birth to a beautiful little girl whom she had named Johnnetta, after Johnny. She had appreciated the way he had been able to put the past behind them and befriend her during the time she had truly needed a friend.

Leigh had also gotten a letter from Ellie in which she apologized for the way she had treated Leigh while they'd been roommates at Howard. Leigh had written Ellie back letting her know she accepted her apology. Not one to hold a grudge, Leigh had decided the best way to handle the situation was to wipe the slate clean. As far as she was concerned, Ellie had gone through enough and had learned from her past mistakes.

Leigh received letters from Noah on a frequent basis and couldn't wait to see him and let him know she was pregnant when she went to Paris in June. She had taken some over-the-counter medication for a cold, not knowing that certain medications could counteract the effectiveness of the birth control pill. After two missed periods she had gone to the doctor who confirmed her suspicions. Although this was not the way they had planned it, she was ecstatic.

Jenna knew that Randolph was also receiving frequent letters from Ross and many times he read them to her. In Ross's letters he told them of the magnificent beauty of some of the places and the stink and filth of others. He told them of the people who you couldn't trust and the women who sold themselves cheap just to get a puff from a cigarette. From his letters they knew about the harsh Asian sun that could literally bring a man to his knees if the bigger-than-life mosquitoes didn't suck all your blood first. Then there was the hardship of having to dig deep holes in the ground which at times were the only cool place to be found, and how at night you had to be alert and on your guard against an enemy who claimed the night as his own.

Jenna knew Randolph missed Ross and was counting the days until he returned. Angela, although nice enough to her whenever Randolph was around, snubbed her otherwise. Jenna mentioned the woman's behavior to Randolph a few times and he told her not to worry about it.

Jenna was excited about her job offer from Smith and Riley, one of the largest architectural firms that had offices all over the world. They had offered her a chance to work at their Memphis office after graduation in May. Since Memphis wasn't that far from Knoxville and the starting salary was more than she had expected, Jenna accepted the offer. Not everyone had a job lined up after graduation so she felt blessed about it.

She and Randolph had talked about how they would handle being apart after she graduated. It was decided that she would work at Smith and Riley and then they would marry once he finished law school next spring.

At the end of March, Jenna and Randolph caught a bus to Chicago, along with one hundred other students from Howard, to participate in a march led by the Reverend Martin Luther King, Jr. Over five thousand anti-war demonstrators, both black and white, participated. Leigh had wanted to participate but Jenna and Ross talked her out of it, telling her she might place the baby in danger if any violence broke out.

On April fourth Jenna and Randolph celebrated their birthdays together at the same hotel they had the year before. That night while the aftershocks of the pleasure they'd shared subsided, they held each other and whispered words of love.

"I don't know how I'm going to handle it after you move to Memphis, baby."

Jenna smiled as she wrapped her arms around his neck and buried her face against his shoulder. "You'll be so busy your final year of law school, you'll be glad to have me out of your hair for a while."

He shook his head as he drew her tighter into his arms. "Don't even think that. I'm going to miss you like hell. You know how hard it was for me last summer when we were apart."

She nodded. It had been hard for her, too. "Time will fly by quickly and before you know it Ross and Noah will be back home, and Leigh will have had her baby. Things are going to be wonderful," she said, smiling happily.

Randolph lifted his hand and caressed her cheek. He wanted to share in her happiness but something held him back. "I hope so, baby. I truly hope so."

A week later Randolph sat in his bedroom and reread the letter he had received that day from Ross.

March 30, 1967

Rand,

I hope this letter finds you well. Happy birthday to you and Jenna. Give her a kiss for me and tell her I appreciate the care packages she's sending me. Toiletries are greatly appreciated over here and the cans of insect repellant are a blessing.

I have so much good news to share with you that I don't know where to start. So I guess I'll just go ahead and say it. I'm in love. Yes, I know it's hard to believe but I am. And it happened just the way you said it had with you and Jenna. I saw her and wham, it was like I had been hit by a freight train or something. She works at the hospital here in Saigon. She's the most beautiful woman I've ever seen. Her mother is Japanese and her father was Vietnamese. When we first saw each other, it was like some sort of soul connection. It wasn't anything I wanted to happen, and knowing I'm engaged to Angela was reason enough to fight the attraction. And for thirty long and hard days I fought it. But the more I fought it, the more attracted to her I became, so I've given up the fight. She's the one, Rand. She's the woman I love and want to marry. Her name is Gia. I know I have to tell Angela and break off our engagement. She deserves better than a Dear John letter from me so I plan to wait until I have R and R in a few months and call her from Rome. When I return to the States in January I intend to bring Gia home with me as my wife. I know Grandmother Julia will have a cow but she can have triple cows for all I care. For Gia I'll gladly face her wrath and then some. I love Gia just that much. Be happy for me, Rand, because loving Gia has truly made me happy.

Take care and I'll do the same.

Your brother,

Ross.

Randolph reread the letter a third time. And later when Jenna came over he let her read it as well. Like he had, she read it a second and a third time.

"He definitely sounds like a man in love, doesn't he?" she asked smiling.

Randolph shrugged. "Yeah, I suppose."

Jenna stared at him over the rim of the eyeglasses she used for reading on occasion. "Aren't you happy for him, Randolph? He's in love."

Randolph sighed. "Yes, I'm happy for him but I was just thinking about Angela and how she's going to handle a broken engagement."

"I doubt she'll handle it well but would you rather Ross marry someone he didn't love?"

Randolph's lips tightened. "No, I've never wanted that for him."

"Well, okay then. You've said yourself many times that he didn't love Angela. And you've always had doubt as to whether Angela loved him."

"Yeah, but I may have been wrong about her feelings for Ross. I think she really cares for him."

Jenna lifted a brow and wondered when Randolph had reached that conclusion. Personally, she didn't think Angela cared for anyone but herself. "Don't worry about it, Randolph. Things will work out. I'm sure when the time comes, Ross will handle the situation with Angela with as much diplomacy as he can under the circumstances."

Randolph nodded, knowing she was right. Angela was Ross's concern and not his. He just hated seeing anyone getting hurt. And he definitely didn't want to think about how his grandmother would react if Ross married a woman from another country, especially someone part Vietnamese.

"Have you gotten a letter from Ross recently?"

Ross looked over at Angela. They had just gotten out of the Judicial Law class they shared and were walking across the courtyard. He knew that she had another class that day but he was through and was heading for home. A part of him had hoped she would not ask him about Ross. "No, not lately," he said.

She looked over at him. "Neither have I. Aren't you worried?"

Yes, but not for the reason you think. "I try not to worry, Angela."

"I suppose that would be best." She glanced down at her watch. "I have a few extra minutes before I have to rush off to my next class. Do you want to grab something to eat?"

Randolph shook his head. "Sorry, but I can't. Jenna is waiting at my place with lunch already prepared."

Angela schooled her features to hide her anger. "Oh. Maybe another time then?"

"Sure. I'll see you later." Randolph quickly walked away. He knew the only reason Angela wanted to have lunch with him was so she could talk some more about Ross, and Randolph didn't want to be put in the position of having to continue to outright lie to her. He was fiercely loyal to his brother but hoped Ross broke the news to Angela soon.

The next day, following his conversation with Angela, Randolph received another letter from Ross.

April 20, 1967

Rand,

Sorry it's taken so long to write since the last letter but I'm sure you've heard by now that things are really starting to heat up over here. I hate it when I have to go out on patrol. One wrong step could be your last because mines are buried all over the place. Last week I saw a guy I had just eaten breakfast with get his head blown off. Oh my God, Rand, it was like one minute he was there and another minute he was missing his head. And if that wasn't sad enough, Danny was only eighteen, just a kid. That morning at breakfast he'd told me that his mom was still his favorite girl. He had just mailed off his Mother's Day card to her last week.

No matter what you've heard about how bad it is over here, I want you to know it's a thousand times worse. I hate it here, Rand, but Gia has made it so much better for me. In her own way she has helped turn hell into paradise. I love her so much. That night after seeing Danny blown up that way, I went to Gia and she comforted me while I nearly threw my guts up. It's hard to remember at times that we're still human even if those damn 'Congs aren't. I said a prayer for Danny. The kid didn't deserve to die that way.

Ross

A week later was graduation day and Jenna and Leigh proudly walked across the platform to receive their degrees. Four years of hard work had finally paid off. Both Jenna's and Leigh's parents, as well as Leigh's in-laws were there for the joyous occasion. Jenna had been touched that Randolph's grandparents in South Carolina had sent her a graduation present and wasn't surprised that his Grandmother Julia still refused to acknowledge her existence.

Leigh was getting excited about her trip to Paris. Jenna had packed already for Memphis. She was supposed to begin work in a week. The night before she was to leave, Randolph took her out to dinner and gave her his graduation present to her. A beautiful diamond engagement ring. In the restaurant in front of everyone, he got down on his knees and asked her to marry him. Through all the tears that ran down her face and with all the love she had in her heart, she accepted. There was no doubt in Jenna's mind that it was the happiest night of her life.

Three days later, Jenna's happiness was overshadowed with gloom when the news media reported that the Oakland police along with federal agents had raided the Oakland Black Panther Party office, arresting fifteen members and killing eight. In the exchange of gunfire between police and party members, a federal agent was killed.

Johnny was the person the police had arrested for the shooting death of the FBI agent.

Seventeen

July 1967

That summer Randolph went to work at his grandfather's law office as a law clerk. Although he and Jenna exchanged letters frequently and talked on the phone at least once a week, he still missed her like crazy. When he didn't think he could take it any longer, he drove to Memphis to see her and to take her to Glendale Shores for the Fourth of July celebration. Besides, he needed a break from Angela. Her concern for Ross was beginning to drive him bonkers. She was turning into a regular basket case in light of the infrequent letters she was receiving from him. She had started seeking Randolph out after classes, calling him at home and had even shown up unexpectedly at his place, asking him if there was anything going on with Ross that he wasn't telling her.

Randolph hated lying to her but knew it was not his place to tell her anything. He knew Ross intended to do that himself and hoped he would hurry up with it.

During the drive to South Carolina, he told Jenna about Angela's behavior, and she agreed that Angela deserved to know about Ross and Gia, but felt the news should come from Ross. In a couple of months Ross would be calling Angela from Rome, and Randolph decided he didn't want to be anywhere nearby when it happened. He made plans to visit Jenna in Memphis during that time.

Randolph then told Jenna about his most recent letter from Ross telling him that Gia was pregnant. Ross had asked him to send the family Bible, and he had done so a few days ago, sending it via air mail.

"How do you feel about him marrying Gia?" Jenna asked when he'd suddenly gotten quiet.

Randolph glanced over at her and smiled wryly. "He's so damn happy, Jen, I can't help but be happy for him, too. You can feel the love and passion he has for her pouring out of every word that he writes. I've never known him to be so happy and so at peace with himself and his feelings. He even mentioned extending his tour of duty if Gia is unable to travel when his year is up since she will still be pregnant." He sighed. "I wrote and suggested that he consider sending Gia home to us."

Shock came to Jenna's face. "Your grandparents in Virginia?"

Randolph shook his head. "No, trust me, that wouldn't do. I was thinking more of Gramma and Grandpa Denison. They would accept Gia and her unborn child with open arms and would take care of them until Ross came home. I hope he considers that idea. That way his child will be born here in America with someone looking after Gia and the baby properly."

Jenna nodded. "So, he's told Gramma and Grandpa Denison about Gia?"

"Not yet. So far, other than you and me, Noah is the only other person who knows about her, and since Noah knows I feel certain Leigh knows as well. Noah got the chance to meet her when his platoon arrived in the same area where Ross's regiment was stationed." There was no doubt in Randolph's mind that it had been a joyous reunion for the two best friends, and that Ross would take the opportunity to marry Gia while Noah was there to stand in as best man.

Jenna told Randolph that she had spoken with Johnny's parents and about the trouble they were having in securing a good defense attorney for their son. It seemed that no one wanted to take on the case to defend him against the State of California and the FBI. Both had charges against him. She had also talked to Ellie who was concerned about what was going on with Johnny as well. Although Jenna had never mentioned it to anyone and neither Johnny nor Ellie had admitted anything, Jenna had a feeling that something had developed between them during the time they had spent together in California.

When Jenna and Randolph arrived in Glendale Shores, she was glad to see the Denisons again and as usual they made her feel welcome. Later that day they traveled by ferry to Hilton Head Island where other family members had planned this huge Independence Day celebration. All during the day Jenna and Randolph were congratulated on their engagement. Randolph told everyone the wedding would take place sometime next summer after he finished law school and Ross returned from overseas.

The weekend had not been long enough and when Randolph returned Jenna to Memphis, he spent the night. The next morning before the break of dawn he left to return to Virginia.

The following weeks Jenna stayed glued to the television since Johnny's alleged killing of the federal agent still dominated the news. The few times she saw a glimpse of him when the television camera would flash his way, she could tell he had lost a lot of weight and he had the appearance of a person defeated and about to give up. Seeing him that way tore at her heart. She remembered him always being fun loving and always full of cheer. Jenna wrote to him in care of the detention center where he was being held while awaiting trial. She was elated a week later when he wrote her back.

July 20, 1967
Jenna,
It was so good getting your letter. It came at a time I desperately needed to hear from a friend, and you have always been that. I've received letters from Ellie and Leigh as well. And my parents have been corresponding with me a lot. They are so supportive, Jen. When I think of what they are going through because of me and all

the money they are putting out in my defense, it brings tears to my eyes.

I'm sure you know by now what the police claim I've done. But I didn't do it. My prints aren't even on the murder weapon. The person who killed that officer was one of their own men. It was a setup and another example of the war the FBI has waged against the Panthers. But of course no one wants to believe our government can be that devious. They have concocted evidence to support whatever they want and right now they want to make an example out of me for the others.

It's too late to worry about my fate. They are determined that I pay the price for something I didn't do. I just pray that one day the truth will come out.

Forever your friend,

Johnny

Randolph approached his grandfather on Johnny's behalf to see if perhaps there was anything that could be done in his defense. Robert Fuller, who had been keeping up with the media's frenzy of the shooting, told his grandson it would be just about suicidal for any attorney to act in Johnny's defense. Especially when the FBI had so much evidence against him, including eyewitnesses who claimed they saw him pull the trigger.

When Randolph talked on the telephone to Jenna that night, he gave her the details of the conversation he'd had with his grandfather. He regretted he couldn't give her any positive feedback.

After talking with Johnny's parents, Jenna knew they had finally found an attorney but weren't all that pleased with him, but they had no choice but to believe the man would do everything in his power to prove their son's innocence.

The State of California along with the federal government didn't waste time in bringing Johnny to trial. The proceedings lasted only a week and the all-white jury of eight men and four women found Johnny guilty of first-degree murder. He was sentenced to death.

• • •

Leigh and Noah met in Paris in late July. He was overjoyed when she told him she was pregnant. After spending an entire day making love, they ordered room service and ate a delicious dinner while discussing possible names for their baby. Leigh wanted to name the baby Zachary, after her brother if it was a boy, and Noelle if it was a girl. Noah agreed with her choice of names.

They talked about Johnny and both felt that he'd gotten a bad rap and was glad his attorney was appealing his sentence. They also talked about Ross and his marriage to Gia. "She's a beautiful person, Leigh, and Ross loves her very much. She's having problems with her pregnancy and he's worried about it and that concerns me."

Leigh lifted an eyebrow, not understanding. "She's his wife. Why does it concern you that he's worried about her?"

"Because when you're in the combat zone, you need to concentrate on one thing and one thing only—staying alive and staying one step ahead of the enemy. If he's worried about Gia then he can't do that."

Leigh nodded, now understanding fully. "He still plans to break the news to Angela next month?"

"Yes, that's his plan. He's scheduled for R and R in Rome then. But with Gia not doing well, he may not take it." Noah sighed deeply. "I'm concerned about him, Leigh. For years I've teased Ross about not being in love and not understanding just how strong the power of love is. Now he knows. He loves Gia very much and if anything were to happen to her or their baby, I don't know what he'd do."

August 1967

Randolph returned to DC since school would be starting in a few weeks. He had seen Jenna again the first week in August when they attended Grampa Murphy's birthday celebration on Glendale Shores.

Now that they were officially engaged, his grandparents weren't as protective of her as they had been during her initial visits. Since his grandfather had not given him a verbal order to stay in his own bedroom at night, Randolph went to Jenna's room each night after his grandparents went to bed and would leave early the next morning before they got up. He knew he would miss her during the school year, but they'd made plans to spend Thanksgiving with his grandparents at Glendale Shores and Christmas with her parents in Knoxville.

They also agreed to give Ross and Gia the support they would need when they came to the States. There would be those who would want to scorn Gia because of her nationality, especially with the war still going on. Although she was only half-Vietnamese, people would see her as an enemy nonetheless.

During the second month of school Randolph was awakened during the middle of the night by the sound of someone pounding on his front door. His housemate was spending the weekend away with his girl-friend in Baltimore. Rubbing a hand over his face as he tried to come completely awake, he made it to the door, opened it and found both his grandparents standing there. The look on their faces was grief-stricken.

"What is it? What's wrong?" he asked as he stared at them. For a long moment neither answered and his Grandmother Julia's eyes began filling with tears. His gaze left his grandmother and settled firmly on his grandfather. A deep knot began forming in his stomach and air slowly began seeping out of his lungs. He could tell from the look of anguish on his grandfather's face that bad news was coming. He inhaled deeply and embraced himself.

"Randolph, your grandmother and I got word a few hours ago from the State Department that one of the enemy's artillery shells scored a direct hit on a marine post, killing twenty-two men and injuring over forty." His voice suddenly broke when he added, "Ross is among those listed as dead."

Randolph closed his eyes, wanting to believe he was still asleep and this was just a bad dream. Ross . . . oh, God, it couldn't be. It couldn't happen this way. With only five months remaining before he would come home, there was no way life could be this cruel. And then there was Angela, the woman engaged to marry his brother who didn't yet know he had already married someone else.

He felt his grandfather's firm hand on his arm. "I know this is shocking news to you, Randolph, as well as to all of us. But we have to pull ourselves together now and think of Angela. Her parents are over at her place now, telling her the news. We can only imagine how devastating this will be to her."

Randolph opened his eyes. He didn't want to deal with anything or anyone. He didn't want the pain he was beginning to feel, pain that was ripping through every part of his body, pain that was piercing his heart.

Ross.

Without saying anything to his grandparents he stumbled out of the living room, somehow made it to his bedroom and slammed the door behind him, wanting to be alone to deal with an amount of grief he didn't think he'd ever be able to recover from.

Jenna woke up to the sound of the phone ringing. She had just gotten into bed after attending a weekend business seminar in Atlanta.

In a sleepy daze she reached over and picked it up. "Hello."

"Jenna, it's Leigh."

Jenna glanced at the clock on the nightstand. It was almost two in the morning. Why was Leigh calling her so late? And from the sound of Leigh's voice she could tell her friend was crying. Had something happened to Noah? "Leigh, what is it? What's wrong?"

"It's Ross."

Jenna's stomach tightened. "Ross?"

"Yes, the Fullers received word tonight that he's been killed."

The words had been spoken so softly, for a moment Jenna thought maybe she had heard them wrong, but Leigh's gentle crying told her that she hadn't.

Oh, no! "Randolph," Jenna said, closing her eyes. Her thoughts immediately went to him.

"Yes," Leigh was saying. "That's why I'm calling. I understand he's in a state of shock. He won't see anyone, talk to anyone and he's been drinking heavily since finding out to drown out the pain. His grandmother is worried sick about him and how hard he's taking it. In fact, believe it or not, she's the one who called me and asked that I contact you."

Jenna was already out of the bed and taking off her nightgown. "I'll be there as soon as I can get a flight out. What about Noah? Have you told him?"

"No," Leigh said sadly. "He hasn't called yet. He told me that he would be flying several missions this week and won't be calling until the middle of next week. I want to get a message to him but I don't know how he's going to take it. He and Ross were very close. I've got to get a grip and think about the best way to handle this."

Later, as she quickly began packing, Jenna continued to think of Randolph and the pain he was going through. She wanted to be there for him. He needed her.

Angela couldn't believe Ross was dead. She had wanted to be free of him, but not like this. She could just imagine the pain Randolph was going through.

After assuring her parents and Ross's grandparents that she was fine, they had finally left. Now she found herself headed toward the house where she knew Randolph lived. According to the Fullers, he was in a bad way and refused to see anyone. Julia Fuller had even broken down and admitted that she had contacted Jenna Haywood.

Angela had been furious, embittered at the very thought that Jenna was on her way to DC to comfort Randolph. Angela didn't intend to have any of that. She had thought of a plan and intended for it to work.

She remembered the conversation she'd had with Kathy before leaving the apartment.

"Kathy, I need you to do me a big favor."

Kathy lifted a brow. "What?"

Angela sighed. There was no need to pretend she was all torn up over Ross's death when Kathy of all people knew she wasn't. "A few weeks ago you mentioned experimenting with speed."

Kathy studied Angela curiously. Drugs were something Angela usually stayed away from. "Yeah, what of it?"

"Tell me some more about it."

Kathy smiled ruefully. Angela had a feeling Kathy had an idea why she wanted to know. "Speed is a harmless stimulant that can give you one hell of a mind-blowing high. The effects will make you forget almost everything, especially your troubles. You began hallucinating, getting absorbed into a world filled with peace and harmony, calm, serenity and happiness."

Kathy's smile widened. "At least you feel those things until the drug wears off, but it's comforting to know the experience is just another pill away whenever you want to get high again."

Angela smiled, bringing her thoughts back to the present. Before leaving the apartment Kathy had given her enough of the pills to accomplish what she wanted to do.

She intended that she and Randolph would get high together.

Angela kept up a steady hard knock on Randolph's door, determined that he would eventually get up and let her in. She just hoped Jenna had not arrived yet. She gasped when he finally snatched the door open. Unshaven, and unkempt, blurry, bloodshot eyes filled with pain stared at her.

"Oh, Randolph," she cried, throwing herself in his arms. "We've lost him! We've lost him," she said, playing the part of the grief-stricken fiancée.

Randolph closed his eyes. The constant drinking had almost made him forget but the effects of all the alcohol he had consumed over the past fourteen hours was beginning to wear off. Now Angela's words were making him remember and he didn't want to remember. He had tried calling Jenna but didn't get an answer at her place in Memphis. Where was she? He needed her. He needed her so damn bad. He wanted Jenna here with him, not Angela.

He gently pushed Angela away from him. "Please go, Angela. I can't handle your being here. Go home and drown in your own misery. I want to be alone. Please leave."

Angela forced more tears to spill down her cheeks. "But I can't leave you like this. Can I get you something? Make you something to eat? I bet you haven't even eaten."

"No, I don't want anything. Please just leave." And with that statement he turned to go back into his bedroom.

"Wait, Randolph! Ross and I were to get married and now I've lost him. You're not the only one who's hurting. I'm hurting, too!" she cried.

Randolph turned around slowly when her grief-stricken words penetrated his mind. She would hurt even worse when she discovered Ross, although engaged to her, had married someone else. Someone would have to eventually tell her the truth. But not now and not here, and definitely not before he got the chance to break the news to his grandparents about Ross's wife and child. A part of him forced his pain aside to help her deal with hers. He walked back over to her. "Don't cry, Angela. Let's talk. Maybe that will help."

She nodded, satisfied he was no longer pushing her away.

"All right. Do you have anything I can drink? I need to pull myself together. Ross would not want me falling apart this way. But I can't help it. My heart feels like it's been ripped in two."

"Yeah, I know the feeling. I'll get you something," he said, turning toward the kitchen. "Will wine be okay?"

"Yes, that will be fine. And please share a glass with me."

Randolph knew after consuming an entire bottle of Jack Daniels that the last thing he needed was another drink. But if joining Angela in a drink would make it easier for her to deal with her grief then he would do so. "All right." He went into the kitchen.

Randolph returned carrying two glasses of wine and found Angela sitting down on his sofa. He sat in the chair across from her and placed the filled wineglasses between them.

"I'm sorry to ask you to get up again, but I could desperately use a tissue," she said, wiping the tears that were beginning to form in her eyes with the back of her hands.

"That's no problem, I'll get you one."

The moment Randolph had left the room Angela quickly dumped the speed into his glass then waited for him to return. Not wanting to take the chance of the pill not dissolving fast enough, she had ground it into a powdery substance before leaving her apartment.

She talked while he sat across from her, telling him how she and Ross had met, like he didn't know the entire story already. She talked nonstop and he listened. And as she spoke she watched him and noticed the exact moment beads of sweat began forming on his brow and when his already bloodshot eyes became even more dazed. The combined effects of the alcohol and speed were working but she could see he was trying to fight both.

"Look, Angela," he said standing, unsteady on his feet. "I'm sorry, but I'm beginning to feel funny. I need to go lie down. Please let yourself out." He stumbled to the bedroom and closed the door.

Angela smiled. She wasn't going anywhere. She sat where she was for several moments before standing. She then slowly began removing her clothes. Leaving them in a heap on Randolph's living room floor she crossed the room to his bedroom and slowly opened the door, closing it behind her.

The drawn blinds made the room completely dark, and the air smelled of musk, alcohol and man. She saw Randolph lying flat on his back, looking up at her as if in a daze.

"Jenna?"

She caught her breath, then answered softly, "Yes, sweetheart, I'm here."

He slowly got out of the bed and walked over to her and pulled her into his arms. "I hurt, Jenna. Please take away the hurt," he said between kisses.

"I will, Randolph, I will."

She let him take her into his arms and carry her over to the bed. She watched as he removed his clothes and rejoined her there, all the while calling her Jenna. And then he was on top of her and a few seconds later, he was inside of her. It didn't matter that she wasn't the virgin that Ross had thought her to be. To Randolph, this was a sweet dream anyway.

Randolph made love to her, bringing both of them to the highest peaks of fulfillment. Then before he could catch his breath, she was on top of him, doing all those things with her mouth and body that she had perfected over the years, just for him. When the two of them could not take any more pleasure, he collapsed from total exhaustion in her arms. She snuggled close to him and wondered how he would handle it when he woke up after the effects of the speed had worn off, and realized that it was Angela, and not Jenna, who had shared his bed and his passion for the entire afternoon.

Jenna's hand tightened around the spare key she inserted into the lock of Randolph's door. She had tried calling him on the telephone before leaving Memphis but didn't get an answer. Then she'd been placed on standby to get a flight out. When she'd tried calling him from the airport, his phone line had been busy. It was a good thing that she hadn't had any problems getting a taxi from the airport, and she was grateful that he had given her a key to his place. If he was as drunk as Leigh said he was, he wouldn't be fit to get up and open the door.

The first thing she noticed after entering the house was the pile of woman's clothing on the floor, a blouse, a skirt, slip, bra and panties. She frowned, wondering if Ben had brought a girl over who'd had the bad taste to undress in the living room. In Jenna's opinion that was kind of tacky for any woman to do since two men and not one lived there.

Placing her suitcase next to the sofa, she softly crossed the floor to Randolph's bedroom and opened the door. The closed blinds made the room dark, so she turned on the lamp next to the bed.

Jenna gasped, not believing what she saw. Angela was in bed with Randolph. Both were asleep. And they were naked. Angela's body was draped over his while he held her in his arms. All the blood from Jenna's body rushed to her head, and then a degree of pain she had never experienced before tore into her when it was apparent what they had done. His betrayal felt like a knife that had been plunged into her heart.

With eyes filled with tears, she angrily shook Randolph awake. When his eyes opened, he looked up at her, confused, with a red, bloodshot gaze. "I don't believe you did this, Randolph! And with her!"

Before Randolph could gather his wits Jenna ran from the bedroom.

Eighteen

The lingering residue from any alcohol or drugs immediately washed from Randolph's mind with Jenna's painful outburst. He quickly pushed at the naked body draped across him and almost froze when he saw it was Angela.

"What the hell are you doing here?!" he asked as he frantically got out of bed and reached down to slip into his pants. He didn't remember a damn thing but right now the one thing he did know was that he had to stop Jenna from leaving.

Without waiting for Angela's response, he raced after Jenna. He found her in the kitchen hanging up the phone. She looked up and appeared further pained by the sight of him. "I called a cab," she said, wiping tears from her eyes. "I'm going to wait outside."

He made a move toward her and she backed away from him. "Jenna, please—"

"Jenna, please what? Listen to your explanation?" she asked as more tears clouded her eyes. "How can you explain having Angela naked in bed with you? It was apparent what the two of you had done. How can you explain that, Randolph?"

Randolph rubbed his palm across the back of his neck as his mind fumbled, trying to find an explanation. He remembered making love to someone, but in his mind it had been Jenna. "Jenna, all I remember is getting drunk yesterday. Nothing else is clear."

"That's not good enough, Randolph," she said, wiping away more tears. "I know what I saw with my own eyes and what's obviously clear to me." She moved to walk past him and he reached out and touched her. She recoiled from him.

"Don't touch me!" she screamed, anger flaring in her features. "Don't you dare touch me after touching her. How could you make love to her when you're supposed to love me? And how could she let you make love to her when she's supposed to be in love with Ross?"

At the mention of Ross's name, pain—deep and sharp—cut into

Randolph's features to the point of puncturing Jenna's heart. Had he gotten that drunk trying to drown his sorrow that he had made love to the first available woman? Or had something been going on between him and Angela all along and she had been clueless?

"Has something been going on between you and Angela, Randolph?" she asked him quietly, desperately wanting to believe otherwise.

The sudden twist of his lips indicated he couldn't believe she could ask such a thing. "No, Jenna, I swear. I don't know what happened. But I do know that I love you, please believe me. I was stone drunk." But he was even more confused by that notion. He remembered getting completely wasted earlier in the day but by the time Angela had arrived he had pretty much sobered up. Or had he?

"You weren't drunk on alcohol, Randolph, but on grief."

Jenna and Randolph turned to the sound of Angela's voice. The woman hadn't bothered to get dressed but stood before them wearing of all things, Randolph's bathrobe. "What happened was that our grief was so great that it made us reach out to each other. One moment we were crying, comforting each other, and then next thing I know you had removed my clothes and taken me into your bedroom. I was so filled with grief that in my mind I pretended you were Ross. I would not have slept with you otherwise."

Tears sprang into Angela's eyes. "I was a virgin holding myself for Ross and our wedding night. But I was too overwrought with grief to stop you."

Jenna didn't know if Angela was sincere or acting. Was she really an innocent victim of circumstances, or was she just pretending, laying it on as thick as she could to deepen Randolph's guilt? At the moment she really didn't want to know. All she wanted was to get away from them. "I'll walk to Leigh's. When the cab comes please have him bring my luggage to her place. I've got to get out of here. The sight of the both of you sickens me."

"Jenna, please don't—"

"No, I need time alone right now and since it seems you've been in capable hands, there's no need for me to stay."

Without giving Randolph an opportunity to say anything else, she left.

For the third time in less than four hours, Randolph was at Leigh's house, pleading with her to tell him where Jenna had gone. Leigh claimed she wasn't there.

"Leigh, please tell me where she is. I have to talk to her! I have to explain things."

Leigh was livid. "And just how are you going to explain being caught in bed with another woman, Randolph? A woman who was engaged to your brother? You hurt Jenna. You hurt her pretty damn bad."

Pain clouded Randolph's eyes. Not only had he lost the brother he loved but he'd lost the woman he loved, too. "I need to see her and talk to her. I don't know what happened, Leigh, but I do know that I love Jenna and unless I was stone drunk I would not have slept with Angela. I've been racking my brain trying to remember and constantly come up with zero. All I know is that there is no way I could have been in my right mind. I would not have intentionally dishonored Jenna like that."

Leigh glared at him. "But dammit, Randolph, you did dishonor her and with a woman who's always treated her lower than low. It wouldn't surprise me if Angela set this whole thing up. She's always wanted you."

Randolph lifted a confused brow. "What are you talking about?"

"I'm talking about the fact that Angela has always been attracted to you. I'm not stupid. I picked up on it a while ago and even mentioned it to Noah before he left."

Randolph shook his head. "You're wrong, Leigh. Angela loved Ross. There was a time when I actually thought she didn't but now I believe she does. And she's taking his death pretty hard. Not only did I mess things up with Jenna but I've messed things up for Angela as well. The only reason she slept with me is because in her grief-stricken state she envisioned me as Ross." He sighed deeply, guiltily. His grandparents and Angela's parents were now aware of what had happened and everyone was taking sides—Angela's. She had been the grief-stricken virgin who had been taken advantage of by the grief-stricken brother.

"When Jenna returns please let her know that I need to see her and talk to her, Leigh. And please let her know that I love her. Totally. Completely." Randolph's eyes became misty. "They're having funeral services for Ross on Saturday." He almost broke down when he said the next words. "His body is supposed to arrive tomorrow."

Without saying anything else, Randolph turned and walked out of Leigh's house.

Leigh stood at the window and watched as Randolph got into his car and drove away. "You know I'm a poor liar, Jenna. Chances are he knew you were here."

Frowning, Jenna came down the stairs, her eyes still swollen from all the crying she had been doing. "I really don't care what he knows."

Leigh sighed and turned around to face her. "I think you should go to the memorial services, Jenna. Not going will make Angela think she's won."

Jenna sighed. Leigh was convinced the entire thing had been set up by Angela to make a move on Randolph. "Leigh, it's not a matter of winning."

Leigh raised her eyes to the ceiling. "Surely you don't think Randolph has feelings for Angela?"

"No, I believe he was either stone drunk or overcome with grief, or both. But the fact still remains that he did sleep with her, Leigh. I found them in bed together."

"But consider the circumstances, Jenna. It's not like he was intentionally unfaithful to you. He was torn up over his brother's death. I know how that feels from personal experience. You'd do just about anything to ease the pain."

"But would you have gone to bed with another man?"

"Jenna, to be honest with you, there were times I don't remember if I was coming or going, I was so full of grief when my brother was killed. But luckily for me Noah was there and unfortunately for Randolph *you* weren't and Angela took advantage of an opportunity."

A part of Jenna didn't want to believe Leigh's theory. She didn't want to believe anyone could be that deceitful and stoop that low.

"But like I said," Leigh continued, "you need to go. You need to show Angela that the love you and Randolph share is pure and true, and nothing can come between you, even her sharing his bed when he wasn't in his right mind."

When Jenna didn't say anything, Leigh kept talking. "I'm sure you couldn't resist taking a peek at him. He looks so pitiful, Jen. He's lost Ross and now he thinks he's lost you, too. He's going through a hard time right now and he needs you more than ever. And you know in your heart that he loves you. Only *you*. I don't think even you can question or dispute that."

Jenna nodded as more tears formed in her eyes. In her heart she knew that she couldn't. Their love had been special from the very beginning. It had even survived Julia Fuller's meddling. "Oh, Leigh, I don't know what to do."

"Yes, Jenna, I think that you do. I know it hurts, but you're going to have to swallow your pride and stand by the man you love—the man who loves you."

No longer wanting to dwell on Randolph and how she would handle the situation, Jenna asked, "How did Noah handle the news?"

"Not well. This is the second best friend he's lost. I'm just grateful he and Ross got to spend time together last month in Saigon. Noah said Ross made him promise that if anything happened to him that he would make sure Gia and the baby were taken care of. And now with Ross gone there's no doubt in my mind Noah will keep his promise."

On October twenty-second more than fifty thousand people—liberals, radicals, black nationalists, hippies, professors, women's groups and war veterans—participated in a massive demonstration in Washington against the United States' policies in Vietnam. The demonstrators marched in an orderly procession to the Pentagon where they held another rally and vigil that continued through the early hours of the next day. A force of ten thousand troops surrounded the Defense Department, standing ready to defend a nation against its own people if they had to.

Not far away a military plane landed, bringing Ross Donovan Fuller home to his country and his family for the last time.

Tan Son Nhut, Saigon

Artillery missiles resembling Fourth of July fireworks lighted the sky not far from the military base, and all around the smell of smoke, fumes and cigarette tobacco permeated the air.

No one noticed the man wearing fatigues as he entered the small freestanding building that served as a chapel. Walking to the front, he knelt before a bruised and battered statue of Jesus.

Noah's heart was heavy and tears suddenly sprang to his eyes as he pulled out of his pocket a group of photographs. They were the same photos he had been looking at during his free time over the last five days.

He knew that back in the States, in Virginia, the services for Ross were about to begin. Taking his time, he looked at one photo and then another, remembering the moment each was taken, just last month. Ross was smiling in every one of them as he stood next to the woman he loved, his bride. The last photo, one taken by another soldier who'd been passing by, had included Noah as well. He stood in the middle with one arm around Noah and the other around Gia. Everyone had been so happy that day, Ross's wedding day.

Then that night when he and Ross had some private time alone, his best friend had made him promise that should anything happened to him, Gia and their unborn child would be taken care of. Noah had made him that promise.

Noah had then made Ross promise that should anything happen to him, likewise, Leigh and his unborn child would be taken care of. Ross had made him that promise as well.

"Damn you, Ross, looks like I'm it," Noah said, trying to joke through the tears wetting his cheeks. "That's just what I need, man, two more mouths to feed."

He wiped at his tears. "But I'll do it for you, buddy. I'll do anything for you. I promise to take care of and hold dear your most precious possessions. I promise."

Nineteen

Jenna stood in front of the small church as the limousines carrying the Fuller and Denison families pulled up. She hadn't told anyone she would be here today, not even Leigh who was already seated inside.

She watched the family members get out of the vehicles and when she saw Randolph her heart ached. He was standing tall, behind both sets of grandparents, taking his place as the lone surviving grandchild in the family procession. Standing by his side where Jenna knew she rightly belonged was Angela, and directly behind Randolph and Angela were Angela's parents.

Jenna studied Randolph. Only someone as close to him as she was could feel his pain. He was about to do one of the hardest things he'd ever have to do and that was to say good-bye to the brother he loved and adored. And knowing how great his pain would be was the reason she had come. A part of her could not let him endure it alone.

Holding her head high, Jenna stepped from behind a group of mourners who had blocked her from view. As if he somehow sensed her presence, Randolph turned and looked her way. This was the first time they had seen each other since the day she had found him in bed with Angela. When their eyes met she saw his pain but then as he continued looking at her, what else she saw took her breath away. She saw his love for her so eloquently stated in his gaze that she stood rooted to the spot. And then, at that very moment, in her heart she knew. No matter what Angela may have thought she had shared with Randolph, she had not shared this—that special connection they had that transcended mere physical contact. For a brief moment Angela may have shared his body, but she didn't share his heart, mind and soul.

Jenna moved toward him and he immediately left Angela's side and met her on the church steps. They exchanged no words. None were needed. His eyes were filled with pain, misery, regret and sorrow. He opened his arms to her and she went into them, and he held her and she held him. Tight. Full of love for each other. A willingness to forgive any transgression. Filled with sorrow and pain for the occasion that had brought them to church today.

He finally released her and gazed down into her eyes. "I wasn't sure you would come," he whispered hoarsely. "I've lost Ross and I didn't know how I would handle losing you, too. I love you so much. I'm sorry, Jenna. I am so sorry for hurting you and for—"

She reached up and placed her fingers against his lips, sealing off his words. "And I love you, too, and here and now, that's all that matters. Come let's go inside, together, and say good-bye to Ross."

Randolph nodded. Taking her hand in his, he walked back over to where his family stood. Angela, in shock over Jenna's appearance, had the decency to step back and join her parents while Jenna took her place at Randolph's side. Jenna glanced up into Julia Fuller's tear stained face, and to her surprise she read deep appreciation and a heartfelt thank-you in the older woman's features. It was evident Julia Fuller was glad that she was there for Randolph.

All through the service as one person after another got up to speak, Randolph held Jenna's hand firmly in his. And when he got up, his voice trembled as he spoke of the brother he would forever remember, admire and love.

During the services Randolph stayed by Jenna's side, as if he didn't want to let her out of his sight. Everyone left the graveyard to return to the church for the repass. Jenna knew most of those present and to those she didn't know, Randolph introduced her as his fiancé, the woman he intended to marry.

Angela played the part of the grieving fiancée which made Jenna think that she hadn't yet been told that Ross was a married man with a wife in Vietnam.

After the repass Randolph hailed a cab at the front of the church and pulled Jenna inside the vehicle with him.

"Where are we going?" she asked when he pulled her into his lap.

"Somewhere where we can be alone."

He took her to the hotel and there in the darkened room, he made love to her. His hands cherished her as they touched her everywhere, creating a raw need within her.

He took her mouth with his and she sank into their kiss, moaning his name softly, repeatedly, and with an urgency that almost brought tears to Randolph's eyes. He loved her so much and had come so close to losing her. "I love you," he whispered when he finally released her mouth.

"And I love you, Randolph."

By the time his body straddled hers, both of them were sexually wired, aching with a need that was filled to the limit with yearning desire. He slipped inside of her, and held there for a moment as her body clutched him and her hands stroked his back.

He closed his eyes, not wanting to move, needing the unity, the link, the connection while they could make it last. But all too soon she moved her body, desperately impatient for hers to be stroked by him.

He leaned forward and captured her mouth again, letting his tongue sweep inside, exploring and tasting while his hands pulled her hips closer. The thundering beat of his heart began to match the rhythm he'd set. But he wanted more. He needed more. And she gave it to him. Everything he wanted. Everything he desired.

When she called out his name again as a climax tore through her body, something inside him exploded, pleasure erupted and his mind shut down. The only thing he could think about was filling her to the rim with his release, making the both of them feel complete, fulfilled and satisfied.

Even when he thought his body was completely drained, he heard her whisper the word, "More," and felt his body get hard again as her legs wrapped tightly around him, to hold him inside of her.

"More," she repeated.

And more is what he gave her.

Hours later, when dawn broke through the hotel's blinds, they were still in each other arms after having shared a night of insurmountable passion. They knew that somewhere Ross was smiling, glad that they had worked out their problems and were back together.

Randolph and Jenna's happiness lasted a little over a month. That was long enough for Angela to make the announcement to everyone that she was pregnant with Randolph's baby.

A distraught Randolph broke the news to Jenna when they met to spend Thanksgiving with his grandparents at Glendale Shores. He told her that Angela's parents, who were still upset about Ross's marriage to another woman while engaged to their daughter, were determined that Angela would not be humiliated again by a Fuller, and were insisting that Randolph do the right thing and marry their daughter.

Randolph assured Jenna not to worry about anything and to continue making plans for their June wedding because she was the woman he intended to marry. But Jenna, after much prayer and soul-searching, knew what she had to do. Especially when she remembered something he had once said to her.

"I'll never have a child of mine born out of wedlock. Ross and I made that promise to our father during our talk about the birds and the bees, and it's a promise we intend to keep. Fuller men live up to their responsibilities no matter what they are and no matter the sacrifices that have to be made."

With Angela expecting his child, Jenna knew there was no way she could marry Randolph. Without telling him of the decision she'd made, she put in for a transfer with Smith and Riley to work at one their overseas offices. The approval for the transfer came less than a month later, at the beginning of the new year. She had sworn her family and close friends to secrecy as to where she was going.

She had also told Gramma Mattie. Over the years Jenna had grown close to the older woman and made a special visit to Glendale Shores to tell Gramma Mattie of her decision.

Mattie Denison understood the painful sacrifice Jenna was making. As the two women walked along the shores with intermittent

bouts of hugging and crying, Gramma Mattie told Jenna that no matter what, she would always be the granddaughter of her heart . . . just
as she knew Jenna would be the woman her grandson would forever
love.

Jenna waited until the day before she was to leave for Paris before
sending Randolph her letter along with her engagement ring.

January 13, 1968
Randolph,
Please accept your ring back. I'm releasing you from our engage-
ment so that you can be free to do the right thing. I refuse to take
you away from your child.

If you love me you will let me go just like I'm letting you go.
Please don't try to find me. I've instructed my family and close
friends not to share my whereabouts with you. It's better this way.
Sometimes we have to think of others before we can think of our-
selves, and that's what I'm doing. I pray you will do the same.

I am also including a check for five hundred and fifty dollars to
repay the money you had loaned me, plus adequate interest. This
wipes the slate clean between us so we can get on with our lives.
Separately.

Wishing you all the best,
Jenna

Book Two

1980 - 1981

Truth stands the test of time;
lies are soon exposed.

Proverbs 13:19

Twenty

November 1980
Twelve years and eight months later

Perhaps it was the expression on his secretary's face, one that indicated she was truly irked to the bone, that told Randolph something was amiss. After an entire week spent in the courtroom against one of the most cold-hearted and apathetic prosecutors he knew, the last thing Randolph needed was some sort of office crisis. Usually the unflappable and forever cool and calm Clara Bradley could handle just about anything that came her way. In fact that was the main reason he'd hired the older woman six years ago. He didn't know of any problem she couldn't deal with competently and efficiently.

Except for one.

"Where is she?" he asked when his mind figured out the obvious.

Mrs. Bradley didn't bother to look up from her typing. "Your wife is waiting for you in your office, sir."

Randolph frowned. "She's my *ex-wife*, Mrs. Bradley."

"Not according to her, sir. She's corrected me on that twice today. She says once a wife, always a wife."

Randolph frowned, deciding not to cite clear reasonable evidence of the opposite with his employee. "Please hold my calls for a while."

"Yes, sir."

Randolph opened the door to his office then closed it behind him. He clenched his jaw when he glanced across the room and saw his ex-wife sitting on the loveseat, flipping through a magazine like she had every right to be there waiting for him. "What are you doing here, Angela?"

She looked up and smiled. "I wanted to congratulate you on winning the Blither case. It's all over the news. Everyone has been talking about what an outstanding job you did."

"Thanks, but you could have called. What's the real reason you're here?"

Angela stood and crossed the room to him. "I'm here about Trey.

He hasn't been himself lately and today he finally told me why. He's upset about that airline stewardess you're dating."

Randolph threw his briefcase on his desk and turned to face Angela, crossing his arms over his chest. Anger was apparent in his features. Ross Donovan Fuller III, named after his brother and whom they called Trey, was his twelve-year-old son. The spitting image of his father, Trey already reached his shoulders and had a muscular build as a result of all the sports he participated in.

"Trey wouldn't get upset about anyone I date if you'd stop filling his head with foolish notions that the two of us will get back together. It's not going to happen." Their marriage had lasted ten years, for his son's sake and no other reason. But Randolph had soon realized that ten years had been ten years too many with Angela, even for his son's sake.

Angela glared at him. "I wonder if you would have been so quick to divorce me two years ago had you known your old girlfriend was somewhere happily married with a family of her own. Don't you think I know that's why you did it?"

Randolph frowned. "Evidently you've forgotten about the issue of your unfaithfulness. That's the reason I did it. No one screws another man under the roof that I'm paying for."

Angela flinched. He had been asking for a divorce and she had refused to give him one. Then one day she screwed up when he returned unexpectedly from a business trip and had walked in on her having sex with another man. To be free of her, he had threatened that unless she gave him the divorce he wanted, he would expose her illicit affair with Tommy Gardner, their neighbor's twenty-year-old son. It hadn't helped matters that she'd been thirty-two at the time.

"And what was I supposed to do, Randolph? You weren't taking care of my needs. You made it clear when you married me that you were only doing it because I was carrying your child."

"But that didn't give you the right to act the part of a whore in *my* house. What if it had been Trey who'd come home early from school that day instead of me?"

For a long moment she didn't say anything. Damn him for having the will to resist her! While married to him for ten solid years, she had tried to seduce him and he'd resisted her at every turn, except for the times he'd awakened during the nights in their separate bedrooms to find her in his bed with her mouth on him. But no matter how good her blowjobs had made him feel, other than letting her finish what she'd started, not once had he ever reciprocated and made love to her. "Tommy Gardner took advantage of me during a weak moment. Is it so hard to forgive me for that *one* time? I was completely faithful to you until then."

"Don't insult my intelligence. I know about your ongoing affair with Harry Connors eight of the ten years we were married. But at least, as far as I know, Harry had the decency take you to hotels rather than screw you under my roof."

She lifted her chin and glared at him, wondering how he'd known about her and Harry. They had tried being careful. Harry was a bank executive she had met long after her marriage to Randolph. When she saw that Randolph had had every intention of keeping his word and not make their marriage legitimate, she had turned to Harry for sexual relief. "Harry loves me."

Randolph smiled but it was a smile that didn't quite reach his eyes. "Then you should marry him, or hasn't he asked you?"

Angela's gazed hardened. "That would pose a problem since I still consider myself married to you. There were those ten words the preacher spoke that day that sounded like . . . what God has joined together, let no man put asunder.'"

Randolph drew in a shuddering breath to keep his anger in check. "There's also a line about not committing adultery. You should have thought of that before you began opening your legs to every Tom, Dick . . . and Harry."

She glowered furiously at him. "I didn't come here to be insulted. I thought I'd let you know about Trey. You may as well get used to the idea that your son won't accept another woman in your life."

"No thanks to you. I'll deal with Trey in my own way. He's going to have to realize that he can't have everything he wants and that we'll never be a family again."

He sat down behind his desk as he continued to stare at her.

"Besides, in a few years he'll be so absorbed in a woman of his own, he'll care less about what I'm doing and who I'm doing it with. What will you do then, Angela, when you won't have him to use as leverage with me? Take my advice and get a life."

Randolph watched her face as her anger rose to the boiling point just moments before she snatched open the door and walked out.

A few minutes after she had left, he leaned back in his chair. His chest expanded and he drew in a deep breath. No man should have to put up with an ex-wife like Angela and if it weren't for his son, he wouldn't either. He loved Trey very much, and Trey loved his mother and thought she could do no wrong.

If only he knew.

But his son didn't know and like it or not, Randolph had always shielded Trey from the sordid truth about Angela. But he refused to allow Angela to use his love for Trey as a way to keep him on a leash.

Randolph stood and moved to one of the windows in his office that faced downtown Richmond. He would never forget the time he'd run into Kathy Taylor, the woman who'd been Angela's best friend, confidante and her roommate in law school. Like him, Kathy had been one of many attorneys attending a four-day conference in Houston. She had joined him for dinner that first night and it didn't take long, after she'd consumed a couple of drinks, to spill her guts.

He could remember that night like it was yesterday . . .

"So, how are things going with you and Angela?" Kathy asked, taking another sip of brandy. Evidently she liked the stuff, Randolph thought, since she was drinking it quite heavily.

"As Angela's best friend I'd think you would know," he responded dryly, taking a sip of his own drink. He wondered why he had asked her to join him for dinner. There were too many things about her that reminded him of Angela.

She smiled as she took another sip of brandy. "Angela and I haven't kept up over the years. She found out I was bumping and grinding a former lover of hers and didn't like it too much, although the man hadn't slept with her in years—at least not since we had graduated from college."

Randolph lifted a brow, thinking Kathy was mistaken. There couldn't have been former lovers for Angela since she had been a virgin when he'd touched her. Unless Kathy was referring to someone Angela had screwed around with after her marriage to him. Not knowing which was the case, the attorney in him decided to dig deeper, especially since Kathy was flapping her jaws with all kinds of information. "I thought Angela was a virgin."

Kathy began laughing so hard, for a moment Randolph thought she would choke on her drink. After a few hearty laughs she was able to recomposed herself. "Virgin! I can't believe you of all people fell for that. Angela was screwing anything in pants while attending Bronson." Kathy giggled. "Hell, she even got it on a few times with the security guard. But her main squeeze was Dean Hightower himself. He showed her all the tricks of the trade and in return he made sure she got good grades. He even arranged her abortion when she got pregnant by him in her senior year of college."

Randolph stared across the table at Kathy. He was shocked as hell. Could she be telling the truth? If she was telling the truth then how had Angela convinced everyone, including his grandmother, that she was a prim and proper innocent? Convincing Ross would have been fairly easy since the two had never slept together, and he remembered nothing of that day they had slept together other than waking up in bed with her and Jenna standing over them.

He watched Kathy, who had stopped drinking long enough to wrap spaghetti around her fork and chew, return his scrutiny smiling. "It's hard to digest, isn't it? What I've just told you about Angela. She started freaking out when she was pregnant with Trey thinking you would find out about the abortion. Her doctor did and he asked her about it and she confessed all. But her doctor assured her that her medical history was confidential." Kathy smiled, taking another sip of wine. "She's been a good actress all these years. In fact, one of the nation's wealthiest men, Robert Morgan, is the one who taught her all about blowjobs when he paid a visit to Bronson while she was there."

Randolph pushed his plate aside, no longer having an appetite. He met Kathy's gaze across the table. He decided to play another hunch. "What about that time she slept with me? Was she being an actress then?"

Kathy chuckled and replied, "Depends on how you look at it. You've *always been an obsession with Angela. She was with Ross but wanted you. In fact she would sleep with all those guys pretending they were you. The more you ignored her the more obsessed she became. She had been waiting for some way to rid herself of Ross and his death gave her a perfect opportunity. She didn't waste any time trading one brother in for another one, including taking some speed off me to drug you with. Your mind was all screwed up over losing Ross, your girlfriend was out of town and Angela's body was hot. She knew what she was doing and did it. Her plan worked just the way she wanted it except she hadn't counted on your girlfriend forgiving you after being caught in bed with her."* Kathy *laughed out loud. "Now that really pissed her off. But she wasn't about to give up. Right after Ross's funeral she slept with a number of guys, intent on getting pregnant from one of them and claiming the child was yours."*

Kathy shook her head, grinning. "Did you know that she wasn't even sure the baby was really yours until Trey came out looking just like you? There was no doubt he was yours. She was so happy she couldn't stand it that you had indeed been the one to get her pregnant. Now that was good timing on her part."

Randolph sat there, not believing what he was hearing. But after listening to Kathy, things were beginning to fall into place, like Angela's insistence that he not go with her to her doctor appointments when she was pregnant with Trey.

Later that night when he'd retired to his hotel room, he had laid in bed and replayed in his mind everything Kathy had told him, especially the part of how he had ended up in bed with Angela that day. She had drugged him.

He'd been furious, madder than hell and the next morning he had checked out of the hotel with the intention of confronting Angela with everything that he had learned. His unexpected return home had been the cause of another revelation for him, when he had walked into his house and found her making love with their neighbor's son who'd been home from college.

Although she had asked his forgiveness about being caught in the act—which he refused to do—Randolph had never shared with her his meeting with Kathy and the fact that he knew how far she had gone to seduce him during the time of Ross's death, and about her sordid past and her abortion. Even now she didn't know he knew everything.

Randolph walked back over to his desk, opened his briefcase and pulled out the envelope that had been delivered to him that morning before leaving for the courthouse. The letter had come from the private investigation firm he had used to find Jenna when no one would tell him of her whereabouts. Although he had honored her wishes and hadn't sought her out after finding out where she had gone, he had to know she was doing all right. So each year the PI firm had reported to him, usually in a one-page briefing.

He'd known about her father's death from with cancer eight years ago, and on impulse had gone to the Knoxville cemetery and had been there, watching from afar as John Haywood was laid to rest.

It had been the first time he had seen Jenna in the four lonely years since she had disappeared from his life and her beauty had still taken his breath away. And on that cold, gray day as sprinkles of snow blanketed the earth, unknown to her, he had been there for her, just like she had been there for him the day Ross had been buried. He had wanted to go to her, talk to her, touch her, let her know he was there. And he wanted to ask her if the same beautiful memories that had sustained him over the years were sustaining her. But he had done none of those things. Instead, he had caught a plane back to Richmond that day to return to the wife he didn't want and the son he loved to distraction.

The following year he had received the letter from the investigation firm advising him that Jenna had married a man by the name of Steven Malone; a guy who worked for the same company she did. And then two years later he'd been told of the birth of her daughter, a little girl that she had named Haywood.

He inhaled deeply as he tore open the envelope and read the contents.

November 10, 1980
Mr. Fuller,

   Please find our annual report on Jenna Haywood Malone. We regret to inform you of the passing of Mrs. Malone's husband,

*Steven Malone, from a sudden heart attack, just one month after
our last report had been sent to you.*

*Mrs. Malone and her daughter now reside in Atlanta, Georgia.
Her change of address is noted on the card enclosed with this letter.*

*Please contact our company if you have any questions. Your next
report will be sent in approximately twelve months from the date of
this letter.*

Respectfully yours,
Aaron Exelberg, Exelberg Investigators

Randolph's breath caught in his throat as he folded the letter. Jenna
was no longer married.

"You know, Jen, it's a sad day for our country when an over-the-hill
movie star can become a United States president."

Jenna smiled but didn't bother glancing up from icing the cake she
had baked. Carol Strong, her neighbor and a woman she considered a
friend, was still upset about an election that had been held over two
weeks ago. "If hearing about it bothers you that much why don't you
turn off the television?"

"I would but then I'll risk the chance of not finding out who shot
J.R. Tonight was the worst possible time for my television to go on the
blink."

Jenna shook her head. Carol was hooked to the nighttime soap
opera, *Dallas,* and had called her in a panic. Tonight was the night that
concluded the cliffhanger and according to the newspapers they
expected the show to draw more viewers than any other show in television's history.

Jenna was glad she'd never gotten caught up watching it. Friday
nights were the time she got to unwind and spend with Haywood. At
six, this was her daughter's first year of school and the report card she
had brought home today indicated she was doing extremely well—
which was the reason for the cake. Haywood had been close to her
father and missed having him around. That was why Jenna had made

the decision to move to Atlanta. She thought the change in location would do them both some good.

"If they show one more commercial, I'm going to scream!" Carol yelled, breaking into Jenna's thoughts.

"They have to make their money somehow," Jenna said, stepping back from the table to view her handiwork. "So what do you think?"

Carol took her gaze off the television long enough to give the frosted cake a cursory glance. "I think it would have been appreciated much more if you had made it with green icing. You know how much Haywood loves green."

Jenna chuckled. That was an understatement. The two most important things in her daughter's life at the moment were the color green and the Cookie Monster from *Sesame Street*.

"Speaking of Haywood, where is she? I haven't seen her but once since I got here."

Jenna decided not to tell Carol that Haywood had come through the kitchen several times but that Carol had been too absorbed in *Dallas* to notice. "Right now she's in my room playing with that Pac-Man game her uncle Jarvis gave her."

Jenna had just placed the cake in its keeper when Carol released a long whistle. "Now that's the kind of commercial break I don't mind," she said, indicating the quick news flash that had spread across the television. "He's one good-looking man and he's winning every case he gets his hands on."

"Who?" Jenna asked as she snapped the lid to the cake keeper in place.

"That hotshot attorney, Randolph Fuller."

Jenna's hands froze. "What about Randolph Fuller?" she asked, trying to sound calm.

"I said he's won another case and it was one everybody was convinced would go the other way. He's dynamite as an attorney and is definitely making a name for himself. This is the sixth high-profile case he's taken on in the last three years and won. He's really something else and to top it off he looks totally awesome. A man like that would definitely make me forget about watching *Dallas*. Look at him, Jenna, and let's see if you don't start drooling at the mouth."

Jenna looked at the television where an interview segment between Randolph and some reporter was being shown. She didn't start drooling but she did feel a strong, stirring sensation in her stomach. In less than six months, both she and Randolph would be celebrating birthdays. She would be thirty-four and he would be thirty-six. And like Carol she had to admit, he looked totally awesome. Time had only enhanced his looks.

She blinked when the television went into another commercial, wishing she had not seen his face on the screen. Seeing it brought back memories too powerful and too painful to dwell on after twelve years.

Later that night after Carol had left and Haywood had gone to bed, Jenna sat in the rocking chair in her room and tried to read a book. The words appeared fuzzy to her mind as her thoughts drifted back twelve years to the last night she and Randolph had shared together. She had known it would be their last but he had not.

Instead of the two spending Christmas with her family as originally planned, Randolph had spent time with his grandparents in Virginia and South Carolina. The holidays had been hard for them since it had been the first without Ross. He had arrived in Memphis two days before New Year's and from the moment he had walked into her apartment, she had tried to absorb him within herself knowing it would be the last time she could do so.

Without bothering to explain why, she had encouraged him to remain inside the apartment with her. She didn't want to go out and do any of the stuff they had planned to do like go to a New Year's Eve party. Instead, in the hours leading into 1968, the need to be a part of him had grown into a clawing ache that had to be filled.

And filled it he had. He had kissed her over and over again, everywhere, touching her, caressing her, preparing her body to take his and by the time she had, she had experienced one mind-blowing orgasm. It had been the first of many.

That night they had made love with their hearts, minds and souls as well as with their bodies. Neither spoke of Angela and the baby she carried or how the situation would affect them and their relationship. All they had wanted was to concentrate on each other and the love they shared. He spent five glorious days with her and a week after he left, so did she. She left for Paris without letting him know where she was going.

When April fourth came around, a day they had shared celebrating their birthdays together for the last two years, she had been so miserable she had gotten sick. It didn't help matters when news reached her that day about the assassination of Martin Luther King, Jr. She had cried her eyes out over such a loss and knew that back home in the States, masses of people were also grieving. She had thought of Randolph and what he had to have been feeling. He had always admired and respected the civil rights leader and after working with Dr. King that summer on the voter registration drive, she knew Randolph's admiration and respect had increased. And then two months later, in June, tragedy struck again when Robert Kennedy was gunned down. It seemed during that time America was losing all of their good leaders. Leaders who had been committed to making a difference.

The ringing of the telephone interrupted Jenna's thoughts, bringing her back to the present. She automatically reached for it, thinking it was probably one of her brothers. All three had remained in Atlanta after graduating from Morehouse. And her mother, lonely after her father's death, had moved to Atlanta to be near her children. "Yes?"

"Jenna? Hi, it's Leigh."

A huge smile touched Jenna's lips. "Leigh, how are you doing? How are Noah and the kids?"

"Everyone is fine. I'm sure you've heard what Castro did. The entire city of Miami is up in arms right now, and as city commissioner, Noah has his hands full."

Jenna nodded. She knew Leigh was talking about the news report that one hundred and twenty-five Cubans had been given approval to leave Cuba for America. Specifically, Miami, Florida. Most were criminals hand-picked by Castro's men.

"Sorry to call so late but Noah heard something that I thought I'd better prepare you for since it will probably make headlines tomorrow. I also plan to call Ellie tonight to make her aware of it as well, just in case she doesn't know already."

Jenna placed her book aside. "What?"

"It's about Johnny."

A lump formed in Jenna's throat. Johnny had been sentenced to die for the murder of a federal agent nearly fourteen years ago and was still on death row. They had exchanged a number of letters over the years and she had even gone to visit him several times, maintaining the close friendship they had shared in college. "What about Johnny?" she asked Leigh softly.

"Since he doesn't have any appeals left a date has been set for his execution." Leigh's voice was beginning to break when she added, "Unless some sort of miracle happens, Johnny will be put to death in sixty days."

Twenty-one

Jenna's fingers tightened around the glass of wine she held in her hand. "There has to be something that we can do. There has to be."

Leigh glanced across the room at Jenna. "Yeah, but what? Noah would step in and help Johnny if he were still practicing law, but he hasn't handled a case in over five years."

Jenna nodded. She knew as city commissioner of Miami, Noah was strategically moving his future toward the political arena with plans of running for the United States Senate in a few years.

Jenna, Leigh and Ellie were in New Orleans on their annual week-long outing together. It was something they had started doing when Jenna returned from Paris, and they saw it as a way to strengthen the bond between them. So every year they selected a different place to go, leaving husbands and children at home.

Leigh and Noah had two kids; thirteen-year-old Zachary, and ten-year-old Noelle. Ellie, the only one who had remained single, had gone back to school and had gotten a degree in education and was teaching at a school in Texas. Her daughter Johnnetta was fourteen. Of the three women, Ellie stayed in direct contact with Johnny the most, and had admitted that during the brief time she had lived in California during the sixties, things had begun developing between her and Johnny, but he had not let them get too serious because of his involvement with the Panthers.

"I think there's a way to help Johnny, Jenna, and if you think real hard I'm sure you know what it is," Ellie said thoughtfully, after taking a sip of her wine.

They all went silent. Yes, Jenna knew what it was, more specifically, who it was. Randolph Fuller. If anyone would be able to step in and fight for Johnny's life with a good chance of winning, it would be him. "Why would he be willing to take on Johnny's case? He'd only met him a few times when we were at Howard. Besides, I doubt Johnny's family has the money to pay whatever retainer Randolph will require."

Leigh waved off her words. "Randolph would take that case in a heartbeat if you were to ask him."

Jenna shook her head. "Why would he?"

"For you," Ellie replied quietly.

For a brief moment, Jenna hung her head and her shoulders stiffened a little. When she raised her head and gazed at her two friends, the look on her face was guarded, haunted. "There may have been a time when he would have done anything for me but that was over twelve years ago. That time is long past."

"He would do it for you now," Leigh said softly.

Jenna met Leigh's gaze. "You don't know that."

"Yes, I do and deep down you do, too. You and Randolph were very close at one time. The two of you shared something very special."

Jenna stood, pretending to stretch her legs when in fact she was trying to find temporary relief for an aching heart. "Like I said, Leigh, that was a long time ago."

"Yes, but there's never a time that he doesn't ask about you whenever I see him since he knows the two of us stay in touch. He used to ask about you even when he was married to Angela, which he isn't anymore, thank God. From what I understand she turned out to be a slut of the worst kind. According to Noah, Randolph actually caught her in bed with a college kid, thirteen years younger than she was. And, over the years he hadn't been the only one. There have been other men."

Jenna's eyes widened in shocked surprise. "What?! You've never mentioned that to me before."

Leigh smiled wryly. "If you'll recall, that was one of your sacred rules, Jen. You never wanted either of us to mention Randolph to you."

Jenna accepted the truth in Leigh's words. She had felt not hearing Randolph's name would ease her pain. Just like she had thought marrying Steven would also do the trick but it hadn't. Steven had been her friend as well as her husband. He had known her heart belonged to another and had asked her to marry him anyway. They had had eight good years together and he had given her a beautiful little girl.

"I'm sorry he had to go through that with Angela. He deserved better," Jenna said angrily.

"Yes. He deserved you, Jen."

Jenna shook her head sadly. "No, he deserved to be a full-time father to his child. I couldn't take that away from him."

"Okay, I understood your reasoning back then but what about now?" Leigh asked as she watched Jenna pace the length of the hotel suite they shared. "Officially the two of you are unattached individuals. He's single and so are you."

Jenna stopped pacing. "Yes, but twelve years have passed. We're two different people. Other than a glimpse of him on television once, I haven't actually seen him in all that time and there's a chance—a damn good chance—he's gotten over what we had and I'm just a faint memory to him. He's a man of the world, in some ways he's almost like a celebrity. A totally different type of woman probably appeals to him now."

"If you really think that, then you shouldn't be afraid to see him . . . unless you still care for him, Jen," Ellie said, gazing intently at her friend.

Jenna opened her mouth to deny such a thing and then her composure wavered under her two friends' speculative stares. "No matter how I feel I can't go back there. I knew when I gave him up that I could never go back and I won't. Haywood is my life now just like I'm sure his son is his."

She waited, knowing Leigh and Ellie probably had a lot to say. But they surprised her and didn't say anything. "What if he won't even see me?" she asked after she couldn't stand their silence any longer.

"He'll see you," Leigh said, taking a sip of her wine.

Jenn nervously bit her bottom lip. "I'll make it clear with Randolph from the very beginning that our meeting will be strictly business."

"Yes, you do that," Ellie said, biting back a smile. "After twelve years that shouldn't be a problem."

Jenna nodded, not seeing the silent look that passed between Ellie and Leigh. "And somehow I will pay him every penny he charges over what Johnny's parents can afford. I should be able to do it without touching Haywood's educational fund if he's willing to work with me on some sort of payment plan."

"And I'll do whatever I can to help financially as well," Ellie said. "Johnny was there when I needed him and more than anything, I want to be there for him."

Leigh pushed herself out of the chair. "And of course you can count me in." She came to stand in front of Jenna. "So have you decided to go see Randolph about handling Johnny's case?"

Jenna's heart thundered in her chest at the thought of coming face-to-face with Randolph after twelve years. But like she'd said earlier, their meeting would be strictly business. "Yes, I'm going to go see him."

Twenty-two

Waiting wasn't an easy thing to do, Randolph concluded as he moved around his office. He checked his watch. He had ten minutes more to wait. Ten minutes before he'd be seeing Jenna again.

When he had checked his appointment book that morning he'd seen the name and had blinked a few times, thinking he must have been imagining things. But after calling Clara into his office to question the appointment, he discovered he wasn't losing his mind after all. According to Clara, a Jenna Haywood Malone had called last week asking for an appointment. There was a case she wanted him to handle for her.

What case? he'd asked himself numerous times since then. He had racked his brain for any possible clue as to what would bring her from Atlanta to see him, and from all indications she wanted to treat her visit strictly as a business matter. Did she actually believe that he could do that, considering what they'd once meant to each other?

He checked his watch again. Eight minutes.

Had she arrived early? Was she sitting out front in the lobby waiting for their scheduled appointment time? He picked up the phone and punched Clara's extension.

"Yes, Mr. Fuller?"

"Has Jen—I mean Mrs. Malone arrived yet?"

"No, sir."

"Thanks." He was as jumpy as a schoolboy about to go on his first date with the most popular girl at school. He sat behind his desk and looked at the report of a case that had just been delivered. A few minutes later, he shoved it aside. He was interested in only one thing. What Jenna could possibly want with him? He definitely knew what he wanted with her. It was what he'd always wanted. To love her forever. He again considered it absurd that she thought things could be strictly business between them. He would play it cool, let her set the pace, and even go so far as to let her lay down whatever ground rules she thought she needed to put in place. But then as smoothly as whipped cream, he would ease back into her life as well as her heart. Then he would set her straight as to how things would be between them. There was probably a chance she wouldn't like it. But he wasn't going to give her a choice.

Fourteen years ago they had spent a week together at Glendale Shores during spring break. It was during that time they had pledged their love for each other as well as bound their lives together. He had explained to her the significance of making a commitment over his great-grandmother's Bible and what it meant. It seemed she had somehow forgotten.

Randolph drew in a long deep breath. And in his own way he was going to make her remember. He had no intentions of letting her disappear from his life again.

Jenna swallowed the nervousness she felt in her stomach. "Good morning. I'm here to see Mr. Fuller."

Clara Bradley peered through the glasses that sat perched on her nose. "Jenna Malone?"

"Yes."

"Please have a seat and I'll let Mr. Fuller know that you're here."

Clara watched the woman cross the room to take a seat. She was pretty, she thought. Very pretty. And for some reason Mr. Fuller was anxious to meet with her. He had called twice asking if she had arrived yet. Clara's ever-observant eyes had noticed the young woman wasn't wearing a ring, which meant she wasn't married. *Umm, interesting.* Clara racked her brain to figure out where she knew the name. *Ahh,* she remembered. Mr. Fuller had a special folder on Jenna Malone in his confidential files. Those were files he personally handled himself. Only once or twice had he given her the key to the locked cabinet to put something away. Now her curiosity was piqued. Evidently Mrs. Malone was someone Mr. Fuller knew. Could she be someone he cared about as well?

Clara hoped so. His ex-wife was a monumental pain, a real witch if ever there was one, and determined to remain a permanent fixture in his life whether he wanted her to or not. Clara thought Angela Fuller's obsession with Mr. Fuller wasn't healthy. There were times when she wondered if the woman didn't have a few screws loose. Already she had called that morning, but as he had instructed she had not put her through and had taken a message.

The phone rang. Mr. Fuller was calling again. Clara picked up, immediately knowing what question he would ask. "Yes, Mr. Fuller, she's here." After a brief pause she concluded the conversation by saying, "All right, sir."

After hanging up the phone Clara stood as she glanced across the room at the young woman. "Mrs. Malone, Mr. Fuller will see you now."

When Jenna entered Randolph's office he was standing across the room at the window with his back to her. His secretary smiled before leaving, quietly closing the door behind her. And as if the click of the door was his cue, he slowly turned around and his dark eyes held her transfixed.

Jenna's breath caught in her throat. Even from across the room Randolph's presence filled the office. He seemed taller, more muscular and if possible, better looking than he had been on television. If only Carol could see him in the flesh she would know that drooling wasn't good enough for Randolph Devin Fuller. He deserved the full slobbering effect.

This was the man to whom she had given her virginity at eighteen when he had branded her as his. He was the man who had been both her dreams and her reality. The man her heart had been conditioned to love forever. A man who had touched and tasted every part of her, and had introduced her to passion of the most prolific and steamiest kind. A man who could turn her on with just a look . . . like he was doing now.

She wanted to feel guilty for having such thoughts when Steven had only been dead fourteen months, but for some reason she couldn't. Randolph had always held a special place in her heart and Steven had known it and accepted it. That didn't mean she hadn't loved her husband, because she had. She had loved him but had not been in love with him. But she knew that the man staring at her from across the room with guarded eyes had branded her heart for a lifetime.

Randolph drew in a deep breath as all his concentration centered on Jenna. He had not forgotten how beautiful she was. He just hadn't counted on her being even more beautiful. The passing of twelve years hadn't taken their toll on her features. In fact there was a lot about her that reminded him of the eighteen-year-old woman he'd immediately fallen in love with at Howard University. The only thing the passing of time had done was give her a serene quality of maturity and sophistication.

She was the woman who'd taken his breath away that night he'd seen her for the first time in the yard. The woman who had given herself to him without reservation and in such a way that made his body tremble to remember it. The woman who had loved him enough to put aside her hurt and forgive him when she had found him in bed with another woman and trusted him enough to know he had not betrayed her. She was the woman who had helped him through the pain of having to say good-bye to his brother.

And the woman who truly believed she had been doing the right thing when she had disappeared from his life.

As he continued looking at her, he felt the attraction. It was even stronger than it had been the night they'd met. Stronger, and in his particular situation, more volatile and explosive. Knowing they couldn't spend the remainder of the day staring at each other, he crossed the room to her slowly, wanting her to feel his approach. He wanted her to be fully aware of him, not as the young man of twenty-two that she had last seen, but as the thirty-five-year-old man she was now seeing. A man who had changed in age and matured in looks but whose wants and desires had basically remained the same.

He still wanted and desired her.

Instead of pulling her into his arms and kissing her like he wanted to do, he stuck out his hand for a formal handshake and said, "Jenna, it's good seeing you again."

●　　●　　●

The pleasure of touching Randolph's hand was so intense, Jenna quickly pulled away as every nerve ending in her body became a mass of sensations. If Randolph had felt them, he did a good job of not letting her know it. "It's good seeing you again, too, Randolph," she managed to say.

Jenna thought she was losing it. She had wanted things to be strictly business between them, but now that they were, she was bothered that he didn't appear to be flustered the way she was. It annoyed her that she obviously was still attracted to him when he didn't seem to be the least bit attracted to her. She had only imagined the desire she'd thought she'd seen in his gaze when she'd first entered the room.

"Would you care to have a seat and tell me how I can help you?"

"Yes, thanks," she said, taking the seat he offered as she fumbled with the straps on her purse. She suddenly felt more nervous than ever before since she wasn't used to seeing him this cool, this reserved. She waited until he had taken the seat behind his desk before she began.

"It's about Johnny Lane."

He lifted a brow. "Your friend from Howard? The one who was involved in that raid with the Oakland Police and FBI agents at the Black Panthers headquarters in 'sixty-seven?"

"Yes. And if you recall he was given the death penalty for killing a federal agent."

Randolph nodded as he stared at her. "Yes, I remember that."

Jenna drew in a deep shuddering breath before continuing. "He was sentenced to die nearly fourteen years ago. A judge has now set a date for his execution and it's supposed to be carried out in the end of January." She paused for a second. "The reason I'm here, Randolph, is to hire you to take on Johnny's case."

He looked pensive for a moment and Jenna held her breath, wondering if he would turn her down outright. After all, he was a well-known attorney and chances were he already had cases lined up to work on.

"You still believe he's innocent and that the FBI framed him?"

"He said that they did."

"And that's good enough for you?"

Jenna met his gaze. "Yes, that's good enough for me."

After a brief second, he nodded. "All right, then it's good enough for me, as well."

Jenna swallowed the lump in her throat. "You'll do it? You'll actually take the case?"

"Yes," he said, reaching for the calendar on his desk. "Did you think for one minute otherwise, Jenna?"

She shrugged, trying to gauge his emotions but couldn't. "To be honest with you, Randolph, I didn't know what to think. I'm sure you're very busy and I figured I'd be taking a chance by coming here asking for your help."

He met her gaze. "I'd do anything for an old friend, especially one who helped me through a very difficult time in my life."

Is that what he thinks of me now? An old friend? She frowned, not knowing why it bothered her so.

"I'm going to have to act immediately if I'm going to appeal the judge's decision."

"Johnny doesn't have any more appeals left," she informed him.

"Just a minor inconvenience that we can work around. I'll block the execution. That will give me enough time to thoroughly review the case. I take it he's still in California?"

"Yes."

"Then how soon can you leave?"

Jenna sat up straight. "Me?"

"Yes. I need you to go with me or join me there. Johnny Lane doesn't know me, at least not personally. He'll feel more comfortable and open up and talk if someone's there he feels he can trust. In order to defend him, Jenna, I'm going to have to build a case, a very strong and solid case, against the federal government, specifically the FBI."

"So you think there's a chance?"

Randolph didn't want to get her hopes up too high. "I won't know until I've thoroughly reviewed the case. I need you to tell me everything you know about it."

"Now?"

Randolph checked his watch. "No, my next appointment is in ten minutes. How long will you be in town?"

"Until in the morning."

"Then how about dinner tonight?"

Jenna wasn't sure having dinner with Randolph was a good idea. "I don't know what I can tell you that might help."

"Have you seen him over the past twelve years?"

"Yes. I try to visit him at least once or twice a year."

"Then you know his mental state. Being in jail almost fourteen years is a long time, especially when you're an innocent man. I need to know what to expect when I meet with him. Plus, I know you told me his version of what happened years ago, but I need to be briefed again. Time is of the essence and could mean whether he lives or dies." Randolph sighed deeply. What he'd just told her was the truth. If the FBI did have something to hide they would want to push for closure.

Randolph knew that the only reason Johnny had not already been executed was because he'd been entitled to a certain number of appeals by law, and then—thank God—there was Jerry Brown, the very liberal governor of California. Brown was known to be an advocate of civil rights as well as a strong supporter of racial integration. What Randolph had to do was convince Brown, as well as the courts, that there was enough evidence to show corruption within the FBI, which would warrant a new trial.

"So what about dinner tonight, Jenna?"

Jenna paused to let everything Randolph said earlier sink in. There was no way she could get out of going to dinner with him. "Dinner will be fine."

If Jenna suspected that Randolph had an ulterior motive for asking her to dinner, that suspicion was shot down the moment he began asking her intense questions about what Johnny had confided to her over fourteen years ago. It didn't take long to understand why he had become one of the most sought-after African-American attorneys in the country.

He knew just the right questions to ask to piece together in his mind the true nature of what had happened to Johnny. He even asked her about the letters Johnny had written during his earlier months with the Panthers. Over dinner he had relentlessly questioned her, deciding what information he could use and what information he could discard as not important enough.

It was only after the remains of their meal had been taken away and dessert had been served that the tone of their conversation shifted when Randolph casually said, "I think we've covered everything that we needed to tonight. However, I would like to read those letters. Is there any way you can bring them to California with you when you come?"

"Yes. I know exactly where they're packed." She didn't add that they were stored along with a lot of her other belongings from college, including a number of photos they had taken together. She had come across them during her move to Atlanta. There were even a few photos that she, Randolph and Ross had taken during her first visit to Glendale Shores that Christmas. Those had been happy times the three of them had shared. There had also been pictures that the three of them had taken together at Leigh and Noah's wedding.

After a few brief moments she said quietly, "I understand from Leigh that Ross's family was never found."

Randolph sadly shook his head. "No, they weren't. However, Noah and I were able to find out that Gia died of complications within a day of giving birth to a baby girl whom she named Adrianna, after my mother. From what we've been able to uncover, after Gia died, Adrianna became the custody of Gia's sister. We were able to trace their trail up to the fall of Saigon, then nothing. We've hired some of the best investigators money can buy as well as worked with a lot of high-ranking government officials, but it's like they've disappeared without a trace. But Noah and I won't rest until Adrianna is found."

Jenna nodded, hearing the frustration as well as the determination in his voice. "I believe in my heart that she will be found, Randolph. Don't give up looking."

"I won't. Neither will Noah. We're both committed to finding her no matter what it takes and no matter how long it takes."

Jenna tilted her head, considering his words and knowing that he meant them. They paused in their conversation when the waiter came and refilled their coffee cups. She lifted her cup and took a sip.

"Tell me about your daughter, Jenna."

Jenna froze from taking a sip of coffee upon hearing the strong emotion that was thick in his voice. If things had worked out the way they had dreamed and planned while students at Howard, her daughter would have been his, just like his son would be hers. The hardest thing for her to get over twelve years ago was the knowledge that Angela, and not she, was going to give birth to Randolph's child. For a long time it had been a bitter pill to swallow, an agony she had prayed away constantly. And now as she looked across the table at him and met his gaze, she knew. She knew that as indifferent as he may have wanted to seem, he was experiencing the same feelings with the knowledge of her daughter Haywood. Another man had gotten her pregnant, and he was trying to deal with it. As close and as much in love as the two of them had been there was no way he could feel otherwise.

She took a sip of her coffee, deciding the best way to handle the situation was to move on and not dwell on the past. Things hadn't worked out the way they had wanted, had dreamed, but then that was life. You took the good right along with the bad, the ups with the downs. And you learned how to get over them how to persevere and how to survive. Over the past twelve years, she had done all three.

She met his inquiring gaze and smiled. "I think Haywood is the most beautiful little girl to walk the face of this earth, but then I'm very prejudiced when it comes to her."

A smile formed on Randolph's lips. "And you have every right to be. With you as her mother there's no doubt in my mind that she's as beautiful as you say."

His comments touched her. "Thanks, Randolph. Would you like to see a picture of her?"

He only hesitated a second. But it was a second that she detected. "Yes, I'd love to," he said quietly.

Jenna reached into her purse and pulled out her wallet. She retrieved several pictures of Haywood and placed them on the table. "This is Haywood at three," she said, pointing to a picture of a little girl who was smiling brightly for the camera.

"She's very photogenic," Randolph said, picking the picture up and taking a closer look.

Jenna chuckled. "Yes, she is that and loves having her picture taken. She also enjoys taking pictures, something she inherited from her father. She's never far from a camera. Steven bought her her very first camera a few weeks before this shot was taken. She had just turned three at the time."

Randolph nodded and took a look at another photo. "How old was she in this one?"

"Five, and this one—" Jenna said indicating the last photo, "—was taken last month at school. She's six and this is her first year and I'm glad that she loves it. Now if she can keep that same attitude about school for the next eleven years I'll be happy."

Randolph chuckled as he studied the photograph. A knot formed in the pit of his stomach. Haywood was a beautiful girl because she was the spitting image of her mother. It seemed all Jenna's features had passed to her daughter. The shape of her eyes, nose and mouth; her smile; her rounded chin and perky cheeks. Yeah, she was a beauty all right. He could just see her at eighteen, the same way he had seen her mother—a young woman who had literally taken his breath away.

"Tell me about your son, Randolph."

Randolph moved his gaze from the photo he'd been staring at to Jenna. He watched as her slightly trembling lips formed into a half smile. Then he knew what the two of them were doing. They were trying like hell, and like mature adults, to handle two very difficult but important issues in their lives. Their children. Trey and Haywood were two individuals that should have actually been just that—*their children*. But things had not turned out that way and they were trying to handle the situation as best they could by facing it head-on.

"He was named after Ross and my father, but to keep things simple and less confusing, we started calling him Trey, which means 'the third.' I don't have as many pictures as you have," he said smiling, as he stood to retrieve his wallet out of his back pocket, "but I do have one." He pulled it out. "Trey is twelve now and started junior high school this year."

Jenna studied the photograph. He looked nothing like Angela and was the exact image of Randolph. And because Ross and Randolph had favored each other, she could see a resemblance to Ross as well. The youth of twelve was tall for his age and already he was handsome. And from the way he was smiling for the camera, it seemed he knew it.

"How did you and I manage to have such conceited kids," Jenna asked chuckling. "He's handsome and I can tell he knows it. I can see him being a heartbreaker in ten years or less."

"And I think just the opposite will happen," Randolph said quietly, as he met Jenna's gaze. "I think he'll do just what I did: meet the woman of his dreams, fall in love and love her for the rest of his life."

Jenna's breath caught with Randolph's words. Silence stretched out between them. A thick lump formed in her throat and a mist of tears touched her eyes. It was there in his gaze, plain for her to see. He still had feelings for her—just like she still had feelings for him.

"Randolph, I—"

"I think we've shared enough for tonight, don't you? As painful as it was for the both of us, we were able to share with each other two people whom we love very much—our children. And I'm sure that no matter what we may have wanted to happen between us in the past, our children were truly gifts from God."

Jenna wiped at a tear that threatened to fall from her eyelid. "Yes, they are."

"And I think the best way to end such a beautiful evening is with a toast." He beckoned the waiter to their table and ordered a bottle of expensive wine. A few moments later he held his filled wineglass up to hers. "To our beautiful children."

Jenna nodded as she touched her wineglass to his. "Yes, to our beautiful children." She then took a sip of wine.

Less than an hour later, Randolph returned Jenna back to her hotel. Although she had told him it wasn't necessary, he was adamant about seeing her up to her room and together they took the elevator to her floor.

"How soon can you join me in California?" he asked, bringing back into focus the real reason she was there; something she was ashamed to admit she had totally forgotten about.

"How soon will you need me?"

"Almost immediately after I arrange to see Johnny. I think it will be best if you're there from the beginning to break the ice, so to speak. Afterwards, I'll be able to handle things from there. I'm sure you wouldn't want to be away from Haywood any longer than necessary."

Jenna appreciated his thoughtfulness and understanding. "No, I prefer not to. Although getting a babysitter isn't hard because Mom now lives in Atlanta, I still prefer not being away from Haywood too often."

Randolph nodded. "I was saddened to hear about your father, Jenna. I really liked him."

Jenna smiled up at him. "And he liked you, too."

"I know. We had a long talk that day I went to him looking for you. He knew where you were but was duty-bound to keep it a secret. But he had known the pain I felt, the pain I was going through. And he talked to me like I believe my father would have talked to me that day. He gave me some pretty good advice although a part of me hadn't wanted to hear it. The only thing I wanted was to find you and get you back."

Jenna knew about that day. Her father had written to her and had told her all about it, including the pain Randolph had been going through after receiving her letter that had ended things between them. "It was hard for us to let Dad go. The only reason we were able to do so was because none of us could stand to see him suffer any longer. I took leave from my job to come back to the States. I was back home a few weeks before he died."

"He was a wonderful person, Jenna. That was one of the reasons I had to be there when he was laid to rest."

Jenna jerked her head up and looked at him. "You were there?"

"Yes. But I intentionally stayed in the background. I wanted to be with you that day, to share your pain and your grief, the way you had shared mine with Ross. Somehow I believed my being there, even without your knowing it, would somehow give you strength."

Jenna nodded. It had. She clearly remembered that day, and the moment when she had glanced away from her father's coffin as it was being lowered into the ground that she thought she'd seen him off in the distance leaning against a tree. But she had convinced herself that she'd only imagined it. But just the idea that he had been in her thoughts had helped her overcome her grief.

"And I was saddened to hear about Grandpa Murphy, Randolph. By the time I got the word in Paris the funeral was over. I did talk to Gramma Mattie though and conveyed my condolences. He was a good man."

Randolph nodded. "Yes, he was."

The elevator door opened and together they walked toward her hotel room. A slight shiver began moving in the pit of her stomach and inched lower to an area that hadn't been touched in over two years. Sex between her and Steven had been good but not frequent due to his travels. It was as if tonight that part of her body recognized the man who had set it on fire years ago. The man who had branded it as his. And against her will, her body was reacting to his nearness. His very presence.

They stopped walking when they reached her hotel room. She opened the door and the two of them stepped inside. Jenna sighed, refusing to dirty what had been something special between them by giving in to overworked hormones. "Thanks, Randolph, for a special evening. And thanks again for agreeing to take on Johnny's case."

He looked down at the hand she was offering him before finally taking it into his. Holding it. Without saying anything, he leaned forward and touched his lips to hers.

The moment he did so, Jenna felt a weakness in her knees, the lower part of her body began to throb and a moan slipped from her throat. And moments later when he slipped his tongue into her mouth, she latched onto it, wanting it, needing it. It felt like coming home. He continued kissing her with a kiss that was tender and passionate.

Randolph slowly lifted his head and stared at Jenna. Her lips were moist and swollen from his kiss. He knew it was time to leave or else he would kiss her again. He was determined to take things slow. They needed to get to know each other again. They weren't the same two people no matter what feelings they may still have for each other.

He dropped his hand and took a step back. "Twelve years ago, Jenna, you thought you were doing the right thing by disappearing from my life. But even with the best of your intentions, you couldn't make me love Angela. Nor could you make me forget you."

Without saying anything else he turned and walked out of the door.

Twenty-three

The end of 1980 was drawing near. Richard Pryor was recovering after getting badly burned trying to freebase cocaine, and on the eighth day of December, former Beatle John Lennon was murdered outside his apartment, leaving numerous Beatles fans to mourn his death.

Noah Wainwright sat behind his desk and frowned at the man sitting across from him. "I hear what you're saying, Jim, but I refuse to give up my search. I have to know something one way or the other."

Jim Rogers sat back in his chair and gazed at Noah imploringly. "Look Noah, I understand your need to bring closure to the issue of whether or not Ross Fuller's daughter is still alive. However, if you're serious about becoming the next senator from Florida, you need to put more concentration into organizing a campaign."

Noah was quiet for a moment. Slowly he stood and walked across the room to look out of the window. It had been thirteen years since Ross had died in Vietnam. It seemed that lately he'd thought of his best friend often. The years he and Ross had shared while in school at Howard had been the best, and he knew if their places had been traded and he'd been the one killed in 'Nam, Ross would fulfill any promise he'd made to him or die trying.

Noah turned around. "Go ahead and organize the campaign and I'll do whatever you need me to do. But I won't give up my search. A part of me believes that thirteen-year-old Adrianna Fuller is alive somewhere and one day she will be found."

Later that evening after spending time helping Zachary with his homework and reading Noelle a story, Noah walked into his bedroom at the same time Leigh was coming out of the bathroom after taking a shower.

Closing the door behind him, he leaned against it and gazed at her. He loved her just as much now as he had when they'd been younger. Now he was thirty-seven and she was thirty-four and as far as he was concerned life had been good to them. They had been blessed with fourteen good years of marriage and two beautiful children.

After Vietnam, he had spent the rest of his military days in Texas. They had returned to Miami when Leigh had been pregnant with Noelle, and by his daughter's first birthday, he had gone into private practice. After practicing law for nearly seven years, he had gotten appointed to the office of city commissioner. Leigh worked as a guidance counselor in one of the Miami high schools and had been doing so for almost ten years. She loved her job as much as he loved his, but he had a burning desire to enter politics. And from recent polls, he had a very good chance of winning.

"The kids are in bed?"

Leigh's question recaptured his attention. "Yes, and I've closed up everything."

"Good."

He crossed the room to her and reached out to let his hand skim up her back. "You, okay? You seemed rather preoccupied at dinner. Is anything wrong?" he asked softly.

Closing her eyes, Leigh relaxed her body against his, reveling in his touch. His hand moving up and down her back was such a soothing motion. "I had Johnny on my mind. I hope Randolph is able to prove his innocence."

"If anyone can it will be Randolph."

"I hope so."

Noah pulled her closer to him. "You're going to have to have faith. It's unfortunate that Johnny has been locked up all this time, but at least now there's a chance he'll be set free."

Leigh nodded. "Thanks for being so supportive when you have a lot on your mind as well. I know that investigator's report wasn't the best news."

Noah sighed deeply. "No, it wasn't but I can't give up. You do understand, don't you? I know we could be doing other things with the money I'm paying out to that agency but—"

Leigh quickly placed a finger to Noah's lip. "You don't have to explain, Noah. Both you and Randolph are paying out a lot of money but one day it will be worth it. One day we will have Ross's daughter here where she belongs."

"You believe that, too, don't you?"

Leigh nodded. "Yes, I believe it because you believe it. And I know that Randolph believes it as well."

Noah sat down with Leigh on the bed. "Speaking of Randolph, from my conversation with him a few days ago I understand he's seen Jenna again. It will serve Angela right if the two of them get back together."

Leigh smiled. She and Ellie had taken bets already that they would. "Yes, it would, wouldn't it? I tried to warn you years ago that I thought Angela had the hots for Randolph but you didn't believe me."

"Yeah, and I regret I didn't take you more seriously. Angela has done nothing but cause Randolph grief and will only continue to do so. She's not above doing anything, not even using their son, to keep her claws in Randolph. I don't put anything past her. Sometimes I actually believe she has a mental problem with this obsession of hers."

Leigh thought that as well. She turned around to face Noah. "I don't want to talk about that woman any more."

Noah chuckled, and the rich sound of his chuckle was like a soft stroke to Leigh's skin. He reached out and touched her cheek with his fingertip. "What do you want to talk about?"

"Nothing."

"All right. There's something I'm interested in doing that doesn't require talking," he said.

The sensuousness in his voice sent shivers of desire up Leigh's spine. She reached out and placed her arms around his neck, bringing her lips close to his. "Show me."

Noah's lips closed over hers as he pulled her down onto the bed with him. They were through talking for the night.

January 1981

On January tenth, Randolph met with Johnny at the California State Penitentiary to discuss his case. What Randolph had told Jenna was true. For the first hour or so, Johnny's attitude had been guarded and filled with mistrust. However, with Jenna's presence, his attitude began thawing considerably, and he began giving Randolph a wealth of information to aid in his defense.

Randolph and Jenna spent all day with Johnny, then afterward they returned to the hotel where they were staying. They agreed to go out to dinner to discuss all the information that Johnny had given them.

"So do you think you have a solid case?" Jenna asked anxiously after they had placed the order for their meal.

"Yes, I believe I do, especially if everything Johnny said checks out. And if it does, we have to be prepared for the federal government's denial of the charges as well as their attempt to keep it under wraps. And more than anything, we can't make it appear that we are accusing the government of wrongdoings, but that our accusations are leveled against certain people within the government. My approach is to place enough doubt and suspicions in the jurors' minds, especially for what I'm pushing for."

"A retrial?"

"Yes."

That night after dinner they had gone back to their separate hotel rooms. Randolph had given her a chaste kiss on her lips before making sure she had entered her room. The next day they had met with Johnny again and it was obvious she was no longer needed since Johnny was beginning to warm up to Randolph. With the possibility of freedom within his reach, Johnny again provided Randolph with additional information.

Jenna's heart was saddened. Johnny had stopped being the happy-go-lucky guy she'd known years ago and it was obvious that nearly fourteen years of confinement had broken his spirit, totally killed his faith in the judicial system and the people who ran it. But now, listening to Randolph defend the government, she realized that the judicial system itself wasn't bad but the people who had been put in place to run it. Often they made the wrong decisions and were corrupted by the power. Randolph was determined to prove that J. Edgar Hoover, who'd been head of the FBI during the time of the Oakland raid, had been that type of individual.

Jenna received a call from Randolph two weeks later. He informed her that his investigators had uncovered some interesting things based on the information Johnny had provided, and that in a week he would be meeting with Governor Jerry Brown behind closed doors. She had not seen Randolph since that weekend she had joined him in California, but he contacted her at least once a week to provide an update on how things were going. During this particular phone call, he mentioned he would be in Atlanta on business and asked if he could look her up while in town.

Jenna had told him that he could.

Moving around the kitchen on Saturday morning, she had just finished placing Haywood's lunch on the table when the doorbell rang. Thinking it was probably Carol, a barefoot Jenna left the kitchen and crossed the carpeted floor to the door and opened it.

"Randolph!"

"Hi, Jenna."

Jenna swallowed, trying not to become hypnotized by Randolph's deep-sounding voice or the dark eyes looking at her. With forced calmness she inhaled . . . then exhaled before speaking. "I thought you weren't going to be in town until sometime next week."

His dark eyes probed hers as he responded. "I hadn't visited Atlanta in a while and thought I'd come up for the weekend. I hope I'm not visiting too early or catching you at a bad time."

"No, it's not too early nor is it a bad time. I'm just surprised to see you." She stepped aside. "Come in. I was just giving Haywood lunch."

Randolph came inside and glanced around. "This is a nice place."

"Thanks. It's just the right size for me and Haywood." No sooner had Jenna said the words then her daughter raced into the living room from the kitchen.

"Is Gramma here, Mommy?" When she saw it was a man who wasn't one of her uncles, Haywood stopped short. "Oh. Hello."

Randolph smiled down at the little girl who was dressed in a Cookie Monster T-shirt and a pair of jeans. "Hello. You must be Haywood."

The little girl smiled as she bobbed her head up and down. She seemed pleased that he knew her name. But then the expression on her face changed and got serious when it appeared she'd suddenly remembered something. "I'm not supposed to talk to strangers," she said, taking a step back to stand beside her mother.

Jenna smiled. Evidently it hadn't hit Haywood that she *had* spoken to the stranger. "He's not a stranger, Haywood. His name is Mr. Fuller and he's a friend of mine from school."

The little girl looked from her mother to Randolph then back at her mother again. "The first grade?" she asked in excitement.

Jenna chuckled. "No, not from first grade but from college."

"Oh," Haywood said, no longer impressed. "Would you like some of my lunch?"

Randolph smiled. "No, I had a big breakfast but thanks for asking."

"You're welcome. Good-bye." She raced back to the kitchen.

"She has a lot of energy," Randolph said, watching the little girl disappear from the room just as fast as she had entered it.

"Trust me, I know all about Haywood's energy. You said you didn't want lunch but can I interest you in a cup of coffee?"

Another smile curved his lips. "You don't have to twist my arm on that one."

"Good. You can join me in the kitchen or I can bring it out here to you, if you prefer."

"I'll join you in the kitchen."

• • •

Randolph kept up a steady conversation with Haywood as she ate lunch and Jenna prepared him a cup of coffee. The little girl never lacked for words. He chuckled, remembering that Trey had been the same way at her age.

"Do you have any little girls, Mr. Fuller?"

Haywood's question made him grin. "No, but I do have a son. His name is Trey and he's twelve."

"Twelve? He goes to a big kids school?"

"Yes, I guess you can say that," Randolph answered, laughing. He found Jenna's daughter very intelligent and a delight to talk to.

"It's nap time, Haywood," Jenna said a short while later. "Tell Mr. Fuller good-bye."

"Good-bye, Mr. Fuller. Will you be here when I wake up?"

Randolph looked at Jenna, saw how she was nervously gnawing at her bottom lip with her daughter's question and said, "I'd love to be here when you wake up but I wouldn't want to keep your mother from doing her work."

"She's done her work already. She did it while I was watching my cartoons this morning. Didn't you, Mommy?"

A number of conflicting emotions raced through Jenna. "Yes, I've done most of my chores but a mother's work is never done. Now go and take a nap, Haywood."

"Yes, ma'am."

A few seconds later Jenna and Randolph found themselves alone. Jenna cleared her throat. "Are there any new developments with Johnny's case?"

Randolph leaned against her kitchen counter. "None other than those I discussed with you the other day. I'm waiting for a call from the governor's office about when I can meet with him again."

"And you think you have enough information to convince him of the need for a new trial?"

"I hope so." He continued to look at her. "Am I making you nervous, Jenna?"

She turned away from him and picked their empty coffee cups off the table. "What makes you think that?"

"By the way you're acting." He walked over to her. "Do you want me to leave?"

Jenna gazed up at him for a long moment, not sure what she wanted. The weekend in California had been tense except when they had been with Johnny. Although she had tried to play it down, the attraction she felt for Randolph was still strong. She wondered why she was fighting it. There was no reason she should be placing barriers between them. He was single. So was she.

"Jenna?"

He reached out and touched her arm. A huge mistake. The heat from his touch when it made contact with her bare skin made her entire body tingle. She took a step toward him, which brought her almost toe-to-toe with him. Too late, she realized what taking that step meant.

"I don't want to rush into anything, Randolph," she said softly when she saw him lowering his head toward hers.

"I don't want to rush into anything, either," he murmured, his voice vibrating against her lips. "So let's take things slow . . . and easy. Just relax, Jen."

All right," she said, parting her lips for him.

Randolph kissed her, taking her mouth slow and easy as he gently reached out and positioned her hips closer to his body. His tongue moved around her mouth to reacquaint itself with the honeyed taste of her, tantalizing her mouth in the process, and making a moan sound deep from within her throat.

This is Randolph, her body seemed to say. *And he's back.* He had kissed her before, that first night he had taken her to dinner in Virginia. But in California, he had held back. But now he was giving her what she wanted. She felt the pressure of his erection, hard . . . real hard . . . pressing against her. The feel of it made her arch into him even more.

Randolph gripped her hips closer and slowly began moving, grinding against her with the same rhythm his tongue was using in her mouth. Slow and easy.

Two years of going without physical release was heating up Jenna's blood and it rushed fast and furious through every part of her body. Her tongue dueled with his, tasting, teasing, tempting. And his body grinding against hers wasn't helping matters. Full sexual awareness for him flooded her head and her mind, replacing the emptiness she'd been feeling.

When he slowly pulled his mouth away from hers, she moaned in disappointment and frustration.

"It's okay, baby," Randolph murmured against her lips. "There's more. As much as you want."

The husky whisper in his voice heated Jenna's insides. Her breath got caught in her lungs when she met his gaze and she saw desire and tenderness in his eyes.

"Come on. Let's go into the living room and talk." Taking her hand in his Randolph led Jenna out of the kitchen and to the sofa. He started to sit with her in his lap, then thought better of it. He didn't want her daughter to wake up and come upon them in such an intimate way. Besides, he needed to get a few things straight with her and the less he touched her, the better. When Jenna sat next to him on the sofa he took her hands in his.

"Do you remember that day we spent on Glendale Shores, vowing our love for each other over my great-grandmother's Bible?"

Jenna held his gaze. "Yes."

"And do you remember the pledge we made?"

Her voice was barely a notch above a whisper when she answered. "Yes. But so much has happened since then, Randolph. We aren't the same people."

He gave her hand a gently squeeze. "No, we aren't. But we owe it to ourselves to try and recapture what we had, regardless of anything else."

"Regardless of Angela?"

His quiet sigh echoed in the room and his hold on her hand tightened. "My life ended with Angela two years ago and as far as our marriage, there never really was one. Our only connection is Trey. He was the reason I married her, the only reason. You of all people should know that. I didn't want to marry her although everyone kept telling me it was the right thing to do; and even though you gave up everything we had just so I could. And I didn't want a baby; least of all a baby from her. But all it took was one look at Trey when he was born, and that fatherly love hit me like a ton of bricks. I couldn't imagine my life without him. He instantly became my heart, a part of what I'd been missing in my life. A purpose."

He decided not to add that from that day forward, Angela had used his love for his child to keep him in a loveless marriage for ten years. "But what I felt for Angela was another matter all together," he said quietly. "As far as I was concerned there was no purpose for our marriage. I couldn't love her. I didn't even try. I told her up front that our marriage would be in name only. That meant we would not share a bed and our only interest would be Trey."

"That wasn't fair to her," Jenna said silently.

"For nearly nine years I thought so too, and felt bad as hell about it. I felt guilty that I was married to one woman but still in love with another. And at one point I had decided I owed it to Trey to make things work between his mother and me, especially since Angela went to the extreme to paint a picture for our son that we were so much in love."

Randolph's eyes narrowed as he continued. "But then I discovered she was sleeping around and had been for a while. And later I found out the truth about what she'd done that time she and I slept together, while at Howard and then felt she got just what she deserved. That day you found us in bed together I had been drugged."

Jenna's eyes widened in shock. "Drugged!"

"Yes. A few years ago I ran into Kathy Taylor, Angela's best friend who had also been her roommate in law school. After quite a few drinks she got loose lips and told me the whole story. Including the fact that Angela wasn't the virgin she had claimed to be. It seems while at Bronson she screwed practically anything in pants and even got pregnant and had an abortion. I verified everything Kathy said by hiring my own team of investigators, so it wasn't just idle gossip I got from Kathy that night. To this day Angela doesn't know that I know the truth. But finding out about that wasn't why I finally divorced her.

The reason I divorced her was because I found her in bed with another man. I had ignored her adulterous behavior until that day. Finding another man in bed with her under my roof was the last straw."

Jenna shook her head sadly. "She never deserved you. But your son did. He still does, Randolph."

"Yes, and Trey has me. He always will have me. Trey means everything to me. I love him very much." Randolph brought their joined hands to his lips and kissed them. "I want things for us, Jenna, but I don't want to rush things, and I want to make sure you want what I want as well. I suggest we take things slow, like we did in the beginning at Howard and get to know each other again. I want to get to know Haywood and I want you to get to know Trey. Will you think about us doing that?"

Jenna looked up at him. She still had feelings for him but she wanted to be sure that renewing a relationship was the best thing for everyone, especially their children. "Yes, I'll think about it."

"Fair enough."

"And you won't put any pressure on me?"

Randolph smiled. "What kind of pressures?"

Her words came out in a throaty whisper when she said. "Pressure of the worse kind and you know what I'm talking about."

A deep smile curved his lips. "Yes, I've got a pretty good idea. How about letting me take you out tonight? A movie?"

Jenna nodded. "All right. There shouldn't be a problem getting Mom to watch Haywood."

"I want Haywood to come, too."

Jenna lifted her dark brow. "Do you know what kind of movie we're talking about then?"

"Yes. But I want to spend time with her and I want her to spend time with me. Is that all right?"

Jenna smiled. "Yes, that's perfectly all right."

That night the three of them went to dinner and then to a movie, Disney's new animated motion picture, *The Fox and the Hound*. Afterward, Randolph took them to an ice cream parlor for Haywood's favorite, chocolate-chip cookie dough.

After Jenna had undressed Haywood and gotten her into bed, she rejoined Randolph in the living room on the sofa. "Haywood enjoyed herself a lot tonight, Randolph. I appreciate you including her in our plans."

He smiled as she came and sat down next to him on the sofa. "I will always include her, Jenna. She is a part of you and I know it's a package deal. I wouldn't want it any other way." He pulled her into his arms. "I'd like to go see your mother tomorrow. How is she?"

Jenna sighed. "Mom's doing fine. She had a hard time after Dad's death and moving here to Atlanta was the best thing for her. The boys keep her busy since none of them have decided to get married. She's hoping that Haywood won't be her only grandchild." After a few moments she said, "And how is Gramma Mattie?"

He leaned back against the sofa.

"She's doing fine. She does a lot of charity work to keep busy. A lot of her relatives have sold their land to developers on Hilton Head and for a long time that bothered her but she refused to sell Glendale Shores."

"And I don't blame her. It's her legacy as well as yours."

Randolph pulled her closer into his arms. "Yes, and Trey's as well. I just hope he appreciates it when he's old enough to inherit it. Angela thinks Gramma Mattie ought to sell it and take the money. She doesn't understand or appreciate the value of something being handed down through generations—especially for black people. There's little we have that we can call ours and can still hold onto."

"And how are your grandparents, Robert and Julia?"

"They are fine. Grandmother Julia had a hard time adjusting to Ross's death and had a light stroke in the seventies. But now she's doing fine and is as feisty as ever, and still refuses to see Angela's true colors. She's hoping for a reconciliation although I've told her countless times it won't happen. Granddad still comes into the office at least twice a week although he's officially retired." Randolph chuckled. "I think he does it just to get away from Grandmother Julia for a while."

He checked his watch. "It's time that I leave. Will you walk me to the door?"

"Sure," Jenna said, getting to her feet. "How long will you be in Atlanta?"

"Through Tuesday. Then I'm flying to Philadelphia to meet with someone who used to be an agent for the FBI. He's willing to testify as to what the FBI was doing against various rights movements in the sixties, especially the Panthers."

"Won't it be dangerous for him to talk?"

"He feels he has nothing to lose since he's dying of cancer."

"Oh, how sad."

"Yeah, but he won't be dying in vain if he knows something that can free Johnny." When they reached the door Randolph pulled her into his arms. "I'd like to spend as much time as I can with you and Haywood while I'm here. For the next three weeks I'm going to be extremely busy trying to put together enough evidence for Governor Brown to review. But sometime during that time I'll be returning to Virginia to spend time with Trey. Due to my busy schedule I try to do that every chance I get."

Jenna nodded. "You will keep me abreast of how Johnny's doing, won't you?"

"Of course." He pulled her into his arms and kissed her in a way that was meant to give her pleasurable memories for that night and a few nights to come.

Twenty-four

February 1981

Randolph spent the next five weeks working extremely hard on Johnny's case. He met with Marvin Crews, a man who'd been a FBI agent for thirty years before retiring at the end of the seventies. He spent a lot of time between California and Virginia and included pit stops in Atlanta whenever he could to see Jenna and Haywood.

After meeting with Governor Brown he filed the necessary papers with the courts asking for a retrial. Word had come to him a week later in Virginia that a new trial would be granted. He leaned back in his office chair and released a huge sigh. They had succeeded and moved past one hurdle but there would be others. News of Johnny's new trial would put the FBI on notice and they would be doing anything and everything to prepare for it. It wouldn't be the first time that a former Panther member claimed the FBI had framed them.

Randolph's thoughts were interrupted when Clara rang him. "Yes, Clara, what is it?"

"Mrs. Fuller is here to see you."

"My grandmother?"

"No sir, your ex-wife."

Randolph frowned. He could hear Angela in the background taking offense at being referred to as his ex-wife. "Did you tell her I'm busy and asked not to be disturbed?"

"Yes sir, I tried."

Frustrated, Randolph rubbed a hand across his face. "All right, then. Please send her in."

No sooner had Clara opened his office door than Angela came storming in. "How could you!" she all but screamed. "How could you take back up with that woman?!"

It didn't take Randolph long to figure out what woman Angela was talking about. Evidently she had found out that he was seeing Jenna—not that he had been trying to keep it a secret—but he wasn't in the mood for one of her tantrums. He stood.

"You have no right to question what I do or who I see, Angela. For some reason you can't get it into your head that we're no longer married."

Tears, whether fake or real, were in her eyes. "But I'm the mother of your son. Doesn't that mean anything?"

Randolph's eyes narrowed. "Yes, it means you're the mother of my son and nothing more."

"Trey wants the three of us to be together."

"I would give my son anything he wants but never that. You and I are finished. In truth, there was never an 'us.' It was all lies from the beginning."

"It wasn't my fault that I got pregnant!"

Randolph walked from around his desk, muttering a curse under his breath. His temper had reached the boiling point. "You think not? Well, I know otherwise. Two years ago I happened to run into the woman who was your best friend and former roommate at Howard. Kathy Taylor. You do remember her, don't you? She got drunk and spilled her guts about your abortion, which I later verified with my own private investigator, so don't waste time denying it. She also told me about what you did to me that day after I had gotten the news about Ross. She told me how she was the one to supply you with the speed to put into my drink."

Shock flashed across Angela's face. "Surely you don't believe that. She lied."

Randolph clenched his teeth to keep from cursing. "No, she did not. She knew too much about it and after listening to her, it all made sense. Grief-stricken or not, I would not have made love to you with a ten-foot pole unless I'd been drugged."

"No, that's not true. You've always wanted me like I've always wanted you."

Randolph looked at her like she was crazy. "I've never wanted you. I've always loved Jenna and you were engaged to marry Ross."

"But I would not have married Ross. I would have found some way out of the engagement. I never loved him. I always wanted you."

A frown marred Randolph's features. He was taken aback by her words. Although Kathy Taylor had mentioned that very thing to him, he had refused to believe that part of her conversation. "What are you saying?"

"Just what you heard. Ross didn't love me so I have no regrets for not being in love with him either. You were the one I loved and wanted any would fantasize about you all the time," she said like he should be appreciative that she had done so. "My only regret is that your grandmother felt I was more suited to be Ross's wife than yours. Otherwise, the two of us would have been together from the start."

"No, we would not have been," he stated in violent protest. "I would never have allowed my grandmother to choose my wife. Don't you understand I was in love with Jenna? In my heart, my mind and my soul, I was already married to her: That's why I could never bring myself to physically touch you all those years we were together."

"But you were married to me!"

"Legally yes, but in every other way possible I still belonged to Jenna. How could you think that you could replace her when she meant everything to me?"

"But I did replace her," she said haughtily. "I planned everything and got just what I wanted. Ross's death was unfortunate but it came at an opportune time."

Randolph became livid. "Get out of my office, Angela, and don't come back. Our only connection will be Trey. Only then can you contact me and only by phone. I don't want to see you unless it's when I come to pick up my son."

Angela's eyes narrowed to slits. "I'm going to tell him what you're doing. I'm going to tell him that you're allowing another woman to come between us and because of her the three of us can't be a family."

Randolph's face turned to stone. "You go do that and while you're at it also tell him about all the men you've slept with while married to me. You can also tell him how you drugged me into sleeping with you when I was already engaged to marry someone else. There is no way in hell that I'd ever get back with you. Now get out of here before I have security throw you out! The sight of you sickens me!"

"You turn your back on me and I'll see to it that you lose your son. Count on it." Angela then walked out of the office, slamming the door behind her.

Randolph rubbed his hand across his face, hating the day Angela Douglass had come into his life.

Jenna, Leigh and Ellie entered the courtroom that was filled to capacity. As Jenna took her seat she glanced toward the front at Randolph. After the courts had made a decision to grant Johnny a new trial, Randolph had worked endlessly, putting together facts, investigating leads and interviewing potential witnesses. She hadn't seen him in the past two weeks and looking at him now, she could see how much time he had put into Johnny's case. Although he was meticulously dressed, the lines of strain around his eyes indicated he was tired, but the sparkle in them indicated he was ready for a good fight.

Ever since he had shown up that Saturday at her house, he had made occasional visits back to Atlanta to see her and Haywood. On these trips he would take them out to dinner, to a movie or just spend time with them. One night, while her mother had kept Haywood, Randolph had taken Jenna to a seventies night club, reliving the music, dress and food of the only decade they had spent apart since first meeting at Howard. They had danced the night away to all the disco sounds. She always enjoyed the time they spent together. Although the attraction between them was very strong, he never pushed for anything beyond friendship. But the kisses he would give her when it was time for him to leave left her breathless and yearning for more. But they had agreed to take things slow and get to know each other all over again. And because he'd been spending so much time working on Johnny's defense, they were taking things even slower.

"Courtrooms always give me the creeps," Leigh whispered to Jenna and Ellie.

Jenna nodded, knowing just how she felt. According to what she had read in the papers, the jury selection had taken almost a week but there they sat assembled, five women and seven men, all of them white. Randolph had told her that he would not be wasting his time trying to paint a picture of the Black Panthers as being a bunch of pure and innocent Boy Scouts. What he intended was to hit hard and heavy, specifically detailing how the FBI targeted the group on several occasions to destroy them, and how in Johnny's particular case there was no physical evidence linking him with the crime. And the one witness they had was flimsy at best.

A lump formed in Jenna's throat when Randolph happened to glance their way. He smiled at everyone but when his eyes met hers they spoke volumes and were filled with desire and longing. His atten-

tion was pulled back when the bailiff indicated the arrival of the judge
and asked everyone in the courtroom to rise.

The new trial of the State of California and the federal government
versus Johnny Lane was underway.

The prosecution, all federal attorneys, tried to paint a picture of
Johnny as being a college dropout, a young man full of hatred against
whites and the war; a man who had left DC and had come to California looking for trouble. They made him look like a militant, a radical,
an extremist and a suspected communist. Their testimony lasted all
that day and part of the next two days. The witnesses they called were
police officers, informants and federal agents who had been involved
in the raid that night. The only eyewitness, an agent by the name of
Frank Miles, testified that he saw Johnny pull the trigger on the gun
that killed federal agent James Johns. He further testified that Johnny
would have killed him, too, had he not wrestled the gun from his
hands.

Jenna had watched as Johnny sat there listening attentively, occasionally taking notes, but not showing any emotion at what Frank
Miles or the other agents were saying.

On the fourth day the defense took over and she got to see Randolph in action. He painted another picture, one totally different than
the one the federal attorneys had painted. He told the jury how the
Panthers had started out as a group of intelligent black men, disen-
chanted with police brutality in their community, and who banded
together to provide protection in their neighborhoods. He told about
the covert FBI COINTELPRO activities that had been aimed at
destroying the Black Panther Party at all cost. He called several past
FBI informants to the stand who told how J. Edgar Hoover was
obsessed with destroying the group, even to the point of deliberately
sending in informants whose sole purpose was to cause friction within
the group. But the surprise came on the fifth day when Randolph
called a white woman by the name of Holly Bell to the stand. She was
the wife of a federal agent who'd also gotten killed in the Oakland raid.

Crying through most of her testimony, Holly Bell told everyone in the courtroom about the letters her husband had written, most of them to appease his conscience regarding the various things Hoover had ordered him to do against certain groups of people. But what Randolph wanted to hit on, and he did so extremely well, was the fact that in one of Oliver Bell's letters to his wife, he told her that his partner, Agent Frank Miles, felt intense hatred for another agent by the name of James Johns.

The prosecution objected, stating Mrs. Bell's testimony was sheer speculation. However the judge overruled their objections and allowed Oliver Bell's letters to be entered as admissible evidence, thus planting a seed of doubt in everyone's mind since the only eyewitness could also be a suspect.

Randolph presented testimony after testimony, letting his skill as an attorney shine through. He showed how the FBI distorted information and depicted them as an agency run by an obsessed tyrant hell-bent on destroying the Black Panther movement, even if it meant sacrificing some of his own men in the process and using unethical and illegal means to do so.

What really was an eye-opener was former FBI Agent Marvin Crews's testimony. He was a man dying of cancer and didn't want to go to hell because of past deeds. He provided in-depth testimony that indicated Johns had become a loose cannon and a decision was made to take him out. Who made the decision was never clear although there was open speculation. Crews's testimony, as well as his taped conversation with other agents, proved that Johns was not supposed to leave the raid alive. Unfortunately, Johnny Lane became the perfect patsy. Crews's story painted Johnny as a victim just like Johns.

On the ninth day Randolph rested his case, hoping that he had created doubt of Johnny's guilt in everyone's mind. But still it wasn't clear just how the jury would vote. The jury deliberated for three days, asking to re-review certain evidence and testimony. On the fourth day they were ready to present their verdict.

They found Johnny innocent of the charge of first-degree murder of a federal agent.

Twenty-five

Johnny wept like a baby. After nearly fourteen years of being locked behind bars he was free to live the rest of his life as he chose.

The federal attorneys and agents, unhappy with the verdict, stormed out of the courtroom while a mass of reporters flooded in. Flashbulbs went off and microphones were shoved in Randolph and Johnny's faces. It had been a case that had drawn national attention. Randolph Fuller had set a precedent for fairness in this country, proving that every individual was guaranteed certain rights and the government had been put in place to protect those rights, not to distort or destroy them. And as Randolph had pointed out, no one man should have had that much absolute power. During his reign as FBI director, Hoover had held more power than the United States president and had maliciously abused it.

After pulling himself together, Johnny answered the reporters' questions then thanked his family and friends for standing by him for fourteen long years and for believing in him. He also thanked Randolph for taking the time to handle his case and knew that no amount of money could ever pay him for literally saving his life.

Not waiting to get the few possessions he had accumulated during his years behind bars, Johnny wanted to get out of California and return home to Alabama. Everyone understood and less than four hours after being set free, Johnny Lane boarded a plane for Birmingham.

That night Leigh, Ellie and Jenna took Randolph out to celebrate his victory in the courtroom. Later Randolph drove Jenna back to her hotel. She was to fly back home in the morning after having been gone nearly two weeks. Her mother was keeping Haywood and although she talked to her every night, she missed her daughter like crazy.

Randolph walked Jenna to her room and asked if he could come inside. When the door closed behind them they stood staring at each other. Jenna noticed the lines of strain she'd seen around his eyes at the start of the trial were gone. She reached up and caressed his cheek. "Thanks for saving Johnny's life, Randolph. I'm so proud of you. I knew you—"

He didn't let her finish. He leaned down and gently captured her lips with his, kissing her like a man starved for his next breath and for hers. Slowly, meticulously, he made love to her mouth, nipping, sucking and stroking; gently at first then with more force, more desperation and less control. She emitted little sounds from deep within her throat as her body gloried in his touch, craving it and wanting it with a passion.

When his mouth relinquished hers, he placed butterfly kisses along her neck and jaw as he held her close to him, not wanting to let her go as he savored her softness, her scent and everything else that was uniquely hers. For twelve long years he had gone without her, but everything there was to know about her returned whenever he held her in his arms. He remembered how her body would feel pressed against his; and just how well the two of them fit together.

Randolph pulled her closer and kissed her again, teasing, tasting. He left her shudder in his arms, which spiked his desire for her even more. When he released her mouth an exasperated sigh escaped her lips.

"I don't want slow and easy anymore, Randolph," she said silkily, lifting her chin a stubborn notch.

He looked down into the depths of her eyes. "What do you want?"

She pressed her body against his as a slow, wanton smile played around the corners of her mouth. She reached out and boldly cupped him through the material of his pants. She felt his hardness, exulted in it. There had always been complete honesty between them. They had always been candid and blunt with each other about what they wanted. She couldn't help but be that way with him now. "This. I want this."

His gaze burned with desire. "And how do you want it?"

Jenna smiled, remembering the many times in the past they had made love, the many positions they'd used and the countless hours of pleasure. "Any way you want to give it to me," she whispered, placing her arms around his neck and molding her body more firmly against his.

"I hope you mean that," Randolph whispered, kissing her again and picking her up into his arms. He carried her across the room to the bed and placed her in the middle. After removing her clothes and then his, he joined her there, pulling her close into his arms and taking the time to reacquaint himself with her body.

"I missed you so much and I've hungered for this as well, Jenna," he said, his voice raspy, his hands attentive as he touched her everywhere.

She felt hot at his touch as he stirred within her a primitive need, an urgent demand. She had almost forgotten how responsive her body was to his, just how receptive. The heat in her reached a feverish peak. She wanted and needed him.

He needed her as well. It had been a long time. Too long. He kissed her. She kissed him back. Longer and deeper. And then he pulled her under him and automatically her body opened to him, as an overwhelming need to be joined with him took over her. The ache between her legs throbbed, wanting him.

"Randolph . . ." she whispered his name when he broke off their kiss.

He straddled her hips, and meeting her gaze and holding, he gently pushed her legs apart with his knee and entered her slowly, savoring the moment. "Ahh, this is home," he murmured as he continued to ease himself inside her, the warmth of her body surrounding him, holding him, clutching him. He continued pressing downward, feeling the very depth of her and going there. He lifted her hips into his hands, loving the feel of her muscles holding him inside of her. He knew he ran the risk of climaxing inside of her without even moving an inch.

He suddenly remembered that he wasn't wearing a rubber and wondered if she was on any type of birth control. He was willing to take his chances, doubting that he would be able to pull out now even if she said she wasn't. He wanted to release his sperm into her, actually wanted to feel it jet into her womb. But she deserved to have a say in the matter.

"Jenna?"

"Umm?" she answered, barely able to get the word out.

"I'm not wearing a rubber."

She didn't respond for the longest time before she said, "And I'm not on the pill."

"Do you want me to pull out?" he whispered, penetrating deeper and hoping like hell that she didn't.

"No," she breathed, wrapping her legs around him to prove her point. He had filled her so deeply it wouldn't take much to push her over the edge. "I want you. All of you, Randolph."

He shut his eyes as her words boosted his primal urges. His body began moving inside of her, as twelve years of holding back took over. She had no idea what she was in for.

Dipping his head he captured her lips as he continued to stroke her body with his, rising to a feverish pitch of desire. Filling her, thrusting in and out, loving the whimpering sounds she made. The feel of being inside of her inflamed him and his body tensed. "Jenna . . ."

Her body erupted into pleasure the same time his did, the force of his release flooding her womb. They trembled in pleasure, rocked into oblivion, taking and giving, and relishing being back in each other's arms. Pushing to the back of their minds the twelve years they'd been separated, they silently acknowledged the power of what they shared and thanked God for bringing them back together.

Hours later, Jenna awoke from a deep, satisfied sleep. Her body was pressed up against Randolph's, curved perfectly next to his. When she felt his fingertips move across her arm she knew he was awake, too.

"Now that the trial is over I want to spend more time with you and Haywood, Jenna," he said huskily. "I want you to get to know Trey and I want him to get to know you and Haywood."

Jenna turned toward him and smiled. "I'd like that, Randolph," she said softly as tears misted her eyes.

"It's going to be a challenge, baby, since you're in Atlanta and I'm in Richmond, but I'm willing to do whatever has to be done for us to be together."

"Me, too." She shivered, partly from desire and partly from the real-ization that they were back together after twelve years and wanted to stay that way. Although they had grown into two different people over the years, one thing had stayed constant.

Their love.

Twenty-Six

The morning sun flowed through the kitchen window as Randolph sat at the table and gazed lovingly at his son who was piling pancakes and eggs onto his plate. He knew, like everyone else in the family, that he spoiled the boy. But then for the past twelve years Trey had been the only thing making his life complete.

"Have you packed everything you're going to need?"

Trey glanced up at him, smiling excitedly. "Yes, sir. It's gonna be cool seeing Ma Mattie again. Do you think this time she'll let me take the canoe out all by myself?"

Randolph smiled. "We'll see. She worries a lot so don't be disap-pointed if she doesn't." He had made plans to go to Glendale Shores for the weekend. What he hadn't told his son was that Jenna and Hay-wood would also be there. He felt it was time for Trey to get to know the woman he planned to marry one day. Soon . . . if he had his way. But Jenna thought it was best to wait and give Trey and Haywood time to accept their relationship. Haywood had already accepted it and had told him many times how much she liked him and wanted him for her new daddy.

Trey's attitude regarding his relationship with Jenna was an entirely different story. Thanks to Angela, he felt nothing but resentment for a woman he had never met, and had refused to meet Jenna although Randolph had told him about her. Therefore, he'd decided to take another approach.

A few hours later, they were getting off the ferry at Glendale Shores.

Plans had been made for the four of them to stay in the home he had inherited from his parents. Jenna and Haywood had come up the night before to spend time on the island with his grandmother. Gramma Mattie had taken to Haywood the first time he and Jenna had brought her to visit and thought of her as a great-granddaughter. Now that his grandmother lived alone, Randolph tried to visit the island every chance he got. Usually he came alone to rest and relax. At other times he'd brought Jenna with him. It was during those times when the two of them stayed in the cottage alone that they remembered happier times, like the week they had spent on the island while in college.

"Can we go fishing, Dad?"

Trey's question interrupted Randolph's thoughts. He smiled. His son reminded him so much of himself at his age—full of life and energetic. But then at twelve he'd had an older brother that he'd adored that he had spent time with. As usual whenever he thought of his brother Ross, a thick lump formed in Randolph's throat. It had been nearly thirteen years and yet the pain of losing the one individual that he'd considered his best friend as well as his brother was still raw— just like it had happened yesterday. And it still bothered him to know that Ross's child—his niece—was somewhere out there. He and Noah had hired some of the best people in the business to find her, yet they had discovered nothing. However, they would continue looking, for the rest of their lives if necessary.

Pulling up in front of the house he noted Jenna's car the same time Trey did. "Whose car is that, Dad?" Trey asked curiously.

"A special friend, whom I would like you to meet," he said, looking at his son.

Trey nodded but Randolph could already feel tension radiating from him. Trey was not one to hide his feelings about anything and it was evident that he didn't like the idea of someone else intruding on their time together. Also, it was evident that Trey had an idea who that someone was.

Randolph decided it was time again to talk to his son so he could be prepared. Fully prepared. He and Jenna loved each other. They always had. Their love was evident for anyone to see whenever they were together. Haywood had gotten used to the open display of affection they shared. Trey would not be used to it. In fact Randolph couldn't remember the last time Trey had seen him with a woman that he'd genuinely liked. Usually their time had been spent together, just the two of them.

Bringing the car to a stop Randolph turned to his son. "There are two people inside that I want you to meet, Trey."

"She's here, isn't she?"

Randolph could hear the deep resentment in his son's voice. "Who are you talking about, son?"

Trey turned angry eyes to him. "That lady Mom told me about. The one who is keeping you from marrying Mom again."

"That's not true. Jenna is not keeping me from marrying your mother again. Even if I didn't have Jenna in my life, I would not remarry your mother, Trey."

Randolph leaned back against the seat, inwardly cursing Angela for putting such ideas in their son's head. "I know it's hard for you to understand, but the only connection your mother and I have and will ever have is you."

"But you used to be married to her which means you had to have loved her once."

Randolph wished he could tell Trey the truth that he had never loved Angela. His heart had always belonged to Jenna, and if Angela hadn't been so deceitful, he would be married to Jenna today.

"Times change and people change, Trey. Your mother and I aren't the same people. She has her friends now and I have mine."

"But she wants to get back with you so we can be a family," Trey said as a sob caught in his throat. "I want you and Mom to be together, just like before. I don't want you to want to be with that other lady."

Randolph reached out and placed his hand on his son's shoulder. "You love me, don't you, Trey?"

Trey looked at him with misty eyes. "Yes, sir."

"Do you want me to be happy?"

"Yes, sir. But weren't you happy with me and Mom?"

Randolph sighed. Trey had a habit of answering a question with a question. Randolph knew he had to choose his words carefully. "Having you as my son has always made me happy, Trey, and that's the way it will continue to be. But things have been different with your mom and me. It has nothing to do with you but everything to do with us. Sometimes after getting married things just don't work out between a man and a woman like they should and they both become unhappy together. Pretty soon they discover they can be happier with someone else." Randolph wondered if Trey understood what he was trying to say.

"You don't love Mom anymore, do you?" Trey asked his father stiffly.

Randolph thought over Trey's question and knew he could and would not lie. "No, I don't."

Time seemed to stretch between them. Randolph knew his words, blatant and truthful, hurt Trey. Because of Angela, he'd been holding out for something that would never happen.

As they gazed at each other, father and son, Randolph saw Trey blink several times to fight the tears that threatened to fall, not wanting to cry in front of him. "I know what I've told you is a lot for you to understand, Trey. But one day you will grow up and fall in love with someone special, and when that time comes you'll know how it is to be really happy."

Trey nodded slowly. He glanced down at his hand then met his father's gaze once again. "Do you love her?"

"Yes, I love Jenna," he said, looking his son squarely in the eye. "I love her very much."

Trey hung his head and began toying with a button on his shirt. "You love her little girl, too?" he asked, raising his chin.

"Yes, I love her, too. But I also love you. You're my son. Don't ever think that I don't love you."

Trey caught his lower lip in his teeth before saying, "Yes, sir." He then threw himself into his father's arms to get the reassuring hug that he needed.

●　●　●

Jenna stood at the window and looked out. She'd heard Randolph's car pull up a while ago, yet he and his son were still outside, sitting in the car, no doubt discussing her. Randolph had shared with her the idea that Angela had allowed to take root in the child's head, the notion that she and Randolph would get back together again, and because of it, his son resented Jenna or any person that he saw as a threat to his parents' reconciliation. Angela had been wrong to try to use Randolph's love for his son as a way to hold onto him. In her selfish obsession to keep Randolph, she had totally overlooked her child's emotional well-being.

It had been two months since that night they had made love again, the night he'd won a victory for Johnny. Since then, he had come to Atlanta on several occasions to see her and Haywood. He had built a very solid, very close relationship with Haywood and she wanted to do likewise with Trey but the boy's feelings for her stood in the way. More than anything, she wanted Randolph's son to like her and to accept her place in his father's life. So far he hadn't done that but she had hoped this weekend would be different. She wanted him to get to know her and to see how happy his father was with her. She wanted him to see that she wasn't the monster Angela had probably made her out to be. She knew she couldn't convince him of all those things overnight, not even over a weekend. But it had to start somewhere and at some time.

"Mommy?"

Jenna turned toward the sound of Haywood's voice. She was standing in the middle of the room. "When is Mr. Fuller going to come inside?"

Jenna smiled. "In a moment, sweetheart. He's talking to his son, Trey."

Haywood nodded. "If Mr. Fuller becomes my daddy will Trey become my brother?"

Jenna smiled. "Yes, sort of. He would be your stepbrother."

Haywood smiled as if the idea of having a stepbrother pleased her. At that moment Jenna heard the sound of the car door closing. She glanced out the window again. Randolph and Trey were walking toward the house and Randolph had his arms around his son's shoul-

ders as they walked. She took a deep breath. At least he wasn't holler-
ing, screaming and refusing to come inside, she thought.

Jenna and Haywood turned simultaneously toward the door when
Randolph opened it. Jenna slanted Randolph a nervous glance and he
smiled and nodded, sending her a silent message that things were
okay. Her eyes moved to Trey. He was standing next to his father, tall
for someone only twelve. And he looked so much like Randolph that it
almost brought tears to Jenna's eyes. There could never be any doubt
in anyone's mind that this was Randolph's son.

Drawing in a deep breath she crossed the room to them. "Hi. The
two of you are just in time for lunch," she said casually, flashing him
her warmest smile. She looked down at Trey who was eyeing her war-
ily. "You must be Trey."

Eyes, duplicates of Randolph's, looked back at her. "Yes, ma'am.
I'm Trey."

"And I'm Jenna." Jenna knew it was important not to push too much
on Trey too soon. She started to open her mouth to ask if he was hungry and wanted something to eat when all of a sudden Haywood raced
over from across the room.

"And I'm Haywood." Not waiting for Trey to acknowledge her presence, she moved next to him and took his hand in hers, linking her fingers with his.

It was as if upon seeing Trey for the first time she had automatically
decided he would be her friend. From the expression on Trey's face it
was apparent that he was surprised by Haywood's action. Surprised
yet accepting. At least he hadn't snatched his hand back.

Randolph cleared his throat, breaking the silence that had engulfed
the room and everyone glanced up at him. "How about if we have
lunch on the boat?" He knew how much Trey loved to go boating. But
in the past it had always been just the two of them.

"I think that's a wonderful idea," Jenna said softly. "What do you
think, Trey? Is that okay with you?"

Instead of meeting her gaze he looked over at his father then back at
her. It was evident that he was dealing with his feelings. "It's okay with
me," he said quietly.

Jenna let out a silent sigh of relief. "Good. I'll get started making lunch."

Randolph placed his arms around his son's shoulder. "And you can go back out to the car with me to get our things."

"Can I come, too?" Haywood asked, still holding onto Trey's hand.

Randolph chuckled. "Yes, you can come and help but you're going to need both hands," he said, thinking Trey probably could only take so much of the little girl's adoring attention.

"Okay," she said enthusiastically, finally letting go of Trey's hand.

Randolph inwardly smiled. The look of relief on Trey's face was priceless. "Let's go then." Opening the door the three of them walked outside, momentarily leaving Jenna alone in the house.

Later that evening, Jenna stood on the porch. She had put Haywood to bed earlier and now Randolph and Trey were putting away the checker game they'd been playing for the last hour or so.

They had had dinner at the big house with Gramma Mattie. She had been elated to see her great-grandson and from the way Trey had hugged the older woman, it was apparent he'd been elated seeing her as well.

Stretching, Jenna thought about their sleeping arrangements for the night. Normally, when Randolph came to Atlanta to visit, he would make up the couch, however once Haywood had drifted off to sleep, he would find his way to her bed and stay until morning, right before it was time for Haywood to wake. Jenna knew Trey wouldn't be that gullible to think they hadn't slept together. Therefore, tonight when Randolph made up the sofa, he would actually have to sleep on it.

She turned at the sound of the screen door opening. Randolph stood in the doorway with a blanket in his hand. "Do you want to take a walk?" he asked in a deep husky voice.

Jenna nodded. Since the time he had arrived, they hadn't kissed and actually hadn't even touched in consideration of Trey's feelings regarding their relationship. "Where's Trey?"

"In bed. I think Haywood wore him out today."

Jenna chuckled knowing that was an understatement. Haywood had not let Trey out of her sight and had been able to talk him into playing a number of games with her. "I think so, too." She smiled. "Yes, I'll take a walk with you, but what's the blanket for?" she asked, but already knowing. She had met his gaze a number of times across the dinner table and had read the strong desire in his eyes.

Randolph chuckled. "You'll find out soon enough."

And she did. Hours later she lay in his arms on the blanket before the pond, satiated. He had made love to her thoroughly and completely, giving her a sense of how much she was desired and loved. "I don't think I'll be able to move," she murmured as she snuggled closer to Randolph's body.

"Then don't, at least not for a while," he said, placing a kiss on her lips. "There's something I need to talk to you about anyway. Something I need to confess."

"What?"

Randolph didn't say anything for a few moments, wanting to choose his words carefully. "I've kept up with you for the past thirteen years. I had hired an investigative firm to provide me with an annual report of what you were doing and how you were doing."

Jenna felt slightly dazed at his admission. "But, why?"

"Because as much as I tried to, I couldn't let you go. I knew why you'd left but I still wanted that connection. The day I found out you were getting married was hard on me. I left home and stayed away for a few days. I spent most of that time getting drunk in a hotel room. And that was the one and only time that I committed adultery during my marriage. I couldn't handle the hurt and the pain at the thought of you belonging to someone else."

Jenna stared up at him as tears began forming in her eyes. "In my heart, I never really belonged to anyone else, Randolph, and the sad thing about it is that Steven knew it and accepted it. I tried to be a good wife to him to make up for my inability to fully let myself go in the bedroom."

Randolph pulled her closer into his arms. "Don't you see then, Jen, that we're meant to be together? God has given us another chance and we should thank him every day for doing so. I know you're concerned about Trey's feelings and I can appreciate that. But we can't let that stop us from being together. He'll eventually come around. And I feel confident that the time he spends around you and Haywood will help. Because of the garbage Angela has fed to him it's hard for him, but he's trying to accept things."

Jenna nodded. Although around her Trey had remained quiet for the most part, Haywood had been able to draw him out to do some things with her and he had genuinely seemed to enjoy doing so. "I know, I just don't want to see him get hurt."

"You're more concerned about his emotional well-being than Angela. She wouldn't hesitate to use him to get what she wants."

Jenna sighed. "And that's what worries me, Randolph. How far will she go to keep us apart? What if she tries to keep you and Trey apart?"

"She can't do that. I'll take her to court if she tries."

Jenna hoped it wouldn't come down to that but she knew Randolph was dead serious.

"What the two of us need to do is to plan our future, Jenna. We need to build that life together we've always wanted and dreamed of having," Randolph continued. "Will you marry me and let me be a husband to you and a father to Haywood?" He sat up and looked down at her. "I love you, Jenna. I always have and I always will."

He reached out and took her hand in his. In a voice filled with emotion, he asked. "Will you marry me?"

Tears filled Jenna eyes as she gazed into his. What he'd said earlier had been true. It was meant for them to be together and God had given them another chance of doing just that. Complete love filled her heart and soul and she didn't think it was possible to be any happier than she was at that very moment.

"Yes," she replied in a voice filled with as much emotion as his had been. "Yes, Randolph, I'll marry you."

Twenty-seven

May 1981

Prince Charles and Lady Diana Spencer weren't the only ones planning a June wedding. Randolph and Jenna decided not to wait any longer and set a date to marry. It would be a wedding at Glendale Shores, outside near the pond where they had first made love and where they had bound their lives together so many years ago; a private affair with only close friends and family attending. Jenna had already given notice to her employer since she would be moving permanently to Virginia. They would live in Randolph's condo until the house they were building was completed.

Angela became enraged upon hearing about Randolph's upcoming marriage. But nothing could have prepared Randolph for the bombshell she dropped on him two weeks before his wedding.

"You aren't the only one getting married, Randolph," she said looking smug. "I've decided to marry Harry."

Randolph wondered if she thought the news she'd just delivered would be devastating to him. It was the best he'd heard all year. "I'm happy for you."

Cold dark eyes met Randolph's. "I never doubted for a minute that you wouldn't be. But there's something I think you should know."

"What?"

"Harry has accepted a position with another banking firm which means we'll be moving to California a month from now."

Randolph's gaze narrowed considerably. "You can move anywhere you want, but Trey stays here."

"No, Randolph, he will not stay here. He goes wherever I go. It will be up to you to maintain a long-distance relationship with him."

Angela's eyes narrowed in anger as she continued. "But we know that won't happen since you'll be too busy playing daddy to Jenna's brat. And while you're doing so, think about what it's costing you."

Randolph's eyes darkened with the fury he felt. "I won't let you do it," he responded sharply.

Angela chuckled. "You can't stop me. I've already checked with my attorney and there is nothing you can do." She smiled sweetly as her eyes glowed with malicious intent. "However, if you were to call off your wedding to Jenna, I'll consider calling off mine to Harry. That way you'll be able to spend time with Trey whenever you want."

Randolph's face turned to stone. "No, Angela. I won't let you use Trey to try and keep me under your thumb."

Angela smiled, looking smug. "No matter what you say, you love Trey and wouldn't want to lose him, Randolph. So, what will it be? Your son or Jenna?"

Without giving her an answer, Randolph walked out of the house.

"Calm down, son. I'm sure there's something we can do. I'll contact Sherman Price and feel confident he'll give us advice as to what our next step should be."

Julia Fuller sat across the room, clearly distressed. The thought that her only great-grandchild would be living three thousand miles away did not sit well with her. "Surely Angela wouldn't go to those extremes," she said, but no longer as certain about what Angela would do. She thought she was acting irrationally, to say the least. Randolph had just finished telling them the whole story, which included Kathy Taylor's claim that he'd been drugged at the time he had slept with Angela, as well as coming home unexpectedly from a business trip one day and finding Angela in bed with another man. But what had clearly thrown her back, and made her feel she'd been had, was the fact that Angela had not been the prim and proper debutante she'd been led to believe. The report Randolph had all but shoved in her face provided proof that Angela had had an abortion at nineteen, as well as accounts of her promiscuous behavior. It had almost been too much.

"Think of what a custody fight will do," Julia said to her husband and grandson. "Especially if you plan to attack Angela's reputation, which I admit I'm appalled at. She really did a good job of pulling the wool over my eyes, which I am not proud of. And to think I wanted a union between her and Ross. But nevertheless, if we go public with anything about Angela, the person who'll be hurt the most is Trey." She shook her head sadly. "I know you may not want to hear this, Randolph, but it might save you and Trey a lot of grief if you give Angela what she wants and don't marry Jenna."

Randolph turned narrowed eyes on his grandmother. But before he could open his mouth to speak, his grandfather did so. "How can you even suggest such a thing, Julia? Haven't Randolph and Jenna suffered at the hands of Angela long enough? I'd be damned if I'll stand by and watch him give Angela the satisfaction of thinking that she can use Trey like that. If Randolph even thinks twice about calling off his marriage to Jenna, I'll take a stick to him myself," the older man bellowed.

Randolph tried putting his best smile forward, truly appreciating his grandfather's support. "Thanks, Granddad, but a stick won't be necessary because I have every intention of marrying Jenna. Angela came between us once, and I refuse to let her do so again." With those final words, he turned and walked out of his grandparents' home.

Sherman Price's words weren't encouraging. "Other than going to court and fighting for joint custody, where you'll have Trey half of the year and Angela will have him the other half, there's nothing else we can do. However, I would think twice before I considered doing that. Most of the time it's the child who suffers by being tossed from one parent to the other, never having any real stability in their life. What I suggest you do is go to court and ask for full summers each year. Getting every single holiday will be somewhat of a challenge, but I would request them, too."

The man then took a huge swallow of iced tea before continuing. "Then there's the other option. You can take Angela to court for full custody rights by declaring her unfit. And trust me, son, you better have solid proof of that claim. Her parents are well thought of and highly respected people. They won't take too kindly to you muddying their daughter's good name. You'll have to call in witnesses to convince the jury that morally, you are a better parent than she is. And it has to be something she is presently doing. You won't be able to bring up anything she may have done in the past. The court will feel that if you knew she did something morally wrong and didn't fight for custody of your son during the divorce proceedings, then you don't have anything to say about it now."

Randolph stood up from behind his desk and walked across the room to stand before the window. Sherman watched him thoughtfully. He had known Randolph from the time he'd been in diapers, since he and Randolph's father had been roommates while at Howard Law School. He could feel the younger man's pain. The worst thing a parent could experience was losing a child. And Sherman was fairly certain Randolph knew there was a possibility that he could lose his son. From all accounts it seemed Angela wouldn't hesitate to poison Trey's mind against Randolph, especially if Randolph didn't give in to her demands. And with Angela marrying Harry Connors, Randolph would run the risk of having his role in Trey's life diminished by a stepfather.

"Randolph, have you mentioned Angela's threats to your fiancée?"

Randolph turned around. "No, and I don't intend to. Jenna wouldn't hesitate to call off the wedding if she thought there was a chance I'd lose Trey."

"She's going to find out eventually."

"Yes, but by that time we'll be married."

Sherman nodded, agreeing with Randolph's decision. "You're determined not to let her get away a second time, aren't you?"

"Not ever again."

Randolph's eyes were hard as steel as he gazed at Angela. "I'm in no mood for games."

"I'm not playing games," she said, spitting the words. "Trey doesn't want to go to Glendale Shores for your wedding."

"When I talked to him last week he wanted to go."

"That was last week. A lot has happened since then. I told him about our move to California."

"And I'm sure that's not all you told him." Randolph glanced around the room. "Where is he?"

"He went camping with my parents."

Randolph glared at her with stormy eyes.

"You had no right to let him go. This was my weekend to have him."

Angela snorted. "Trey is not a little kid anymore, Randolph. He's old enough to speak his own mind and make his own decisions about what he wants, and he didn't want to be there when you got married. I merely honored his wishes. If you don't like what I did then sue me."

Randolph put his hands into his pockets. A part of him was aching to place them around Angela's neck instead. He wondered what Angela could have possibly said to Trey to make him change his mind. Over the last three months Trey had warmed to Jenna and Haywood considerably, and Randolph knew that for him to suddenly have a change of attitude, Angela must have said something to him. "I'll never forgive you for what you've done."

"Do you think I care when you have the nerve to marry that woman and bring her here to live, in this town among our friends? How dare you expect me to take it!"

"I thought you'd have enough pride and not cling to a man who doesn't want you; a man who never wanted you. One day all of this will blow up in your face, Angela. Trey will find out the truth. He'll know everything you've done, and when that day comes, he'll regret ever having you for his mother."

For a brief moment Randolph saw the look of fear in her eyes at the thought that she may one day lose her son. She quickly recovered and lifted her chin. "I'll never lose my son, Randolph. You'll be the one who will lose him. Now got out."

When Randolph turned to walk out the door, she added sneeringly, "Oh, and congratulations. I hope what you're getting is worth what you're losing."

Jenna glanced up at Randolph with brows that puckered in confusion. "What do you mean Trey didn't come with you to the wedding?"

Randolph didn't want to go into a lot of details so he quietly said, "Something came up and he couldn't make it."

Jenna gazed at Randolph, considering. "What aren't you telling me, Randolph? The last time we talked you said Trey wanted to come and that he would be here. What happened?"

She noted the strain around Randolph's eyes, and when he didn't say anything, a light flashed through Jenna's mind. "Angela! What has she done now, Randolph?" she asked angrily. "I guess it was too much to hope that she would finally leave us alone and let us be happy."

Randolph pulled Jenna into his arms. "We *will* be happy, sweetheart, trust me. We'll spend the rest of our life together happy. We've gone through too much not to be."

"But what about Trey?"

Randolph forced a smile. "Trey will be fine. When we return from our honeymoon, I'll have a long talk with him." He took Jenna's hand in his. "Angela is trying to use him against us and we won't let that happen, Jenna." He leaned down and placed a kiss on her lips. "Whatever problems there are concerning Trey, you and I will deal with them together, *after* we're married. We won't let Angela come between us ever again, no matter what. Agreed?"

Jenna looked up at him, knowing at this moment how much she loved him. In less than twenty-four hours, they would be committing their lives to each other.

"Agreed," she said.

"By the powers invested in me by the state of South Carolina, I now pronounce you man and wife. You may kiss your bride."

Surrounded by close family and friends, Randolph lowered his head and his mouth covered Jenna's to claim what he knew awaited him. Her response was quick and complete. Afterwards, the minister had them turn to face their guests and said to all in attendance, "I present to everyone, Mr. and Mrs. Randolph Devin Fuller."

Across the glen with tears in her eyes, Leigh leaned over and whispered to the woman sitting on her left. "At long last."

Ellie nodded in agreement with tears filling her own eyes. "Yes," she said softly. "At long last."

● ● ●

"May I speak to you privately, Jenna?"

Startled, Jenna turned around and met Julia Fuller's gaze, eyeing her uneasily. Standing before her was the woman who had never approved of her relationship with Randolph. The woman who thought she was unfit to become a Fuller because her mother had worked in the school cafeteria and her father had been a meat cutter. This was the woman who hadn't said a kind word to her in all the years she had been with Randolph. Not a single one. And to be quite honest, she had been surprised when she had come to their wedding, although Randolph had told her she would.

"Yes, Mrs. Fuller, you can speak with me privately," Jenna said. She turned back to Ellie and Johnny, with whom she'd been conversing and said, "Please excuse me for a minute." Inwardly she was nervous but she refused to let it show.

"We can go into the guest bedroom I'm using," Jenna said to the woman, leading the way through Gramma Denison's home where the reception was being held. She glanced across the room at Randolph. He was in a group talking to Noah and her brothers. She saw him lift his brow questioningly. Jenna nodded and smiled, letting him know that everything would be fine, and that she would deal with his grandmother. After all these years, it was about time.

She closed the door behind them, then looked over at the other woman. Every time she had ever seen Julia Fuller she'd been the epitome of grace and refinement. Today was no different. There was no doubt in Jenna's mind that the outfit she wore had cost a pretty penny. It screamed expensive with a capital "E".

"What did you want to say to me, Mrs. Fuller?"

"I wish to heaven I knew," the older woman said softly, looking at her. "I know what I should say, but it's hard." Julia sighed deeply. "It's hard admitting you were wrong—completely wrong—about something or someone, and I've been guilty of both."

The older woman looked thoughtfully around her before walking over to look out of the only window in the room. A few seconds later she turned around. "I owe you an apology, Jenna. It is one that I hope you can and will accept. For years I thought I knew what was best for the men in my life. It didn't matter what they wanted, if what they wanted wasn't in tune with what I thought they should have. In a nutshell, I literally gave them grief. At least all but Randolph. He always stood up to me. He tried to make me understand from the beginning how much he loved you, but I just couldn't see it. In fact I really didn't understand it until a while ago."

Julia crossed the room to come to stand before Jenna. "All it took was a look into his eyes while he was repeating your marriage vows to know he meant every word. The look on his face was priceless, such a treasure and he was looking at you that way—like you were the greatest gift he could ever receive; one that was long overdue. And in a way, you are."

She sighed deeply. "I just want you to know, Jenna, that you are welcomed into our family. And I will do everything to make you feel a part of it. I saw something on my grandson's face today that I hadn't seen in a long time, a very long time, and that was a smile of true happiness. And I want to thank you for putting it back there, and I believe in my heart that you'll keep it there."

Tears misted Jenna's eyes. "I'm going to try."

Julia nodded as tears misted her eyes as well. "And I believe that you will."

Right before they were to cut the wedding cake, Randolph pulled Jenna aside. "Are you okay?"

She smiled up at him. "Yes, I'm fine. After all these years your grandmother discovered that she and I have something in common."

"What?"

"Our love for you and wanting the best for you and making you happy."

Randolph chuckled. "That should be an easy task for you to do."

"Easy and fulfilling." Jenna's gaze studied him closely. The lines of strain were still around his eyes. She couldn't help but wonder what or who had put them there. She knew it had something to do with Trey but she wouldn't question him about it. She would wait for him to tell her what was going on.

"I can't wait to start our honeymoon," he said, turning her around to him in his arms.

She smiled up at him. "Neither can I."

They didn't have far to go. Randolph and Jenna had decided to spend their first few days as man and wife in a place that meant a lot to the both of them, the cottage on Glendale Shores. Gramma Mattie had made arrangements to spend time with her relatives on Hilton Head so the couple could have complete privacy.

It was late evening when everyone finally left the island leaving them alone. The sun had gone down and dusk nearly covered the land. When they reached the door to the cottage, Randolph opened the door then stopped her from going further. He took her hands in his and carried them to his lips.

"I have dreamed of this moment, Jenna, for so long. Even when I thought I had lost you forever. But even then, you were a part of me. I love you and will always love you."

With tears glazing her eyes, Jenna raised her hand and framed his face. "And I have always loved you, Randolph. Even in my darkest moments you were never far from my thoughts. Loving you, losing you, now having you back with me is truly a special blessing from God; one I will never take lightly. We were given another chance and I intend for it to last forever."

She leaned toward him and kissed him. Slow. Deliberate. Sensuous. And he returned her kiss in like form then picked her up in his arms and carried her over the threshold.

Once inside he placed her on her feet and only then did they break the kiss. His gaze locked with hers and he knew she was thinking, as he was, what they had endured since that night in nineteen-sixty-five when they had first met on Howard University's campus.

As he continued to watch her, study her, absorb everything about her into his entire being, he felt the atmosphere in the room change as it became electrically charged and intensely passionate. And at that moment he wanted her in a way he had never wanted her before. All he could think about was that now, today, forever, she was his.

His.

He had waited so long for this moment. But first there was something he had to do, something special he had prepared just for her to erase the years they had been apart.

Placing a kiss on her lips he crossed the room to the stereo and pushed a few buttons.

Jenna raised a brow. "Music?"

He returned to her side and smiled. "Because we didn't spend time together in the seventies, I want to relive that time with you, especially a song that always made me think of what we had shared."

"Our Love" by Natalie Cole began playing softly. Randolph offered Jenna his hand. "Come, sweetheart, dance with me in celebration of our love," he whispered huskily.

Jenna went into his arms and he pulled her gently to him as they began moving around the room in tune to the music.

Our love.

She closed her eyes as her mind and heart absorbed the words to the song he had selected for them. Their first dance as husband and wife.

Jenna's breasts felt tight, sensitive and achy pressed so close to Randolph's chest. She felt his hands, firm and possessive, rest against her bottom, kneading her softly, provocatively. As the sound of Natalie Cole floated around them she rested her head against his shoulder and shifted her hips against him and he shifted his against hers as they continued to move slowly.

"Open your eyes, Jenna, and look at me. I want you to see my love. I want you to actually feel it. I love you."

Jenna opened her eyes, leaned back in his arms and met his gaze. The look on his face was so full of expression it made her drag in a deep, consuming breath. His eyes were filled with love, devotion and desire. She swallowed thickly. No woman could ask for more from the man she loved and whom she knew loved her. She felt the strength in him as well as his weakness and knew that even now, as well as in the past, she had always been both.

A shudder of love rippled through her and she knew the man who held her in his arms would have her heart forever. And on this special day, on this special island where he had proclaimed his love to her over fourteen years ago, he was reaffirming, reclaiming, restating.

Tears began filling her eyes and she knew she had never felt as loved as she did at that very moment. "And I love you, too, so very, very much, Randolph Devin Fuller."

Book Three

The Present

The wicked man is doomed by his own sins; they are ropes that catch and hold him.

Proverbs 6:22

Twenty-eight

September 2002
Los Angeles, California

It wasn't hard to tell she was an easy lay.

That thought went through Trey Fuller's mind as his gaze lingered on yet another woman his mother had arranged for him to meet. He wondered if she would ever tire of playing matchmaker.

Checking his watch he noted it was almost nine o'clock. Although he had arrived late to the dinner party his mother had given for the Barfields—business associates of his stepfather—Trey had all intentions of leaving early. Across the room his mother met his gaze and scowled her disapproval, evidently having read his mind. He decided to allow her this one concession tonight and hang around a little while longer.

"Trey, isn't it just wonderful hearing about those exotic places Marva has traveled?"

He glanced at his mother and then glanced at Marva, noting that she, too, was waiting for his response. "Yes, I find her travels utterly amazing," he said smiling. "Which place did you enjoy visiting the most, Marva?"

As Marva began talking Trey noticed his mother, stepfather and the Barfields conveniently departing the room, leaving him and Marva alone. After she'd finished telling him about a recent trip to Egypt, she placed the wineglass she'd been holding on the table beside her.

"I can't believe they think we're that dense," she said, obviously amused.

Trey shrugged. "I take it you're no more interested in their match-making schemes than I am."

Marva looked like she was about to gag. "Not in the least. I find the very thought of settling down with anyone and getting married quite revolting."

Trey chuckled, deciding he actually liked her after all. "Same here. I keep telling my mother that I'm thirty-four and not eighty-four. I have plenty of time to settle down and get married later but have no desire to do so now. I'm totally enjoying myself as a single man."

Marva shifted positions in her chair. "My parents can't get it through their heads that I'm no longer a child. I'm twenty-eight and doing quite well by myself. I have a job that takes me all over the world and pays a very good salary." She shifted positions in her chair again. "They would die if they knew the only thing I want from a man is sex."

Trey wasn't shocked by her bluntness. It was the only thing he wanted from a woman as well, and he did believe in equal rights. "Is that the reason you're sitting across from me with your legs wide open, showing me that you don't have on any panties?"

Marva smiled, a hot sultry smile, opening her legs some more. The way she was sitting was not ladylike at all but from the way his eyes had darkened she had gotten the effect she wanted. For the past two weeks her parents had been singing the praises of Ross Donovan Fuller III, who was called Trey by family and friends. He was a hot-shot corporate attorney for his stepfather's financial corporation. Her mother called him a good catch. Her father indicated he was a young man with a good head on his shoulders. His mother claimed he was an eligible bachelor who the right woman could turn into a family man. But the first thing that had gone through her mind when she'd first seen him was that with a body like his, he would be dynamite in bed.

"The reason I'm being so forward is because I want you to know just how hot and ready I am. And now that you know it, what are you going to do about it?"

Trey slowly stood as a smile curved his lips. "I plan to give you the only thing you want from a man." He placed his wineglass on the table next to hers. "I'll let our parents know that I'm taking you home."

Marva grinned. "You know if we leave together they're going to assume their little matchmaking scheme worked."

"Let them think whatever they want. You and I will know differently, won't we?"

Trey couldn't wait to see Marva completely naked. And she couldn't wait for him to see her naked. She began taking off her clothes the moment they entered her apartment. He'd known she wasn't wearing panties and soon discovered she wasn't wearing much of anything else, either. When she had gotten completely naked, he watched as she strutted into her bedroom and stretched her lush body out on the bed to wait for him.

He took his time removing his own clothes, knowing she watched his every move and was getting even more turned on. Before he was through with her, she would think twice about being a temptress and sitting across from him with her legs wide open exposing herself.

"You're taking too long."

He looked at her, holding her gaze. "Am I?"

"Yes. Need any help?"

He chuckled. "No, I think I can manage. I've done this several times in my lifetime." He had taken everything off but his briefs. And she watched, licking her lips, as he took his hands and began lowering his underwear down his legs. He smiled upon hearing the sharp sound of her indrawn breath. "That about does it," he said moments later after putting on a condom. He moved to the bed to join her.

Trey didn't think he would ever forget the look on her face when he placed his body over hers and slowly entered her. He hadn't gone all the way in when she began panting and moving her body to meet his, softly saying words in a language he didn't understand. He had wanted to start off by taking things slow, initiating foreplay, but she had other ideas. She became an acrobat beneath him, moving her body this way and that. The more she moved, the more he tried pinning her to the bed with his body in an attempt to keep her still. She was hot. Greedy. Hungry. And she was liable to end things before they began. He was already on the edge of going off.

"Slow down, damnit, I'm not going anywhere." His words were useless as she kept up her aggressive pace. After a while when he saw there was no stopping her, he wrapped her thighs firmly around his waist and flipped her over, letting her take the dominant role and give him the ride of his life.

She did.

His body became sensitized as she pulled everything out of him until he couldn't bear it anymore. If he didn't know better he would think she hadn't had a man in months. But then he hadn't had a woman for just that long.

When he felt her body jerk atop his, he knew a climax was coming. Quickly changing positions, he placed her beneath him and slipped his hand under her hips, making sure he had gone as deep as he could, feeling her tremors, shivers and liking the way her body was clutching him.

"Don't fight it. Let it go," he whispered in her ear as one climax after another rammed into her. She moaned loudly, alternating in English and what sounded like Chinese or Japanese. Or was it Russian? It could have been a language from another planet for all he cared. At that moment he was feeling too good to give a damn. Closing his eyes he arched his back to go deeper as a climax tore into him as well.

He gulped for air. She did too, but kept her body moving. Trey knew she'd come twice already and was going for a third, taking him with her.

"Mercy!" The last thought that infiltrated his lust-induced mind before another orgasm struck was that Marva Barfield definitely knew how to get all the sex she wanted from a man.

The ringing of the telephone roused Trey awake. He blinked his eyes several times before remembering he was not in his own bed. He turned and nudged Marva awake. "Your phone is ringing."

Marva peered at him through sleepy eyes before his words registered. She then quickly reached across him to answer the phone. "Yes?"

She slowly lifted her brow. "Yes, he's here. Just a moment." She handed him the phone saying, "It's for you. Your mother. And she says it's important."

Trey sat up. He didn't have to think twice as to how his mother knew where to find him. "Yes?" After a few moments a frown marred his forehead. "When?" For the longest time he didn't say anything, then, "I'm going home to pack. Yes, I'm flying out as soon as I can.

There's no discussion about it, Mother, I'm going." He then hung up the phone.

Marva reached out and touched his arm. "Trey? You okay?"

He looked at her with sad eyes. "My mother called to let me know she'd just received word that my great-grandmother who lived in South Carolina has died."

"Sir, please prepare for takeoff."

Following the flight attendant's instructions, Trey snapped his seat belt in place wondering what to expect when he arrived in South Carolina for Ma Mattie Denison's funeral service. There had always been a special place in his heart for Ma Mattie and he had managed to stay in contact with her over the years. A year ago while on a business trip to Charleston, he had rented a car and had taken the scenic drive to Glendale Shores. She had been surprised yet pleased to see him and he had spent two days with her. That visit had made him realize just how many memories he had of visiting her as a young boy. They had been good memories.

His relationship with his father's family had begun to fall back when he and his mother moved to California because of his stepfather's job. Especially when his mother had told him the truth about a number of things, including the role his father's wife had played in the breakup of his parent's marriage. His mother had sworn him to secrecy, too full of pride to want others to know that another woman had taken her husband away from her.

Trey rested his head against the seat as the plane left the Los Angeles airport headed for South Carolina. He couldn't help but recall those lazy days spent with Ma Mattie on Glendale Shores. Those had been very special times for him. She had been a very kind woman who had always made him feel special. And now, against his mother's wishes, he was going back to be there when she was laid to rest.

Richmond, Virginia

"Do you think Trey will come?"

Slipping into his dress shirt, Randolph gazed across the room at his wife. He thought that at the age of fifty-five, she was still the most beautiful woman he knew. "I really don't know, Jen. More than anything I'd love to see him but Trey made a decision years ago not to have anything to do with this family and as much as that decision hurt, I've learned to live with it."

"But he doesn't know that what Angela told him were all lies."

"No, but I wasn't going to be the one to tell him the truth about his mother. He wouldn't have believed me anyway. Angela did just what she said she would do. She turned my son against me."

Jenna crossed the room to her husband. Even after all these years she could still hear the pain and hurt in his voice whenever he spoke of his firstborn. She had given him another child, a daughter they had named Randi, who was eighteen and about to enter her first year of college at Howard University.

Randolph reached out and pulled Jenna into his arms, still loving the feel of having her there. It was hard to believe that they had been married for twenty-one years. And they had been twenty-one wonderful years. His thoughts then shifted to his stepdaughter Haywood. She had been six when he and Jenna had married and he thought the world of her.

"How did Haywood take the news?"

Jenna released a deep sigh. She had reached her daughter in Paris where she was working as freelance photographer—a love she had inherited from her biological father. "She didn't take the news well. For once I was glad that Aaron was there with her. She and Gramma Mattie were very close."

Randolph nodded. "Yeah, I know. Gramma adored Haywood."

Jenna smiled. "And Haywood adored her. I spoke with her again earlier today. Her plane will land sometime later tonight. She said not to worry about anyone picking her up at the airport. She'll take a taxi." Jenna placed a kiss on her husband's lips. "I hope Trey comes. It will be the first time we've had all our children together at the same time in years."

Randolph nodded. "But let's not get our hopes up about Trey. There is a chance he won't come."

Jenna nodded. "Yes, but there's that chance that he will. He was close to Gramma Mattie."

"Yes, but even she couldn't get the truth through that hard head of his about you and me. Angela has convinced him that you're the reason his mother and I got divorced."

She sighed and laid her head on his shoulder. "One day he'll find out the truth."

"Yeah, but when? It's been over twenty-one years and he still doesn't know it."

Jenna's arms around her husband tighten. "But one day Angela's lies will catch up with her and I wouldn't want to be in her shoes when they do."

Twenty-nine

Washington, DC

Zachary Wainwright glanced across the ER waiting room, frowning at his sister. "I can't believe I let you talk me into coming here. It's just a scratch."

Noelle shook her head, grinning. "Is that the reason you were bleeding all over my kitchen? Stop being a wimp. All the doctor will do is put in a few stitches and send you home with a prescription. Then you'll be good as new."

Zach glared at her. "I don't like doctors."

"Who does? But you're going to have to suffer through it anyway. How would it look in tomorrow's paper if it read, 'Senator Noah Wainwright's thirty-five-year-old son bleeds to death after helping his sister fix her garbage disposal'?"

Zach smiled. "Sounds rather funny, doesn't it?"

"It won't be funny if you stick with your plans to enter politics yourself in a few years. That's the kind of stuff the tabloids enjoy printing. And to make it juicy they'll come up with their own version—which won't be comical."

Zach shook his head, grinning. "Yeah, you're right about that."

At that moment, the receptionist called Zach's name. "The doctor will see you now."

Zach stood. So did Noelle. "Do you want me to go back there with you?"

He shook his head. "No, I plan to take it like a man."

Noelle rolled her eyes to the ceiling. "At thirty-five I hope so." She kissed his cheek. "Go on, break a leg." Then she smiled sheepishly. "Sorry, I guess that wouldn't be the right terminology to use."

"You're right on that account, kid. I'll be back."

Noelle watched as the brother she simply adored walked off. She was proud of him. He was considered a one of the brightest attorneys in Washington and had a promising career in politics like their father. He was slowly rejoining the living after the wife he had loved and adored had been one of the victims in the September 11 tragedy a year ago. She had been a flight attendant, leaving Washington for Los Angeles. The plane had crashed into the Pentagon instead. And for a while it seemed all of Zachary's hopes and dreams had died that day along with Shaun. But with strong family support and love, he was slowly getting back to his old self again.

She sat back down, hoping Zach didn't embarrass her or himself by fainting when they gave him a tetanus shot. She hadn't warned him about that since everyone in the family knew that he had an aversion to needles. A part of her felt downright sorry for the doctor who would be attending him.

Back at his apartment, Zach began packing, mindful of his injured hand, grateful it wasn't as serious as it could have been. He closed his luggage at the exact moment the telephone rang. "Yeah?"

"Zach?"

He recognized the voice immediately. "Haywood?"

"Yes."

He heard the tears in her voice. "Are you okay?"

"Yes, I'm fine. It's just that I just saw Ma Mattie last month before I flew out for Paris and she was doing fine, messing around in her garden as usual."

"She was almost ninety, honey. It was her time to go and I'm glad she did so in her sleep and didn't suffer, aren't you?"

"Yeah, I suppose."

Zach knew that Haywood, the daughter of his mother's closest friend from college, had been close to the woman who'd been her stepfather's grandmother. "Are you in Virginia?"

"Yes, I got in last night. We're leaving for South Carolina in a few hours."

He shifted the phone to his other hand. "Dad, Mom, Noelle and I are leaving later today. We should arrive on Glendale Shores this afternoon. Any word on whether Trey is coming to the funeral?"

"No. I'm surprised you don't know since the two of you used to be as thick as glue. A part of me wishes that he won't come. He's caused Dad a lot of unnecessary pain."

Zach sighed deeply. "For the past few years Trey and I haven't kept in touch like we should have. But regardless of how you feel about him, Haywood, Mattie was his great-grandmother."

"I know. I know. It's just makes me furious how he's treated Dad over the years."

Zach smiled. The one thing he knew about Haywood was that she was fiercely loyal to the people she loved. The two of them had dated a few years back, before he had met and married Shaun. After going out a few times they had decided the only thing they wanted was friendship. He had become one of her closest friends, although not the best. Noelle was her best friend.

"I tried calling Noelle today and couldn't reach her. Is she okay?"

"Yeah, she's fine. You probably tried reaching her the same time she had taken me to the emergency room."

"The emergency room? What's happened?"

"Nothing serious. I cut my hand at her place earlier today fixing her dilapidated garbage disposal and had to get it bandaged, not to mention a tetanus shot."

"You had to get a shot?"

"Yeah, and lived to tell about it. Noelle is suffering with a guilty conscious and wants to play mother hen. I had to force her to go home a few minutes ago, so you can catch her there in an hour."

"All right."

"Haywood, how's Aaron?"

Haywood sighed. She knew Zach couldn't stand the man she was currently involved with. "Aaron is fine but I left him in Paris."

"Good."

She couldn't help but smile. "You really should try and get along with him, Zach."

Zach snorted. "Give me one reason why I should."

"Because it would mean a lot to me. Aaron has his faults but—"

"He's a first-class jerk and that's being kind. Look, I'll see you later this afternoon on Glendale Shores, all right?"

Haywood blew air through clenched teeth. She knew that nothing she said would change Zach's opinion of Aaron so she decided not to bother. "All right. I'll see you later."

Glendale Shores, South Carolina

It was late when Trey arrived in South Carolina. He had called Ma Mattie's home from the Hilton Head Island airport and his half-sister Randi had answered the phone. He could tell she had been surprised to hear his voice. She had been born a few years after his father had married Jenna, and the last time he had seen or spoken to Randi had been ten years ago, when he had graduated from law school. She could not have been any more than seven or eight at the time. Now she had finished high school and was starting her first year of college. Randi's voice had been rather friendly although she'd indicated that they hadn't expected him to come.

He sighed as he stepped off the ferry and noted a car parked near the pier. As soon as the man got out of the vehicle he recognized him immediately, although it had been ten years since he'd seen him. But there were some things about some people you just didn't forget. Especially if you'd been a young boy who had loved your father as much as he had. That deep love had made the hurt and pain of his father's desertion that much harder to bear.

Randolph deeply inhaled the scented ocean air. No matter how much he'd tried to prepare himself, once he'd known for certain that Trey was coming an intense amount of pleasure had overtaken him. Automatically, tears came into his eyes when he saw him. The son he loved with all his heart was now a thirty-four-year-old man.

He inwardly accepted that too many years had passed, and too many lies were deeply embedded for him to convince Trey that his mother had not told him the truth, and that she had deliberately set out to destroy their relationship because of her obsessive jealousy.

Randolph had suspected something was wrong the first summer Trey had returned to Virginia after moving to California. He had seemed withdrawn and unhappy and no matter how much he and Jenna had tried, they hadn't been able to get him out of his funky mood. And when Angela had called later that year to say Trey didn't want to spend the holidays with them, Randolph knew Angela had made good on her threats to build a wedge between him and his son. The following summer when Trey turned fifteen proved him right.

Trey had arrived with a horrible attitude, a chip on his shoulder and no matter what he or Jenna said or did, he let them know he wasn't happy to be there with them, and preferred being in California with his mother and stepfather. They had tolerated his attitude until the day Randolph had walked in on Trey telling Haywood that her mother was nothing but a home-wrecking slut. At nine years old Haywood hadn't known exactly what the term fully meant but had been old enough to know it wasn't flattering. That had been Trey's last summer visit since after that he refused to come again and no amount of coaxing and pleading had made him change his mind.

During the remaining years Randolph had been the one to initiate any type of communication between them. Most of the time he was the one to fly out to California to visit with Trey since he had let it be known that he would not visit his father in Virginia as long as he was married to Jenna.

The last time he had seen his son was when Trey had graduated from law school at twenty-four. Instead of following the tradition of Fuller men by attending Howard University, Trey decided to remain on the West Coast and attend Stanford. Randolph, Jenna and Randi had attended the graduation ceremonies. Haywood had taken a trip with her paternal grandparents to Paris and had been unable to attend.

Trey had been cool to everyone and had broken Randolph's heart by making it obvious that he considered his stepfather to be his father. When Randolph had left California to return home, he had made up his mind that the next attempt at some sort of a relationship would have to come from Trey. Emotionally, he could not handle any more animosity from his son.

Gramma Mattie, on the other hand, had been determined to keep Trey a part of the family no matter what he thought he wanted. The summer Trey turned sixteen, she invited him, along with Noah's son Zach, to spend the entire summer with her on Glendale Shores. The two boys had enjoyed themselves so much they had returned the following two summers after that, partaking in all sort of fun and adventures that teenage boys do as well as building a close friendship between them.

Randolph signed deeply as he crossed the short distance to meet his son. He fought the knots that began forming in his stomach. Trey was here, for a sad occasion, but Randolph's heart sang a song of happiness at seeing his son again after all these years.

"Dad, how are you?" Trey greeted his father cordially when the two finally stood face-to-face after exchanging handshakes.

Randolph was immediately filled with pride. It was like seeing himself all over again twenty years ago. "I'm fine, Trey. What about you?" he asked, as he helped him load the few pieces of luggage he'd brought into the back of the Lexus SUV.

"I'm doing fine."

"And your mother and stepfather?" Randolph asked out of politeness.

Trey's eyes didn't waver when he met his father's. "They're both fine. Thanks for asking. How is everyone here?" Trey knew their conversation sounded so distant, detached and formal.

"Considering everything, they're fine. Gramma Mattie meant a lot to everyone."

Trey nodded. She had meant a lot to him as well. He enjoyed those summers he had spent with her.

"Zach is here."

Trey smiled. "Is he? I'd like to see him again. It's been a long time since we've seen or talked to each other."

"I'm glad you came, Trey."

Trey met his father's gaze. "Ma Mattie was a special woman. Nothing could have kept me away. Nothing and no one."

Haywood sighed as she moved around in the kitchen. "I can't believe Mom let Dad go pick up Trey alone."

Noelle raised her eyes to the ceiling. "Don't you think you're overreacting, Haywood? Zach offered to go with your father but he said he wanted to go alone. Trey is his son. Although this is a sad occasion, it might be the perfect time for the two of them to reconcile any differences between them."

"I wish that were true but I can't forget the animosity Trey felt toward my mother. It was completely uncalled for."

Noelle slanted a glance over at Haywood as she put the dishes away. "You seem to go out of your way to protect your parents and what they have together. Why?"

Haywood knew she couldn't answer Noelle's question. No one knew that at sixteen she had done the unthinkable when she'd stumbled upon her mother's diary in the attic one day and read it. It had taken her only two weeks to read what had covered a huge span of time that started with the night her mother had met Randolph Fuller at a college social function. She could feel the love pouring off each entry. She knew about the week the two of them had spent on Glendale Shores alone during one of their spring breaks, becoming lovers, and how over a family Bible they had committed their lives to each other. She had read how Trey's mother's treachery and pregnancy had ultimately led to the breakup of the couple.

Her heart had gone out to her biological father who had married a woman still in love with another man. He had never been able to replace Randolph in her mother's heart. At first Haywood had had a tough time dealing with that, but then, had accepted that it was predestined for Randolph and her mother to be together. That belief had made her more determined than ever to protect what they shared.

Because she knew Noelle was waiting for an answer, she said, "Because I think what they share is beautiful. Just like what I think your parents share is beautiful, too. Just think of how long they've been together. That's a long time for any couple."

Noelle smiled. "Yes, that is a long time and I hope my marriage to Donald lasts just as long."

Haywood returned her best friend's smile. "And it will. Have the two of you decided on a date yet?"

Noelle sighed. "No, not yet. He's supposed to be returning home from South America next month. We plan to talk about dates then."

Haywood nodded. Don was a fighter pilot in the navy and had been gone six months already. She thought that he and Noelle made such a beautiful couple. As she wiped down the countertops she couldn't help but think of her relationship with Aaron. It didn't bother her as much as it used to that he was holding back and not letting their relationship progress to where she wanted it to be; where she felt it should be after an entire year. Aaron owned the publishing company where she worked as a photographer for his elite magazine line. She knew her mother and Randolph, not to mention Zach, didn't approve of her relationship with Aaron, a man sixteen years older than she was, especially since it was obvious the relationship was headed nowhere. Aaron had been married before and had teenaged children. Although he'd told her he had no intention of marrying again, that didn't stop her from trying to get him to change his mind by seeing that she was the best thing that ever happened to him. So far he hadn't gotten the picture.

The sound of car doors opening and closing gave Haywood pause. She turned from the sink. "I heard a car."

"I did, too. I think your stepfather's back with Trey."

When Randolph and Trey entered the house it was Zach who thwarted what promised to be a very tense moment. Genuinely glad to see each other, Zach and Trey's friendship was quickly and easily renewed.

Trey's acknowledgement of everyone was warm and friendly. However, it was obvious to everyone that his approach to Jenna, though polite, was rather cool.

Haywood had entered the living room and watched him from a distance, not letting her presence be known. She had intended to take her cue of how to accept him from the way he accepted her mother. Seeing that after all these years he still believed the lies his mother had told him made her angry.

At that moment Randolph glanced around the room and asked, "Where's Haywood?"

"Here I am, Dad."

Trey turned around at the same time Randolph did, hearing the sound of the soft feminine voice. Trey stood still. For a moment, just for one moment, he remembered her as the young girl of nine that he had last seen. But she was no longer a young girl. She was a woman. A very beautiful woman.

Trey watched as she crossed the room to his father. The look she was giving Trey was cool. Just as cool as the look he knew he was giving her.

"Trey, you remember Haywood, don't you?"

He nodded. "Yes, I remember." *The other woman's daughter,* he thought. "Haywood."

"Trey."

Zach, forever the peacemaker, came up beside Trey to throw water on the fire he detected was about to burst into flames. "I'll help get your things out of the car, then the two of us can drink a couple of beers while we catch up on everything."

Trey turned his attention away from Haywood and smiled at Zach. "I'd like that."

A few hours later everyone had gone to bed except for Trey and Zach who sat outside on the porch drinking beer. They had spent the better part of the night bringing each other up to date on what had been happening in their lives as well as recalling fond childhood memories.

Trey glanced over at Zach. He took another sip of his beer before asking, "What's the deal with you and Haywood?"

Zach leaned forward. "Haywood?"

"I picked up on something between the two of you." And he had. The two had seemed pretty friendly toward each other, almost too friendly to be just friends.

Zach shook his head grinning. "Before I married Shaun, Haywood and I tried to make a go of it for a few weeks then decided we do better as friends."

"Than lovers?"

"Never got that far, man. Haywood's too damn bossy, in addition to being stubborn, bullheaded and opinionated."

Trey laughed. "Sounds like the type of woman any man would want."

"Yeah, if he's suicidal. But seriously, all jokes aside, Haywood's okay and is a close friend. I know there's some animosity between the two of—"

"What gave you that idea?"

"I felt it earlier, when you first arrived and I feel it every time the two of you are in close proximity to each other. She knows how you feel about her mother and is very protective of her. She's also very protective of your father."

"And she has a right to be since he was so willing to turn his back on me to take up with her and her mother."

"You still believe that, Trey?"

Trey remained silent for a few minutes. "Yes. I'll never forget the day my mother broke the news to me that Dad was making excuse after excuse for why I couldn't fly out for the holidays." He shrugged. "But that's the way Jenna wanted it."

Zach shook his head, not wanting to be the one to tell him that he'd heard an entirely different story. "Have you ever talked to your Dad about any of this?"

"No, and I don't intend to, either. That was years ago and I've put it behind me. All I want is to pay my last respects to my great-grandmother and return to LA."

Zach looked at him, long and steadily. "No, Trey, I don't think you've put it behind you and maybe it's time you did. There're two sides to every story and I think it's time you heard your father's."

Thirty

Every pew in the Sycamore Baptist Church on Hilton Head Island was filled to capacity as people came from all around to pay their last respects to Mattie Denison. The congregation made it a happy occasion, a joyous home-going, and an uplifting church service more than a funeral. They all knew she would have wanted it that way.

A ferry transported everyone back across the waters to Glendale Shores where she was laid to rest in a grave next to her husband of over sixty years. The repass lasted well into the night where family members and friends ate, drank and ate some more before finally leaving.

The man who had served as Ma and Pa Denison's attorney for years, Theodore Jernigan, and his grandson Colt, were the last ones remaining. He surprised everyone when he called them together. "I know this has been a difficult day for you all, but now I have to shed my coat as a friend of the family and put on the one I wear as an attorney."

Randolph lifted a brow at the older man. "What's this about, Ted?"

Theodore Jernigan smiled slowly. "The reading of your great-grandmother's will. She requested that it be read immediately after the repass if everyone was here that needed to be." He glanced around the room. "And everyone is here. Everyone she considered family. Now if you'll follow me to the main room we can get down to business." He held up a finger. "And I promise it won't take long."

"Now then, let's begin." Colt Jernigan took over once everyone was seated. Like his grandfather he was tall and dark. But where his grandfather's face showed his years, Colt was blessed with the gleam of youth. At twenty-five he was fresh out of law school and had returned to South Carolina to work in his grandfather's law office.

"According to her request, Miss Mattie also wanted us to make this as informal as possible because she knew all of you had jobs to return to." He glanced up and met everyone's gaze. "She became a very wealthy woman after her family sold the land they owned on Hilton Head to developers. Since Miss Mattie never agreed to the sale of that property she never used any of the money she received. Instead, she decided to bequeath it to those she loved."

Colt pulled out a folder. "Instead of reading the will word for word," he continued, "I will get to the heart of the matter." He pulled a number of documents from the folder in front of him. "First to Noah Wainwright and his family. Miss Mattie has included this letter she wants me to read.

"Noah, from the first time Ross brought you to Glendale Shores while on a summer break from college, Bush and I adopted you into our hearts as another grandson. Your friendship and dedication to Ross continued, even beyond his death, and for that I will be eternally grateful. Your wife, Leigh, and your children, Zachary and Noelle, were special to me as well. Therefore, I want to leave you and your family collectively the sum of four hundred thousand dollars."

Deeply touched by Mattie's gift, Noah could only nod.

"To Randi, my beautiful great-granddaughter whom I love dearly, I leave you the sum of five hundred thousand dollars to be used wisely. This amount will be held in a trust for you until your twenty-fifth birthday."

"Wow," Randi said, her eyes getting big at the amount her great-grandmother had left her.

"There's a handwritten statement, one addressed to Adrianna Fuller that Miss Mattie wanted read," Colt said.

"There's a strong possibility that when this is read my granddaughter, Adrianna Fuller, still will not have been found. But in my heart I believe that one day she will be. And when she is found, I want her to have her share of what I would have left to her father, Ross Donovan Fuller, Jr. My only regret is that I never met her during my lifetime, but one day all of us will be together, and when I see Ross at the pearly gates, I will let him know that his loved ones are still searching for the daughter he left behind. And when she is found, the family Bible will be restored to its rightful place."

"Miss Mattie left a list of things she wants Adrianna Fuller to have when she is found," Colt said, after clearing his throat.

"To Randolph and Jenna Fuller. There are separate letters to the both of you that she wants you to read privately. As far as what she wanted you to have, collectively she has left everything she didn't specifically bequeath to anyone else to the two of you. If the two of you have any questions after reading your letters and reviewing her bank statements, please let me know."

Both Jenna and Randolph nodded.

"Now, moving right along," Colt said smiling. "There's only one document left to be read and that's her letter to Haywood Malone and

Ross Donovan Fuller III." He looked at one and then the other before he began reading.

"To Haywood and Trey. Words can't express how much the two of you mean to me. Haywood, from the moment I first met you when you were a mere six years old, you became special to me. And Trey, although I didn't get to spend as much time with you as I would have liked over the years, you've held a special place in my heart. Not only are you the one remaining male Fuller from your generation, but you are also the one remaining male Denison as well. And because I believe you and Haywood will do the right thing and carry out my wishes, I leave to the both of you Glendale Shores, the entire island except for the south portion of land Ross and Randolph inherited from their parents. This land is to be shared equally and to be used as you please but only after the following stipulation. Because this land has been a part of the Denison family for over one hundred years, I don't want you to make the same mistake my siblings made when they sold land on Hilton Head to the developers. Before either of you entertain the idea of selling any portion of Glendale Shores, I want you to spend two weeks here and enjoy the beauty of the island. You are to commit yourselves to stay on the island without any outside interference of other family members or friends. I don't want either of your decisions influenced in any way. I prefer that you make arrangements to do this within three weeks of my passing to pack up everything I have listed on a separate sheet of paper and given to Ted. Some things I want donated to the South Carolina Historical Society and others to Goodwill. I'm leaving the two of you responsible for carrying out these wishes of mine. After the two weeks the two of you must agree on what to do with your portion of Glendale Shores. It is my desire that you will come to love it as much as I have and will want to keep it, but the decision is yours."

Colt lifted his head and looked at Trey and Haywood. Both were speechless. "Do you understand what she is asking the two of you to do?"

"Yes," Trey said, amazed. Astonished. He'd always assumed his father would be the one to inherit all of Glendale Shores one day. It touched him deeply that Ma Mattie wanted him to have part of it. He wasn't concerned about Haywood's share. He would just buy her out. Even as that thought entered his mind, he glanced over at her and met her gaze. She frowned as if knowing what he'd been thinking.

"And Miss Malone, do you understand?" The question grabbed Haywood's attention. She shifted her gaze from Trey to Colt. "Yes, she wants me and Trey to dispose of her things."

Colt nodded. "Yes. And do you also understand about the two weeks?"

Haywood nodded although she really didn't understand. Ma Mattie had known that she would never sell Glendale Shores to anyone because she'd known how upset Ma Mattie had been when her family had outvoted her to sell land on Hilton Head to developers. Although Ma Mattie had subsequently made a lot of money off the sale, she had been left with a broken heart that greed for money instead of love for the land had driven her siblings to sell their family legacy. She never wanted the same thing to happen to Glendale Shores.

Haywood was also aware that Ma Mattie had gotten a lot of letters from various developers who wanted to turn Glendale Shores into another Hilton Head, but she had flatly refused each and every one of their offers time and time again. Haywood felt she didn't need two weeks on the island to make up her mind about anything. She would never agree to sell her part of Glendale Shore.

"What if my mind is made up as to what I want to do with my share of the island? Will the two weeks still apply?" she asked Colt.

"Afraid so. The two weeks is a stipulation which must be met, Miss Malone."

She nodded, knowing that somehow during those weeks she had to convince Trey not to sell. If that didn't work she would buy him out.

She glanced over at Trey. He was frowning at her; probably pissed that he had to share a piece of the island with her. She sighed deeply. The time she spent with him on Glendale Shores would be two weeks of pure hell.

Thirty-one

"I forbid you to go, Trey."

Trey looked at his mother with narrowed dark eyes. They seldom had arguments but when they did, they were doosies. "Mom, first of all I'm thirty-four, too old for you to forbid to do anything. Secondly, I have to go. It's within the terms of Ma Mattie's will."

"You're an attorney. You can fight it. She must have been out of her mind to even think about sharing something that rightly belongs to you with that woman's daughter. It's my understanding that Glendale Shores can only be left to a blood relative."

Trey glanced at his watch. "There is one exception and that is if a Denison legally declares someone as their godchild or adopted child. According to Ma Mattie's attorney, she legally claimed Haywood as her godchild when Haywood was ten."

"But it's not fair. That island should belong to you and only you."

"It may still belong to me if I can get Haywood to sell me her share."

"Don't hold your breath for that to happen. Everyone knows Glendale Shores is a gold mine. Just look at how exclusive Hilton Head is. Any developer would pay plenty for that island. You'd be set for life if you were to get complete ownership of that land."

Trey nodded as he continued packing. Now was not the time to tell his mother he had no intention of selling Glendale Shores. He knew how much Ma Mattie wanted the land to remain in the family and that's where he intended for it to stay. If Haywood wouldn't sell her part to him then he would have to convince her not to sell out to developers, either.

He then realized his mother was still talking.

"I still think Mattie Denison was up to something when she drew up that will. As far as I'm concerned she was a crazy old woman. Why would she want you and Haywood on that island alone for two weeks?"

Trey glanced over his shoulder, not liking the fact that his mother had called his great-grandmother crazy. "There was nothing crazy about her or about her request. She wants me and Haywood to pack up her things, and at the same time make a sound, unbiased decision. And she knew the only way we could do that would be to spend time on the island away from our family and friends. Haywood will be living in the big house and I'll be staying in Dad's cottage. I also intend to rent a boat while I'm there and will spend time on it."

"I don't care what you say, Mattie Denison was a little touched in the head. Otherwise why would she leave something in her will for Ross's daughter when she'll never be found?"

Trey turned and look at his mother questioningly. "What makes you so sure of that?"

Angela rolled her eyes. "Because it's been over thirty years and she hasn't been found yet. Your father and Noah Wainwright hired some of the best investigators around. No one knows if she's even still alive."

Trey thought about something that Zach had told him. "Noah and Dad think she's still alive."

"That just goes to prove what big fools they are."

Trey shook his head as he shut his suitcase. He'd never noticed before just how negative his mother could be when it came to his father's family and friends. "If an emergency comes up, call me at this number," he said, handing her a piece of paper. "And I mean a real emergency, Mom. Otherwise, just wait for me to call you. I'll check in each week and I'd appreciate if you didn't share any of your opinions about the island when we talk. To sell or not to sell will be my decision."

Angela looked up at him with a bemused look on her face. "What are you talking about? Surely you're not thinking of keeping that land?"

"Mom, I can't discuss this now. I have to finish packing."

"What about Marva?"

Trey flashed a confused look. "What about her?"

"Will she know how to reach you if she needs you?"

Trey arched a brow. "Why would she need me?"

Angela looked confused again. "But—but I thought the two of you were seeing a lot of each other."

"We only had three dates. We're nothing more than friends."

Angela narrowed her eyes. "Nothing more than friends? You spent the night at her house all three times."

Trey raised his eyes to the ceiling. "And your point is?"

Angela walked over to stand in front of him. "My point, Ross Donovan Fuller the Third, is that she's the daughter of very good clients of your stepfather's. I would hate for him to lose the Barfields' business because you couldn't keep your pants zipped."

Trey shook his head. The Barfields' daughter couldn't keep her legs closed any more than he could keep his pants zipped. "Marva and I know where we stand with each other. Don't lose any sleep over our relationship because there isn't one. Now if you don't mind, there are a million things I have to do before I leave."

Angela stared at the man towering over her. He was the one and only person she cared about in the world. The thought of ever losing him . . .

"Promise me you won't believe anything they tell you about me."

Trey sensed her fear as he noted the lines of anxiety etched in her face. Her voice was oddly shaky as well. He felt a surge of concern. "Who are they?"

"Any of them, the Fullers and the Wainwrights. They hate me and will try to do anything to turn you against me."

"Mom," he said softly, reaching out and touching her shoulder. "You're my mother and no one could turn me against you. You should know that."

"They might try."

"Let them. But I have no reason to think that they will. Why would they?" He looked at her intently. "Unless there's something I should know that you're not telling me. Is there?"

"No, of course not!"

"Then don't worry about it. Besides, the only person I'll see over the next two weeks is Haywood and she doesn't even know you."

Angela nodded, deciding not to say anything else and fearful she may have already said too much. "Take care of yourself, Trey," she trailed off in a soft voice.

He smiled as he pulled her into his arms for a hug. "I will and you take care of yourself, too, Mom."

"Haywood, you got a minute?"

Haywood smiled as she looked at her mother standing in the door-way of her bedroom. "Sure, Mom, come in."

Jenna glanced around the room. "Are you sure you'll be gone for just two weeks? It looks like an entire year's supply of stuff here."

Haywood chuckled. "Most of it is my camera equipment. I plan to take a lot of pictures while I'm there. Glendale Shores is such a beau-tiful place."

Jenna nodded. "Yes, and Gramma Mattie knew just how much you loved it. That's why she left it to you."

"Then why do I have to stay on the island if she knew how much I loved it?"

Jenna got a faraway look in her eye when she said, "Sometimes, when we love something . . . or someone . . . we'll give it up if we think it's for the best."

Haywood shook her head. "Well, that's not me. No one's going to take care of Glendale Shores like I would. I have no intention of let-ting some developer come in and destroy the natural beauty of the island so they can build hotels and condos." She sighed in disgust. "Just look at Hilton Head. It's a beautiful resort area, true enough, but just think of what they did to the island to get it that way. And it both-ers me when I think of all those African-Americans who sold that land and now it's too expensive for them to even go back there to visit. I don't want that to happen to my land."

"You may have a hard time bringing Trey around to your way of thinking."

Haywood shrugged. "I'm going to have a hard time bringing Trey around period. He hates me."

Jenna shook her head sadly. "No, I don't think Trey hates anyone. He just thinks he does."

Haywood glanced at her mother, incredulously. "How can you say that after the way he's treated you? Even at Ma Mattie's funeral he was cold and indifferent toward you."

"He thinks he has a reason to be that way."

"Well, it's time for him to stop."

"He will when the time is right." Jenna took a deep breath. "Randolph and I were talking and we want to make sure you're okay with spending two weeks on Glendale Shores with Trey. Sometimes he can be a rather angry young man."

Haywood chuckled. "Don't worry about me. I'll be able to handle Trey and his anger. I'm sure we'll get along since I probably won't see much of him after we finish packing up Ma Mattie's belongings each day. That island is big and I overheard him tell Zach that he plans to rent a boat, so I imagine he'll be busy enjoying himself."

Jenna nodded. "Yes, I guess he will. How did Aaron handle the news about this trip?"

Haywood shook her head as she put one piece of luggage aside and began packing another. "Although he gave me the time off work he wasn't happy about it." She decided not to mention that to her surprise, Aaron had shown signs of possessiveness and said he didn't want her to go. He'd even given her an ultimatum that if she didn't return to Paris, things were over between them. She was sure she had surprised him when she'd said that suited her just fine. Now was not the time to tell her mother that she and Aaron had ended their relationship. She'd wait and tell her parents at breakfast in the morning.

"You'll call me and Randolph if you need anything, won't you?"

Her mother's words reclaimed Haywood's attention. "Yes, but I'll be fine."

A few minutes later when she was alone in her bedroom again, Haywood thought about calling Aaron then decided not to. He was the one who had acted like a jerk, not she. She decided the best thing to do when she got back to Paris would be to look for another job. With her skills as a photographer that shouldn't be hard to do.

After she'd finished packing Haywood made a decision. Somehow and someway while they were together, she was going to get Trey to listen to what she had to say about their parents. Then he would know the truth about his mother's lies and betrayals. As far as she was concerned, it was time he knew the truth.

Thirty-two

Zach had just finished jotting some notes down on a legal pad when his secretary buzzed him. "Yes, Mrs. Summersfield, what is it?"

"Your father is here to see you, Mr. Wainwright."

Zach smiled as he tossed the legal pad aside. "Please show him in." He was proud of his father, who at fifty-nine didn't show any signs of slowing down. He was in great shape and enjoyed his job as a senator. He believed his father had accomplished more in his lifetime than most people. He was a hero of the Vietnam War, had worked in private practice as an attorney in Texas and had returned home to Florida where he'd been selected by the mayor as a city commissioner. He'd then run for the office of senator and that was almost four terms ago. He claimed he had one term left before retiring.

Zach's office door opened and his father and his secretary walked in together, laughing and talking. Senator Noah Wainwright was a born politician and had a way of handling people that was genuinely sincere and caring. He was a good man—fair-minded, open-minded and dedicated, and had a definite patent on charisma. He was loyal to those he loved and those he served. Zach also had to give credit to his mother, who was an excellent politician's wife, one who complimented his father well. At fifty-six she was still a beautiful woman, devoted to her husband and her children.

"Dad, this is a surprise," Zach said, crossing the room and giving his father a bear hug and a firm slap on the back. Open displays of affections were common in his family.

Noah smiled. "A good one I hope."

"You know it is. Have a seat, Senator."

Noah smiled and shook his head. "Don't try getting too big for your britches, Zachary."

"Ouch," Zach said, grinning. Everyone in the family knew he preferred being called Zach to Zachary, although he was proud of his name since it had been given to him in honor of his mother's brother and a man who had been his father's best friend. At least one of them. His father was always proud to boast that he had been blessed with two best friends during his lifetime, Zachary Murdock and Ross Fuller, Jr.

Senator Wainwright leaned back in his chair. "We haven't seen you since the funeral so I thought I'd better come and investigate to make sure you're doing okay."

Zach smiled. He wasn't fooled one bit. He knew his mother was the one who'd been worried and had sent his father to make sure he was doing all right. "Tell, Mom I'm fine, Dad. I've just been busy lately."

Noah nodded as he studied his son. "Yeah, we've noticed. We're also concerned."

Zach knew what his father was referring to. It had been a year since Shaun's death, but the pain of losing her was still raw. "Don't worry about me Dad, I'm fine." Wanting to change the subject, Zach asked, "Any new developments with Adrianna Fuller?" Adrianna Fuller was his father's goddaughter. He and Randolph Fuller had been looking for the woman for over thirty years.

Noah leaned back in the chair and met his son's gaze. "Yes, in fact when I leave here I'm meeting with Patrick Sellers, the son of one of the investigators. His father died a few months ago and he took over the case. According to him he may have a new lead."

Zach smiled. "I hope it's good news for you. Finding her has become an obsession, hasn't it?"

Noah shook his head. "No, Zach, not an obsession but an overwhelming desire to fulfill a promise made to my best friend."

* * *

"I was sorry to hear about your father, Patrick. He was a fine man."

"Thanks, Senator. He never came back around after losing Mom. It was hard for him the way she died, so sudden, senseless and tragic."

Noah nodded. He'd known that Matthew Sellers's wife had been a victim of a car accident where teenagers had stolen a car and gone joyriding. He'd never gotten over the death of the woman he'd been married to for over forty years, and over the last year had basically given up on life, eventually dying of a broken heart.

Noah signed deeply. He didn't want to imagine how he would handle it if anything ever happened to Leigh. "You indicated there may be a new lead?"

Patrick smiled. "Yes, sir. Unfortunately, it came across my father's desk earlier this year but as you know he wasn't in the frame of mind to deal with a lot of stuff. Therefore, I'm working overtime to make sure things are taken care of right away. One of those things is this letter Dad received from a detective agency in Saigon that he'd been working with to locate your goddaughter. As you know, the problem we've always had is not having a name for the aunt who raised her after her mother died in childbirth."

Noah sat up straight in his chair. "You have a name now?"

"Yes, sir. It seemed she married and we were able to get a name for her. A lot of the records had been destroyed with the fall of Saigon."

Noah shook his head. That had been the main reason they had not been able to locate Adrianna. Most of the birth records of Eurasians had been deliberately destroyed. That, coupled with the fact that the government had not known the identity of Gia's sister.

"I sent an investigator to talk to the woman we believe is the aunt. She claims that she gave the child to the orphanage when she was four."

Noah frowned. "Why?"

"The man she was engaged to marry would not accept Adrianna due to her mixed heritage."

Noah tried to downplay his anger upon hearing that. How could anyone hold something like that against anyone? Especially a child? "Have we contacted the orphanage?"

"One of my contacts is doing so as we speak. I hope to hear something from him in the coming weeks. Usually church groups from different nations or individuals sponsored those kids. Also, a number of them, those who could prove their mixed American parentage, were allowed to come to this country as United States citizens. Most of them settled in the California area. That may have been the case for Adrianna Fuller. All that is uncertain. However, there is one thing we are certain about."

"What?"

"She's not going by her American name. Doing so would have made our work a lot easier for us."

Noah nodded in agreement.

"There is something else that we discovered that we think you should know."

"What."

"The aunt claims that after her sister died she contacted the American embassy, right before the fall of Saigon. She wanted to send Adrianna to the States to Ross Fuller's family. She felt she would have a better life here."

"What made her change her mind?"

"She didn't. She claims a reply from the Fuller family indicated they didn't want the child, and would not acknowledge her as their grandchild and signed full custody of the child over to the aunt."

Noah sat up in his chair, angry. "Are you telling me the Fullers turned their back on their grandchild when they had an opportunity to claim her?"

"Yes, sir, it appears that way."

Noah stood. "I don't believe that, Patrick. Although the Fullers weren't happy with the fact that Ross married a Vietnamese girl, they wanted their granddaughter found as much as Randolph and I did."

"Not according to the aunt and she claims there's a signed document proving it."

"Were you able to get a copy of this document?"

"Unfortunately, no. She left any and all paperwork as well as any of

Gia's belongings with Adrianna at the orphanage. If this document exists, Adrianna has it in her possession."

"So if she's still alive then she's known the identity of her father's people all this time?"

"Possibly. But she may not have wanted to contact them since they had clearly indicated they didn't want her."

Noah shook his head. He had to talk to Randolph immediately. "I want you to stay on top of things, Patrick. I think we're close to finding her. Lord, I hope so."

The young man smiled. "So do I, Senator. Thirty-four years is a long time to be searching for someone."

Randolph leaned forward in the chair with his hands braced on his thighs. "There has to be a mistake, Noah," he said angrily. "There has to be." He had made the drive from Richmond to DC after receiving Noah's call and after immediately visiting with his grandparents. He had to find out if they knew anything about Patrick Sellers's claim that someone in the family had not acknowledged Adrianna as Ross's child and had gone so far as to sign papers giving up any rights to her.

A few moments later when Noah didn't say anything, Randolph added, "And I know what you're thinking but even my grandmother wouldn't stoop that low."

Noah sighed deeply. "Can you really say that with all certainty, Randolph? She was hell-bent on Ross marrying Angela and never approved of him marrying Gia."

"Yes, but regardless of that, had she been contacted she would have told us about it. I asked her about it today and she denied knowing anything. And I believe her mainly because Ross's death was hard on her, and she wanted his baby found as much as we did."

Noah nodded as he stood. "Well, if Sellers's claim is true, someone did do it and every time I think about it I get madder than hell. Who would do such a thing, especially knowing how much Ross loved Gia and how much he wanted his daughter here with us?"

Randolph shook his head. "I hope it's all a mistake and Sellers got his information wrong."

Noah looked at him for a long moment then said, "And if it's not a mistake and his information is right?"

Randolph stared hard at him. His jaw clenched and clearly defined anger clouded his eyes. "Then that person will have to deal with me personally. Count on it."

Thirty-three

"Hey, that box is too heavy for you to pick up. Play Superwoman some other time."

Haywood turned and glared at Trey. If looks could kill he would be dropping dead immediately. She didn't know how they would survive the two weeks it would take to pack Ma Mattie's belongings without doing each other in first.

Instead of saying anything she walked across the room to the sofa and sat down, crossing her arms over her chest to let off steam. It was either that or slapping him stupid. "Evidently you don't want or need my help since you have something to say about everything I do."

"I was trying to keep you from hurting yourself."

"Don't do me any favors."

Trey, who'd been leaning over a box, straightened to his full height. "Next time I won't. I'll just let you break your damn back."

"I prefer if you didn't curse around me."

"Saying the word 'damn' isn't cursing."

"In my book it is."

"Then you need another book."

Haywood stood and threw up her hands. "I don't know how Ma Mattie could have possibly thought you and I could do this. We don't even like each other."

Trey shook his head. "Don't like you? Hell, I don't even know you."

"Well, I don't know you either."

After a few minutes Trey said, "Look, other than proving we have a good pair of lungs, we won't get anywhere yelling at each other. Can we call a truce until we get this finished? Afterwards, we can cuss and fuss all we want."

Haywood couldn't help but chuckle as she came back over to the box. "Okay, I admit I'm a little uptight." When he lifted a brow she said, "Okay, so I'm more than a little uptight. But I just don't feel comfortable doing this."

"And you think that I do?"

Haywood sighed as she looked at him. Ma Mattie had meant a lot to him, too. "No, I guess you don't but for some reason, we're the ones she wanted to do it." She glanced at her watch. "Do you want to call it a day?"

"Why not? We've been at it half a day already." He glanced around the room. "We've packed four boxes. That's a box an hour."

"I think we've made good time."

He nodded in agreement. "How many more boxes do you think we have to do of this stuff?"

Haywood picked up the list containing the items that were being sent to Goodwill as per Ma Mattie's instructions. "At least another twelve boxes."

Trey shook is head. "How can any one person accumulate so much stuff?"

"Beats me. I consider myself a pack rat but this is beyond my wildest imagination. And there's just as many boxes that we have to pack for the South Carolina Historical Society. When Ma Mattie's will said it would take two weeks she was right on the money."

Trey nodded. "What are you going to do for the rest of the day?"

Haywood smiled. "I'm going swimming, what about you?"

"I'm going to check my e-mail on my laptop, see if I can get some work done. I plan to stay in for the rest of the day taking care of a few business matters."

Haywood nodded. "All right then, I'll see you in the morning, bright and early."

•   •   •

Breathtaking, Trey thought, when he came upon Haywood half an hour later near the water's edge. She had changed out of her tank top and shorts into a two-piece bikini and looked simply breathtaking.

He tried not to stare as he crossed the distance separating them but didn't like the uneasy feeling hitting him. Okay, so he was attracted to her. Big deal. Such an attraction was normal since he was a virile male with an abundance of hormones and she was a good-looking woman with a nice set of body parts. And no matter how much he wanted to dislike her, that didn't call for a sudden freezing of his blood. His blood was too hot for that.

His blood grew hotter the closer he got to her. She was stretched out on a blanket and her pose was to die for. Laying flat on her back she had one gorgeous leg raised that was bent at the knee giving him a nice view of her thighs. This was the first time he'd seen a woman that he knew personally be bold enough to wear a thong bathing suit in public.

"Do you mind company?"

Haywood quickly sat up and looked at him in surprise. "I thought you were going back to the cottage to work to work on your laptop for the rest of the day."

"That had been the plan but I got bored."

Haywood could believe that. Who wanted to be stuck inside when they could be outside enjoying the beauty surrounding them? She watched as he sat down on the edge of her blanket, thinking had she known she would see him again that day she certainly wouldn't have worn her two-piece, and definitely not this one. It was the one she had purchased last year with the deliberate intention of seducing Aaron. It had worked. At least for Aaron it had worked since he had enjoyed getting her out of the skimpy bathing suit. But it hadn't gotten her any closer to the altar with him than before. Now that they were no longer together she could see her parents had been right. Over the past year she had been involved with a man who had no intention of ever marrying her no matter how good she'd looked to him and no matter how much she had pleased him. There was no way she would have ever gotten him to change the way he felt about getting married again, and now she was glad she no longer had any intention of trying.

"I love it here," she finally said to Trey by way of conversation.

In an attempt not to stare at her body, Trey decided to look out over the water instead. A horde of birds was flying overhead searching the ocean for worthy prey. He glanced back over at her. "When was the last time you were here before Ma Mattie's death?" he asked softly.

Haywood lay back down on the blanket, instinctively reaching for a huge beach towel to cover her bottom area. Wearing such a provocative bathing suit around Aaron was one thing but around someone else entirely another. "I was here three months ago. I came to see her before I left to return to Paris."

"You've been in Paris long?"

"I moved there a few years ago. My father lived there for a number of years and still had friends living there so I went to stay with them until I found my own place."

Trey lifted a brow. "Your father used to live in Paris?"

"Yes. For a good fifteen years or more. In fact that's where he and my mother met. They were married in Paris and I was born there as well. We didn't move back to the States until after he got sick."

"And when was that?"

"When I was five."

He nodded. "But your mother, she came back to the States for extended visits pretty frequently, didn't she?"

Haywood knew what Trey was getting at and did her best not to let her anger take over. Instead she decided to pretend she didn't know where his line of questioning was leading. "No. She only made a trip back to the States once a year to visit her family and would stay for a couple of weeks. She never took extended trips back to the States, except for the year her father died. That was the year before she had married my father and two years before I was born."

She knew she had placed confusion into his mind as to when and how her mother and his father could have been having the ongoing affair as his mother claimed. There was no way his father and her mother could have had a long-distance romance like that. She was glad she had given him something to think about.

She stood and wrapped the towel around her. "I think I'm going inside. Too much sun isn't good for the skin. I'll see you tomorrow." Without saying anything else to him, Haywood started walking back toward the big house.

Trey watched her leave thinking she had the best-looking backside of any woman he knew, even with a thick towel wrapped around it. He smiled. She had seemed uncomfortable around him in that two-piece suit, and she should have been. A pair of panties and bra covered more than that thing she had on. But he had to admit she'd looked pretty damn good in it.

While talking to her he had tried not to notice a few things. Like the way her hair curled around her face and the way her eyes lit up with fire when she got bent out of shape about something. Then there were those lips she liked to moisten with the tip of her tongue. He could count the number of times she had stuck her tongue out to rub over her lips when they had been packing those boxes earlier that day.

He sighed deeply, disgusted with his thoughts. His father had made a mistake by getting involved with Haywood's mother but he had no intention of making a mistake by getting involved with the daughter. For the rest of his remaining days on the island he would do what he'd come here to do and keep his attraction to Haywood in check.

Thirty-four

Haywood stood back and looked at the boxes stacked in the room, feeling mighty proud of their accomplishment. "Hey, this isn't bad for one week's worth of work."

Trey also stood back but he thought what he'd experienced was one week's worth of torture. And to think he had another week to go. He took a quick glance at Haywood and doubted he would make it. She was not a "drop-dead gorgeous woman" but was definitely a "you got to take a second look" one. And during the past week he hadn't just taken a second look, he'd gotten an eyefull.

They had worked well together, usually in silence. They'd known what they had to do and had done it. Besides, they had nothing to talk about and she had proven that like him, she was not into idle chatter. So she had scanned the list and had assisted him by making sure Ma Mattie's wishes were carried out. The twelve packed boxes were ready to leave Glendale Shores by ferry for the Goodwill agency tomorrow.

He couldn't help but notice Haywood dressed each morning in a different tank top and a pair of shorts. It made him wonder just how many outfits she'd brought with her. It also had him wondering what sort of sleepwear she had brought along. He could visualize her being a silk and satin woman, all soft, cuddly, warm and—

"This calls for a celebration, don't you think?"

Her words broke into his thoughts and considering where they'd been headed, that was a good thing. "A celebration for what?"

"For completing one week of work. Don't you feel good about it?" she asked smiling.

He shrugged, thinking about his week of torture. "I suppose."

"Don't you know?"

Trey raised his eyes to the ceiling. One thing he did know was that she liked being specific. "Okay, I guess I do feel good about it, so how will we celebrate?"

Haywood stretched her body, and as he watched her he couldn't help but stretch his mind with all sorts of things. None of it good.

"Umm, I'm dying for seafood," she finally said after he assumed she had worked the kinks out of her body. "I suggest throwing out the net and seeing what we come up with."

His brow lifted. "You want us to fish for our own food?"

A smile touched her lips. "No, I want *you* to fish for our food. I'll volunteer to cook whatever you catch, granted it's something that can be cooked. I don't do old shoes and beer bottles. So are you game?"

Trey thought that at the moment, he would do just about anything to get away from her. "Yeah, I'm game."

"Good, Captain Trey, now go catch our dinner."

Trey caught more than enough for dinner—he caught enough for a feast. The net had been overflowing with an abundance of shrimp and blue crabs. Then, using the fishing pole once owned by his grandfather, he had caught a number of nice-sized fish.

True to her word, Haywood cooked enough for their dinner and put the rest in the freezer for next week. There was no need to make pigs of themselves. They decided to eat outside on the porch and the warm air carried the scent of the ocean and the smell of the roses from Ma Mattie's prized rose garden.

Trey glanced down at Haywood's plate and took note that like him she was a hearty eater. He liked that. A lot of the women he dated were too concerned about gaining weight. Evidently Haywood had no such fear. One thing he did know about her was that she was into physical fitness. He had noticed her jogging every morning while he sat at the kitchen table in the cottage enjoying his cup of morning coffee. He also saw her run occasionally in the afternoons. Other afternoons she'd walk around with a camera slung across her shoulders. She had taken enough photos of Glendale Shores to last a lifetime.

"Well, what do you think?"

For some reason his smile came easily. "About what?"

"About the food. Can I cook or what?"

With a half sigh he finished off the rest of his hush puppy. "Yes, you can cook and I find that amazing."

"Why?" she asked with a gleam in her eye. "Can't the women you date cook?"

"I don't know. I don't date them for their cooking abilities."

"What do you date them for?"

Trey chuckled before saying, "Their minds."

Haywood's smile widened. "And you really expect me to believe that?"

"Yes."

Haywood studied him as she considered what he'd said. He was handsome, there was no doubt of that. He was also tall, dark and built. She had noticed just how built he was with the shorts and T-shirts he'd worn each day. He had a naturally athletic body, one a person didn't get by lounging around all day but from hours spent at some spa or health club. She wouldn't be surprised to discover that he worked out at least two to three times a week. He was a healthy man and no doubt had a healthy sexual appetite. Therefore, she couldn't buy into his lie that he dated women for their minds. But if that's the lie he wanted to tell then so be it. She could just imagine some woman openly flirting with him and then later going home with him. She could also imagine that he would know how to undress a woman in the right way. There was something about the way he had folded up a Ma Mattie's things before placing them in a box. He had been neat and tidy, like he'd had all the time in the world. He hadn't rushed. She'd also noticed his hands. They were large and firm. Hands that appeared capable of bringing pleasure.

"What are you thinking, Haywood Malone?"

Haywood shook her head in disbelief at what she *had* been thinking. She picked up her glass of wine and took a sip. Her eyes met Trey's over the rim. "I was thinking how this place can spoil me if I'm not careful," she lied, knowing that hadn't been what she'd been thinking about. She quickly decided not to feel guilty about lying since he had a penchant for lying, too.

He glanced around. "It is beautiful here, isn't it? I always enjoyed coming here as a child with my father."

"What about your mother?"

He took a sip of his wine and said, "I don't ever remember her coming here with us. I don't think she and Ma Mattie got along."

It was on the tip of Haywood's tongue to say that Ma Mattie was the type of person who got along with everybody so that in itself should have told him something. "Do you remember Ma Mattie's husband?"

"Papa Murphy?" Trey asked smiling. "Yes, I remember him. He used to take me fishing as a little boy all the time. Do you remember him?"

Haywood shook her head. "No, he died before I came on the scene. She used to talk about him all the time though. She always referred to him as 'her Bush'. I gather they had a very close relationship."

Trey nodded. "They did. I could actually feel the love flowing between them. It was volatile enough for a child to pick up on."

Haywood smiled. That's the way it was for her mother and Randolph. Anyone could clearly see just how much they loved each other. Even her friends used to comment on how well suited they were and how affectionately they treated each other. That's the kind of relationship she wanted with a man. One that wasn't reserved and fake.

Suddenly realizing that Trey had been speaking, she looked up at him. "I'm sorry, what did you say?"

"I asked if you wanted to take a walk around the island after we did the dishes?"

Haywood lifted a brow in surprise. "You're helping me do the dishes?"

"Of course. I helped you eat didn't I?"

She nodded. Aaron had never offered to help her with the dishes no matter how many times he'd eaten at her place.

"All right then. Let's do the dishes then take a walk. What do you think about that idea?" Trey asked.

Haywood smiled. "I think it's a good one."

Later that night as she got into bed Haywood couldn't help but think about the walk with Trey around the island. For the first thirty minutes or so they had walked side by side talking about a number of things. She had told him about her love for photography. He had shared with her his love for law and how much he enjoyed working as a corporate attorney for his stepfather's company.

At one point while walking he had reached out and held her arm as he guided her around a fallen tree limb, then automatically, like it was the most natural thing for him to do, he had taken her hand in his and held it. And they had continued their walk holding hands.

Turning in bed she leaned back against the propped pillows, not feeling sleepy, although the clock indicated it was close to three in the morning. She wondered if Trey was still up. Getting out of bed she crossed the room to the window. From the second-floor window she could see the distance across the treetops to where the cottage sat. The lights were on which meant he was still up. She couldn't help wondering what he was doing and if he too was having a restless night.

Since tomorrow was Saturday they would rest. She didn't know what his plans were but hers included sleeping late, especially since she wasn't getting much sleep tonight. On Sunday she would explore the island and take more pictures. Then on Monday she and Trey would start packing the boxes that would go to the Historical Society.

She crossed the room and got back into bed. Closing her eyes she imagined a pair of sexy eyes looking at her and a sensually ripe mouth coming toward hers.

Haywood wondered why she was in such a bad mood Monday morning and tried convincing herself it had nothing to do with the fact that she hadn't seen Trey all weekend. After all, she'd been free to do her thing like he'd been free to do his. At one point she'd even thought he had left the island for the weekend, but at night the light had come on inside the cottage as usual. So she could only assume he had decided to stay indoors and work on his laptop. But that didn't help the nagging urgency she felt of wanting to see him, even a glimpse.

And it sure didn't help matters that each night he had somehow managed to creep into her dreams. For the first time in her life she had awakened in the middle of the night aroused.

Her mood Tuesday wasn't any better and Wednesday was even worse.

"Are you going to help pack or are you going to stand there and daydream?"

Trey's sharp words broke into Haywood's thoughts. "Don't mess with me today, Trey. I'm not in the mood."

"That makes two of us. So how about we finish up here?"

"Fine."

Trey frowned. It was fine with him as well. He didn't want to be around her any more than he had to. Taking that walk together Friday had been a mistake. And because of it he had stayed inside all weekend trying to screw his head back on straight. And then to top things off, she'd been acting moody for the last three days and he was getting sick and tired of it. "Look, Haywood, if you'd rather not be doing this, I'd rather do it myself than put up with your bitchiness."

"My bitchiness!"

"Yes!"

Perhaps it was a direct result of the sleepless nights she'd been having lately. Perhaps it was the plain and simple fact that he'd had the nerve to say she'd been acting bitchy. Or perhaps it was just because. Whatever the reason, she acted on it and shoved hard against him, which sent them tumbling to the floor.

Caught off-guard by her actions he cushioned their fall and landed flat on his back with her sprawled on top of him. "Are you nuts or something, Haywood!"

"No, I'm not nuts! I'm bitchy, remember?"

Oh, he remembered all right. But what he didn't remember was her feeling this soft and cuddly atop him. Or her being nose-to-nose with him. Or eye-to-eye, hip-to-hip and thigh-to-thigh. She shifted her body to get up and immediately his arms latched around her waist. "Don't move."

Haywood raised a brow at the same time her body began responding to the purely male body beneath it. Looking into his face she saw those same dark sexy eyes and sensually ripe mouth she had been dreaming about for the last five days, and a flash of arousal rushed through every bone in her body.

"Let me up," she said softly but without much conviction in her voice.

Trey looked at her. He didn't want to acknowledge this attraction he'd tried so hard to ignore, but was helpless to stop it. "No, stay."

She was lying on top of him between his legs. It was an indecent yet perfect fit and they both realized it the same time. "Let me up, Trey," she said lightly. "Don't forget we have a lot of work to do before the ferry comes on Friday," she reminded him.

For a moment Trey wondered, because of the calmness in her voice, if he was the only one on some sort of adrenaline high; the only one whose body was experiencing a mega-shock of excitement and desire.

He stared up at her and took note of the deep darkening of her pupils and the faint blush tinting her cheeks. For the longest time neither of them said anything. Then Haywood broke the silence by saying. "If you're going to kiss me then go ahead and get it over with so we can—"

Trey didn't let her finish. Instead he tightened one hand around her and with the other gripped her hair, pulling her mouth down to meet his. He saw the moment she closed her eyes, then he closed his.

The moment their mouths touched, electricity flowed through their bodies. She opened her mouth beneath his to let him taste her like she wanted to taste him. With his hand firmly planted in her hair he held her mouth in place while his tongue took, possessed and pleasured her mouth. And she couldn't do anything but melt under him, and let him continue to drive her over the edge with his tongue.

When she felt his hand slipping beneath her blouse she pulled back. She hadn't meant for this to happen, then remembered that she had all but invited him to kiss her so she couldn't play the part of an innocent now. But she could try and get control of the situation. "Okay, you've had your fun for today. Let's get back to work."

She knew her words were like ice water thrown on a blazing fire but at the moment that couldn't be helped. They had crossed a line and she wanted to get back on the other side as soon as possible.

She let out a sigh of relief when Trey released her and gently pushed her off of him. Instead of saying anything he stood and walked out of the house.

Thirty-five

Kissing Haywood had been a mistake.

But something in him needed to know what her mouth tasted like. And now he wished he hadn't found out. He let out a little hiss of breath when he made it to the pier. What was wrong with him and Haywood? Why were they trippin'? Why were his hormones raging to the point where she was like a craving he had to have? How had she managed to get to him so fast? He breathed deeply, wondering if the saying, "like mother, like daughter" was true. If Jenna's allure had been anything like Haywood's, his father hadn't stood a chance. But still, nothing should have been that tempting to make a man turn his back on his wife and child.

Bitterness flooded his mind. He would never forget the day his mother told him why she was marrying Harry and moving to Los Angeles. She had given up hope that she and his father would get back together because she'd discovered that for the past five years he had taken back up with an old girlfriend from college, and had been secretly having an affair with her. Now the woman's husband was out of the picture and the two wanted to marry. But the woman didn't want a visual reminder of Randolph's marriage to another woman, which meant there wouldn't be a place for him in his father's life anymore.

At first he didn't want to believe what his mother had said. He wanted to believe she was wrong. But when his father had asked that he not be present at the wedding he had been crushed and filled with bitter resentment. It was resentment that even now he hadn't been able to let go of.

He stood on the pier and looked out over the water. From the conversations he and Haywood had had while walking he knew she had been close to her own father. He wondered how she had handled her mother remarrying so soon after his death. Did she know her mother and his father had been having an affair while they were married to other people?

A part of him didn't want to bring up the past but he wanted to deal with the anger he was feeling each and every time he thought about it. Taking another deep breath he decided to talk to Haywood once and for all about something that had festered inside of him over twenty years.

Haywood was sealing up the last box that she intended to pack that day. Trey had not returned and she doubted that he would. She rubbed the ache at the back of her neck admitting that she *had* been acting downright bitchy with him since Monday and admitted further that he hadn't deserved it. But there was this thing between them where they could be nice to each other one minute and at each other's throats the next. And she was sick and tired of it.

A sound behind her made her turn around. When she did so she met Trey's gaze. He stood leaning against the door looking at her. His face and stance appeared calm but she had a feeling there was a storm brewing; a storm she was about to get caught up in. Even the air surrounding them was filled with tension.

There was something else in the air, flowing between the two of them. Temptation. They had kissed once but the need, the desire to do so again was there as he looked at her. Would kissing him again be so bad, she wondered? She studied him as she considered it. She also considered the possibility that she was stone crazy to want to do such a thing.

Her gaze moved over him and she took in what he was wearing, a pair of jeans and a sweatshirt with an expensive pair of tennis shoes on his feet. She thought he had pretty good taste. When she lifted her gaze to his face, his mouth in particular, she remembered he also tasted pretty good.

She inhaled deeply and tried to ignore the pulses of desire shooting through her body. "You weren't supposed to come back," she finally said, breaking the silence surrounding them.

"Did you actually believe I that wouldn't?" he questioned huskily.

She thought of their kiss and the passion it had stroked to life inside of them and shook her head. "No, but one of us has to keep our head on straight," she said, softly.

"Usually my head is on straight," he replied throatily. "I've just never had to deal with someone like you before. You're different."

She didn't know if what he said was a compliment or an insult. She decided to find out. "In what way other than bitchy?"

He couldn't resist the urge to smile and that smile, Haywood thought, tugged at her insides some more. The tension that had surrounded them all morning began evaporating with that smile. "We're crazy, you do know that, don't you?" she asked quietly.

"Yeah, but maybe it's not us, but it's this place instead. People claimed Ma Mattie had some sort of mystical powers that were linked to her Gullah ancestry."

Haywood nodded. She had heard that, too. She wondered if it was true and if there was a purpose to her and Trey being here on this island together other than packing up Ma Mattie's belongings. Had Ma Mattie decided to do what she felt had to be done to end the Denison-Fuller curse, and was she using Haywood and Trey to do it?

"But what would be gained if the both of us lost our minds?" she asked, trying to keep her voice calm and her senses intact. "We have a decision to make."

He lifted a brow. "About the island?"

She nodded, then decided to be truthful. "Yes, about the island and about us as well."

She waited for him to say there was no "us" but he didn't. And in not saying anything, he was acknowledging that something was going on between them. Something neither of them understood but both were willing to own up to.

She watched as he pushed away from the door and slowly walked over to her. "Ahh, Haywood, what are we going to do?" he asked when he stood directly in front of her.

She never let her gaze leave his face when she said, "Kissing again wouldn't be such a good idea but I'm willing to chance it."

"Yeah, I'm willing to chance it, too." His voice was low, sensuous, and then he leaned toward her and captured her mouth with his and immediately began feasting on her.

Haywood rose onto her toes to get closer as he mated with her tongue so relentlessly that she felt that same urge to mate in the lower part of her body. His kiss was deep, drugging, all-consuming, If the two of them were under some sort of spell, then it was definitely an erotic one that was meant to dull their senses and stimulate their passion.

And it was working.

That thought quickly intensified when she felt his hand move up and down her backside. His hands felt good on her, like that's where they belonged. For the first time in her life she knew how it felt to be completely absorbed by a man. Aaron's kisses had never made her feel this way. This was the kind of kiss that could knock you flat on your butt and dare you to get up. Passion was spinning out of control all around them. One of them had to pull back; Haywood quickly concluded it wouldn't be her. The taste of him was like an aphrodisiac, making her body hunger for things beyond a kiss.

Trey heard her moan a low, throaty sound and it triggered a desire to have more of her. For the first time in his life there was this reckless power within him. His blood was raging and his control had snapped. With this kiss she was tearing down a wall he had built, brick by brick. It was a wall that was supposed to be solid as a rock.

He pulled back as a semblance of control seeped in and he slowly let go of her mouth. But not completely. The tip of his tongue began caressing the outline of her lips, liking the way she shuddered in his arms. Moments later he rested his forehead against hers as his breathing tried to return to normal.

He took her hand in his. "Come on, let's go for a walk so we can talk."

"Are you seeing anyone?"

They had stopped walking for a brief moment and he turned his head to look at her. That was not what he'd meant to talk to her about. But now he wanted to know.

"No, not any longer."

"But you had been seeing someone seriously?"

He felt her hand stiffen in his. "I thought it was serious but I don't think Aaron did, although we'd been together a little more than a year. He owns the company I work for and is sixteen years older than me. Mom and Dad don't like him."

"I can understand why."

She looked at him and smiled. "Now you sound like Zach. He doesn't like Aaron, either. He thought he was taking advantage of me but the truth is that I was taking advantage of him. I knew he had no intention of ever marrying again but I was determined to change his mind about that."

"I take it you didn't change his mind."

Haywood inhaled deeply. "No, so I decided to cut my losses and move on."

Trey said nothing for a while then asked, "Are you still working for him?"

She nodded. "Yes, for now. But when I return to Paris I'm turning in my resignation. It will be pretty awkward for us to continue to work together." They began walking again. "What about you? Are you dating anyone seriously?"

"No." Now that he had appeased his curiosity about her love life he said, "Haywood, we need to talk about my relationship with your mother and why I feel the way I do."

Haywood had wondered if he would ever bring the subject up. She concluded that he figured she didn't know the whole story since she had only been six when her mother had married his father.

"It doesn't bother you that they are together?" he asked her.

"Why would it bother me, Trey? Our parents have been married for almost twenty-two years. Don't you think it's time you let whatever way you feel about them being together go?" she responded in a gentle voice.

"What about the way they got back together and the people they hurt? Don't you feel angry at the way they treated your father? Your mother was unfaithful to him."

Haywood shook her head. "No, she wasn't. My parents had a loving relationship. And although I now know my mother never truly loved him, at least not the way she'd always loved your father, I'm okay with it because of what Randolph and my mother gave up."

Trey frowned. "And what did they give up?"

Haywood smiled. "The most beautiful and the most passionate love any two people could ever share."

Trey stopped walking and crossed his arms over his chest and glared angrily at her. "And just where did my mother fit into the mix?"

"She didn't. My mother and your father had already committed their lives together more than a year before he married your mother. They did it here, on this island in your father's senior year of college during spring break. And it was done over the family Bible. In their hearts they were as married as two people could be, Trey. Maybe not legally but they were married just the same."

Trey had heard about the family Bible and that all Denisons were to commit their lives to the person they loved over it. He also knew it had gotten lost to the family when his father had sent it to his Uncle Ross to use when he had married his Vietnamese bride. It had not been returned with Ross's belongings when he'd died in Vietnam. "If what you say is true and they felt they were already married, then why did he marry my mother?"

"Because she was pregnant with you."

He'd already known his parents had married after he'd been conceived. Their anniversary date in correlation to his birthdate had indicated that. "In my book that meant he was not faithful to your mother. I know my mother was originally engaged to my father's brother. I also know about how the two of them ended up sleeping together one night when they were both mourning Uncle Ross's death. My mother told me everything."

"I doubt she told you everything."

He frowned. "What's that supposed to mean?"

"It means there are still things that you don't know."

"Your mother's version of it?"

"No, the truth, Trey. You're an attorney and are aware that diaries can be admissible as evidence in certain court cases. My mother's words in her diary depicted what really happened. She doesn't even know that I found it one day and read it. That's how I learned the truth. It's time that you learn the truth, too. Go to your father and listen to his version of what happened. You owe him that, Trey. He has been hurt so much by all of this."

"He's been hurt? What about me? I'm the one he turned his back on for you and your mother because that's the way she wanted it. She didn't want me around because I reminded her of his marriage to my mother."

"That's not true and if your mother told you that she lied. My mother is not that type of person. And no matter what you want to believe, she did not break up your parents' marriage. My mother broke off her engagement to Randolph so that he and your mother *could* marry and then she moved to Paris. They didn't see each other again until almost twelve years later. By then he was already divorced from your mother."

"Your mother and my father began having an affair three years before my parents divorced. She's the reason he divorced my mother, Haywood."

Haywood frowned. "That's not true and if you talk to your father you will find out what's true and what's not. If you don't want to talk to him then talk to your grandparents, the Fullers. They both know what really happened. You owe it to yourself to find out the truth once and for all."

Her words may as well have fallen on deaf ears, Haywood thought, as she got into bed later that night. Their talk hadn't accomplished anything but had made them angry and frustrated with each other once again. They had ended their walk and had gone their separate ways. They had two more days of packing left and she dreaded seeing him again. He was convinced that his mother had told him the truth. Haywood wondered how he would handle it when he found out what she'd told him had been nothing but the lies of a spiteful and hateful person.

As Haywood drifted off to sleep she prayed that whatever reason Ma Mattie had had for placing them on the island together was worth all the anger, hard feelings and frustration that she was feeling right now.

* * *

Private Investigator Patrick Sellers read the report for the second time. The information was still incomplete but at least he seemed to be headed somewhere other than a dead end.

There was reason to believe that Adrianna Fuller was not only alive but was living in San Diego, California.

He had been able to track the American church that had sponsored her to come to the United States and had paid for her schooling. According to their information, she was a doctor. The only thing he did not have was the last name she was using now.

Patrick checked his watch. It was late and time he called it a day. But he was determined to find the final piece to a thirty-four-year puzzle.

Thirty-six

He didn't stand a chance.

Trey knew it when he arrived at the big house the next morning and Haywood opened the door with sleep-filled eyes, wearing her robe. Some things were supposed to look good early in the morning, but a woman whose face had that "just got out of bed" look was not one of them.

"I'm sorry, Trey," she said between yawns. "But I didn't get much sleep last night and overslept this morning. You can start packing and I'll join you as soon as I get dressed."

He nodded as he leaned in the doorway. "Have you had breakfast yet?"

"Breakfast? Are you kidding? I just rolled out of bed. I haven't had a chance to even wash my face or brush my teeth."

He quirked an amused brow at her as he straightened his stance. "All right, go do both and I'll fix you something to eat." He entered, closing the door behind him.

Haywood tilted her head up and looked at him. "I like your offer but I don't want to put you to any trouble."

"It's no trouble at all. Eggs, toast, bacon and coffee. That's simple enough."

"You sure?"

"I'm positive."

She smiled at him, finding it hard to believe this was the same man she'd had a disagreement with the day before. He was in a good mood and she decided to take full advantage of it. "Do you mind if I add taking a shower to washing my face and brushing my teeth?"

"Nope, don't mind if you do."

"Thanks." She was halfway up the stairs when she stopped, turned around and looked back down at him. "You didn't ask how I wanted my eggs."

He grinned. "I only know how to cook them one way. Scrambled."

She laughed. "That will work." She then continued walking up the stairs.

"I've made up my mind to talk to my father."

Haywood lifted a brow over her cup of coffee. She hadn't expected to hear him say that. "When did you make that decision?"

"Last night. I thought about everything you said and admit that there are too many inconsistencies for me not to ask questions."

She nodded, glad he had made that decision. "When are you going to talk to him?"

"Before I return to California."

For the rest of the day they packed up the boxes, working together in peaceful harmony the majority of the time.

"So what do you plan to do now that we're finished here?" he asked as he sealed the last box they were to pack, thus finishing up a day early.

Haywood shrugged. "Since I have only three days left on the island, I thought I'd go around and take more pictures. What about you? What will you be doing?"

"Don't know what I plan to do the other days, but today I'm going to shoot a few hoops. That basketball net is still standing that Pa Murphy put up years ago for Dad and Uncle Ross."

"I know. I always used it whenever I came to visit."

Trey lifted a brow. "You know how to play basketball?"

"Sure," she said grinning. "I'm a girl with three uncles who're basketball fanatics."

"Do you want to shoot a few hoops with me later today?"

"I'd love to."

"Okay, so you won. Try not to gloat too much, will you?"

Trey smiled. "It will be hard but I'll try. And I have to admit, Malone, that you play a mean game."

"But not mean enough to whip you, Fuller. Right?"

He laughed. "Remember you said it. I didn't."

Haywood eyed Trey. He was just as sweaty as she was. They had been battling it out on the basketball court for two solid hours and she had enjoyed every minute of it. "I'll remember." She took a swig of water out of the bottle. "It's going to be nice sleeping late tomorrow morning."

"Is that a hint?"

"Yes and I'm glad you caught it. Don't bother coming over since we finished packing everything up today."

Trey chuckled, then asked, "What do you plan to eat for dinner?"

"Nothing big. I thought I'd throw a pork chop in the oven and have a salad. Want to join me?"

"Only if you let me grill the chops."

"That's not a problem. Let's say we both go to our respective residences and take showers. Then you can come on over to the big house."

Trey's lips curved into a smile. "Sounds like a plan."

The sun was just going down when Trey arrived at the big house. Haywood opened the door, saw him and smiled. He was wearing a nice pair of trousers and a crisp white shirt. "Well, well, Mr. Fuller, you didn't have to dress up on my account."

He shook his head, returning her grin. "I didn't. I just wanted to wear something other than shorts or jeans."

She gave him a thorough once-over. "And you plan to grill in that?"

"Sure."

"Okay, it's your decision," she said, stepping aside to let him in. "You know where the grill is, don't you?"

"Yes. It won't take but a minute to get things set up. Did you find a bag of charcoal?"

"Yes. I put everything you'll need on the patio table."

A few moments later, Haywood thought that the two of them worked well together. In addition to the pork chops and salad, she had decided to bake a couple of sweet potatoes and dinner rolls. By the time they both sat down to the table they were hungry.

"It's beautiful out here, isn't it?" Haywood asked him as they sat at the patio table enjoying their food as well as the view of the Atlantic Ocean. Since Ma Mattie and Pa Murphy had been the only ones living on the island for the past fifteen years, other than the clearing where the big house and cottage sat, the rest of the island was wooded.

"Have you made a decision regarding what you want to do with your part of the island?" Haywood turned and asked Trey when she felt him looking at her.

He nodded, holding her gaze. "I know how much Ma Mattie loved this place and how much she wanted to keep it in the family. I also know how hurt she was when her family sold out to the developers on Hilton Head. I don't feel right doing the same thing, Haywood." He leaned back in his chair. "What are your thoughts on it?"

She smiled over at him, relieved he felt that way. "I feel the exact same way you do. It's so beautiful here. So peaceful. I love it here. Always have. Ma Mattie knew that I could never in good conscience sell this place. I'm glad the two of us are in agreement on that, Trey. I knew what my decision would be the moment the will was read. I just didn't know yours." Her smile widened. "I really thought I would be faced with a legal battle."

He shook his head. "That's the least of your worries. Now that we've decided that we're going to keep our share of the island, what are we going to do with it?"

Idly she tapped her fingers on the table. "Find a way to keep it up. Most of that will fall on you since I'll be returning to Paris."

"And how long do you plan to live over there?"

"I haven't decided yet. I like it there but then I'd like to spend more time with Randi. She'll be going off to college and I feel as a big sister I should be here for her. The first year of college was hard for me."

"In what way?"

Haywood grinned. "I thought I could go there and just party. After all, I wanted to learn how to perfect my photography and figured I didn't need biology, history or English to do that. Mom and Dad soon convinced me otherwise when they got my grades."

"So you weren't the typical good girl?"

She turned her head and looked at him. "Typical good girl? Heck no. But I wasn't a holy terror, either. I'd just inherited a bit of my father's wild streak, as my paternal grandparents termed it. And their prediction came through that after the first year I would settle down and do what I was sent to college to do."

"And how did Dad and Jenna handle your behavior?"

"The one thing I appreciated about them the most was that although they did the usual parent thing with the lectures and stuff, they never forgot how it was to be young. After that year I tried being a perfect daughter and it worked until they found out about my affair with Aaron. They didn't like that too much. Although Aaron had been divorced more than five years, they had a hang-up with our ages."

"Have you told them that you and Aaron have broken up?"

Haywood laughed. "Yes, and there were signs of the words 'good riddance' in both of their eyes. Like typical parents they want me to settle down, marry and give them grandchildren."

Trey took a sip of his wine then asked, "And what do you want?"

Haywood looked out over the ocean again. "To settle down, marry and give them grandchildren," she said softly.

"Yet you wasted an entire year with a man who had no intention of giving you what you wanted?"

Haywood smiled as she twirled her wineglass with her fingers. "Crazy, isn't it? The only reason I can think of for doing that is because I thought I loved Aaron and I always liked a good challenge."

"You don't love him anymore?"

She met Trey's gaze again. "Now I don't think I ever did. I loved the glitz and glamour of the lifestyle he introduced me to. I remember the first time he took me to Iman's house for dinner and to discuss the layout he wanted me to do for her cosmetic line. Oh, my gosh. She was absolutely radiant and it was easy to see why she was a supermodel. There were other celebrities that he did business with on a regular basis and I enjoyed hosting his parties and being known to everyone as his companion. Then I got greedy and wanted more and that's when our troubles began."

A part of Trey wanted to tell her that he thought she was just as radiant as Iman but decided not to. "It's getting dark. We better clear the table and go inside before we become the mosquitoes' dinner."

Cleanup was easy since they had used paper plates. Afterward, they continued drinking wine and talking inside in the living room. "And how is your relationship with your mother and stepfather?" she asked him.

Trey thought about her question a few minutes before answering. "Harry is wonderful. Always has been. He loves my mother deeply. Sometimes I don't think she knows just how much and it bothers me because at times I don't think she actually cares. I think Dad is the only man she ever really loved."

He took a sip of his wine before continuing. "My relationship with my mother is I guess the typical mother-son relationship. We agree and then we disagree. She tries playing her hand in my love life, and I have to let her know in no uncertain terms that I won't tolerate her interference. She's strong-willed and likes to have her way. Harry indulges her too much for fear of losing her. I indulge her every once in a while as well, but unlike Harry, I know how far to take it."

Deciding to change the subject, Haywood asked, "When do you have to go back to work?"

"I took the entire month off. I'm even thinking about remaining on the island for another week."

"Alone or have you made plans for someone to join you here?"

He met her gaze over the rim of his wineglass. "Alone. Not unless you want to hang out another week with me."

She smiled. "Doing what?"

A smile curved his lips. "Anything but packing. I've packed enough boxes over the last two weeks to last a lifetime."

"Hey, I share your pain." She thought about his offer. Another week doing absolutely nothing on the island sounded blissful. "Are you sure you won't mind the company if I decided to stay?"

"I'm positive. We can do fun stuff like take the boat out every day."

She nodded. "Sounds like fun."

"It will be. How about giving it some thought?"

"Okay, I'll do that."

Trey checked his watch then stood. "It's getting late and I'd better go. And I promise to let you sleep late in the morning."

"Thanks. I plan to be up by noon if you want to get together for lunch."

He gave her a thoughtful smile. "I may follow your lead and sleep in late myself."

Haywood put down her wineglass and stood. He automatically reached for her hand when she walked him to the door. "Good night, Trey."

He let go of her hand and reached up and touched her face as his dark eyes raked over it. His finger gently caressed her jaw. "Good night, Haywood."

Haywood's heart began to beat faster and her mouth suddenly felt dry. Instinctively, she stuck out her tongue to moisten her lips with the tip of it. She saw him watching her actions, saw the exact moment his chest expanded as his breathing increased beneath his shirt and saw—almost in slow motion—his head begin lowering toward her.

Trey didn't give her a chance to put her tongue back in her mouth. He swooped down on it and sucked it into his own mouth like it was the very lifeline to all of his wants and desires, and to his soul.

Haywood felt her entire mouth being absorbed and vanquished by his. And she felt every part of her body energized, mesmerized, and hypnotized. The effects had every nerve ending charged. And when he curved his hand around the nape of her neck to feast upon her mouth more deeply, she felt pure raw desire. His tongue was doing anything and everything to her mouth and then her arms came down around his neck to join in the play that was arousing her beyond madness. His erection, pressed against the fly of his pants, made sensual contact with her midsection but that wasn't enough. So she shifted her body against his to find that perfect spot and when she found it, she heard him groan, a guttural sound from deep within his throat. Then the grinding began. Moving his hands to her hips, he held the lower part of her body immobile as he moved sensuously against her—rubbing, stroking, massaging—as he rocked his loins methodically against her. Moments later when he slowly released her mouth, her eyes met his. They were filled with hot desire, hooded with longing, darkened by passion. And without saying a single word he began unbuttoning her blouse.

She looked down and watched his fingers as they slowly eased each and every button out of its hole, like the task took all his concentration. She watched his jaw tighten as he pushed her shirt off her shoulders and let it fall to the floor. She inhaled deeply the moment his hands went around her to unhook her bra and let it join her shirt on the floor, freeing her breasts. More heat than ever before surged through her when he leaned toward her and buried his face in her chest, absorbing her scent.

A jolt of electricity shot through her when she felt the tip of his tongue touch the tip of her breast for a taste. It was a taste he evidently liked when he began flicking his tongue against the sensitized peaks with incredible intensity. She felt her knees about to give out and held onto him as he continued his assault.

"Trey . . ."

His name came out as a sensuous moan. Never in her life had she experienced such tremendous pleasure. And when she felt his fingers at the zipper of her shorts, a fierce sense of longing and desire swept through her. Moments later, when she felt those same fingers push past her skimpy underwear to touch her intimately, she felt the beginnings of an orgasm take place deep inside of her.

A whimper of a sound, a groan, possibly a moan escaped her and she felt her body instantaneously react to his touch as sexual desire shot straight from where he was kissing her breasts to where his fingers were engaging in foreplay, the likes she had never encountered before. She quickly concluded in her mind that only he could do this to her. Only Trey had the mouth and fingers to elicit this kind of response. Only him.

When one of his fingers touched her in a oversensitized spot, she cried out softly as sensations rocked her, making her hungry for more. She reached down and stroked his thick erection through his pants, pleased when she heard that same deep groan from within his throat. Thinking two could play his game she unzipped his pants—which wasn't easy due to his enlarged state—and she reached inside to touch him through his briefs.

"Ahh, Haywood," he said, finally releasing her breasts and moving up to her neck and lightly biting it in retaliation. "We've got to stop."

"Easier said than done," she responded as she tightened her hand around him and began squeezing and stroking. "I don't think I can stop."

He inhaled sharply before saying, "Neither can I."

He quickly pulled back and began stripping off his clothes. When he stood nude before her he began pulling her shorts down over her legs. "It has to be this place that's making us crazy," he whispered with a laugh when he gathered her up into his arms. He stopped long enough to retrieve a pack of condoms out of his wallet before carrying her up the stairs.

"Yes, it has to be," she agreed, feeling reckless, too consumed in desire, as she wrapped her arms around his neck. He took her into the guest room and placed her on the bed, then after preparing himself he joined her there. His mouth latched onto hers as he quickly moved over her body.

"Trey . . . please."

She felt ready, absorbed in heat, flooded to the maximum when she felt him entering her, the sweaty coating of perspiration on their bodies a slippery surface that help glide him inside, and she immediately lifted her legs to wrap around him, to lock him in place. What she felt was extraordinary. It felt right.

"Hang on, baby," he warned as his body began to thrust deep into hers.

Haywood didn't take his warning lightly. She gripped his shoulders as he mated with her with an intensity that made her want to scream, shout, and holler out loud. She did all three, not caring if her voice carried across the waters to Hilton Head or all the way to St. Simons Island. He pumped and she bucked. He nibbled at her neck and she clawed at his back. He groaned and she moaned.

"Ohhhh, Trey. Ohhhh."

She gripped his shoulders tighter as a climax rocked through her at the same time one rocked through him.

"Haywood . . . ahhh."

Even as his body began to tremble in ecstasy, he didn't slow down. Instead the tempo of his body increased and he pumped harder as they shared the ultimate in mating. Neither fought the tidal wave of exhilaration that tore into them and Haywood's hips undulated and continued to lift up to meet the force of him as he moved relentlessly in and out of her.

They both fell over the edge into deep sated waters and drowned in a sea of excruciating pleasure, and at that moment neither cared if they resurfaced again.

Thirty-seven

"Are you sure everything is all right, Haywood?"

"Yes, Mom, everything is fine," she said into the telephone. "Trey and I finished all the packing that needed to be done and decided to stay another week just to wrap things up." She glanced up when she heard the bathroom door open. Trey's heated gaze immediately met hers. She swallowed. It was hard to believe all the passion the two of them had been sharing over the past two days.

She cleared her throat when she remembered she'd been talking to her mother. "Yes, Mom, Trey and I have decided to keep Glendale Shores. We know that's the way Ma Mattie would have wanted it." She scooted over when Trey came and sat next to her on the bed. "Mom, Trey wants to talk to Dad for a second. Okay, Mom, and I love you, too, and I hope you and Dad enjoy your trip to Atlanta. Tell everyone hello for me."

She handed Trey the phone. Thinking he would want to talk privately with his father, she stood to leave the room and was surprised when he caught hold of her hand and brought her back down beside him.

"Yeah, Dad, if it's possible I'd like to meet with you before I leave to go back to California." After a few minutes he said, "Yes, that's right. Haywood and I plan to return to Virginia on Saturday morning. Thanks, Dad, and yes," he said looking at Haywood and smiling. "Everything is fine. All right, I'll talk to you later."

He met Haywood's gaze. "He seems as anxious to talk to me as I am to talk to him."

Haywood smiled. "I figured that he would be. A talk between the two of you is long overdue."

Trey nodded. "You're probably right."

He then lowered his mouth to hers and pushed her back on the bed.

Later that day Trey placed a call to his mother to tell her of his plans to extend his trip.

"What do you mean you aren't coming home this week, Trey? I was expecting you and so was Harry." The tone of her voice was a clear indication that she was upset.

"I'm sure the office can do without me for a while."

"That's not the point."

"Then what is the point, Mom?"

"I missed you and was expecting you."

"And I miss you. But there's a few more things that I need to wrap up before I return to Los Angeles."

He heard his mother's agitated sigh. "All right, if you feel it's necessary."

He thought of the meeting he had scheduled with his father. "Yes,
Mom, I do."

Angela angrily clicked off the phone and turned to her husband. He
was naked in bed, ready for her. Before Trey had called she had been
naked in bed ready for him, too, but now, she had more important
matters to deal with.

"Something is going on and I don't like it, Harry. Why would Trey
want to spend any more time on that island?" she asked, pacing
around the room.

"Maybe he likes the place, Angela."

She stopped her pacing. "Or maybe he likes the person he's with. I
wouldn't put it past Jenna's daughter to have seduced my son."

Harry chuckled. "Trey is a hot-blooded young man, Angela, and you
know it. If she did seduce him I'm sure he didn't put up a fight."

Angela found no humor in Harry's words. "I don't want them
together. She might try and convince him to bridge the gap between
him and Randolph."

"And of course you wouldn't want that to happen since he'll find
out the truth about what you did and the lies you told."

Angela sighed deeply, suddenly feeling the walls closing in all
around her. She had to do something. She could not lose her son now.
"I'm going to find out everything there is to know about Haywood Malone."

Zach didn't say anything for the longest moment, then he met Patrick
Sellers's gaze and wanted to make sure he had heard correctly. "You've
actually found Adrianna Fuller?"

Patrick Sellers nodded, smiling. "Yes, I'm ninety-five percent certain it's her and in my line of business that a pretty high percentage. I
tried contacting both your father and Mr. Fuller and can't reach
either of them. The last time I met with the senator he gave me your

name as the person to contact if the two of them were ever unavailable."

Zach nodded. "Yes, my parents are in Florida on business and won't be returning until Tuesday, and it's my understanding that Randolph Fuller and his wife are out of town visiting her relatives in Atlanta for a few days." He leaned back in the chair. "So, please tell me what information you've discovered."

Patrick smiled as he opened the folder. He was pretty pleased with the investigative work he'd done. "She's an emergency room trauma doctor living in San Diego."

"What name is she using?"

Patrick grinned. "Now that's the kicker and what made it so hard for us to find her. Although she hasn't made any claim on the Fuller family, believing they basically disowned her because of the documentation she has, she had just enough spunk and tenacity not to let the Fuller family deny her the right to claim her father's name. She goes by the hyphenated name of Ross-Fuller."

Ross-Fuller. Zach smiled. "And what first name is she using?"

"She shortened Adrianna to Anna. At San Diego General Hospital she's known as the competent, compassionate and very dedicated Dr. Anna Ross-Fuller."

Zach rubbed his chin in deep thought. "Has anyone approached her about the investigation?"

"No, and that's why I wanted to talk to your father and Mr. Fuller. I needed to know how they wanted me to proceed."

Zach stood and went over to the window and looked out. After a few moments he turned back around to Patrick. "I'd prefer it if you didn't mention your findings to my father or Mr. Fuller just yet. I want you to leave your report with me and I'll go over it in detail. Then, unless there is something in the report that indicates it would be in the best interest not to go, I plan to catch a flight to San Diego tomorrow and meet with Dr. Ross-Fuller."

He walked back over to his desk and met Patrick's curious stare. "For thirty-four years my father and Mr. Fuller have searched for Adrianna Fuller, and she needs to know that. Regardless of what documentation she has, she needs to know that someone did care about her and that she was wanted by the Fuller and Wainwright families."

He inhaled deeply. "My father's sixtieth birthday is next weekend and my mother has planned a big gala for him. I can't think of a better surprise than the goddaughter he has spent more than half of his life looking for."

Thirty-eight

Wishing he were someplace else, Zachary glanced around the ER waiting room. Hospitals were not his favorite place. According to the receptionist, an older woman who reminded him of his secretary—stern and efficient—it would be another thirty minutes or so before Dr. Ross-Fuller was free to see him. So he had decided to wait it out.

Leaning back in the chair he stretched his legs out in front of him, thinking about the report he'd read. Patrick Sellers's investigation had been thorough. There was very little about Anna Ross-Fuller that he didn't know.

He knew that because of her mixed heritage, being a child living in Vietnam after the war hadn't been easy for her. She'd been made to feel like an outcast and was often called cruel names. The Vietnamese people's hatred of Eurasians hadn't just stopped with her. It had extended to the aunt who had raised her after Gia had died in childbirth. And when her aunt's fiancé declared he would not marry her as long as Adrianna was in her care, her aunt had taken her to the orphanage and left here there, although there were recorded accounts of her visiting Adrianna at the orphanage occasionally.

The report further indicated Adrianna lived at the orphanage until she had reached the age of seventeen. It was then that she had been sponsored by the Lutheran Church Alliance to come to the States to further her education. She had attended UCLA and later moved to

San Diego to attend medical school and had remained there for her residency.

He also knew that she had been engaged to marry a fellow medical student but the wedding had been called off a mere two weeks before the scheduled date. That had been almost eight years ago, and since then Dr. Ross-Fuller had only dated occasionally.

"Mr. Wainwright, the doctor will see you now. She's in her office down that corridor."

Zach pushed his thoughts to the back on his mind when the receptionist spoke. He stood and picked up his briefcase, hoping that Dr. Ross-Fuller would listen to what he had to say.

Dr. Anna Ross-Fuller stood at the window in her office and looked out. It had been a busy day; not as busy as others but busy nonetheless. And now she was free to meet with Mr. Zachary Wainwright.

She had been surprised and curious when she'd gotten the message from her secretary that he had called wanting to meet with her, indicating he was a family friend of her father's.

Family friend of her father's?

She had pondered the message before returning his call. Their conversation had been brief and the only thing he'd said was that he knew she was the daughter of Ross Fuller and needed to meet with her to clear up a few things about her father. That in itself had come as a shock since she had never revealed her father's identity to anyone. So she couldn't help wondering what, after thirty-four years, the Fuller family, or any acquaintance of that family, could possibly want with her.

She sighed deeply when she heard the knock at her office door. Leaving her place at the window she crossed the room and stood behind her desk. Taking another deep breath she decided it was time she found out. "Come in."

Zachary opened the door and entered, his gaze focused on the woman standing behind the desk as he closed the door behind him. He couldn't help but stare at her. With the deep slant of her dark eyes, and her hair—more straight than curly—it was evident she was part

Asian. But her cocoa-colored skin tone, full lips and straight nose strongly reflected her African-American heritage as well.

The first thought that came to his mind was that Anna Ross-Fuller was a strikingly beautiful woman. The other thought was that even with her Asian features, she strongly resembled pictures he had seen over the years of Ross Fuller. She definitely had that Fuller forehead, full lips, austere chin and high cheekbones.

He cleared his throat. "Dr. Ross-Fuller?"

She came from behind the desk and accepted the hand that he extended to her. "Yes, and you're Mr. Wainwright, I presume?"

"Yes."

She nodded. "Please have a seat. I must admit I'm more than mildly curious about your visit."

Zach eased down in the chair she offered then watched as she went behind her desk and sat down. "I appreciate your agreeing to see me, and I guess my call came as a surprise to you."

She studied him thoughtfully before answering. "Yes. I was surprised that you knew Ross Fuller was my father, and secondly, I was surprised that you acknowledged that fact since it had never been done so before."

He raised a brow. "Because you assume the Fuller family disowned you?"

Anna stared at him, wondering what game he was playing. A frown filled her eyes. "I don't assume anything, Mr. Wainwright. I know they did."

Zach nodded. "Because of a certain document you have in your possession?"

She leaned back in her chair and continued to stare at him. "Yes. My aunt left a number of my parents' possessions at the orphanage for me. Among their things which included pictures, their marriage certificate, a family Bible and letters they exchanged, there was also a signed document, a disclaimer so to speak, that clearly stated the family of Ross Fuller refused to acknowledge me as his child."

Zach leaned forward. "What if I presented you with solid proof that no one in the Fuller family has knowledge of signing such a document?

What if I presented you with strong evidence that for thirty-four years there have been private investigators paid to find you and bring you home to the Fuller family? They were investigators who were paid by my father, Noah Wainwright, and your uncle, Randolph Fuller."

She lifted a brow. "Noah Wainwright? The senator?"

"Yes. He's was your father's best friend and he is also your godfather."

Uncertainly flowed like a chill through Anna. She refused to believe after *not* believing for so long. She drew in a deep breath as she considered his words. Slowly she stood and crossed the room to the window and looked out. From her office she could see the beauty of the Pacific Ocean. For the past eight years San Diego had been her home. A place where she had felt appreciated and wanted. Being appreciated and wanted had meant a lot to her, especially after her breakup with Todd and his family's rejection of her because of her Vietnamese heritage, like it had been her fault that his uncle had gotten killed in the war.

She turned back around to Zach. Drawing in a deeper breath she said, "Even if you were to present me with proof, Mr. Wainwright, I would be hard pressed to believe it."

Zach held her gaze. "Why?"

The steel beneath that one word he had spoken didn't escape her. She walked back to her chair and sat down. Her eyes flared. "I just would. It's not like I've been in hiding for thirty-four years. I lived at the orphanage in Vietnam since I was four."

"Yes, but a lot of records were destroyed with the fall of Saigon."

Anna nodded, acknowledging that to be true. "Yes, but even so, it should have been easy enough to trace my whereabouts."

Zachary smiled wryly. "Trust me, it wasn't. While at the orphanage you did not carry the Fuller name. You were registered in your aunt's name, which was different from your mother's since they had different fathers. And then when you moved to this country and started college, you took on your father's full name instead of his surname."

Anna tilted her head defiantly. "I knew Ross Fuller was my father, Mr. Wainwright. I had all the proof I needed in the papers my aunt had given me, and in the letters my father and my mother exchanged.

There was no doubt in my mind that my parents loved each other and that my father wanted me. Regardless of what his family refused to acknowledge, I am his child. I felt justified and felt I had every right to honor my father by taking his name. So I did. All of it."

Zach inwardly smiled. Patrick Sellers had been right. Anna Ross-Fuller certainly had spunk. "Yes, you had every right." He then reached down and picked up his briefcase. Placing it across his lap he opened it and pulled out a folder. She held his gaze steadily when he stood and handed the folder to her.

"Please accept this, Dr. Ross-Fuller. It contains all the proof I indicated I had. I'll be in town for another two days and I hope during that time you'll review all the information that I'm leaving with you. I'm staying at the Marriott two buildings over in room three-fifteen. Please call me if you think these papers are proof enough for you."

He hesitated a moment before continuing. "Somehow a grave mistake was made. Whether intentional or unintentional will soon be determined, you can bet your life on it. I'm four months older than you, Dr. Ross-Fuller, and for as long as I can remember, I've watched my father and your uncle become obsessed with finding you. Even when investigators said they should give up, they refused to do so."

He regarded her and smiled. "And I'm glad they didn't." Turning, he walked out of her office.

Hours later in the privacy and comfort of her home, Anna's chest expanded as she drew in a deep breath. Tears she couldn't contain any longer clouded her eyes. Everything Zachary Wainwright had claimed was true and was there in the reports he had given her to read; thirty-four years of investigative work that often led nowhere.

But Noah Wainwright and Randolph Fuller had refused to give up.

She closed the folder on the last report. Zachary Wainwright had also been correct in stating a grave mistake had been made and now she wondered if it had been intentional. Standing, she crossed the room and got on her knees to seek out the cedar chest that she kept under her bed.

Pulling it out, she unlocked it and looked at the items she had placed inside—things her aunt had given her. At seventeen, she had been resentful of the things her aunt had told her; and of her father's family that had not wanted her. She had purchased the chest and locked the things away and until now had never taken the time to actually go through them.

Sitting back on her haunches she picked up the Bible, well-worn with age and use, yet the leather cover was still intact. Opening it she read the names recorded there:

John Anderson weds Mariah Slater, May 11, 1901
Murphy Denison weds Mattie Anderson, October 2, 1922
Ross Donovan Fuller weds Adrianna Denison, July 8, 1942
Randolph Fuller pledges his love to Jenna Haywood, March
*   18, 1966*
Ross Donovan Fuller, Jr. weds Gia Wang Fu, June 18, 1967

She slowly closed the Bible and picked up a photograph that had aged over the years. Two American soldiers, one standing on each side of the woman she knew was her mother. She was wearing a white dress and according to her aunt, it had been her mother's wedding day. The soldier whose arm was around her mother's waist was her father, she could see her resemblance to him, and the other man she knew had to be Zachary Wainwright's father, also because of the resemblance. Like his father, he was a very handsome man.

Placing the picture aside she looked through other papers, seeking one in particular. Specifically, the document that clearly stated that the family of Ross Donovan Fuller, Jr. refused to acknowledge her as his child.

She studied the signature. It was all the proof she needed. She wondered how Julia Fuller intended to explain to Noah Wainwright and Randolph Fuller why she had acted in the family's behalf and refused to acknowledge her own grandchild.

Zachary looked up when he saw Anna enter the hotel's coffee shop. She had called him that morning asking that he meet with her.

He stood when she approached his table. Her eyes were red and slightly swollen. "Are you okay?" he asked, pulling the chair out for her.

She nodded as she sat down. "As okay as a person can be who for most of her life thought she wasn't loved or wanted by her father's family, only to discover that was not the case. Do you know how many wasted years that's been?"

He smiled wryly. "Yes, too many. When I was four my father had a special Christmas ornament made with your name on it that he placed on the tree. It was the first time I had heard the story about you. That ornament is still placed on the tree every Christmas."

She smiled sadly as tears mistied her eyes. "Tell me about them, your father and my uncle. I reread my father's letters last night and I know he was close to his brother as well as to your father."

Before Zachary could respond to her request a waitress came to take her order. She didn't want anything. After the waitress left Zachary told her everything she wanted to know about the two men.

"So, as you can see, both will be elated that you've been found," he finished by smiling.

Anna leaned back in her chair. "I'm still not sure I want to be found, Mr. Wainwright."

Zach smiled. "It would be much easier if you were to call me Zach."

Anna returned his smile. "And please call me Anna."

Zach nodded. "After reading that report, why wouldn't you want to be found, Anna?"

She sighed deeply. "Mainly because I also read over that document again, the one signed by a member of the Fuller family, and it wasn't a mistake."

Zach frowned. No one had admitted to signing such a document. "Do you mind if I take a look at it?"

Anna studied him thoughtfully. "Why? You don't believe me?"

He gave her an assuring smile. "Yes, I believe you, but I want to see with my own eyes the signature of the person who outright lied to my father and Mr. Fuller."

Their gazes held for a moment then Anna nodded. "All right. It's at my apartment."

Zach placed money on the table for his coffee. "You're not working today?"

Anna shook her head. "It's my day off." She stood. "Are you ready to go?"

He took one last sip of his coffee. "Yes."

Zach grimaced as he read the signature. He then handed the document back to Anna.

"Well?" she asked as she placed it back in the chest.

Zach shook his head. He knew Randolph had personally spoken to his grandmother about the document and she had denied having any knowledge of it. Her signature proved otherwise. "All hell's going to break loose in the Fuller household, that's for sure."

Anna shook her head. "Not if I'm not found."

Zach sighed deeply. "No, Anna, you have every right to be found and your grandmother is due her day in court over what she's done. I don't think your uncle and grandfather will ever forgive her."

Anna stood and paced the room. Then she stopped and looked at Zach. "You can go back to Washington and forget you've met me."

Zach returned her stare and hesitated for just a heartbeat before saying, "I don't think that I could forget meeting you even if I wanted to, Anna."

Her lips curved into a smile at the compliment she read in his words. "Thank you, Zach."

"In fact," he decided to add, holding her gaze, "if possible I'd like you to go back with me. My mother is giving my father a birthday party Saturday night, his sixtieth, and I can't imagine a more perfect gift than you."

She returned his stare and then her lips firmed. "What about my grandmother, Julia Fuller?"

Zach's gaze hardened at the thought. "It's my understanding she will be there along with your grandfather. I think it will be the perfect time to expose her for the liar that she is. After what she did, you owe her nothing, Anna. But you do owe those who wanted you found and prayed each night that one day you would be."

Anna sighed. It was something she had to think about. "I need to think things through, Zach. You've given me so much to absorb at once."

He nodded, then stood and walked over to her. "I know I have, but remember, my father and your uncle have been waiting thirty-four years. Do you think it's fair to make them wait any longer?" He smiled. "Just take your time and think about everything; especially what you think your parents would want you to do." He reached out and gave her hand a reassuring squeeze. "You know where I am when you make a decision."

He released her hand, then walked out the door.

Zach received a call late that evening. Anna had made a decision. She would go back to Washington with him.

Thirty-nine

Haywood glanced around the room that had been hers as a child. No matter where she went it was always good to return to the place she considered home.

She and Trey had arrived back in Richmond less than an hour ago, and he was downstairs talking to his father in his office. Her thoughts drifted to the time they had spent on Glendale Shores, specifically, the last week. Surrendering to all the raging needs inside of them, they had been ravenous as if it had been years since either had enjoyed that kind of pleasure.

A soft knock at the door interrupted Haywood's thoughts. "Come in." She smiled when her mother entered her bedroom. For the first time in a long time she felt a little uneasy as her mother studied her. "What is it, Mom?"

Jenna tilted her head and smiled at her daughter. "Oh, I don't know. You look different somehow. A little more relaxed maybe."

Haywood shrugged. The last thing she planned to do was volunteer information that she and Trey had spent an entire week together doing very little other than eating, sleeping and making love. "Glendale Shores can do that for a person," she said calmly. "Relax them."

"Yeah, I bet."

Haywood smiled, knowing she couldn't pull too much over on Jenna Haywood Malone Fuller. "Okay, Mom, evidently you want to talk to me about something."

Jenna came further into the room and sat next to her daughter on the bed. She was concerned. She felt certain that Trey and Haywood had slept together while on Glendale Shores. The signs were all there. The smiles, the innocent touches and the heated looks when they weren't aware others were watching. There was enough sexual awareness flowing between them to bottle it.

"I want to talk about you and Trey," Jenna finally said.

Haywood lifted a brow. "What about me and Trey?"

Jenna met her daughter's inquiring gaze. "There's something going on between the two of you. I can feel it."

Haywood had no intention of indulging in any conversation with her mother about her love life. After all, she was a twenty-seven-year-old woman. Too old to be explaining or defending what she did to anyone, including her mother. But she saw the concern and love in her mother's eyes and decided to make an exception.

She stood and walked over to the window and looked out. It was the middle of October; the middle of fall. In Richmond the air was already a bit chilly. But in some places like Glendale Shores, the days were still hot. She smiled. And the nights were hot as well, if you made them that way.

Sighing deeply, Haywood turned around to face her mother. There were no accusations lining her mother's face. There were no signs of disappointment or disapproval. What she saw in her mother's gentle smile—pure and simple—was understanding and support. Understanding for whatever it was she had done and support for whatever decisions she would make.

"Yes," she finally said softly. "There is something going on between me and Trey."

After a few minutes Jenna nodded then asked, "Is it serious?"

A smile touched Haywood's lips. "It was last week." Things had been so perfect and had felt so right that more than once she and Trey had teasingly commented that they were under some sort of spell. But now it was time for a reality check. Trey would be returning to California in a few days and she would be returning to Paris.

"And what about now, Haywood? Is it serious now?"

Her mother's questions invaded her thoughts. "I don't know, Mom. We didn't do much talking."

"I see." Jenna shifted positions on the bed to study her daughter. "Then let me ask you this. How do you feel about Trey?"

Haywood shrugged. "I don't dislike him anymore if that's what you mean."

Jenna shook her head. "No, that's not what I mean."

Haywood had known that it wasn't. She slowly walked back over to the bed and sat down beside her mother. "Mom, do you believe it's possible for two people to connect together in such a way that . . ."

"That what?"

"That they feel so attuned to each other? Like it was meant for them to be together?"

Jenna nodded slowly as she remembered how things had been for her and Randolph. "Yes, I believe that's possible."

"Well, that's the way I feel. For me it was more than just sharing a bed with Trey. I felt some things with him that I've never felt with anyone, not even Aaron. I'd been with Aaron a little more than a year, yet thoughts of him didn't even cross my mind. When I'm with Trey I think of no one else."

"So what do you suppose that means?"

Haywood's forehead furrowed. "I don't know. A part of me wants to think it's too early to consider the possibility that I've fallen in love with him but then . . ."

"But then what?"

"I know I'm going to miss him when he goes back to California and I return to Paris. I also know I would jump at the chance to continue what we have." She met her mother's direct gaze, deciding to be completely truthful. "And I'd sleep with him again, in a heartbeat, if he gave any sign that he wanted me."

Haywood sighed. If her words had shocked her mother, she didn't let on. The one thing she had always appreciated about their relationship, now that she was a woman, was her mother's ability to treat her like one and not like she was still a child. They could speak mother to daughter, yet woman to woman.

Jenna patted her daughter's hand. "I think things will work out."

Haywood lifted a brow. "Why do you think that?"

Jenna smiled. "Because this entire thing, your and Trey's stay on Glendale Shores, was orchestrated by Gramma Mattie. And a part of me believes she had a reason for doing what she did. One good thing out of this is that you got Trey to talk with his father."

Haywood nervously gnawed on her lower lip. "Yeah, and it has me worried."

"Why?"

"What if Trey doesn't believe what Dad tells him? Or what if he does believe him? How will he handle the fact that his mother lied to him all these years?"

Randolph looked across the room at his son. Trey had sat silently while he had told him everything. Not once had he interrupted him or defended his mother. He had sat there and listened.

But now as their eyes met across the room he knew there would be questions and denials. The two things he hadn't told Trey and never intended to ever tell him was that Angela had drugged him the night they had slept together which had resulted in her getting pregnant, and about the time he had come home for a business meeting and found her in bed with another man. He felt neither was relevant to what his son needed to know. And what he needed to know more than anything was that Jenna had not destroyed his marriage and that he had not turned his back on him.

"Are you trying to tell me that you never once saw Jenna during the entire time you and Mom were together?"

"Basically yes, Trey. I saw Jenna only once and that was at her father's funeral. I saw her but she didn't see me. She hadn't known I was there until I told her when we got back together."

Randolph walked across the room to his safe and opened it up. "I want you to look at these," he said, handing him some documents. "Understandably, considering the circumstances of my and your mother's marriage, I was still in love with Jenna. However, she had broken our engagement so I could marry your mother. But a part of me couldn't let her go completely, although I knew we would never get back together. I wanted to make sure she was all right. For the first two years I had no idea where she had gone since no one would tell me. So I hired a private investigator to find her. Once he found her and I was assured she was all right, I kept him on the case to send me yearly updates as to how she was doing."

Randolph inhaled deeply, remembering those times before continuing. "As you can see, the last report came to my office two years *after* your mother and I had gotten a divorce. Two solid years, Trey. I wasn't even aware that Jenna was a widow until then. This proves that I didn't have an affair with Jenna while I was still married. Nor did I rush out and break up Jenna's marriage before the ink dried on my own divorce. I had accepted my fate. For some reason, which turned out to be a blessing, God brought Jenna back into my life a little more than two years after my divorce from your mother. By then I had already started dating other women."

"But Mom was hoping that the two of you would get back together."

"Yes, but I never gave her reason to think that we would. In fact I made it absolutely clear to Angela that we would never remarry. I even made that point clear to you that day I took you to Glendale Shores to meet Jenna."

Randolph sighed. "You're old enough now to accept that the only reason I married your mother was because I had gotten her pregnant. She was engaged to marry my brother and I was engaged to marry Jenna, a woman that I loved completely. After being married to Angela for ten years I knew that I could never love her the way she wanted and needed to be loved. That's why I gave her her freedom."

"And what about me?"

Randolph met his son's gaze. "There was never a time I didn't love you, Trey. In fact the reason I stayed married to your mother as long as I did was because of you. You were all I had, all I ever wanted and Angela knew it. I allowed her to use you to get to me, to keep me on her leash. But then I couldn't deal with it any longer. She always hung the threat of taking you away from me over my head if I got too involved with anyone. And she made sure you didn't like any woman I dated after our divorce."

Trey nodded. He knew that much was true.

"But at no time did I turn my back on you. You don't know how upset I was when I went to pick you up for my wedding to find she had sent you on a camping trip with her father. The only reason I didn't come after you was because I let her convince me that you really hadn't wanted to go."

Trey's eyes widened. "That's not true. I wanted to be there. I had begun to like Jenna and when I heard that she had been the reason you and I couldn't spend any more time together, I began despising her."

Randolph nodded. "Jenna is not that type of person. Just like I accepted Haywood as her child, she accepted you as mine. She would never have done anything to come between us."

He walked over to the window and looked out a few minutes before turning back around to face his son. "Your mother threatened me numerous times with what she would do if I didn't call off my wedding to Jenna. My mistake was in not believing she would carry any of them out. When I discovered how wrong I was, it was too late. I have documentation of the times I took her back to court after you had moved to California just to have visitation rights."

Trey shook his head sadly, still in shock over the things he had heard. "And she led me to believe just the opposite. For all these years I thought you didn't want me."

Randolph's misty eyes met his son's. "I wanted you, Trey. You were my son and I loved you with all my heart. I wanted you more than anything. And each time I couldn't have you, it was like a knife going through my heart and your mother knew it."

Trey rubbed a hand over his face. His entire body was shaking. He felt a part of him ripped in two. How could his mother do such a thing? How could she feed him all those lies? How? Had she been that obsessed with his father that she would have done anything to keep him away from Jenna? Even go to the extreme of turning his son against him?

He stood, needing to get away for a while. "Look, I—I need to go someplace to think. I'm going back to the hotel."

Randolph nodded. "You're welcome to stay here, Trey."

"Thanks, but I can't. Not right now."

Randolph nodded in understanding. "Will you be attending Noah's birthday paty later?"

"I'm not sure about that, either. Right now I'm not sure of anything, Dad."

Randolph sighed deeply. "All right." He walked his son out of his office at the same time Haywood and Jenna were coming down the stairs. He saw Haywood take one look at Trey and rush over to him. He watched as she wrapped her arms around him. He then watched as Trey held onto Haywood as if she were the only person in the world.

Randolph frowned. What he was seeing was not a regular embrace between two people. He felt something. An instinct, an intuition, a natural inclination that something was going on between Trey and Haywood. And as he continued to watch how they touched each other with clear familiarity, he knew with all certainty that they were sleeping together. He looked past them to Jenna and saw the tears in her eyes. She met his inquiring gaze and nodded, knowing what he was silently asking.

He cleared his throat and spoke when Trey and Haywood finally broke apart. "Trey is going back to the hotel for a while."

Haywood met Trey's gaze. "I'm going with you. Wait a minute while I grab my purse and jacket." The three of them watched as she raced up the stairs.

Trey's glance went to the woman on the other side of the room. A woman he had hated needlessly for the past twenty-two years of his life. He squared his shoulders and slowly walked over to her. "It seems that I owe you a big apology, Jenna," he said softly, seeing the tears lining her eyes.

She smiled at him through those tears. "No, all is forgiven, Trey. Unless . . ."

He raised a dark brow. "Unless what?"

The gaze that met his was unwavering and completely serious. "Unless you hurt my daughter."

Trey tried calling his mother the minute he was back in his hotel room. He couldn't get an answer at her home or her cell phone.

"Maybe it's not a good time to talk to her right now, Trey. You should chill a while and think about why she did what she did, and try to reach some kind of understanding."

He looked at Haywood and frowned. "An understanding? How can there be an understanding, Haywood? For twenty-two years I didn't have a relationship with my father because of her."

"Yes, but there has to be a reason for what she did. Maybe it stems from something in her childhood, or maybe—"

"Why are you trying to find excuses for her?"

Haywood shrugged. "Because she is your mother and I believe she loves you and doesn't want to lose you. After thinking about all of this, I think the reason she did what she did was because she didn't want to lose you."

"She wouldn't have lost me."

"But she had no way of knowing that. According to Randolph she's an only child. Maybe that had something to do with it."

"All I can see are the actions of a manipulative and spiteful woman who didn't stop at anything to hurt my father, even using her own son."

Haywood knew at that moment there was nothing she could say in Angela's defense. It would be up to the woman to save face with her son . . . if that was possible. She had been caught in the worse type of lies.

Haywood walked across the room to Trey. She smoothed her hands down his chest then leaned up on tiptoes to kiss him. He returned her kiss with a hunger that she knew bordered on need and pain. And then he picked her up in his arms and carried her to the bed.

Trey released her long enough to undress her then undress himself. And when he joined her on the bed, nothing else mattered other than getting inside of her and being a part of her. His attention was focused only on her. He saw her as something wonderful. Something fascinating. Something that he wanted more than life itself. And suddenly, he knew why.

That knowledge made him look at her in a whole new light. No longer did he see her as the woman sharing his passion but he saw her as the woman who shared his heart. His breath caught when he moved his body in place over hers and kissed her in a way he had never kissed another woman. Surrendering himself completely.

And then he made love to her in a way he had never done to another woman. Totally and without reserve. He entered her slowly, going as deep as he could as the scent of her body entranced him. The sensations of being inside of her were flooding every part of him when he began to move inside of her.

Pressing her hands on his shoulders she helped guide him to where she wanted him to be and he took full advantage of it. With intimate slowness he moved in and out, feeling each and every shiver of pleasure her body made as it mated with his.

He could feel her bare breasts against his hairy chest and feel her stomach completely lined with his. They were connected from head to toe and he couldn't imagine her not being a part of him forever.

He broke off their kiss. He had to see her this time. He had to look into her eyes while he made love to her. "Open your eyes for me, Haywood. I want to see you."

He watched her lids flutter open and saw the darkness of desire that clouded her pupils. He looked closer and wanted to see if he saw in her gaze what he knew was in his, whether she could decipher it or not. He saw her blink and refocus on him. And finally as that part of him went even deeper inside of her, stroking harder, he saw what he wanted to see. Passion and love.

Then he completely lost it as sensations, to a degree he'd never felt before, rammed through him. He automatically exploded inside of her as she bucked wildly, almost out of control. Her eyes seemed to have rolled to the back of her head when she screamed out her pleasure at the same time he groaned out his. He pushed further inside of her, wanting her to feel him. Know him. Want him and love him.

And as their passion began subsiding, he held her tightly in his arms, knowing there was no way he would ever let her go.

Forty

"So," Leigh said as she blew out a breath after listening to what Jenna had just shared with her regarding Trey and Randolph. "What's next?"

Jenna shook her head. "I don't know. I'm just glad Trey has finally learned the truth. But even so, Randolph didn't tell him everything. He didn't tell him about the drugging or coming home to find her having sex with another man."

"Don't you think he should have told him everything?"

"No, I think Randolph did the right thing by not telling him. Those two things really don't involve Trey. What Randolph wanted was to make sure Trey understood that I didn't break up his marriage and that he didn't turn his back on him."

"How did Trey take the news?"

"Not well. He went back to the hotel and Haywood went with him."

Leigh lifted a brow. "Haywood? You mean they've learned to tolerate each other that much on Glendale Shores?"

"You don't know the half of it." Jenna shook her head, smiling. "But maybe you will later if they still come tonight."

Before Leigh could ask what she had meant the doorbell sounded. "Excuse me for a minute. I have to take up my post as hostess." She glanced around. "By the way, where is the man of the hour? I haven't seen him since you and Randolph arrived."

Jenna chuckled. "That should tell you something. They're in Noah's office talking business as usual."

Leigh crossed the room and opened the door. She smiled when she saw it was Randolph's grandparents, Robert and Julia Fuller. She gave Robert a kiss on the cheek and gave Julia a big hug. As usual the older woman looked stunning. "Come on in. Randolph and Jenna arrived a few minutes ago. Can I get the two of you something to drink?"

Jenna helped Leigh place trays of hors d'oeuvres on the table.

"So, how does it look?" Leigh asked, eyeing the table.

"Gorgeous as ever."

"Did I tell you that Zach is bringing some young lady tonight?"

Jenna shook her head. "No, you didn't mention it. He's back to dating again?"

"I guess so. He arrived in town today from a business trip and called to let me know he's bringing a guest. I have no idea who she is or how they met."

Jenna grinned. "Does it matter?"

Leigh smiled in a way that told Jenna she was pleased about something. "No, I'm just glad he's seeing someone. Shaun's death was so hard on him." She glanced across the room at Haywood and Trey. They had arrived a few moments ago. "Are you going to tell me what's going on with Haywood and Trey?"

Jenna smiled. "Oh, so you've noticed something?"

Leigh lifted a brow. "How could I not notice? They have all but been in each other's pockets since they got here. And I can't help noticing how they keep smiling at each other and they're so touchy-touchy." She smiled. "They remind me of you and Randolph when the two of you were a hot item at Howard."

Jenna shook her head laughing. "We weren't ever a hot item."

"I thought so and so did others." Leigh checked her watch. "I hope Zach hurries up and gets here. I can't wait to see the girl he's bringing with him."

Jenna glanced across the room to where Haywood and Trey stood. Haywood had laughed at something he'd said, moments before holding a piece of food up to his mouth for him to bite into. They seemed happy together and she hoped everything worked out for them.

The first thing Anna noticed about Zach's family's home was just how big it was, and then she noticed how many cars were parked out front. "I thought this would be a small birthday dinner, Zach," she whispered as they strolled up the walkway leading to the front door.

"This is my mother's definition of small," he said as he pressed the doorbell. He looked at her thinking she looked absolutely stunning in the outfit she was wearing. They had arrived in town earlier that day and he had convinced her to stay at his apartment and use his guest room. He knew she still had misgivings about coming tonight but he knew it was time the thirty-four-year search ended.

He took her hand in his and squeezed it lightly. "Nervous?"

Anna nodded as she smiled at him. "Yes." She liked him. Over the past few days they had become friends.

His hand on hers tightened. "Everything will work out, Anna. You'll see."

The door opened and Noelle gave her brother and the beautiful woman at his side a squeaky-clean smile. "Well, hi, Zachary."

Zach grinned and said to Anna, "This is my sister Noelle." To Noelle he said, "I'd like you to meet Anna."

Noelle extended her hand to Anna. "It's nice to meet you, Anna." Zach had told Anna all about the younger sister he adored.

Anna took Noelle's hand in hers and returned Noelle's warm welcoming smile. "Thanks."

Zach looked down at Anna and his smile widened. "Ready to meet everyone?"

She nervously smiled back at him. "As ready as I'll ever be."

"I think that was Zach at the door," Leigh whispered to Jenna. "I'm glad he's finally here."

No sooner had she said the words, Zach and a beautiful woman dressed in a stunning white dress entered the room. Leigh's attention was diverted when she heard the sound of a plate crashing to the hardwood floor. She looked to her right to see that it had fallen from Julia Fuller's hand and there was a look of total shock on the older woman's face. The room became deathly quiet as everyone tried to figure out what had startled the woman so.

Leigh followed Julia's fixed gaze to where Zach stood with his date and when she looked into the young woman's face—which was at the same exact second Jenna did—both women simultaneously uttered a quick intake of breath. Except for her slanted eyes, the woman who stood at Zach's side was the spitting image of Ross Fuller. The features were distinctively clear, and like Trey, her features had the Fuller print stamped all over them.

"Go get Noah and Randolph quick!" Leigh whispered to Jenna. "They're still in the study."

Leigh placed her hand over her heart, not sure how much excitement she could take. Knowing that as hostess she had to bring order back to the party, she began crossing the room to her son and the woman with him.

Anna nervously glanced up at Zach when the room became deathly quiet. "This may not have been such a good idea," she said, grabbing hold of his hand.

He leaned over and whispered, teasingly, "Just think of how dull the party must have been before we arrived." He had seen the shocked look on Julia Fuller's face and didn't have any pity for the woman.

He saw his mother walk toward them at the same time his father and Randolph Fuller came out of his father's study. He turned to Anna. "Here they come. Just let me handle the introductions."

She nodded nervously, tightening her hold on his hand. "All right."

He turned when his father reached them with Randolph Fuller at his side. His mother and Jenna Fuller quickly joined them. Everyone's eyes were on Anna.

Noah shifted his gaze from Anna to Zach and looked up at him, questioningly. "Who—who is this?"

Zach smiled widely. "Dad, Mom and Mr. and Mrs. Fuller. I'd like all of you to meet Dr. Adrianna Ross-Fuller." He then placed a hand on his father's shoulder. "Happy birthday, Dad."

A light sheen of tears suddenly formed in Noah Wainwright's eyes. He glanced over at Randolph and saw tears had formed in his eyes as well. He looked back at his son and the woman by his side. Shock was evident on his face. "But how?"

Zach chuckled. "We'll talk in your office later, after the party is over."

Noah nodded. He then returned his full attention to Anna, and taking her hand in his, he asked, "Do you know how long your uncle and I have been looking for you? You are the best birthday present I could ever receive. This is more than I could ever wish for. My prayers have been answered."

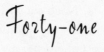

Forty-one

"Are you sure you don't want anything to drink, Anna?" Zach asked before sitting beside her on the leather sofa in his father's office.

"No, I'm fine, just don't leave me," she whispered, holding his hand tightly as she nervously glanced around the room. The senator and Randolph had wanted answers immediately and had refused to wait until after the party to get them. She and Zach, along with a few family members, had quickly been ushered into the senator's office.

Zach smiled down at her. "Don't worry about that. I won't leave you."

The clearing of someone's throat made the both of them look up. The senator was looking down at them, still smiling in utter disbelief. "I apologize if I made you nervous a few minutes ago, Anna. It was just such a shock seeing you after all this time."

Anna nodded and drew in a deep breath. "I admit things were overwhelming at first but I'm fine now."

Tension was beginning to slowly leave Noah's shoulders. Zach had

told them about receiving Patrick Sellers's report while they were away
and how he'd made the decision to go to San Diego and meet Anna
himself. "I know tonight has been taxing for you, Anna, but if you
don't mind we would like to ask you a few questions."

"No, I don't mind."

Noah then took the time to introduced the other people in the
room. "This is Randolph Fuller, your uncle, and his wife Jenna. This is
my wife Leigh and this couple here is Robert and Julia Fuller, your
great-grandparents. The young man sitting on Randolph's left is his
son and your first-cousin Trey. But his real name is Ross Donovan
Fuller III. He was named after your father."

Anna nodded, smiling softly at Trey, noticing how much the two of
them resembled each other. "I see."

"And of course you know me," Zach said teasingly.

Anna turned and captured his gaze, grinning fondly at him. "Yes, I
know you, Zach."

With introductions made, Noah sat in the large chair behind his
desk and faced Anna and Zach. "My question to you, Anna, is that if
you knew all along who your father was why didn't you ever try to contact his family?"

Anna met Noah's stare. "It was my belief all these years that the
Fuller family had rejected me once by not acknowledging my existence. I had no desire to be rejected a second time. I do have my
pride."

"Of course you do. You're a damn Fuller," Zach grumbled teasingly,
trying to keep the mood in the room light although the issue at hand
was serious.

Noah smiled at his son's attempt and looked over at Anna. "And
you believed they rejected you?"

Anna didn't want to look at the others in the room so she kept her
gaze solely on Noah. "Yes. My aunt told me when I was a little girl,
and she told me again right before I left Vietnam to come to America.
She also gave me a piece of paper that was signed stating I was not
Ross Fuller's child."

"Do you have a copy of that paper?"

"Yes. It was in my father and mother's belongings that my aunt kept for me."

Randolph Fuller, with barely restrained anger in his voice, spoke up and asked, "Was there a family Bible with their belongings?"

Anna met his gaze and thought about how much he resembled the picture of her father. "Yes. There was a family Bible. There were also letters and a picture of my father and my mother." She glanced around the room at the large picture that was framed on the wall and pointed. "It's that same picture but mine is only a snapshot."

Noah smiled. "That's the picture taken the day your parents got married. I'm the third person in that picture."

Anna chuckled softly. "Yes, I know. I figured that out after meeting Zach. He favors you a lot."

Noah smiled brightly. "Yes, he does, doesn't he?" he said, looking at Zach and taking note that Zach had his full attention on Anna. He cleared his throat again to regain Zach's attention. "Earlier you mentioned something about a document, Zach."

Zach nodded then turned to Anna. "Tell them about the document you have, Anna," he said. "The one you let me look at."

Anna tensed and the hand holding Zach's tightened. "Yes, it was among the things, too, and it clearly stated that the Fuller family did not wish to claim me as Ross Fuller's child."

Randolph's jaw tightened and he crossed the room to stand in front of her. "And can you tell us whose signature is on it?"

Anna hesitated a moment before answering. "Yes."

"Whose?"

Anna's gaze moved from Randolph to Zach. Pain flared in her dark eyes. "Go ahead, Anna, it's okay. You can answer his question," Zach said quietly.

Anna's gaze returned to Randolph's but only briefly. It moved across the room to someone else. "It was signed by a Julia Fuller." She held the older woman's gaze, challenging her to deny it.

Julia did. She quickly got out of her seat. "No! That's not true!" she said when all eyes turned to her. "I swear it. I would never have done that to Ross! I loved him! I finally accepted how much he loved

that girl after Randolph shared his letters with me," she said, dragging in a pained breath as tears came into her eyes. "I wanted my
great-grandchild home as much as anyone. I would never have done
that."

Randolph's body began shaking in anger as he stared across the
room at his grandmother. He remember her doing some devious and
malicious things in the past, but a part of him could not believe she
would be that cruel and turn her back on Adrianna. Mainly because
one thing she had said was true. She had loved Ross. There had never
been any question of that. And even with her prim and proper ways,
she would not have defied his wishes and prevent his daughter from
coming home as he would have wanted.

Randolph turned his attention back to Anna. "Do you remember
what year the document was signed, Anna?" he asked quietly.

She met his gaze and nodded. "Yes, it was signed in nineteen seventy. June twenty-fifth, nineteen seventy."

Randolph frowned. He turned around to his grandmother and saw
her tear-stained face that pleaded for him to believe her. He turned
back to Anna. "My grandmother had a stroke in February of nineteen
seventy which left her slightly paralyzed in both her hands. She
remained that way for a year. She didn't get the full use of her hands
back until November of nineteen seventy-one. Are you absolutely sure
the document was signed in nineteen seventy?"

Anna nodded her head. "Yes, I'm sure."

"That means someone forged Julia's signature," Noah said angrily.
"Who would have done such a thing?"

"Angela," Robert Fuller's deep voice filled the room. He stepped
forward. "During the time of Julia's illness I had asked Angela to handle any type of correspondence that may have come in as a way to help
out. I didn't see anything wrong with it at the time. After all, she was
your wife, Randolph."

Before Randolph could respond, Trey stood. "Hey, wait a minute!
There's no way my mother would have done something like that! What
was done to Anna was cruel, devious and malicious. I admit Mom was

wrong in keeping you and me apart all those years, Dad, but this is something altogether different. She wouldn't have stooped that low."

"Oh, yes, she would have," Julia Fuller came before her grandson. She was filled with fury at the thought that Angela had forged her name on a document that had kept her from being a part of her great-granddaughter's life for thirty-four years. "Any woman who would drug a man to sleep with her with a devious plan to get pregnant, would do anything."

Shock appeared on Trey's face. "Drug a man? What are you talking about? What man did she supposedly drug?"

"Your father! He would never have slept with her any other way, since he was in love with Jenna," Julia all but screamed, clearly getting hysterical. Pain tore at her heart, knowing all those years her great-granddaughter had thought that she had been the one to keep her from the family.

Stunned, Trey's gaze left his great-grandmother and moved to his father. "Is what she's saying true, Dad? Did Mom drug you?"

Later that night, Haywood snuggled closer to Trey in bed. "Are you sure you're all right?"

Trey said nothing for a few moments and then he pulled Haywood into his arms, "I'm all right for a man who found out more about his mother in one day than he's known in his entire lifetime. And the sad thing about it is that I discovered I don't know her at all. The woman who did all those things isn't the woman I know."

Haywood released a deep sigh. "So, what are you going to do?"

"I'm flying back to California tomorrow to confront her about all of this."

"What if she denies it?"

"She can't, Haywood. There's too much proof that says otherwise. Seeing that paper Anna brought tonight from her childhood nearly twisted my gut. When I think of what a better life Anna could have gotten over here while growing up, compared to what she got, I feel sick."

Haywood nodded. It sickened her as well. "Do you want me to go to California with you?"

"No, this is something I have to do alone."

"All right." A part of her wanted to ask him if he was coming back but she couldn't. He hadn't made any promises for their future or even said that they had one. "I'll be leaving myself in a few days to return to Paris," she said softly.

"Do you still plan to turn in your resignation?"

"Yes."

"I'm glad." He pulled her into his arms and held her. There was so much he wanted to say to her but could not. He couldn't commit himself to her until he got beyond this thing with his mother.

Forty-two

Angela looked up and smiled when Trey walked into the living room. "Trey, I didn't know you were coming back today!"

"Hello, Mother," he said, coming to stand directly in front of her. "Can we talk for a minute?"

"I was just about to go shopping. Can it wait until later?"

"No. It can't."

Angela raised a brow as she looked at her son, suddenly feeling chilled inside. "Is everything all right? You seem bothered by something."

"I am." He took her hand. "Please, let's sit down and talk."

The message in his tone was unmistakable, and Angela allowed herself to be led to the sofa and sat down next to Trey. She wasn't sure what he had been told but she knew he had been told something. Deep down she felt she had nothing to worry about. After all, she was his mother and deserved his loyalty, no matter what.

"What's this about, Trey?" she asked him, noticing the firm set of his jaw.

"I know, Mom," he said, staring hard at her.

"You know what?" she asked, trapping his angry gaze.

Trey's eyes narrowed. "I know what you did to Dad thirty-four years ago, the day I was conceived. I know you drugged him to get him to participate."

Angela's eyes flashed. "I did no such thing!"

Trey ignored her outburst. "I also know that he *did* want to be a part of my life while I was growing up and that Jenna did not come between us. You did."

"Lies! Those are all lies!" she said angrily. "I can't believe you let them convince you I did any of that, Trey!"

"So, you're denying it?"

"Of course I'm denying it. What sort of woman do you think I am?"

Trey looked long and hard at her. "To be totally honest with you, I really don't know. You sit here next to me and lie to my face, Mom. I know you did those things because I have proof."

"Proof? What kind of proof?"

"I saw documentation of the many times Dad tried taking you to court for visitation rights."

"Oh, that. Your father is an attorney, Trey. He can come up with any bogus form that he wants. He has friends in high places."

"And what about that signature you signed regarding Adrianna?"

"I didn't sign that. I wouldn't put it past Julia to have someone sign it for her but it wasn't me. No one can prove that's my signature."

Trey stood and walked to the window and looked out, deciding to call his mother's bluff. "Someone already *has* proven it. Noah took it to a handwriting specialist, a friend of his who works for the FBI. The man confirmed it was you and not Grandmother Julia who signed it."

He saw the color literally drain from his mother's face. Then suddenly her composure returned and she said, "Okay, I admit I did sign that form, but only after Julia asked me to."

Trey shook his head in disgust. "I don't believe you."

Anger flared within Angela. "What do you mean you don't believe me? You would take their word over mine? How dare you! They are nothing. I even had a report run on Jenna's daughter, the one you've been sleeping with—and yes, I know the two of you have slept together because she's as much of a slut as her mother was. The report I got indicates she's currently screwing around with her boss, who happens to be an older man. So it looks like she's banging her way to the top."

Trey's eyes flashed anger, nearly ripping him from reality as his jaws clenched like stone. "Jenna is not a slut. And I know all about Haywood's past relationship with her boss," he said, his anger having reached boiling point.

"And you accept the kind of woman she is, Trey? Are you so taken in by her that you would take her any way you can have her? Don't try defending her because she's nothing but a slut just like her mother!"

"And what does that make you, Mom, a woman who would drug a man to get him to sleep with her?"

Angela stood, clearly upset. "Like I said before, that's a lie. Your father had no right to tell you that!"

Trey shook his head sadly. "He didn't. That was the one thing he didn't tell me about you. That, and the fact that he caught you in the act of being unfaithful. He respected how I felt about you enough not to tell me that. But he didn't have to. The truth came out after all. So, Mother, as you can see, secrets aren't secrets forever." He turned to leave.

Panic surged through Angela. "Trey! Wait! Where are you going?"

"Right now I don't know. All I know is that I'm going as far away from you as possible. You are my mother, but I don't know you. You are heartless, cruel and calculating. You were willing to let Adrianna stay in—"

"Adrianna! Who cares about her?! Yes, I did it and would do it again to protect you."

"To protect me?"

"Yes! To protect you and what you were due! You were supposed to be the Fuller heir. If Ross's child had been found then everything would have gone to her, since she was the oldest. Don't you see I did it for you?"

Trey stared at her and then uttered a disgusted sound. "For me! You cause someone undue pain and grief for me? Don't even try it. You did it for yourself and your own selfish greed. You didn't do anything for me."

Angela's eyes suddenly filled with tears "No, that's not true. Everything I've done was for you and Randolph. Do you know how long I wanted your father? How long I've loved him? He's the only man I've ever wanted and he hurt me by going back to that woman. I'll never forgive him for that. I'm the only woman for him and one day he will realize it and when he does, the three of us will be a family again."

Trey shook his head sadly. There was no doubt in his mind that his mother needed psychiatric help. It seemed that she was having a nervous breakdown right before his eyes. Deciding not to make her anymore hysterical than she was already, he coaxed her into lying down in her bedroom by telling her everything would be all right.

Closing her bedroom door behind him, he then went to the phone and called his stepfather. "You need to come home right away."

Four hours later Trey sat in his apartment after returning from the hospital where he and Harry had taken Angela and had her admitted. Sadly, while sitting in the waiting room for the doctor to give them feedback on her condition, Harry had admitted that he had known of his wife's emotional state for a long time but had ignored it, hoping things would eventually get better and her obsession with Randolph would come to an end. He loved his wife and was going to make sure she got the best medical care possible.

Trey had told Harry that he would help with Angela any way he could; after all she was his mother and he loved her, too. He just hated the things she had done.

For the third time Trey reached for the phone, wanting to talk to Haywood. And for the third time he didn't make the call. He wondered if she was still in Richmond or if she had returned to Paris.

He again reached for the phone. This time he was determined to make the call. His father picked up on the third ring. "Hello, Dad."

"Trey? How are you, son?"

"I'm fine."

After a few brief moments, Randolph asked, "And how are things with your mother?"

Trey let out a deep sigh. "Not good, Dad. She was admitted to the hospital a few hours ago. The doctors agree she needs psychiatric help."

"I'm sorry, Trey."

"I know, and I'm just glad Harry agrees that Mom needs help. He really loves her, Dad, and she's going to need him now more than ever."

"You know what they say. Behind every good woman is a good man."

"Yeah, and behind every good man is a good woman. Speaking of good women, how's Jenna?"

Randolph smiled. "Jenna's fine. She and Randi are out shopping."

"And what about Haywood? Has she returned to Paris?"

"No, not yet. In fact she's back at Glendale Shores."

Trey lifted a brow. "Alone?"

"No, not exactly. Noelle and Anna went with her. They wanted to return the family Bible to its rightful place. Noelle and Anna came back today but Haywood decided to stay a few days longer."

"Oh."

After a few minutes, Randolph said, "Trey, can I give you some fatherly advice?"

"Yes."

"If you're in love with Haywood, let her know it."

Trey's chest tightened in response to what his father had said. "Thanks for the advice, Dad. I think I'll take it."

Haywood lay facedown on a blanket beside the pond. The calming sound of the rippling water and the gentle rays of the afternoon sun made her eyelids grow heavy as she felt the weight of sleep pressing against them.

Her eyelids snapped open at the sound of footsteps on broken limbs and crunched grass. She sat up at the exact moment a figure stepped from among the trees.

"Trey!"

He stopped walking as his eyes took her all in. The two-piece bathing suit she was wearing wasn't as revealing as the one she'd had on that first day but it was still eye-catching. "You like living dangerously, don't you?" he asked in a husky voice.

"What do you mean?"

"You shouldn't be out here alone dressed like that."

"There's no one else on this island."

"You can't always be absolutely sure of that, so try and be more careful."

"All right."

She looked at him expectantly and he suddenly realized that he hadn't told her why he was there. "I called Dad and he told me you had come back here."

She nodded. "Yes. I thought it would be a good time for Anna to see the place since she'll be sharing it with the two of us. Besides, she wanted to return the Denison family Bible to its rightful place."

Trey nodded, then crossed his arms over his chest and looked down at her. "I understand Noelle and Anna left yesterday. Why didn't you go, too?"

"I wasn't ready to go back yet."

"Any reason why?"

Haywood shrugged. "I just wasn't ready. How's your mom?"

Trey came and sat down beside her on the blanket. "I don't want to talk about my mother right now."

"Okay."

After a few moments he looked over at her and said, "I missed you."

Her lips curved into a smile. "And I missed you, too."

Trey decided to take it one step further. He looked out at the pond then back at her and met her gaze. "And I love you."

He heard Haywood's sharp intake of breath and saw the mistiness that suddenly clouded her eyes. "Oh, Trey. And I love you, too."

He shifted his body to reach into his back pocket to pull out a box.

He flipped it open as he handed it to her, a beautiful diamond ring. "Will you marry me?"

"Trey," she reached out and hugged him as she began to cry in earnest. Somehow through it all he was able to place the ring on her finger. Then he kissed her the way he had wanted to kiss her from the moment he had seen her drifting off to sleep on the blanket.

"You know what, Haywood?" he asked, moments after breaking off the kiss and while still holding her in his arms.

"What?"

"I think Ma Mattie had all this planned. She knew this place would get to us and break down our resistance."

"You think so?"

"Yes, I really think so."

Haywood nodded. "I think you're right," she said as she kissed him again and pulled him down to her, to show him just how right she thought he was.

Epilogue

Glendale Shores
Six months later

It had been a beautiful day for a wedding.

Jenna smiled as she glanced across the way at her daughter. She had been a beautiful bride in such a beautiful place. The wedding had been held outside, in the same spot where she and Randolph had exchanged their wedding vows.

In one heartbeat Haywood had walked down the aisle on Randolph's arm, and in the next, she had been standing beside Trey, facing the minister as they repeated their vows, pledging their lives together forever. Noelle had been her maid of honor and Randi and Anna her bridesmaids. Zachary had been Trey's best man and a couple of his frat brothers his groomsmen.

So many had come out to witness another union between a Haywood and a Fuller, and like her, everyone thought it was a blessed occasion.

Jenna's breathing became ragged when she caught her husband's eye. Every muscle, every angle, and every line in his face shone with happiness. Over the past six months he and Trey had slowly rebuilt a relationship that had taken Angela twenty-two years to destroy.

Trey had told her earlier that Harry, deciding it would be best if he and Angela stayed away, had sent words of congratulations and best wishes. Although part of Jenna wanted to hate Angela for all she had done, she couldn't find it in her heart to do so. Angela was a sick woman and was still undergoing psychiatric help. Besides, the love she and Randolph shared had survived the test of time. Living proof was there in her daughter and his son.

Jenna reluctantly moved her gaze from Randolph to Leigh and Noah. It was rumored around Washington that Noah's name had been thrown about as a possible vice presidential nominee for the next election. The good news was that he was giving it considerable thought . . . in case the rumor was true.

Ellie and Johnny were standing together talking with Johnnetta, Ellie's thirty-six-year-old daughter. Ellie and Johnny had gotten married a few months ago. Johnny, who had finished college while incarcerated, had since gone on to get his masters and his doctorate and was now a professor at Morehouse College. He had also written a book detailing his time with the Panthers, and the fourteen years he had been locked up for something he didn't do. The book had been a bestseller.

Jenna turned slightly and watched as Zachary carried a cup of punch over to Anna, who was sitting on a bench facing the pond. The family had accepted Ross's daughter with open arms, glad to see that the search, which had taken thirty-four years, was over. Leigh had mentioned that Anna was thinking of moving to Washington to be near her father's family, who she now considered her family, as well. According to Leigh, Zach and Anna had been seeing a lot of each other whenever she came to town, and although Zach said the two of them were just close friends, she knew the family was hoping it blossomed into something more.

Something pulled at Jenna and made her turn around. She glanced through the trees and in the distance she could see the big house, looming tall and stately. She blinked. Then blinked again and her eyes flew wide.

"What are you looking at, sweetheart?" Randolph appeared by her side and followed her gaze through the trees.

Jenna's head snapped around and her eyes met those of her husband's. "I thought . . . I could have sworn I saw . . ." She shook her head, collecting her wits, knowing it wasn't possible.

"Gramma Mattie?"

Jenna's mouth dropped as she watched Randolph's lips form into a smile. "How did you know?"

His smile widened. "There have been a few times today that I imagined seeing her myself. She was such a vital part of this place you can't help but feel she's here and will always be here."

Jenna smiled, knowing that was true. "She's happy. I can actually feel it."

"And she has reasons to be," Randolph said, taking Jenna's hand in his. "Today her great-grandson married her goddaughter, her long-lost great-granddaughter has been found, the Bible has been returned to where it belongs and last but not least, Glendale Shores will be kept out of developers' hands. Knowing my grandmother, I believe she is extremely happy."

He held his wife's gaze steadily as he added, "Just like I am happy. When I think about all we have gone through, all we lost and restored, I can't help but thank God."

Jenna's smile widened. "And I feel the same way. I thank God for our families and friends, but most importantly, I thank him for the ties that bound us together all those years ago, and still bind us today."

Randolph grinned. "So what do you anticipate next, Mrs. Fuller?"

Jenna chuckled. She glanced over at Randi, who was talking to Noelle. "Trying to get our daughter through college without losing any of our hair."

She moved her glance over to where Zach and Anna sat talking. "Possibly another wedding in a year or so."

Her gaze left the couple to go rest on the bride and groom. "A grandchild in less than a year."

Randolph, who had been following the movement of her gaze, chuckled. "That soon?"

Jenna turned her head and met Randolph's gaze and smiled. "Possibly sooner, less than nine months from now, and if that's the case, act surprised."

Randolph paused when her words sank in. "Are you saying that you think . . . ?"

Briskly, Jenna nodded. "He's a Fuller. She's a Haywood. Together that's a combustible combination. If anyone should know it would be us."

Randolph couldn't deny that. Nor could he deny feeling more love for Jenna than he thought was possible. She was and had always been everything to him.

He lifted his wineglass up to her in a salute. "To the ties that bind."

READING GROUP GUIDE

1. Who was your favorite character in the book? Who was your least favorite? Why?

2. Do you think Ross should have seen through Angela's duplicity?

3. Do you think the love Jenna and Randolph shared was special? Why?

4. Did Julia Fuller have the right to interfere in her grandsons' lives?

5. Did you see Ross as weak because he was more tolerant of his grandmother's interference than Randolph?

6. Do you think Jenna did the right thing by breaking off her engagement with Randolph when Angela got pregnant?

7. Should Randolph and Noah have stopped looking for Ross's daughter years ago? Why or why not?

8. Do you think the historical detail was critical to the story? Why or why not?

9. Should Randolph have told Trey the truth years ago instead of letting him think the worse about him and Jenna?

10. Did Trey handle the situation properly in dealing with his mother once he discovered all the things she had done? Why or why not?